FINDING EVER AFTER SERIES | BOOK FOUR

THESE GRAVE HEARTS

K E BARDEN

Paperback ISBN: *978-1-7635308-9-8*

Ebook ISBN: 978-1-7643297-0-5

Hardcover ISBN: *978-1-7643297-1-2*

Cover design by Etheric Tales

Chapter Artwork by Etheric Tales

Map designed by AdrianoBezzera

Typography and Formatting by Flutterby Formatting

Trim: 5.5 x 8.5

Publication Date: 14.02.2026

Registered Under: K E Barden Author

OTHER BOOKS BY K E BARDEN

Finding Ever After Series
The Gilded Mirror
These Grimm Fates
A Glass Darkly

To Jared,
For dream weaving with me.

N
NW
NE
W
E
SW
SE
S
Beast Cove
CRULLFELL
ASHENFELL
Lake Moss
The Luna Lighthouse
The Tower and the Mage
Cawdor
XERSAILLES
ARDENBEAUX
The Lantern Lighthouse
Annice
Lake La Belle
White Bridge
The Channel
Waters Keep
The Cove
THE ISLAND OF MYORCAI
THE EVER AFT
THE REALM

LE'S
The Northern Lighthouse
THE REALM OF DRAGONS AND GIANTS
THE CORAL COAST
AURELIA
'S KEEP
Butterpond
Blarney Forest
The Briar Rose
The Marshes
MINES OF PARADOR
Hasleholme
MAELSTROM
Ellendale
CARNELL
PEAKS OF CARFELL
Eastborne
MOUNTAINS OF EYRIE
W FOREST
Arrow's Den
Ivywood
The Crystal Lake
THE SILVER CITY
Bell's Peak
THE DARK FOREST
ERRIDORM
Roserock
Dove Port
Witches Hut
The Elysian Fields
The Skinny Piglet
BELLATORRE
Wolf's Den
YN
TEAL COVE
The Queens Mines
ATLAS
NYSA
THE ISLE OF NYSA
Lighthouse Luvon

*Faraway, within the murky depths
of the wild sea, lived two rivalling
kingdoms. One kingdom was etched in
sea glass, the other in pearl. Both were
a promise. The beating twin-hearts of
the great abyss, and though their kingdoms
shone in beauty and light, a seed of
darkness had been buried. And with it,
the burden of blood.*

Prologue

The breeze was crisp, the air bitter as it frosted over the ground. Eve drew her knees close, the chill seeping through the thin stretch of her leotard under a starlit sky. The cobalt fabric itched at her skin, the material caught in a weak blue glow of the lantern beside her. The platform of the raised tent where she sat bit into her thighs, each movement causing the wooden slats to creak.

The fire near the smaller tents crackled as it died, its sparks whispering into the dark. Crickets sang somewhere amongst the forest, their rhythm broken by the low rumble of beasts locked deep in their cages. The circus never slept, not even when the world grew still at dusk.

The same was said for the sounds of those who lived within the circus. Light spilled out the tent door behind Eve onto the grass, coating it in shadows from those moving within. A harsh cough echoed through the entryway, reminding her that death was close.

A male voice echoed through the half open tent flaps, murmured and hushed. 'You must drink.'

She'd been hearing the doctor's voice all night, a crackle to it she didn't fully trust. But it wasn't his voice that made her hug herself tighter. It was Dante's. Occasionally his rasp would filter through to the outside where she sat, her name sounding foreign on his tongue. *'Eveline.'*

His wheezing voice sounded far away, as if it floated along the wind.

She pressed her palms to her eyes, pushing down hard as if she could make the horrible sounds go away. Make it all stop.

'Eveline,' Dante said again.

She sucked in a breath. It was all she could do to hold back the whimper crawling up her throat.

The voice is not his, she told herself.

Another rasping cough tore through the night, clawing its way from the lungs of the man inside, raw and relentless.

Eve trembled. She knew those sounds. That same sickly rhythm had haunted her dreams, night after night. It stirred in her blood now, rising like a memory she couldn't bury. Another face flickered behind her eyes, caught in the broken candlelight of her old home in the glen. Her mother's skin had turned paper-thin, her eyes hollow and distant, fixed on nothing.

Eve had shut it out back then, too. Told herself it wasn't her mother; not that shadow of a woman lying disturbingly still in the bed.

No.

Her mother had been life. She had been song, and light, and warmth.

Like Dante.

And now both had become something else. As though every trace of light had been drained, leaving only ghosts behind.

The darkest part of the night had begun to seep in.

Shadows stretched from the trees, growing closer, the silhouettes trying to cover what little light gleamed.

It isn't happening again. It can't be. You have to wake up, she thought. Open your eyes and the dream will fall apart.

But no matter how many times she told herself the lie, it never became truth. Life didn't work that way. It tore you apart. Tested you. Then recycled trauma all over again. Maybe, if she stayed calm, if she still kept the warmth in her chest, she could pass it. That was what the heroes did in the stories. They endured. They believed.

The light shifted as deft fingers opened the tent flaps. Eve peered up into the eyes of Madame Viper, her coat the colour of old blood. Her gaze swept over Eve. 'I thought I told you to sleep.'

Her straight black hair was still pristine despite the long night, her velvet coat clean, the golden buttons glimmered as if they'd been freshly polished. Normally, the woman terrified Eve. Terrified all her employees. But this night, Eve couldn't muster it. That fear.

Not with who lay inside.

Tonight, she was more terrified of death. Of what happened next. Of the end that neared. Perhaps Viper saw that, because for the first time in the year Eve had been here, the circus master's eyes softened.

Viper sighed and disappeared back inside for a moment. She returned with a blanket in hand. Eve felt the weight on her shoulders, the gentleness of the touch before Viper lifted Eve's quivering chin. Viper's manicured nails dug into her skin, but Eve didn't dare look away. Didn't dare allow her lip to wobble.

Viper's face was grim as she said, 'Just don't get sick. I still need you in the show tomorrow.'

Eve nodded. It was the only kindness Viper would offer. Her circus always came first and foremost.

The Cirque Magique.

Eve scuffed her shoes against the wood, worn from years of use. Viper didn't upgrade much. She liked to keep her coin on hand, using it sparingly and only when completely necessary. Still, the woman lived and breathed this circus. It was all she had. All she'd ever loved.

But Eve had more than the circus. She had Dante.

Sweet, bronzed Dante. Who stargazed with her and sang her to sleep. Who protected her from a fall when the tightrope was too high. Who threw knives and juggled like a prince. Dante, who cooked terribly and spoke of gods and monsters and magic.

Her thoughts jolted as another wheezing cough slipped through the tent flap, and the fabric rustled as another figure stepped out. Broad shoulders, a strange mask coloured like bone with weeping paint. The scent of death and alcohol hit her, sour and thick. A gloved hand curled around a cane as he limped down the stairs, his left leg dragging slightly under the weight.

Eve tried to look brave as he approached, but her eyes fixed on the cane. She was afraid of what she might see, of what she already knew he wore.

The mask was horrific in the half-light, carved into the long face of a weeping man. His eyes glinted through narrow slits, unreadable.

Her muscles clenched as his voice reached her, crackled and rough. 'You can go in now. But cover your mouth with this,' he said, holding out a silver-threaded scarf. The fabric a small flutter in his large, gloved hand.

Eve gingerly took it, her fingers grazing over the soft material, the threading loose along the sides.

Viper mumbled something to the man and Eve's gaze caught on the entryway. The tent flaps swayed with each breath of wind, the thin canvas trembling as if something terrible waited on the other side.

The doctor spoke again. 'He won't last the night.'

Eve turned her head towards him. Towards that terrifying mask.

'Make it count.'

She gave him a tight nod, and tied the scarf over her nose and mouth, Viper's sharp gaze assessing each movement. Eve was sluggish as she stood, her feet slow and unwieldy. As if she waded through mud only to continue sinking.

It took Eve's eyes a moment to adjust as she entered. The room was warm, brushing across her skin like the hearth of a fire. Despite the scarf, she wrinkled her nose at the smell.

Decay and death.

Eve followed the wheezing coughs and shallow breaths. The short walk was an eternity as she rounded a sheer curtain, arriving at a cot layered with blankets and pillows. Dante's cot.

Though it wasn't him. Not really.

Not when his skin was yellow. Not when he was coated in a sheen of sweat. Not when the bones protruding from his shoulders made him look like a skeleton. His ribs poked through his chest, his elbows sharp and lanky.

He was a stranger. A shadow.

Everything was wrong. He was *wrong*.

She couldn't help the step she took back, her breath halting somewhere inside her chest.

His eyes fluttered, the movement soft and delicate like the quiver of fairy wings.

A wide smile spread over his features as he took her in. The leotard. The blanket. The messy braid. 'My Eveline,' he said quietly. 'Don't you look pretty.'

Her mouth went dry. She didn't feel pretty. She felt sick. Like if she swallowed too hard, her insides would fall out.

He reached out his bony fingers. She noted the thin joints, the taut skin. His knuckles still had scars from training. From the long years practicing with knives and dancing with heights. It loosened something inside her, allowing her a long breath. At least those scars remained unchanged.

With a hesitant step, she took his hand. It was clammy, and the calluses rubbed against her own. Familiar but different.

'I'm glad you came,' he wheezed, the sound like scraping rock.

Blood dribbled down his chin and his chest heaved, another coughing fit wracking his body. She tried not to flinch. To waver. She would be his strength when he had none.

She began to untie her scarf, to give it to him, but he held his hand up, stern and resolute. 'No, Eve. Keep it on.'

His eyes crinkled at the side as he smiled. The same warm brown eyes that had embraced her day after day.

Her bravery waned, and her chest tightened. She tried not to shake. To crush the terror threatening to break through the surface of her thin façade.

Dante wiped his chin on his sleeve before pointing to a box in the corner. 'I have something for you,' he said. 'Can you bring it over?'

She eyed the wooden box, and tried to regain what little control she held. It lay by the corner table. Unremarkable. Plain. The only decoration was a small carved bird on the surface, the animal's wings outstretched in mid-flight. She walked over and, with unsteady hands, picked it up. It was lighter than she expected, shiny, and smooth.

She placed it in his lap, her eyes wary as Dante smiled at her hesitation.

His voice was faint as he said, 'Open it.' She paused, but he waved away her concerns. 'Just open it.'

With shaking fingers, she lifted the latch, finding silky cloth inside. Carefully, she folded the cloth back, revealing two golden knives.

Her stomach dropped.

The blades glittered in the lantern light.

She bit her cheek hard enough to draw blood. This was too much. *Too final.*

Eve shook her head as she stepped back. Her nostrils flared, the silence roaring in her ears.

His knives. Dante's treasure. Laid out for her in a gift. A parting gift. Her eyes watered, silently begging him not to do this. She couldn't take them. Couldn't own them. They were his. *Only his.*

Eve shoved them away and the box clattered to the floor. The knives slid across the wood, halted by the worn rug. But it didn't dull their shine. The gold glittered. As if waving to her. Warning her.

Her heart hammered in her chest, the need to run fierce. But a soft, skeletal touch halted her.

'Eveline,' Dante wheezed.

She turned slowly, hating the way her name was a plea on his lips.

'*No,*' she said. But it came out as a garble. Something violent was carving through her chest. It stole her breath. Her words. Her heart.

'Eveline,' Dante said again, his voice croaky. '*Please,* nobody else can have them. Nobody else deserves them like you.'

'I don't want them,' she whispered. 'I don't want any of it. I just want *you*.'

His eyes softened. 'You'll always have me.'

'I don't believe you.'

He pulled her close as her body shook, panic beating beneath her skin. He stroked her hair, letting the silky strands run through his fingers.

'I'll be with the stars,' he said. 'Even after I'm gone, I'll still be guiding you, wherever you go.'

Eve hiccupped. 'But you'll be gone.' She closed her eyes, focusing on the comforting touch as he kissed her hand.

'I know you're scared,' he murmured.

She wasn't scared; she was terrified. It was happening again. All over again. As if the realm had not punished her enough.

Another cough took hold, blood dribbling down Dante's chin as he failed to control it. Sweat shone on his brow, and she gripped his hand harder, each violent shake reverberating through the touch.

Eve prayed to the Godmother. To the stars. To any being who would listen.

Not him. Anyone but him.

She eased Dante back into the bed, his coughs finally ceasing.

'Please take them, Eve. They're all I have left to give you.' He offered her another smile, but she saw the pain behind his eyes. The cruel beast inside tearing him apart little by little. 'Gold is my favourite, remember?'

'I remember,' she said, running her thumb over his palm. His fingers were bare, the rings he so fondly wore missing.

She let go, and collected the box from the floor, carefully placing the knives back inside. They were only slight. Toothpicks against some of the others' knives wielded in the circus.

But she didn't mind. That was the beauty in them. Their golden hilts and plain décor were practical yet beautiful. Easily balanced. Perfect for throwing. And stunning enough to put on a show.

Just like him.

Dante panted. 'Magic lingers in everything, but love lingers too. It sits inside your very soul.' He closed his eyes. 'Water.'

Another cough shook his body, and Eve ran for the jug. The metal was cool against her palms. She lifted it with both hands, arms trembling as the water sloshed inside. It caught the lantern light as she poured, a thin stream flashing silver before spilling over her fingers and soaking the boards beneath her knees. She reached for a cloth, hissing at herself for being so clumsy, when she noticed the silence.

Eve turned slowly, the air somehow holding its breath. She heard Dante's rasp. The slowed heartbeat.

The final breath.

'Dante?' she whispered.

But Dante's chest did not rise again. His fingers did not twitch. And his eyes ... his eyes had gone flat and unseeing. Nothing but a lifeless ghost.

The jug slipped from her hands. It struck the boards and shattered, the sound thick and distant, as though heard through water. Shards skittered across the floor, glinting in the lantern light. Eve pressed a hand to her chest, checking for a heartbeat but only finding a chasm. It cracked, splitting her open from the inside.

A strangled sound escaped her lips. It carved through her heart, her chest, her soul. Scraping her raw.

The silence was deafening.

Too heavy.

Too demanding.

Her feet moved of their own volition. She had to get out. Out.

Eve stumbled from the tent and tore off the scarf. She sucked in air as if it could wash away the pain, the grief. But it wasn't enough. It would never be enough.

Instead, she ran. As if she could somehow outrun the shadows. Outrun her fate. Outrun her pain.

Her feet guided her towards the forest. As she entered the trees, the vines twisted around her in a welcome embrace. And from the darkness, the only light came from two sharp knives with golden hilts, grasped in her small, blistered fingers.

I

The Queen's Poison

The golden knife sat comfortably in Myrenna's hand, its handle brilliant against the light from the chandelier. She lounged on her throne and lifted the dagger, her eyes narrowing at the workmanship. It was a tiny thing, the blade coming to a long, thin point, etched with a decorative frame. The rubies on the hilt glinted, the red bright against the black husk of the throne room.

Anger bubbled under the surface as her thumb caressed the

cherry stone of the blade, her nails ruined and chipped against its crimson gleam. It reminded her of blood.

Myrenna tried to think of the last time she'd held a weapon like this, but her mind came back blank. She'd long lost the thirst to use such mundane weapons; she'd never had the need, really. Not when her magic was far more powerful than anything a blacksmith could craft. But it was still impressive workmanship. Delicate and dangerous.

Her eye twitched at the thought.

The knife was a reminder of Eveline. Of the little *bitch* whose words stained Myrenna's tongue. The Seeker had become more than a thorn in her side. She had become an infection, slowly polluting every one of her plans. Unravelling them piece by piece.

Myrenna's recovery from the Ancient One, a magical tree in the Shadow Forest, had taken days. Her magic had been slow to regenerate from the Nightkiss flower, the power of the crushed petals enough to subdue any magic. It had been agony, being mortal. Worse still, being smothered by the tree's roots.

She remembered sinking, her lungs burning.

But what she remembered most was the desperation.

And the fear.

Myrenna was a survivor. She'd proved that time and time again. So, when she'd found a trickle of magic, a black pearl lost in the depths of the deep, she'd grasped onto it with every fibre of her being.

Pain had ricocheted as her nails snapped, bleeding and sick against the Ancient One's power. She'd screamed and clawed, rabid as she raged in its greedy grasp.

The dark memory made her shiver. When she'd made the bargain with the Sisters Grimm all those years ago, it had been with a promise to make her all powerful. To make her *invinci-*

ble. A power that would only succumb to those who granted it. She'd traded her very soul to do so.

'And yet,' she muttered, 'I was almost killed by a bloody tree.'

It pissed her off.

When she'd first been granted her power, the revenge had been sweet. It had been easy to kill. To watch as the light left the eyes of all those who had made her suffer. Her father and Annabel had been the two she'd savoured most. Their screams were a sick lullaby that made her dreams so much sweeter.

After that, it had been about finding a way to halt death. The hearts were the key to her very long life. But with her consumption of hearts came more maidens. More death. More sorrow. She ate hearts in droves now. Staving off her promise to the Sisters Grimm.

And they hated her for it.

Sometimes she hated herself.

She growled in the silence, her knuckles white against the golden hilt of the Seeker's blade. Myrenna had taken kingdoms, had honed magic so powerful that it failed the comprehension of most living things in the realm. She had built an army, forged her future with hearts and stolen back what had belonged to her. But it was not enough. Nothing was ever enough.

Still, she did not have the heart she needed. She did not possess the secrets hidden within the grimoire. Nor did she have the mirror she so desperately searched for in the mines.

The wrath of the Sisters Grimm would be mighty once they found out she had cheated death.

Again.

Without the mirrors, she would be vulnerable to them.

They were the only things capable of stopping the Grimms. Capable of taking away what they had given.

Pain throbbed behind her eyes, sharp and familiar. The headaches she was prone to had returned, creeping in like something long buried come to the surface. If she was honest with herself, she needed more than what she had. More protection. More power.

She needed to make the Grimms mortal. To make them crawl. To hear them beg.

Her shoulders cracked as she turned to the gilded mirror, still flawless and gleaming amid the ruin of the throne room. Behind her, she felt the weight of the Tinker's corpse, a blackened husk, his velvet robes reduced to ash.

He hadn't been moved yet. She hadn't had the energy to order his removal. Not when her rage upon her return could have burnt cities. Even now, the flame of her ire licked her insides. Smouldering through her veins with such vibrance that it took everything to leash it.

The mirror remained still. The usual shadows behind the glass asleep.

Screams careened from the city below through the open windows – the hangings and backlash from the fires Dread had started, echoing towards the castle. What was once a vibrant city now reflected something cold. Something grey.

She thought of Dread. Of his desperation and fear. His pathetic grovelling and his thirst for power. She usually admired those qualities. Today, she *loathed* them.

It wasn't the hangings, or the screams, or the fire, that set on her edge. It was the insolence. The powerplay. Dread had found a solution that was short term. That would instil fear but would also breed hope. Dread had acted on a whim, without thought or permission, leaving *her* to fix it.

'What a fool,' she hissed.

With a shriek, Myrenna threw the gilded knife towards the mirror's golden frame. The half-burnt curtains behind the throne flying in the wind.

The blade fell with a clatter on the stone floor.

I missed.

Her breathing was laboured, her chest heaving with dark rage. A memory flashed. One where power had raced through her as a Grimm handed her the mirror in the cell under King's Keep. The Grimm had smiled at her with those keen eyes and blackened teeth. And as Myrenna had devoured hearts, the Grimms had devoured souls. Each one's potency different from the last.

Suddenly, Myrenna's corset was too tight. The red of her dress too bright against the ash. Out of place. Her neck flushed, the room's temperature rising as she tried to swallow. To breathe.

Her hands shook as she scrambled for the ribbons that tied her gown together, her broken nails scratching against the silky material. Myrenna let loose a strangled sound as she ravaged the material. The ribbon uncurled, but it was too slow. Too tight.

Trapped.

The seams gave way at her shoulders first, the fabric splitting beneath her fists. She clawed at the bodice, nails catching on the threads until the dress ripped down her side. Air hit her skin and she gasped, dragging in colour and light with every breath. She dropped to her knees, the torn fabric hanging from her arms like shed skin. Her fingers were stained black from the coal and dust, but she didn't care, not when she needed to breathe. Myrenna peeled the dress from her skin, before throwing it across the room.

Myrenna clutched her stomach in the silence. In nothing but a thin slip, her breathing began to finally slow.

A hiss echoed along the walls as the mirror came alive, its silky voice slicing through whatever reprieve she'd found. *'Though she holds a crown, she still feels weak, powerful she is, but cannot grasp what she seeks.'*

Myrenna didn't turn around, she didn't need to. His cruel taunts always hit the mark. 'Shut up,' she wheezed. It was all she could manage.

The mirror laughed, as if she were a child playing a game she did not understand.

As her chest finally slowed, her breath steadier, Myrenna looked over her shoulder.

Eyes came into focus through the haze, blinking at her through that gilded frame. *'Power comes with a price, my Queen, and not all payments are as they seem. The Seeker, the Princess, and the mutiny grows, yet you focus on knives and books and crows.'*

Her voice was low as she said, 'I'm prioritising.'

With effort, she picked herself back up. Her knees were a little wobbly as she eyed the discarded red dress stained with dust and ash.

She wiped her hands on her undergarments, soiling the ivory silk, and faced the mirror. Her heart thrummed but she kept her face implacable. She'd been playing this game with the mirror for an age. By the cauldron, she could keep doing it now.

'Tell me, mirror, in all of your truths and wisdom and advice, have you ever seen anything like her? The Seeker, that is?'

The mirror's fog crept forward, slithering over Myrenna's

toes as the glass warped. The image transformed into the Queen.

Her, but not.

Myrenna wore the same crown, with the same undergarment she wore now. Yet she was not the Queen who stood on the podium. The face looking back at her was wrinkled, the black hair etched with grey. The lines worn into her skin blended into sunspots, speckling her face. It grinned at her, flashing blackened gums and milky, filmed teeth.

Myrenna recoiled. She hated seeing this version of herself. Hated what the mirror promised. It was a tactic it used often.

Even Myrenna had to admit it worked.

She knew the mirror only did it in times to remind her of where she stood. Of whom truly held the power here.

She snarled. The reflection echoed the same.

Amethyst eyes met each other as the reflection spoke. *'You once heeded my voice, now you choose to ignore, you forged your own path but must settle a score. Without my advice you have failed every avail, your enemies are free and your mortality frail.'*

Her breath halted at the words, but the mirror wasn't finished. It never truly was.

'You have forgotten your path and forgotten our deal. My Queen, without me, you are a broken wheel.'

Myrenna clutched the anger inside her and used it to burn the hopelessness threatening to break in. But it didn't stop the sting in her eyes, the bitter tears brimming just below the surface.

She'd failed at every possible angle. Her store of maidens was almost dry. Her only hope of immortality was running wild in Perridorm – in a battle she was barely winning. She hadn't yet found what was buried, and now she had the Seeker on her tail. Her ex-lover was hidden, no doubt plotting her demise. Not to mention, the spindle and Rumple had been taken. The Tinker was dead. The rebellion grew as the people rallied against her reign, and her magic only pushed so far. Her crow had burnt her city. Had given the people more reasons to fight back.

The pressure suffocated her.

She was alone. As she had always been. The flour girl, a dreamer, living in a nightmare.

She traced her fingers along the lines etched beside her eyes. Her breath came out in a rasp as she asked the mirror, 'What do I do?'

The reflection smiled, but it wasn't kind. *'A kingdom is nothing without its regal queen. Let's remind the realm of what real power means.'*

She nodded quietly. 'Tell me where to start?'

They would start with her city. Then she would deal with Dread. Then she would address the battle at the border. Tricky pieces of her own puzzle she could control. Moving pieces she could contain. But her power was slipping. She was desperate now.

And when one became desperate, they were terrifying.

Mist dusted over the ocean like a low-forming storm. Eve huffed as she shivered from the chill, her clothes sticking to her frozen skin. She trekked up the shoreline from the beach, her pride slightly broken. She was tired, soaking wet, and the beach was about as cheery as a stab to the gut.

Waves crashed along the cliff in savage waves. Though she'd tried to see through the mist, she couldn't find what she was looking for. Her father had told her tales of intimate islands dotted amongst the sea, where the sea nymphs dwelled. Eve had only dealt with a few sea nymphs in her time – Cyrene being the most prominent over the years, but even that had been a disaster. She envisioned the blue, scaled skin and the stark, red hair as the female creature sat across from her in the Skinny Piglet; the nymph's fingers cooling the warm brew Eve had failed to touch that night.

The same night she'd met Hansel.

An ache in her heart stirred at the thought, and she frowned, her breath hitching. She reached the edge of the beach, and started the climb towards the cottage on the cliff. It had been a few days since she had dived under the waves, a few days of staring off into the distance and wondering how in the cauldron she ever thought diving into frigid waters was a good idea.

After she'd entered the depths, she'd almost drowned from the frost-bitten water as it ravaged her and left her soaked, shivering, and defeated on the coastline. Since then, she had been at an utter loss.

Eve wished Nona was here to tell her what to do. The pain of Nona's death still lingered somewhere deep within Eve. Another person gone. Another piece of her childhood vanished.

Just like Dante, and her father, and her mother.

She missed the old woman and at the same time wanted to punch her. Or hug her. She wasn't entirely sure which option appealed more.

Smoke curled as it exited the chimney ahead, the cottage still patiently waiting for her upon the hill. She'd already checked for a boat, for anything that could help her cross the waters and maybe find Nysa's location, but that's when she'd begun to doubt whether her cause was lost before it had even begun. Nysa was in the ocean's depths; even if she found it, there was no way she could survive going there, not without drowning.

She was wary to enter the cottage again for a while after she'd first entered the waves. What if it disappeared to a new location again? What if it left her stranded? Would it take a week to project back here, or would it be years? She hadn't yet figured out whether its location jumps could be controlled, but she lacked the energy or time to figure it out.

Eve sneezed as the wind surged, tugging at her clothes with impatient fingers. In her pocket, the stone Hansel had given her began to vibrate, warmth blooming against her hip. She hissed through her teeth and fished it out. The deep blue glow pulsed in her palm. Silver veins shimmered across its smooth surface from when she had shattered Rapunzel's mirror. The heat offered a brief comfort, but it did little to ease the knot in her stomach.

With the Princess no longer hidden and the Queen possibly on a rampage, Eve was a wanted criminal and stuck in the middle of a prophecy involving the most powerful beings in the realm.

Reaching the Queen of Nysa was one thing. Convincing the royal not to slit her throat was another.

She could ask for the mirror and the sea nymphs could blatantly laugh in her face. She had nothing to trade. Nothing to offer. She was merely human in a world destinated to destroy her.

Cyrene's cold warning from the Skinny Piglet surfaced in

her mind. *'Something wicked brews. Even my queen keeps deep within our caverns. Something evil is coming, Seeker.'*

Worry curled inside her and it made her uneasy. She would have to find another way.

Taking a deep breath, Eve shoved open the cottage door with her shoulder and paused on the threshold. The house looked the same as before. Her messy scrawl on the sign near the door read: *The Cottage of Convenience.*

The fireplace blazed, the broth in the cauldron above the flames perfectly cooked. Her mess with the potions still remained, botched cures and vials scattered over the tabletop. Papers littered the floors from when she'd raided the Spindle's room and had found all those lost items and missing people. Her eyes lingered on the spare room by the back, the effervescent glow swimming under the door gap.

A familiar *thump* came from above and the sound of running water filled her ears. She'd spent enough time in the cottage to accept that it was enchanted. Her limbs were leaden as she hiked up the stairs towards the bathroom, the defeat of the ocean still lingering in her veins.

Her clothes came away stiff with dried salt and sand, scattering grit across the tiles. She eased herself into the bath and hissed as the heat met her skin. Scars pulled tight across her arms, pale lines against bruised flesh. The apothecary's salve had done its work, though the memory of the Queen's strike still burned beneath it. She sank lower, quietly thanking Nona's Grimoire for having the information she'd needed at the time.

When she surfaced, Eve ran her fingers along her cheek, carefully feeling the raised skin lining her jaw. The scar on her face wasn't her first. Her whole body was an array of pale white nicks and cuts. Some came from battles or the slip of her knives when she'd been training. But others, hidden in places she couldn't reach, were from Rapunzel. Her punishments.

She blinked away the memories and dunked her head, letting the water wash away the grime. Grains of sand fell into the water, leaving a trail as she pulled her fingers through the tangled mess of her hair.

Another *thump* came from her left. Tiny fingers darted past, snatching her worn leathers and leaving a folded shirt and trousers in their place. Eve smiled faintly. The hands always came and went before she could thank them.

Days had begun to blend together, the rhythm of this place settling into her bones. Mornings at the training grounds, afternoons by the sea. It was a pattern she hadn't meant to fall into, yet it held her all the same.

Sometimes, she would read the grimoire – mostly just staring at the sketches and the cursive print of Nona's hand-writing, the ache in her heart never quite fading. Sometimes, she uncovered more knickknacks and names from the suitcases of lost belongings shoved into the tight places of this cottage.

And other times, the glow from the Spindle Room called.

Steam curled around her as she leaned back, tracing the rim of the tub with one finger. The water had cooled, its warmth spent, and the thought of the room below tugged at her. She rose, wrapped herself in a towel, and watched the bathwater darken with ash and grit before it drained away.

Eve padded downstairs in clean clothes and slumped onto the couch. Her face itched, but she resisted the urge to scratch, nose scrunching as the skin pulled tight. The three puncture marks from the wolf were still there, a constant reminder etched into her cheek. She knew she should be grateful they hadn't become infected, and they'd healed quickly enough, thanks to the traveller's Halopods.

Outside, a storm churned across the sky. She wrapped her arms around herself.

Why did it always feel like she left ruin behind her? Like every person she touched either vanished or died?

She squeezed her eyes shut.

She could still feel the memory of Dante's hand on her cheek. Calloused, rough, and yet impossibly gentle as he'd said, *'Magic lingers in everything, but love lingers too. It sits inside your very soul.'*

She tried to recall that love, to let it fill her again, but all she could feel was the ache that followed. The bone-deep tear left in the world after his final breath.

The night he died, she ran.

Just as she ran from every corner of her life.

From her destiny.

From Hansel's love.

From Nona's teachings.

But she couldn't run forever. Sooner or later, her legs would give out, her will would bend. And in the end, she would lose everything because of it.

She flicked through the pages of Nona's grimoire, stopping at the sketch of Dante. His eyes sparkled with joy, captured in a moment that no longer existed. Drawing her knees to her chest, Eve stared at the image. Something tender and aching began to curl inside her.

No, she couldn't keep running. None of them would have wanted that.

Beneath the thunder-heavy sky, Eve wept until the last flickers of the fire faded into ash.

II

The Fairy Tongue

Blood was everywhere.

It soaked through the bandages faster than Bryn could replace them. He muttered a curse under his breath. The wounds weren't clotting. Red gashes tore down the injured dwarf's back, open and raw.

The mines were growing more violent by the day.

Another escape attempt had failed. This time, the punishment was public. Brutal and deliberate.

Bryn had stood in the pits with the others, watching in

silence as six prisoners were dragged to the decaying podium. He'd tried to look away, tried to swallow the sick churn in his gut, but the sound of the lashes had anchored him there.

That was when he saw him.

The Queen's crow.

He watched from a high window, a wicked smile curling his lips. His long, matted hair hung like tangled vines across his shoulders. But it was his eyes Bryn remembered most. Cold, knowing. They had locked onto Bryn's like a hunter marking prey.

The gaze still lingered, a tingle down his spine that felt too much like a caress.

Somehow, Bryn had become a target. And he didn't like it.

The changeling beside him – Erick – brought more bandages and sliced new strips with his taloned nails. Bryn hadn't known him for long, but somehow in the weeks he'd been imprisoned here, they'd begun working together, helping those who bled like the dwarf before him.

Erick's hands were quick, his sharp nails doing most of the work as his dark skin shone against the waning light.

Bryn offered a hopeful smile to the half-conscious prisoner, though he doubted the dwarf could see it. His eyes hung low, lids heavy and vacant. A wheeze escaped the prisoner's cracked lips, thin and rattling, as if the last threads of life were slipping through his chest.

'Hang in there,' Bryn whispered.

They crouched inside one of the ramshackle buildings lining the edge of the Queen's Mine caverns. Each structure held up to fifty souls, crammed together without blankets or beds. Bodies pressed shoulder to shoulder in the stale dark, trying to sleep while the elements gnawed at their bones.

Bryn had been told he was lucky it was spring, that most of

them didn't survive winter, not with the harsh frozen wind and nothing to cover their wounds. If the mines didn't kill them, starvation, weather, or untreated injuries did.

Erick's dark fingers sliced another bandage, though that was a pleasant way of saying it. They didn't have any supplies here, just their wits, and the bandage was the stolen clothing of a dead prisoner. They hoarded whatever they could, made whatever they needed. Another survival tactic to pass through another night in this horrid place.

Bryn was good with his hands, building what he could. He was a creator. An inventor.

But he wasn't a healer.

Bryn's fingers stung as he kept pressure on the wounds. His throat was dry, his muscles sore from the day's work, but he didn't relent. Didn't let go.

Erick replaced another bandage, and his frown deepened as he eyed the empty bucket beside him. 'We're out of water.'

The prisoner quivered, his skin pale and eyes hollow as he let out a soft groan. The whites of his eyes rolled to the back of his head.

'I don't think he's going to make it,' Erick said quietly.

'Not again,' Bryn mumbled, gritting his teeth.

The prisoner shuddered, then went still.

Bryn knew he was gone. He felt it in the air, as if the soul had grazed his skin on the way to the Ever After.

A warm hand rested on his elbow, nails digging into his thin tunic. 'Let him go, Bryn,' the changeling said softly.

But Bryn kept applying pressure. Kept trying to staunch the blood.

Not another.

Another soul taken. Another one lost to the dark.

'You cannot save him.'

Bryn choked back a sob. His hands were stiff as he finally released his hold.

Erick gave him an encouraging nod, his eyes sad. *You did what you could.*

Tried to save a life. And failed.

Bryn looked at his blood-soaked hands. After the colonies in Carfell had been destroyed, Bryn felt like blood washed through his very pores. The red stains etched into the sand of his cousin's home playing on repeat through Bryn's every dream. Forever dripping. Forever flowing.

'*Murder,*' Bjorn had said.

Bryn tried to save who he could. Tried to wipe it clean. To become someone whole. If he could help at least one dwarf, one creature. Then that was one less death. One less wound in the realm.

He clenched his fingers as he took a step back. Erick moved forward and covered the prisoner's face with the remnants of a ripped shirt. His voice was hushed, his tone calm as he lowered his head. 'May the Ever After hold you close.'

Eyes peered at Bryn from the dark, but no other voices spoke. The dirty, sick captives observing yet another prisoner perish.

Death in the mines wasn't uncommon, but giving the vows of the dead was. And while Bryn hadn't known the other prisoner well, he could at least provide one last chance at peace. It was a small blessing.

Bryn was worse for wear. He woke at the crack of dawn to vicious growls of dark creatures, and his days were spent underground, cutting through rock in unstable tunnels. The tools were blunt, the meals were few, and between the harsh conditions his body was failing.

In a few short weeks he'd lost significant weight, his body

covered in dozens of new scars. Blisters coated his hands and dark circles rimmed his once bright eyes. But despite the darkness and the brutality, he'd also found something miraculous here.

He'd seen secret messages. The wink of one miner to another. Food shared. A pickaxe sharpened. He'd seen fingers graze each other in the dark, prisoners who huddled close to share warmth.

He'd seen it in the little things.

Hope.

He turned to the dead prisoner as Erick lifted the body. His blood still flowed, leaking from the dwarf's torn back. He would be carried to the back, to the place where Erick and Bryn had dug a large hole.

Normally, a pyre would be set. But here, amongst the blood, the torture and the pain, he would remain beneath the soil, just as he had in the mines. It was all they could offer.

Prisoners made way for Erick as he carried the body, the quiet whispers of the Ever After following him.

One last gift.

'He shouldn't have done what he did,' a witch said in the dark. Bryn stopped in front of the woman, but Erick kept moving, his head bowed. Bryn eyed the owner of the voice. The woman's eyes were hollow, the bones on her chest peeking through her stained white dress. From memory her name was Maleny. She held the hand of a witchling, the little girl's wide dark eyes glistening with unshed tears. Her long dark hair was matted, her skin pale from living underground. Both were broken and battered, proof of the hardships they endured here.

'To expect anything but death was a fool's hope,' Maleny said.

Bryn understood. Knew why the words made the crowd murmur. 'At least he still had hope,' Bryn whispered back.

The woman shook her head, her eyes dim. 'Hope doesn't exist here.'

'That's not true,' the witchling girl said, her voice soft. 'We have each other.'

'Hush, girl.'

Bryn tried to ignore Maleny's tone, the defeat lacing those words. Instead, he looked towards the little girl. He had seen her around, hidden by the coven of witches imprisoned here. He didn't know if she'd been mothered by one of them, but children were rare anyway.

Bryn fingered the stone carving he'd made the week before. It was little more than a token, the rough shape of a deer taking form but not quite finished. Not his finest work, but it was all he had to offer.

Bryn raised the carving towards her. 'You're right,' he murmured. 'We're safer together, better. But if you should find yourself alone, you will always have a companion.'

She looked to Maleny, who pouted her lips but she complied with one stiff nod. The girl took the carving from his hands and turned it over, inspecting every inch.

'Thank you,' she whispered.

'My pleasure,' he replied.

Maleny tugged her away and Bryn found his space on the floor, the dirt rough underneath him as the silence lingered. He still had Rabbit to save. A princess to protect.

He also had the Seven.

He would not lose hope. *Could* not.

Erick eventually laid beside him, his breath heavy. And as with every death, they did not speak.

Nor did they sleep.

So, when the horns broke out as the sun begun to rise, they were both already standing. Waiting for their chains to be clasped, Bryn held his head high. Ready to step into the hollowed-out maze known as the Queen's Mines.

Dread's legs were unsteady but at least he could walk.

After his battle with Flynn, he'd been trapped in a chair for a week, watching from his tower like a useless overlord. There had been no word from his Queen. And after Flynn's betrayal, he'd avoided talking to Trik.

He was hiding, but desperation clawed at him.

He had burned the city. Let the Tinker die. His brother had turned against him. And still, the secret behind the bone door remained out of reach.

The wooden walkway linking one shelf of rock to another trembled beneath his weight as the reaper led the way, tracing the path towards the eastern caverns of the Queen's Mines. Screeches tore through the open air as shaiths beat their enormous bat-like wings. He watched them slash at each other, their cries sharp and terrible, echoing through the void.

The reaper hissed when a prisoner stumbled past and collapsed, his thin frame crumpling onto the dirt. He lay motionless, blocking the path. Dread glanced down, noting the hollow of the man's chest, the wheezing breaths swallowed by the clatter of stone and machinery.

Another broken body.

Dread kicked the prisoner over the edge and watched him vanish into the depths below.

Dread pressed on. Flames flickered against his skin as he neared the shaft that would lower him into the darkness. He kept clear of the forges, avoiding the curling smoke and the sickly stench of sulphur and decay.

The reaper scraped its claws into the earth beside him, tongue flicking over sharp teeth. Dread glared at its twisted limbs, eyes drifting over its taut black skin and elongated ears.

The thing was hideous. But so were the mines.

With long strides, Dread stepped onto the lift, the wooden platform groaning under his weight. It hung within a narrow shaft that split the cavern from roof to floor, open to the sky where light pooled and shadows tangled below. He grasped the lever, and the platform shuddered before beginning its slow descent. The grinding sound was muted against the clangs and shouts of prisoners. Human, dwarf, witch, changeling – each one looked emptier than the last as they sank into the dirt. Most averted their eyes as Dread passed, hoping to remain unseen, forgotten.

A scream split the air.

Dread turned sharply, eyes locking onto a ledge where one of his hounds stood, blood dripping from its jaws. An elf knelt in the dirt below, shrieking as he clutched at the place where his arm had been, ripped away at the elbow.

Dread frowned, then turned away. This place devoured the souls of those who dwelled here. Unfortunately, it had claimed his too.

He hated the underground. The fires, the smells, the screams, the death. But what he hated most was the thick, undiluted magic lingering in the lower eastern reaches.

The lift crept deeper, the sun swallowed behind a dusty outcrop jutting from the open cavern. Though he had steeled himself, the magic still hit him like a blow. A heavy pressure settled over him, humid and distorted. He cracked his neck, trying to shrug it off, but the sensation seeped into his pores, crawling like ants beneath his skin. A dull, persistent headache began to throb behind his eyes.

With gritted teeth, he stopped at the bottom. The workers skittered away, cutting a path through the tunnel. Despite his headache, he smiled as he arrived. They had made progress. The large square surface of the bone door came into view. Gone were the half-covered markings and forgotten bones. It now sat in a neat square, etched into the wall as if it belonged in a temple. They'd cleared the dirt enough to see sharp ivory steps leading downwards towards its towering entrance. They looked to be made of marble or some kind of white stone.

He eyed the strange flowers dotting the walls in small clusters, crawling up the rock like a little garden. They only grew in areas with heavy magic and the further they dug, the more they grew.

Like weeds.

Dread plucked a white flower free, twirling it in his hand before he crushed it between his large fingers, the pale pigment staining his fingers. 'When can it be opened?' he asked the diggers.

One of the shaiths sat perched on a wooden beam above, her black skin shiny amongst the lanterns, her wings tucked in tight. She picked her teeth with her nails, her keen eyes twinkling as she watched Dread. 'They say it needs a key.'

'What kind of key?' Dread asked.

If Myrenna came and the door wasn't open, she would tear them all limb from limb. This was progress, a step in the right direction. If all it took was a key, then Dread would pull apart the whole damn realm to find it.

'The dwarves say it needs to be of bone. But not any bone. The bone of a witch.' She chuckled.

'The bone of a witch?' he mused, turning to the dwarves. 'Is this true?'

The group of dwarves shivered, their sallow skin and terrified eyes roving over Dread. They held each other close, and he growled at them.

'Speak,' he demanded.

One of the older dwarves stepped forward, tapping another dwarf's arm in comfort. His beard was singed, his head bald. The shirt he wore was covered in dust, but so was his skin, each piece of ash and mud ingrained in his wrinkled body.

'Well?' Dread asked. His beasts growled, and the older dwarf swallowed, licking his cracked lips. 'If you stay silent any longer, I'll make sure you stay silent forever. The shaiths are due for a little playtime.'

The shaith above him leaned down and screeched in joy.

With a shaking nod, the older dwarf pointed to the bone door. 'The bones have been hard to uncover because they're so frail. Some turned to dust under our touch and others caved.'

'Louder,' Dread growled.

The dwarf's shaking voice rose as he said, 'Using the brush has been the only way to reveal it without damaging its design. If you look here and here, the symbols etched are from the original fairy folk. The ones born at the beginning of time.'

Dread eyed the shallow symbols, the swirls, and symbols in sharp patterns.

'Not many beings can read this language anymore,' the dwarf continued, 'but I was a scholar in Parador, back when we still had scrolls with the same language, yet even what I know is minimal. This symbol here means bone, this one witch and that one up there means key.'

The shaith cackled, 'The bone key of a witch!'

The dwarf nodded. 'That's what we believe but we can't be certain. We need someone else who can read the symbols.'

'And who can do that?' Dread asked.

The dwarf swallowed and smoothed the front of his shirt, a measured gesture to steady himself. 'Some changelings can. Their blood remembers the tongue of the fairies.'

Dread considered his words before he turned towards the shaith. 'Mistress.'

She leaned forward and snarled hungrily.

'Round up the changelings.'

'Alive?' she asked.

'Alive.'

With a cackle, she unfurled her wings, snapping them wide as she jumped from the platform. Her screech echoed as she called to the others.

Within moments the horns blared.

And Dread grinned at the bone door before him.

III
The Ties of Death

Snow woke to the melody of songbirds. Grey light filtered through a wide window set into the ceiling. Beside her, someone snored. She tried to turn her head, but pain bloomed behind her eyes like someone had carved out part of her skull.

She winced.

The sheets rustled and the snoring ceased. The bed shifted as she pulled her blanket back, revealing dark hair and pale green skin. Half of Malak's body slumped over the side of the bed, still perched awkwardly on the chair.

Before she could speak, Malak jerked upright, blinking in a daze. His hair stuck out at wild angles, his shirt rumpled and threadbare. She tried to smile, but it caught in her throat as the smell of stale sweat reached her nose.

'You're awake,' Malak said, voice low.

She was. And every inch of her ached. 'You stink.'

He shrugged and gave a crooked grin. 'It's a troll's prerogative.'

'Or you just need a bath.'

'That too,' he said with a laugh. 'How do you feel?'

She groaned. The pillow felt like rock beneath her head. Stranger still, she couldn't feel her feet.

'I felt better waking up from the coffin. The Queen's poison was kinder than this.'

'That's what war feels like.'

War.

Visions flickered behind her eyes. Scrabbling limbs clawing through broken soil. Artemis, grinning as she almost killed Malak. The black-clad stranger, sword gleaming, slicing through flesh and bone.

And Snow, moving through it all like a warrior queen.

Malak reached for her hand and gave it a gentle squeeze. 'You've been through a lot,' he said. 'What we saw was … horrific. A nightmare.'

'A nightmare,' she repeated under her breath.

But the word didn't sit right. It tasted wrong. Incomplete.

It hadn't felt like a nightmare.

It had felt like a dream.

She had been alive. Free. In control.

She licked her cracked lips as Malak went to the table and poured her some water. 'We survived. That's all that matters. We made it to Perridorm.'

'Perridorm,' she repeated. She took a sip, the water crisp along her throat.

'The Prince is the one who found you,' Malak said, watching her drink. 'He freed you. His name is Odion. His sister is here too. She's the one who controls the dead.' His voice was calm, but his fingers trembled slightly as he took the cup from her. His dark eyes held warmth, his smile unguarded and real.

She tried to return it, but moving her mouth felt heavier than it should have. 'How long have we been here?'

'Not long,' he replied, fixing her pillow. The movement pulsed through her throbbing skull. He was like a mother hen.

She clamped her mouth shut.

'Nothing has happened,' he continued. 'We've all been waiting for you to recover. The rest of us got out pretty easily, but you took some serious injuries. You could have bled out.'

His mouth formed into a tight line at the thought.

'I was always going to be fine,' Snow said, swatting away his concerns. 'You and Hansel prepared me for this, remember? I'm not a delicate child.'

He fluffed the pillow again and it was a hammer ringing against her head. 'Stop that, would you!' she snapped, and he halted. 'You're making it worse.'

'Sorry,' he mumbled.

Footsteps echoed across the room. Snow had barely turned her aching head when an obnoxious voice broke through the silence.

'Well, if it isn't her royal highness, awake and full of joy,' Pip chimed as he rounded the corner. 'I could feel your positive energy radiating before we even stepped in the room.'

Snow gave him a scathing look before she noticed his company. While Florian skulked behind him, it was the young man with deep ochre skin and piercing eyes that made her pause. He looked different without the black outfit. He wasn't as covered; his prominent features now open for display. His arms were chiselled and trained for battle. And there, peeking under the sleeve of his shirt, was the dark ink of a large tattoo. A feather and a stone.

His eyes settled on her. Mismatched colours of gold and brown.

He tried for a smile, but it was more of a grimace. She was distracted by the screech of wheels, revealing a girl in a strange contraption.

A chair made of wood, with wheels.

It was pushed by a young maid on the plumper side.

The girl was pretty and had the same coloured skin as Odion, except it held a slight pallor of grey. Her hair was long, smoothed into curls, but her eyes were the same. Mismatched.

Odion's sister.

Adanna, if her memory was correct.

'It's a pleasure to meet you, Princess. Welcome to Perri-dorm,' Adanna said.

Snow should be glad. Relieved she'd made it here alive. But her head hurt too much to care. 'Is this my welcome party?' she asked, her body tensing at the gathering of people around her.

The group was smothering. Too large in the small space.

Malak noticed her discomfort and stood. 'I think Snow needs rest. Perhaps we can give her a moment alone?'

Pip rolled his eyes, but complied, tugging Florian with him. Odion gave her a sharp nod before following the others, including the maid, but paused when he saw his sister hadn't turned. She looked at him, a placid smile plastered on her face. 'I think I'll stay.'

Odion looked back at Snow, frowning, before deciding his

sister was safe and disappeared. That left Snow with Malak and Adanna.

'You too, Malak,' Snow said.

'I thought you might want me to stay.'

She slid her eyes towards him. He was covered in nicks and scratches, but otherwise he was okay. Healthy.

She took his large hand, massaging her thumb in his palm. 'Thank you,' she said, 'but I need a moment with Adanna. Perhaps it's time to take that bath.'

'I'll come back later.'

'Only if you bring chocolate,' she said, softly.

A flush rose on his cheeks. 'I'll see what I can find.'

As he left, Adanna's sharp gaze settled on Snow. 'You know me?'

Snow hesitated. She knew the name – the princess had come up in her studies, alongside tales of Perridorm's lord system and the dead army that haunted its borders. But it wasn't until she met Florian that the realm had begun to unfold in full. He had shown her the scars left by Myrenna's warmongering, the battles waged far beyond her stepmother's court. The Elysian Fields. The shattered alliances. The quiet ruins.

She might have recognised Odion, had he not been cloaked in black and lost to the battlefield.

'I know your name,' Snow said. 'But I don't know you.'

The Princess wheeled herself forward and Snow assessed her. Adanna smiled, amused at whatever look Snow had on her face. 'It's a wheelchair.'

'A wheelchair,' Snow repeated, but the words sounded funny.

'It's for those who can't walk.'

Snow frowned. Wheelchairs didn't exist in Bellatorre. If

you didn't walk, you died. Unless you had someone to care for you. Sometimes, if you were lucky you were killed at birth by the Queen's orders.

'Can I ask you a question?' Adanna said, interrupting her thoughts. 'Why did you ask your friends to leave?'

Snow shuffled under her curious stare. She'd never met another princess. Only princes.

Once, when she had been a child, the royal family had visited from Carnell. The twelve brothers had come with their father and Snow had seen them bully and beat each other. It was how she knew Florian and why he'd not been a complete stranger when she'd woken up in the grotto.

'I'm not used to so many people around me,' Snow replied. 'It was … uncomfortable.'

The Princess rested her chin on her arm, thinking for a moment. 'You know, as a royal, it comes with the territory? Especially for one who plans to be a queen.'

Snow didn't like her eyes, the way they seemed to pierce deeper than they should. 'That's a future me problem.'

Adanna chuckled.

Snow stared at her chair again. 'Why can't you walk? Are your legs broken?'

'My legs are fine. I'm just too weak,' Adanna replied. 'The feather to my brother's stone.' She smiled to herself, like she was remembering some inside joke.

Snow didn't know what to say, so she sat there silently. Her eyes scrunched as the throbbing in her head worsened.

'I'll have a healer sent, to help with the pain,' Adanna said. 'For now, I just wanted to check in on you. Make sure you were okay. I also wanted to give you an update. I've sent word to the rebellion about your survival. They know you're alive.'

Snow frowned; she'd been sent here by Flynn. Sent to rally

an army. To gain an ally. If they were already in contact with the rebellion, then why hadn't they come to her aid? Adanna and Odion knew of her kingdom's hardship. They knew what the rebellion represented. Why had they ignored the stakes?

'I know why you're here, Snow,' Adanna said, her eyes turning soft, as if she could read her thoughts. 'I know the journey has been hard. That your past has been a burden. I also know why you chose to fight.'

Adanna lowered her head. 'But I also know we can't give you what you want, though it is nice to finally meet in person.'

Snow's mouth was dry. Her head throbbed. The words a blur in the streaming daylight. The voices inside her mind hissed.

Adanna waved her arm, and a healer came into the room, mixing a powder into Snow's water. 'We cannot leave our lands vulnerable,' Adanna continued. 'We don't have the luxury of coming to another kingdom's aid when we wage our own war.'

The healer raised the glass to Snow's lips. She took steady sips, and the taste of citrus hit her tongue.

Snow's headache began to recede, and she sent a small thanks to the Godmother.

Adanna sighed. 'I'm afraid to tell you that your journey would have been more fruitful if you had gone to your own people. To your rebellion.'

The words rang in Snow's ears. The rejection of a proposal before it had even begun.

'Thank you, Andre,' Adanna said to the healer before turning back to Snow. 'You are welcome to stay here as long as you like. What we can offer, we will. But further support in this war is impossible. I hope, with Odion saving you, we can come to an alliance of peace, a way to help each other through hard times.'

Something cold sliced through Snow's veins.

'An alliance,' Snow repeated quietly. '*If* we win.' She straightened her spine, ignoring the pull in her aching muscles. 'All I hear, *Princess*, is that you offer no aid and expect to reap the rewards without lifting a finger.'

Adanna stilled. 'That's not what I'm saying.'

'That's exactly what you're implying.'

'You misunderstand.'

Snow didn't misunderstand. She didn't want to hear it. Didn't want to face the idea of going home alone. No proof of her leadership. No support. No alliance.

If she returned empty-handed, how could she expect anyone to follow her? How could she lead without something to show for her strength, her sacrifice?

She needed Perridorm. She needed their power.

Adanna's words echoed in her mind.

Failure before it had even begun.

You were always better alone, the little voices whispered.

And she was inclined to believe them.

'Get out,' Snow said, her voice flat.

Adanna blanched.

The healer gently pressed a cloth to Snow's sweat-soaked forehead. 'She is unwell, Majesty,' the healer said quietly.

Adanna hesitated, her expression pinched with concern, then gave a shallow nod and began to retreat.

Snow turned her eyes to the wheelchair again.

Weak, her mind echoed.

Snow turned away, her eyes resting on a cot nearby.

You will not fail, the voice inside her said, stroking her. *Power can be found in the smallest of cracks.*

Snow let the voices in, let them comfort her as they had in the forest.

She would not fail. She couldn't. Not if she wanted Hansel and her crown. She had been born into greatness. With or without Perridorm, she would win.

Hansel was out there and so was Myrenna. And she would fight with every pore of her being to do what she had to do.

We will not fail, the voices murmured.

'No,' Snow whispered back. 'We won't.'

Malak was outside the room when Adanna shut the door to the infirmary, leaving Snow to recover. His face was pained, and his eyes heavy.

Adanna knew he had been listening. She supposed she would have done the same if it were Odion.

'I assume you think I was too hasty,' she began.

Malak shook his head, his eyes lingering on the door for a moment before he said, 'I guessed the conversation would come, I just thought it would happen after a negotiation.'

A negotiation. As if they had all the time in the world.

Adanna couldn't help but feel the weight of her powers. How the lifeblood of those souls on the field felt. How even now, when she wasn't using the sword, she still felt them and each of their deaths.

Slumbering and cold beneath the earth.

She pulled at the hem of her sleeve. 'We have nothing to offer,' she said, her voice quieter than she'd like.

The troll's politeness had thrown her off more than she cared to admit.

He shuffled on his feet, his eyes roaming the door. But

there wasn't any sense of dismay from him. His shoulders were hunched but his eyes had a steadiness she'd seen rarely in others. Something akin to faith.

Faith in Snow.

'There is always something to offer,' he said. 'More to give. It's the way of the realm.'

'You are far more diplomatic than your princess,' she mused. 'Has anyone ever told you that?'

A rough laugh escaped his lips. 'Nobody paid me enough attention to render advice.'

His green skin, gold earrings, and warm smile sat strangely against the backdrop of the creamy dust covered halls. Despite his gruff appearance, there was something disarming about him. She wondered if a troll had ever set foot in the castle before. Had one ever been allowed this far, or even dared to come?

She'd have to look it up in the library, if Petrella – the librarian – would allow her access. Given the last incident of her visit.

Malak looked down at her, at the meek body contained inside her wheeled chair. Adanna did not lower her chin. She knew what she looked like to him. Trivial. Pale. Weak. Feelings she tried to keep at bay inside herself.

But as she met his eyes, they held no pity. No judgement. Just pure curiosity.

She couldn't help but like him.

'Perhaps if advice was given,' she answered, 'you may not have heeded it anyway? Much like your princess.'

He pulled at the gold earring looped through his ear. 'I'm sorry,' he said, nodding to the door. 'She's usually not that hostile.'

'I suppose we all have our traumas.'

She felt Malak's stare as he took in her pallor, the scars she couldn't quite hide. She wore long sleeves and a high-necked dress. It wasn't that she concealed them, not exactly, but she knew they unsettled Odion.

Odion hated that she was the one to bear the sword. That it marked her, hurt her, each time she stepped forward to protect the kingdom. But the burden had always belonged to their joint bloodline. The family curse. To wield the blade that would guard their home.

What Odion despised most was that it wasn't him. That he couldn't make the sacrifice too.

The stone to her feather.

Adanna's skin had lost its colour, her body worn, but she was still strong. Still stubborn.

Perhaps, too much so.

Adanna reflected on her conversation with the Princess. Perhaps she had been too hasty. The girl was barely recovered, after all.

She hadn't matched Adanna's expectations in the slightest. Pale, with tangled hair cropped short. Her features were soft, almost delicate, but her eyes were sharp, a piercing blue that held more strength than her body could show.

Adanna blurted the words before she could consider them, 'I'd like to extend an invitation to dinner.' she said, her mouth a little dry. 'We still have some help around here, though it's not a lot. Do not fear the silent halls too much.'

'I quite like the silence,' he replied. 'Thank you. We accept.'

'I might not have put her in the best mood,' Adanna joked as he gave her a slight bow.

'That's okay,' he said. 'I'm used to brooding royals.'

She nodded towards the infirmary door. 'I'll leave you to it, then.'

His hand lingered on the handle before entering, his fingers twitching as he carefully opened it.

Adanna couldn't help but follow his movements, curiosity getting the better of her. It had always been in her nature to look further than others could see. It happened mostly in her dreams, the way shadows moved through her thoughts and predicated strange events.

Events like the Princess's arrival.

As Malak entered the wing, she rolled her chair down the decorated corridors, the wheels creaking with each turn. Dust had settled in the corners, and cobwebs clung to the ceiling. This castle had once been beautiful. The carvings vibrant, the painted walls glowing under the light, filled with the hum of life as people wandered its halls.

Malak might have found comfort in the silence, but some deep part of Adanna missed the noise. Missed the cries of children. Missed the laughter.

She loosed a breath. It did her no good to think of what had been. It only ever lulled her into a melancholy mood.

Lost in her thoughts, she veered towards the central courtyard, where she caught sight of Prince Florian leaning against a window in the hall. His pressed shirt was neatly tucked into black pants, his hair combed and clean.

She didn't have time to turn before he looked up. His golden hair shined against the morning sun, but his eyes were hollow, dark circles blooming underneath. Red blotches were scattered across his skin, but she recalled Pip mentioning that the prince suffered from extreme allergies.

'Prince Florian,' she greeted, stopping next to him.

The view overlooked the gardens, which were a little unkempt. The rose bushes were fat with the hedges splaying branches in all directions. The vines had grown out of control, and Adanna wondered how many snakes now lay in the long grass.

She tilted her head. Though it was chaotic, she thought she rather preferred it this way. A bit wild and untamed.

Odion would disagree.

'Princess Adanna,' Florian replied. His eyes were a shade of light brown, and she noted a small freckle in each iris. 'How was the visit with Princess Snow?'

She should find a polite response, tell him it was pleasant. But his eyes told her that he would know she was lying. After all, he had been travelling with Snow.

'It was an experience,' she said.

He chuckled. 'It always is with her.'

'Do you know her well?'

He waited a moment before answering. 'I thought I did. But I find now ... *Achoo!*'

Adanna reached into her pocket and produced a handkerchief. He took it gratefully.

'Sorry,' he mumbled.

'Go on,' she urged. 'You find what?'

He tried to hand the handkerchief back, but she shook her head.

He pocketed it, smiling sheepishly. 'I find that who we are as children can be amplified as adults. When I first met Snow, it was on a political visit with my parents. When my brothers bullied me, she'd watched. And when it had become enough, she picked up a stick and chased them away.' He laughed. 'It was a sight to see. This tiny girl, up against older boys, and yet they still ran away. I was in awe of her.'

His eyes sparkled against the reflection of the window. Adanna looked away and straightened her skirts.

'I suppose it sounds silly now, a boy getting saved by a girl,' Florian said.

She scoffed. 'Why would that be silly? Can't women show as much strength as a man?'

'That's not what I meant,' he said, shaking his head.

Adanna lifted her brow.

The Prince sputtered, 'I'm trying to say I'd never seen that before. My father and brothers never saw value in women's opinions. Men inherit the land. Men take the throne. *Men are what make a Kingdom,*' he mimicked in a deep voice, and sighed. 'What I meant to say is that Snow is fierce. She was a storm when my mother was a calm day. I'd never seen anything like her before'

Adanna assessed him. 'And what have you seen now, Prince?'

'I've seen giants. I've seen a troll break a curse. I've seen the Seeker do impossible things. And I've travelled across three kingdoms.'

Adanna tilted her head again, her curiosity piquing. For someone so ... forgotten, those eyes had seen more than she'd ever known. Ever felt. It was a different kind of sight to her own. One that was tangible and not lived through others. She wanted to know more.

'Will you take a stroll in the gardens with me?' she asked.

'I don't—'

'I'd like to know more of what you've seen. If you'd share it with me.' Refusing to take no for an answer, Adanna pointed to her chair. 'I find myself rather tired, do you mind?'

He shook his head as a blush crept along his cheeks. He took the handles of the chair and began to slowly push her. The wheels creaked along the floor as Adanna cupped her hands in her lap. 'Let's start with the giants.'

IV

The Crossroads of War

Hansel stood at the balcony of the Sanctuary and watched the crowd below. Hands exchanged food, bedding was folded, weapons sharpened. A few fairies darted through the air, playing tag.

It was an odd sight, something that clawed at his chest.

Nowhere across the realms had he seen such peace between species. Nothing like the bigotry and racism rife in the kingdom beyond these walls, where royal families measured worth by what each race could offer. For fashion, for labour, for food.

The sight blew a cautious breath of hope into his chest. One he guarded closely.

Eve had once told him he had a hero complex. It had been the last day he'd seen her. Perhaps she'd been right. Or perhaps he was just a dreamer.

In truth, he was neither. Hansel knew what he was. Had known since the day his sister died. He was broken. Damaged.

He'd once believed peace was possible. That good would outshine the bad. But the longer he stood in the shadow of war, the more that belief frayed. His ember of hope flickered, dimmed bit by bit.

A breath from his sister's death.

A drop of water from Myrenna's betrayal.

A cold wind from losing Eve.

Each moment chipped away at the flame. He could feel himself cupping his hands around it, shielding it. Begging it not to go out. Because without hope, he was lost. Just a lifeboat, adrift in a vast, empty sea. And what now? Torn between Snow and Eve. Between duty and love. Between fighting and fleeing.

Laughter rang out from the far corner. Hansel followed the sound and met Viper's gaze. She smirked, eyes gleaming, as a ring of children gathered around the illusion she'd conjured, a spectacle of shifting light and shadow that held them captive.

'She's been recruiting,' Piccadilly said, her voice dry as dust behind him. 'Like the ringleader she is.'

Hansel turned. Her presence cut through the noise below. Silver hair spilled down her back in loose waves, catching the light like moonlit silk. Nothing like the woman she'd been yesterday, standing beneath the podium's glow, singing for the dead.

They'd held a memorial. For the ones lost in the city's fires. For the Queen's victims. For every shadow that had crept into their lives. Names had been written, folded, and fed to the flames. One had been for Gretel. For the fairies of the grotto. The dwarves. Lady Nona. Beetle.

Beetle's name had stung the most. After Bonyx's rescue, he'd told them what had happened in the throne room. The truth had settled over them like ash.

The ceremony had been quiet, heavy. But necessary. Grief, left unspoken, would rot them from the inside. Even now, each name was a drum. A memory.

Piccadilly stopped beside him, her eyes piercing the crowd as he watched her. From the outside, she looked relaxed. But her shoulders were tight, and her fingers tapped along the railing. She exuded strength and grace but there was vulnerability there too. She was the Commander, though she held all her power on a lie. They were treading muddy waters without a map to guide them.

If Hansel was being honest, he could admit he was lost. He was unsure on what to do next or who to help. Nona's words rang in his mind whenever there was a moment of peace, reminding him to *Find her at the end.* Whatever that meant.

One of the performers below did a backflip, the crowd clapping with encouragement.

'She looks to be a good teacher, at least,' Hansel said. 'One of her better qualities.'

Piccadilly leaned against the rail to face him, her skin luminescent in the light. She held no weapon, choosing instead to wear a dress of deep blue.

'The Silver City is in shambles,' she said quietly. 'The fires took a third of the city. Hangings still line the square, the bodies piling up. Between yesterday's ceremony and all the blood and loss ... any form of happiness is welcome.'

She was right. But something inside him went rigid. All he could see was the dead yet to come. The pleading eyes of families ripped apart. The stench of burning flesh clinging to the air as the flames crawled through the streets. The screams in the night as death rapped on their doors.

He couldn't face another massacre. Another casualty.

Another name on paper to burn.

'You sang beautifully,' he murmured, not taking his eyes off the crowd.

She sighed, accepting his change in topic. 'The rebellion needed to mourn. At least for a little while.'

That was all they had. Only a little time. A smidgen of hope. Fleeting moments, captured.

There was always more to give. More to sacrifice.

Hansel studied her. The way her brow furrowed, how her eyes stayed distant, as if plans upon plans ran like clockwork through her mind. Piccadilly was kind, despite her talent with blades. But she was also cunning.

'What do you hope to achieve?' Hansel asked, his tone edged.

Anger simmered beneath his skin, coiled with nowhere to go. No target. No clarity. They were hidden away beneath the city he used to love. The one he used to dream in.

Piccadilly blinked, the only sign she'd registered his shift in mood. 'I hope it can be used to drive them. To bring them closer. To make them fight for the same cause.'

Always to fight. Never for peace.

'Vengeance isn't the answer,' he muttered.

'Not vengeance, no,' Piccadilly said, carefully. 'Something

more. A push for peace. For safety. And one day … freedom. But I didn't come here to talk about mourning and moral codes,' she added. 'Can I borrow you for a moment?'

He breathed through his nose, forcing the tension from his chest. He needed to move. To train. To do anything.

Hansel exhaled, long and low. 'Sure.' And followed her down the corridor.

He glanced at the stone underfoot, his steps heavy where hers floated like smoke. He tried not to stare at the sheen of her skin, the lean muscle shifting beneath her dress as she walked.

Lanterns flickered within alcoves built into the wall. Heat radiated from the fireplaces of each room they passed, casting long, warped shadows.

He ran a calloused finger along the wall as they turned another corner. The paint flaked beneath his touch.

As the voices of the crowd faded and the echo of his footsteps took over, Piccadilly stopped at a pair of tall double doors. She drew a key from her pocket, slid it into the lock, and turned it with a quiet *click*.

Darkness met them.

Then came the flare of a match in Piccadilly's fingers. She touched the flame to a lamp in the wall, and the room bloomed with soft light, spilling across the wooden floors.

It was not what he expected.

The shadows flickered over him as he entered, his eyes landing on a high ceiling with hanging chandeliers. Furniture was covered in sheets, setting an eerie glow that made him think of the wraiths roaming through Parador.

'What is this place?' he asked.

She gave him a smile. 'Welcome to the Commander's Hall.'

She glided across the room, fingertips skimming the edge of a white sheet draped over the furniture. Piccadilly gave it a sharp tug, and the cloth came free, sending a cloud of dust spiralling through the air.

The dust caught in Hansel's throat, and he coughed, waving a hand as the haze settled.

Beneath lay a dining table, its surface dulled by time. Chairs stood like sentinels, their backs carved with curling patterns, round cushions faded but intact. The wood held a quiet dignity, as if waiting for voices that hadn't filled the room in years.

'So, if this exists, then why didn't we have our meeting here?' Hansel asked, taking a seat. He thought back to their makeshift meeting. The uneven tables and cramped space.

'I hadn't yet admitted I was lying, that the Commander wasn't here, remember?' she said, rummaging through her pockets until she pulled out two cups. 'Plus, this room gives me the shivers. Like something lurks in here.'

He glanced toward the dark. The shadows shifted with the flicker of light, and for a heartbeat he thought he heard something thrumming within them. Like a heartbeat inside a chest.

Piccadilly pulled the chair out, the legs scraping against the floor. The sound snapped him from his thoughts.

'Drink?' she asked.

He nodded, stretching his legs beneath the table. A faint breeze moved through the wide room, cool against his skin. Piccadilly poured what he assumed was liquor into the drinks, and with a soft clink, they both swallowed.

The liquor burned his throat, warming him and easing some of the tension in his shoulders.

They sat in silence for a while, each sifting through their own thoughts before Piccadilly said, 'I want to seek counsel from you,'

She reached over to refill his glass. Her hands lightly shook, enough that Hansel couldn't hold back his frown.

'You and I both know I'm at a bit of an impasse,' Piccadilly said. 'The dwarves have saved our coffers, but our morale is the lowest it's ever been. People are missing, missions are halted, information is minimal, and our communities are being hung on the other side of these very walls.'

Her eyes lifted to the ceiling and her shoulders sagged. There were bags under her eyes, the bruises of battle staining her skin. The weariness.

'I need help, Hansel. I have few people I can trust.'

'I thought Flynn was your counsel,' Hansel said, swallowing his second glass.

'I know you don't like him, but he can be trusted, you know.'

Hansel snorted. 'Then, where is he?'

They'd broken out Rumple and Bonyx from the castle days ago, exploding an entire wall of the dungeon at the base of the castle to do so. Flynn had gone missing when Hansel and Piccadilly had been captured. Since then, he hadn't returned. Nor had any messages been sent, as far as Hansel knew.

'Everyone has secrets,' Piccadilly replied. 'We don't pry for yours, so don't pry for his.'

'But you know his secrets, don't you?'

She smiled again. 'I know many things.'

He hated that. The lies and deception. It was always a guessing game. With Myrenna. With Eve. And now Piccadilly.

He shook his head, holding out his glass as Piccadilly grabbed the flask.

'That's what I wanted to talk to you about,' Piccadilly said. 'Not Flynn, but some information he gave me before he went missing.'

Hansel kept his face neutral as he swallowed the liquor.

'He thinks he met the Princess,' she said. 'He was sure of it.'

Hansel snapped his attention to her. 'What?'

'We don't even know if it was her,' Piccadilly said with a shrug. 'He was on a mission, collecting stardust and weapons from our contact at the Skinny Piglet. I believe you know him, actually.'

'Marcellus,' Hansel grumbled. 'He helped us with the spindle.'

'Well, Marcellus and Flynn were interrupted during their dealings by a troll and a young woman.'

Hansel sat up straight. He hadn't heard from Malak since they'd left the grotto. Hadn't seen the Princess since he'd dived into that chasm.

'The woman *claimed* to be the Princess.' Piccadilly snorted and took another shot. 'She met the physical description, of course. But a lot of girls do. Flynn said he'd been hesitant, but she'd answered questions nobody else would know. *Couldn't* know. I don't think she knew the weight of what she was saying.'

'What kind of questions?' Hansel prodded.

'Questions about the castle. Things that happen behind closed doors,' she said softly.

Raven silk hair brushed his skin, the scent of jasmine clinging to the air. Cushions sank beneath him, warm and heavy, and the Queen's breath grazed his neck – slow, deliberate, close enough to steal his own.

His stomach lurched at the uninvited memory. But Snow wouldn't share what happened to him with the Queen. She would have shared something else. Something she'd seen within the vast tunnels of the castle.

Piccadilly watched him carefully. Her eyes never missed anything. 'She said things that nobody else knows. Except for Flynn. She travelled with an axe, and the troll was small for his kind, spoke in clear Bellatorrian with no hint of an accent.'

Hansel leaned back, his heart thrumming wildly in his chest. Humans didn't travel with trolls. It was an oddity; one Eve had pointed out from their first meeting in Roserock. Besides Hansel, Snow was the only other person who would do so openly. Especially if it was Malak.

He smiled to himself. 'They're alive.'

Piccadilly poured another glass. At the rate they were going, they'd be drunk in half an hour.

'I thought it was all fairy shit, but from your reaction I'm now reconsidering,' she said. 'This changes everything.'

'What do you mean?' he asked.

'You're not going to like this,' Piccadilly said, offering him another glass. Hansel shook his head, declining. 'Flynn sent her to Perridorm.'

The words barely landed before Hansel was on his feet, his chair crashing backward. 'HE WHAT?!'

In a blink, Piccadilly was alert, a knife in her palm. He had no idea where she'd drawn it from. And he didn't care.

'That spineless soldier sent her to a battlefield?' Hansel roared. 'She's not ready for that. She's barely even been outside!' He ran both hands through his hair, heart thundering, panic clawing up his spine. 'We have to find her. Bring her here. She's not—'

'Huntsman.' Piccadilly's voice cracked like a whip, sharp with command. 'I haven't finished.'

He was pacing now, his breaths uneven, muscles coiled and ready to sprint through stone. He couldn't save Eve. That failure had branded itself into his bones. But Snow ...

Malak ... He could still save them. By the Godmother, he would.

'I'll kill him,' Hansel said, his voice low, trembling with rage. 'I swear, I'll *kill* him.'

Piccadilly rubbed her temples, muttering under her breath, 'Men never cease to amaze me.' She looked up. 'She's already made it, you idiot. She's *in* Perridorm.'

Hansel froze. The words hit like a slap.

'We received word this morning,' she continued, pulling a scroll from the folds of her dress. 'From the Princess.'

She handed it over. Hansel snatched it, fingers trembling as he unrolled the parchment.

Just a few lines. Simple. Direct.

Snow had arrived. With the Prince of Carnell. An elf. A troll.

'Pip and Malak,' he murmured, disbelief in his tone.

They'd made it. *Alive.*

Hansel stood there, scroll in hand, silent. Letting it sink in.

They were in Perridorm. *Perridorm.*

'What do you think?' Piccadilly asked.

'I think—' he started, his mouth going dry. 'I think once Myrenna finds out, she'll kill them all.'

'Perridorm has a strong army. One of dead soldiers and magic. The twins have been holding off the Queen for years.'

'Which means the young twin heirs are likely depleted,' he retorted, fists gripped above the table. 'Fighting an army for decades takes a toll. Perridorm was weakening when I was still in the castle, before Carnell joined the Queen's forces. What army could the twin heirs likely give?'

'What if I were to suggest we help them?'

'Then I'd say this is another one of your very stupid ideas.'

She laughed. 'The last plan worked, didn't it?'

'Barely,' he said through clenched teeth. Her last plan had almost gotten him killed. 'How would we help them? We have our own problems here. We're being hunted like animals. The Queen will have a fit when she sees the condition of the city. Zacariah still wants to free the prisoners in the Queen's Mines, and half the rebellion isn't trained. They aren't soldiers.'

Piccadilly downed her drink. 'The problems will always remain here. We are in the heart of the Evil Queen's domain. It was always temporary. I fear we've outlived our welcome in these city walls anyway. Once Myrenna returns – if she hasn't already – she will slaughter us. I know that.'

'Then what's your plan?'

She leaned forward, her elbows resting on her knees. 'I'm already working on evacuation plans; relocation sites are getting back to me daily. But I'm also considering another location. The Queen's already been there but I hope that means she'll forget it was ever a threat. As long as the ghosts will let us in.'

'What is it you're actually asking me, Piccadilly?'

'What I'm asking, *Hansel*, is whether we hide or fight.'

He sighed. 'If we hide, they'll end up weeding us out eventually as they always do. And if we fight ... How many more ceremonies will we need? Half of them have never even held a sword or a weapon in their whole lives.'

He crossed his arms, watching dust drift through the air, each mote turning slow circles in the light.

They couldn't hide forever. They would have to fight eventually. They had little choice. With the scouts not coming back, and the mines, they were done for.

The rebellion was small. He didn't know how big the pockets were, but Piccadilly had already said the Sanctuary held most of them. If nobody taught them to fight, then they'd have no chance. Nona had asked him to help the rebellion. To go to them.

Perhaps this was what she meant.

'We have to start training. Even if it's only a few. At least give them the basics,' he conceded. 'We start on a voluntary basis. Nobody is forced into anything.'

She nodded. 'So, we fight?'

'Not yet,' he replied. 'But we can at least prepare. With some help, we can use this room for the space.'

'Some of the dwarves may be willing to help.'

He nodded. 'Bring anyone who can fight. The more trainers we have, the more of a change we'll see. As for running to Perridorm or attacking the mines, let's see what we're working with before we do anything rash.'

'I'll look at relocation efforts, continue to see where we have the best advantage.'

He nodded as she poured him another glass. He could already see her mind at work, the plans shuffling through her brain.

'We can start as soon as tomorrow.'

Piccadilly smiled and gave his arm a squeeze. 'It's a good start.'

'It's something,' he replied.

V
The Lure of Dreams

Eve stared at the appalling mess she'd made.

The vials she'd concocted – filled with pain killers and energy serums – remained in order, but the cauldron and the ingredients were strewn about, resembling a break-in. With a sigh, she started on the cauldron first, the stains from her latest failed attempt at potions sticking like tar to its side. Her hands were raw by the time she finished.

With quick work, she tidied the table until all that remained on the bench was a stack of books and her measly belongings. Her knife glinted in front of her, the ruby stone a deep blood red. She'd lost the other one when she'd faced the Queen at the Ancient One.

Her heart sunk at the thought.

They were a set. A twin pair. Losing both was one thing, but having one whilst her greatest enemy held the other felt like a betrayal to Hansel.

She fingered the ruby, her mind wandering to the lingering kiss she'd given Hansel after he'd gifted them to her. The hurt from losing Dante's knives had been great, but Hansel had soothed it somehow. Soothed *her* somehow.

Her things lay where she'd left them, neat enough to count at a glance. The stone from Hansel sat by the window, pale in the weak light. Beside it, the wolf's tooth rested on her folded shirt, its edge dulled from handling. Her mother's mirror caught a sliver of her reflection as she passed, and the piece of wood from the Ancient One leaned against the vials she'd filled that morning. Not much, yet enough to trace the path she'd taken.

She supposed having so little was a good thing. Less to carry. Less to lose. But as she looked about the cottage, the cosy lounge, and the array of belongings, her heart ached. It almost reminded her of her old home. The one in the glen with her father.

The compact mirror caught the light, flashing like an eye, urging her to peek. Her fingers lightly grazed her cheek, the mark of her scar thinner than expected but still taut against her skin. The mark didn't change who she was – she knew that. But there was still an underlying current of fear.

Eve was a mess of scars, inside and out. It proved she was a survivor. A warrior. But there was truth to the term that not all scars were physical. She held some inside. Ones that were hidden, marred across her heart from loss. Kept away from the prying eyes of strangers.

Her hands shook slightly as she brought the compact towards her face. the latch opening with a click. On the unblemished side of her face, her skin remained soft next to her full lips, her eyes still warm. Surprisingly her eyebrows only needed a minor pluck.

Slowly, she lifted her gaze to the ruined side of her face. The scar ran from beneath her eye to the curve of her chin, a thin, jagged line of pink edged with bruising. The skin puckered beneath the light, tender to the touch. It gave her features a sharper cast, her usual glare cutting harder than before. She snapped the mirror shut. She hated mirrors anyway.

At least that's what she told herself.

A light *thump* came from her left, and a book appeared. Happy for the distraction, Eve picked up the leather-bound cover: *Legends and Creatures of Magic.*

She played with the cover, tracing the smooth lettering with her fingers and peeled back the front page. At the top of the contents, it read 'Sea Nymphs'.

The rain still poured outside, the sky a deep grey against the angry sea. Eve watched it for a while, tracing the path of a raindrop as it slid down the glass. 'You're as miserable as I am,' she murmured.

A soft thump broke her thoughts. A mug of tea sat before her, steam curling into the air. The scent wrapped around her like warmth after a long chill, and despite herself, she smiled.

Cottage of convenience, indeed.

The window creaked as she looked towards the sea. The angry waves crashed against the shores, digging into the black rock with veracity. She knew if she tried to swim today she'd end up drowning. The thought was not inviting.

With a crackle from the fire, she pulled her tea close and read the page. It didn't give her much about the sea nymphs. Mainly stated the obvious facts she'd already learnt from Cyrene years ago. As she yawned, a glint caught her eye. The gold lettering of the dream book she'd been reading the night before stared at her, stacked amongst the grimoire on the coffee table. Its pages lay open, displaying a picture of two spindles, one large one from the room next door, and another for the smaller one she'd collected for Rumple.

Forgetting the nymphs, Eve wandered over to the dream book. Picking it up, she eyed the neat lines and read the first passage.

Dream Weaving is considered an erratic magic with sub-components. Memory Walking and Dream Walking. Each sub-component differs from past to present.

Memory Walking focuses on past moments, where the viewer may delve into lost moments and memories without altering the scene.

Dream Walking, however, focuses on real time and is far more dangerous. When Dream Walking one can create a Dreamscape. A Dreamscape allows one to create unique surroundings and connect with the one who is unconscious. When one uses intent, it is possible to manipulate those surroundings and those who inhabit it, including the unconscious victim's mind.

Without proper precautions, reality and dreams combine in a way that one may lose one's mind, with the risk of one floating through dreams to never be seen again.

Preferably, to Dream Weave, one may have a guide on these journeys, or a tether to their reality. In some cases, one can weave alone. However, this is not recommended.

'I wonder if Rumple wasn't the only Weaver,' Eve whispered, sipping her tea.

The room with the spindle and tapestry glowed softly, the call of it pulsing through her veins like a heartbeat. She tapped her fingers nervously on the grimoire's page, her bottom lip caught between her teeth. If she had survived memory walking once, surely she could do it again. Right?

Her eyes lingered on the open page, where Dante's lip was curled in a tentative smile. His cheekbones were sharp, his crooked nose from all his falls flawed but perfect all at the same time.

She slammed the book closed. She was foolish. Completely idiotic to even consider testing the spindle again. But still, she found herself drawn toward the door bathed in filtered light.

What if?

What if this could change everything? Including the war.

They were all dreamers, after all.

What if dreams and memory held the key – not the mirrors?

The door to the Spindle Room creaked open silently as she pushed it, the glow from the tapestry flooding the space. With careful steps, she settled onto the bench before the spindle, placing the open leather-bound book beside her. The great wheel hung above, the tapestry to her right shimmering with ethereal light. In the corner was a chipped piece of wood, shavings from a carving on the floor, as if someone had stolen a piece of it.

Eve's hands trembled as she drew in a deep breath. And began to thread.

The magic brushed over her as she pieced the strands together, her eyes flicking back and forth between its threads and the book. She thought of Dante, of his kind smile and strong hands. She focused on the pattern, envisioning it was him, a tether to this world and the next. As the picture began to form, her body shuddered.

And she fell.

Colours and light drowned Eve. Her skin stretched, tearing from bone. Bile crept up her throat and just as she thought she would spew, she hit solid ground.

Her knees cracked as she landed, and pain rippled up her legs. She spat in the grass, her head throbbing.

The sky was light blue, the clouds fluffy and white amongst the open space. Spread across the field were tents of all shapes and sizes. Vargos sprawled intermittently, and in the middle sat the biggest tent of them all, made of swaths of red and gold.

She'd fallen into another memory.

Eve took a shallow breath as a young man whistled, pitching one of the last tents. His hair was tied in a bun, his skin tanned against the bright sun. A little girl ran after him holding an array of tools.

Eve choked in air, her mouth dry.

Dante.

His skin was the same, dark, and bronzed against the sun. He was healthy. Fit.

Eve clutched her chest as the little girl stepped forward. Her hair was braided and freckles scattered across her skin.

Eve knew that girl. Knew what it felt like to be a part of Dante's world. To play a role in it. Something inside her broke and remade itself all at once.

'Do I have to go again?' younger Eve asked Dante as he pinned down another cloth for a new tent.

'Nona isn't as scary as you think,' he said. 'I know she's old, but she's very wise.'

'I know,' the girl said, twisting her head towards a vargo at the edge of the clearing. 'She just says strange things.'

Dante held out his hand, 'Like what?' he asked, taking the hammer from her outstretched hands.

'I'm not supposed to say.'

He chuckled. 'Well, don't tell me then. If the Seer says not to, then you listen to her, okay?'

She tapped her foot. 'Why?'

Dante finished securing the tent and stopped to look down at her. 'Because she sees things others can't. Things that will happen and things that have already been. If she's taken an interest in you, then it's a good thing.'

Young Eve paused before answering. 'She scares me with the things she says.'

He kneeled in front of her, pulling away the tools before he placed them in the grass. Taking her hands, Dante stared her into her eyes. 'Being scared is okay, but being too afraid that you remain frozen is not. Does she hurt you?'

'No.'

'Does she treat you badly?'

The girl shook her head.

'Then you must heed her words,' Dante said. 'What have I taught you?'

She shuffled her feet in the dirt. Staying silent.

'I've taught you to learn. To gain knowledge wherever you can. How do you do that?'

She huffed a breath. 'By watching.'

'How else?' he asked.

She frowned. 'By using whatever resources I have. Like books, or my surroundings, or people.'

He nodded. 'That's right, and Nona has a lot to teach you.

Not many have the opportunity to work with a Seer. They are rare.'

'But I don't want to hear stories. I want to learn to fight, like you.'

He chuckled. 'I'm an entertainer, not a fighter. But I'll teach you what I can, and Viper's fighters can teach you the rest. For now, I want you to listen to those stories. I want you to memorise them, to lock them in that big brain of yours.'

Young Eve's lip wobbled. 'I don't like stories anymore.'

Dante pulled her close, his lean arms enveloping her. 'You like my stories.' He stroked her hair, letting the loose strands slide through his fingers before he pulled back, the smile gone. 'I know Nona's stories aren't like the ones your father told you, but maybe if you give the Seer a chance, she might surprise you.'

'... Okay.'

Eve's stomach dropped and her body was flung back as she was swallowed into colour.

She landed on the bench with a thud. The book scattered to the floor, the pages folding over themselves under the tapestry's glow.

Eve's body shook, her mind feeling like it was being pieced back together after turning to soup.

Her eyes stung. Her head throbbed. And her body ached.

But as she looked up at the looming tapestry, the spinning wheel shiny and solid before her, she croaked out a laugh. She was finally getting the hang of this.

Bryn twined the decaying rope around the head of a pickaxe, tightening it over the handle and metal. Erick's talons had been helpful with the steel, his own iron tips unbreakable, leaving the metal sharp. Bryn handed it back to an elf when he was done. The creature gave him a quick nod of thanks before he disappeared down the tunnels.

It was a small act, an easy fix, but at least it would make carving into the dirt one less strain for him to endure.

'You're good with your hands,' Erick commented, leaning against the opposite wall, the roof low enough to graze his scalp.

'You're good with your talons,' Bryn answered.

The tunnel they stood in was narrow, the rock jagged and hot. One lantern had been allocated to their group, the fire fairy sprawled along the bottom of the glass cage providing light. Her chest rose and fell with shallow breaths, her skin paler than normal.

Bryn hissed as he dug a splinter from his palm. Another one to add to the pile.

'Can you fix anything? Or is it just the pickaxes?' Erick asked, lifting an axe for another recruit.

'Most things,' Bryn said. 'I like to create and figure things out. Mostly it's just to use my hands, but when I was back in Parador, I made things for the others. Toys for the younger ones, carved bowls and the like. Small stuff.'

It seemed like an age ago now, the green ferns and glowing lights a distant memory.

He'd always been useful with his hands. Either cooking or carving or fixing things in the glen. He remembered sculpting out a little wooden fairy for Rabbit and Beetle a while ago; their eyes had shone at the creation. But whilst Rabbit had kept his, Beetle had grown out of it, wishing instead for adventure.

Bryn gnawed his lip at the thought of Rabbit lying in the shadows of the Doc's ward at the Sanctuary.

Originally, Bryn had left to go find more Vox Leaf, escaping the Silver City and filling his pouch. But where he had been stuck was finding a specific flower. One that only grew near the mines. On his journey, he had been captured after borrowing a horse from a farm. And now he was here. Locked in the mines.

'I made a crystal coffin once,' Bryn said.

Erick snorted as he used his talons to sharpen another axe. 'That doesn't sound useful.'

'It was beautiful,' Bryn remarked, smiling at the thought.

Erick shook his head.

When Bryn had arrived, he'd been alone. Most of his comrades disappearing or dying in his first few days. He'd learnt to remain silent, watchful of the creatures that roamed in the dark. Then one night, everything changed. A prisoner was dragged into the huts and thrown to the floor, bleeding and broken. No one moved to help. The sound of his breathing filled the room, strained and wet, until even that began to fade.

That was the day Bryn stepped up, feeling for a pulse, checking the extent of the prisoner's wounds. And whilst the hollow eyes of the other recruits watched him, Erick had been the only one to assist.

Since then, they'd been inseparable. A team working together to help with weaponry and the injured. Not that made it much of a difference. The beasts took liberties with the recruits and at any sign of weakness, you became a target.

This place bred hopelessness.

Bryn and Erick did what they could, no matter how minor, because it was still *something.*

Bryn hit the rock, his muscles shaking as the lantern gave an eerie glow. The growls of the beasts echoed through the walls and Erick's piercing eyes followed the sound.

Erick had been here a year, longer than most. His skin was dark as midnight, his eyes sharp and watchful, reminding Bryn of the night sky. Quiet, vast, and full of hidden motion. He moved with the grace of something coiled, lithe and ready.

Though a changeling, he bore little resemblance to Piccadilly. No two changelings were ever the same. Piccadilly shimmered with silver skin and hair pale as moonlight. Erick, by contrast, carried talons that curved like blades and a faint pulse of magic that clung to him like mist. His hair was cropped close, his left ear lined with piercings made of jade, gold, and silver catching the light with every turn of his head. Hunger had carved lines into his face, sharpened his jaw, but it hadn't stripped him of presence. There was a quiet power in Erick, something that drew others in without effort.

When Bryn had enquired about his home, Erick had merely snorted, saying home was a fairy tale. He was a traveller; he held no home. From what Bryn had gathered, Erick had been a raider, seeking refuge with other lost souls and stealing from those unawares on the main roads.

Bryn usually feared the raiders on the road, terrified that whatever supplies he'd gathered would be stolen on the way back to Parador. But Erick had laughed, saying his victims could always afford to be robbed.

The comment didn't ease Bryn's caution about raiders, but he trusted the changeling.

'See anything down those dark tunnels?' Bryn asked, taking another swing at the wall.

Erick grunted. 'Nothing.'

His ears twitched, the growls reverberating around them as a scream echoed from somewhere far below.

'I just like to make sure I'm prepared for when one of those *things* come near.' Erick's voice was rough, like forged steel.

Bryn hated the beasts too. The reapers, the shaiths and the blood hounds were twisted, as if they'd been made in some dark place deep within the cauldron itself.

'I don't suppose you'll want to pick up that free axe and help me?' Bryn asked. 'You know we'll get a beating if we haven't made enough progress.'

Erick flicked his eyes back to him. 'Progress in what?' he motioned his hands around them. 'This is all for show, anyway. We're not here for the pretty minerals or diamonds. We're here for whatever lies in the eastern tunnels.'

Bryn wiped the sweat from his brow, his stomach grumbling. Erick had been obsessed with the eastern tunnels since Bryn's arrival, the changeling adamant that it felt *wrong*. Cursed.

Erick's eyes shone in the dim light. 'Whatever the Evil Queen wants, it's not what we're digging here.' He looked back towards the shadowed tunnel. 'Something has changed. The magic is stronger. I can feel it from here.'

'What do you think it is?' Bryn asked, curious.

He frowned. 'I don't know, but I think the magic is dangerous.'

A horn blared through the tunnels, raising the hairs on Bryn's arms. Erick shifted as the beasts came, followed by a small group of guards. Shouts tore through the dark. A whip cracked, sharp as lightning, and Erick flinched. From the gloom stepped a burly man, his black eyes narrowing in disgust towards Erick.

Erick stood in front of Bryn, but the guard only laughed.

'We're not here for the dwarf. We're here for you, changeling. Get to the pits.'

Erick growled as the man stepped forward, his shoulders taut, when some of the blood hounds and reapers stepped from the shadows. The guard ran his hand over his whips, causing blood to splatter on the floor.

Bryn placed his arm on Erick's elbow. 'I'll be fine. Just go with them.'

Erick stared the guard down before he eventually nodded. The man smiled, his teeth the colour of sand.

And as Erick left, followed by the mine's keepers, Bryn couldn't help but feel that something was very, very wrong.

The storm stayed for days, and Eve found herself drawn more to the spindle. It was like a drug she couldn't quit, nauseating but satiating at the same time. She pored through memories like she was drinking the finest wine from the richest vineyards.

For days, she tumbled through mountains where Dante told her about the stars. She spun through forests with Porchid. She wove through markets, laughing as her father tickled her belly.

It was glorious.

And terrifying.

And *free*.

On some days it was like learning to swim again, as if she'd dipped in her toe and begun a slow paddle. But with each memory she entered, with each dream, she became more confident. More daring.

And as the rain bucketed outside the cottage's windows, she would spend hours weaving, the tapestry glowing, drinking her in just as she became drunk on it.

And as she slipped through each memory, trying it on like a new pair of slippers, she began to forget.

She forgot the time weighing on her. Forgot the mirrors. Forgot the grief.

So lost she had become in those moments, that she didn't notice the presence of a stranger entering the cottage to escape the rain.

VI
The Uncertainty of Rulers

Piccadilly sifted through the scattered papers in the commander's office. Ledgers, lists, and accounts blurred together in dark ink. His neat handwriting crossed off meetings and problems with sharp precision.

She remembered his hard eyes and rough hands. The firm nod that had turned her world upside down. His quiet acceptance of her. Of her skill.

He hadn't been warm, but his heart had been kind.

She'd seen it in the portions of food he quietly donated to

the hungry. In the stillness of night, when he rescued survivors slipping through the cracks. His tired eyes weighed down by the burden of keeping others alive in a realm determined to destroy them.

He'd been a teacher once. It was his claim to the castle. That he had taught Princess Snow herself. Until the Queen had banished him after the dark days came. The days after the king died and Myrenna tore away the carefully crafted mask of the baker's girl with the apple pie.

Piccadilly clenched her fist, calluses rubbing raw against her palm when she remembered his corpse in the Queen's dungeons.

Piccadilly had been so young when she arrived here, running from home after her family was lost. She had never known her father but had stayed with her mother in the mountains, hidden away, until raiders found them and burned their home to the ground.

Food had been scarce, and she had not yet honed her skills with the blades or bow. She'd not yet learnt the signs of death as her mother withered away in the foothills of the snow-crusted landscape.

The Commander had been the only one to show her kindness. To show her how to fight. To believe in something better. Something more.

The prison cells in the castle flashed across her mind, the Commander's blank eyes and shrivelled body in the corner.

How had I not known? How had I not heard he was taken?

The Queen had been sly in her kidnapping of the Commander. Little had she known, Piccadilly had been the thread holding the seams together while he was missing. Leading, while he faded away into nothing.

Guilt rattled her, but she palmed the papers, the ink

smudged in some places with the red stains of the Commander's favourite wine.

She was alone now. And though the rebellion was barely holding on, she still grasped onto the hope her companions were true. That the small fortune of gems Bjorn had gifted might save them. She faced the same problems despite his donation. The rebellion had more refugees than warriors; they were more a charity than a force to be reckoned with. Piccadilly swore she could hear Myrenna laughing at her from the castle.

What a pitiful resistance. A fledgling group amongst the queen's skilled and terrifying army.

Hangings still rang throughout the city, the cobblestones stained with the death of so many. The once vibrant city was lifeless against its old bright memories. The colours of the buildings had dulled, as if the paint itself had grown tired. Cracked shutters hung loose, and roofs sagged under years of neglect. Myrenna ignored it all, her silence saying more than care ever could. The soul of the city was charred and smoke-ridden like the beating heart of the Queen herself.

Piccadilly rubbed her eyes. The candle's wick had almost burnt down to a dying flicker. She was stuck, unsure on the next move, on the next mission.

The tiny piece of hope in the rebellion was dying, withering away slowly as the Queen closed in on them. As family and friends were slaughtered at the stocks. She'd considered telling the rebellion the Princess was in Perridorm, and that she lived. If only to rally them.

But what if she told them Snow lived, only for them to watch her die?

Piccadilly groaned. She had relied on Hansel, and Flynn. She had prayed to the stars and the Fairy Godmother with every inch of her being. But the more she fought, the more lost she felt. Like she was wading through a stream before the dam broke and snatched her away.

It was a suicidal war. An attempt to cleanse a world that would ultimately kill them all. They were untrained, undecided, and surrounded by enemies. Snow was a tool, but one Piccadilly didn't yet know how to use. Hansel had offered to train them, but they barely had the space. Or the privacy.

Her finger roved over a map of the realm, stopping along the line of trees lingering beside the Skinny Piglet. The forest held monstrous things, like witches who preyed on children. The coast was too far and too open for such a large group to hide. The mines of Parador were filled with wraiths and hidden corners even she feared to tread, despite Bjorn's assurance he could track the halls. But she also doubted its security after Myrenna's attack on Beetle and Bonyx. Not to mention her massacre of the fairies in the grotto.

Bjorn had admitted defeat at that point, but he had raised something that tickled in the back of Piccadilly's mind.

The Gilded Mirror.

'The Queen will always find us,' he'd said, as they sat around the makeshift room. *'That mirror of hers is a reflection of the realm. A window to wherever she wants to look.'*

'Then why has she not found us yet?' Piccadilly had asked.

'Because she has bigger things to focus on,' Flynn had replied, his eyes darkening. *'But when she gets bored, when she finds what she wants, and her eyes fall elsewhere. We'll be the first thing she wipes out.'*

The rebellion had been a minor nuisance to Myrenna, nothing else. A fly buzzing around her head while she found more powerful allies, and even more powerful objects. And right now, they were waiting for her to feast on them.

Unless they could manifest a shield of some kind, but that

was power Piccadilly had not encountered. The small number of witches amongst them were healers, utilising plants and modest healing magic to help Doc. They hadn't the knowledge nor the power to provide such a thing.

Where could we go with protection? Where it didn't matter if we were found.

Piccadilly's finger lingered on the foothills near Ivywood. Where the border of Carnell and Bellatorre met. The dwarves had said the Peaks of Carfell were well fortified. The tunnels from the old dwarven city ran deep, the traps built by the ancestors who created the colony. It had already been ravaged by Myrenna, but they had made the mistake of opening their doors to the Queen. What if they hadn't?

The mirror would find the rebellion wherever they hid. Then, like an addict crushing the last of their popium, it would snuff them out.

And when it did, the Sanctuary had nothing to protect them.

She lingered on the curves of the hills. The mountains at the back, a wall of impenetrable heights. The lake sitting to the south shone on the page.

A tug pulled at Piccadilly. The one that urged her towards a destination. The one she had relied on to survive.

Piccadilly tore down the map, her mind already plotting. If they were to survive, they would have to brave it outside the walls of this city and find safety in the Peaks of Carfell.

Or run.

VII
The Unexpected Encounter

Eve jolted awake to a crack of thunder that rattled the cottage to its bones. Her neck clicked as she straightened, joints stiff from sleeping on the bench. Pins of pain shot down her spine when she stood.

'I sound older than the Sisters Grimm,' she mumbled, rubbing the sleep from her eyes.

The air was thick and black, the kind of dark that swallowed corners and blurred the edges of the room. Only the faint glow of embers hinted at the hearth. She shuffled forward, breath misting in the cold, and rubbed her arms against the chill. Rain lashed the windows, the pitter-patter loud in the hush.

Eve was used to storms, to the fierceness of them. They came with the territory, part of the price for roaming the realm in search of work. Years of wandering had carved resilience into her bones and sharpened instincts that rarely failed her.

Now, something prickled along her spine. A warning. The kind that didn't shout, but whispered.

She turned slowly. The room felt both known and strange, like a memory half-remembered.

Darkness blinked. Lightning split the sky. And there, by her favourite chair, stood a cloaked figure. Silent. Watching.

Shit.

Eve dived for her lone knife by the door. Just as fast, the stranger was up, a weapon of silver appearing from within their black robes. Eve grabbed the hilt of her knife and twisted, just as a long spear swung for her. She ducked, lifting the blade when it was knocked clean from her hand.

Eve jumped back, her shoulder grazing the wall as the spear swung towards her face. She felt it lift her hair, the point a pixie away. Eve dodged the next blow and ran, bolting over a table as the stranger came for her.

They were like water. Moving quickly. Desperately.

Eve didn't understand how she'd been found. How the cottage had been revealed to whoever this was. She'd believed herself safe. Watched over.

That had been her mistake.

Her eyes scanned for a weapon, a fork gleaming dully before her in the light. She smirked at the house's attempt to help, and snatched it in her palm. She braced herself, the room too dark to see clearly, but the stranger moved quickly. Eve pivoted around furniture, narrowly missing the spear's point as the stranger jumped, prodding the weapon forward. Eve's fork clanged against the weapon, missing the second swing by a pixie as she spun, carefully avoiding the blow. Already her breath was laboured, her body still aching from her dive beneath the ocean outside the cottage.

Eve's heart thrummed in her chest like a thousand fairy wings. 'Get out of my house!'

A crack of thunder roared through the sky, lighting the room for a split moment. It was enough for her see the stranger was lean, tall.

The windows cracked, the house shook. And the stranger dived.

Eve rolled, the spear crashing into the wooden floor. The fork fell as she twirled, running towards the lounge. A spatula appeared mid-air and she grabbed it. 'An actual weapon would be better,' she muttered.

If she could get to the fire, maybe she could grab a poker or something heavy. The stranger didn't hesitate. With feline grace they ran for the couch, their limbs stretching out like a flying shadow as they dived over the edge. Eve gasped, fumbling with the spatula only for it to bend when the spear came for her again. Scrambling back, Eve groped for a fire poker, for *anything*. But not even a kitchen utensil was available.

'Give me a weapon,' she shouted towards the ceiling.

The space was small, with a table in the centre. Eve knocked the table over, using it as a barrier, and thanked the Fairy Godmother. It was her only reprieve. A shield against her attacker.

The stranger let out a curse as they stumbled into the wood and Eve crawled towards the fireplace. Her fingers fumbled in the dark, finding nothing, except for a baking tray.

Seriously?

As the stranger stood and readied themselves Eve gave up on the fireplace and threw the tray behind her.

Surprise had always been her specialty. The clang from the tray distracted her attacker for a moment. Desperately, Eve tackled them into the couch, hitting the stranger with a deep grunt as they collided. She'd expected the cushions to break the fall, but it seemed the lounge was daintier than Florian's best apology. With a loud crack, it snapped under them, the wood shattering. Eve tried not to think about it as the splinters flew, cutting into her skin.

More scars.

Eve dragged herself across the floor, a groan slipping from her lips. The front door rattled under the storm's fury, nails groaning as wind clawed at the frame. She whimpered, pain blooming across her body like bruises already forming beneath the skin.

She pushed herself upright, breath ragged, and turned to face the stranger.

They circled each other in the dark, silent and deliberate. Lightning flared, casting fleeting shadows that danced across the walls.

Eve cracked her knuckles, the sound sharp and defiant. Blood trickled down her side, hot against the chill, her clothes damp with it. Whoever had found her wasn't using magic.

If they had been, she wouldn't still be breathing.

She remembered her father's warning. *'True strength lies in the crevice of one's heart. It is found in one's wit and skill and soul.'*

She was fast. She was strong.

It was time to prove it.

With a wicked grin, Eve lunged forward, looping her arms

around the stranger's torso. They landed with a thud, smacking against the wooden floor like two flailing fish. It wasn't neat, but it didn't need to be. Eve just had to win.

A fist cracked against Eve's jaw, snapping her head sideways. Pain flared through her skull, hot and immediate, and blood pooled in her mouth. She growled, twisting violently, limbs locked in a frantic struggle.

Her foot slipped on the slick floor as the stranger shoved her face away, forcing Eve's neck into an unnatural angle. The cloak tangled around them, wrapping their bodies in folds of fabric as they rolled, breathless and clawing for advantage.

Eve drove her elbow back with a snarl, landing hard. Only to be met with a stinging palm across her face.

The stranger moved like smoke – fluid, fast, unforgiving. Eve ducked, breath rasping, as the strike skimmed her cheek, a whisper of pain left in its wake.

She gasped, lungs burning, just as her attacker seized the moment. The cloak twisted around her limbs, pulling tight, dragging her down. Eve clenched her jaw. She wasn't finished yet.

With a desperate shuffle, she broke free, only to be met with a knee to the gut. Her body folded, the bruises already stitched across her skin flaring anew. Her head throbbed from using the spindle, her vision blurred at the edges. She'd let her training slip. Now it showed.

Her fist lashed out, bone cracking beneath her knuckles. The stranger rolled off, tumbling towards the lone spear.

White light split the room. Eve barely found her footing before the stranger's blue hands closed around the weapon and hurled it. The spear tore through the air.

Eve ducked. It slammed into the wall, sending jars crashing

from the shelves. She twisted, reaching for the pale metal shaft, but it held firm, unmoving beneath her grip.

She cursed under her breath.

The stranger didn't falter. They surged forward, feet pounding, cloak trailing like shadow.

Eve's gaze snapped to the knife by the door. No hesitation. She lunged, vaulting over the bench, scrambling across the floor. Her fingers curled around the hilt, the cold metal grounding her.

She spun just as the spear sliced past her again, the wind brushing her cheek like a kiss. Her hair whipped sideways, and she whispered a prayer.

Her eyes locked on the weathered cloak. Her grip tightened.

The Seeker spun her blade.

Once.

Then twice.

'My turn,' Eve said with a wicked grin, before letting her knife fly free.

It was an extension of herself, a shot so true that she'd done it a thousand times. And as time slowed, the golden hilt flying towards her target, they flinched. The knife embedded into the creaky wooden wall, nicking the stranger's hood.

I missed.

But as thunder roiled again and the room glowed a pale white, the hood fell with a jolt. Eve didn't hesitate as she ran, her feet pounding hard against the wooden floor.

The stranger pulled at their cloak, the neckpiece refusing to unclasp before the Seeker's fist collided into the stranger's jaw with a crack. Fire raced down Eve's arms as sharp nails clawed into her skin, tearing flesh free.

Both of them let out strangled cries but Eve didn't halt. She swung again, slower than normal, less efficient, but she hit her mark. Her fist collided with the intruder's shoulder and they howled.

Blood coated her hands, the sting from her injuries a faraway thing when another crack rolled through the sky, blaring light onto the stranger's face.

Blood. Teeth. Blue skin. Shimmering scales.

... And hair the colour of red wine.

Eve froze.

With a loud rip, the stranger broke free from the cloak, and in one vicious motion smashed their fist into Eve's face.

Eve barely had time to think, barely had time to process what she had seen as their bodies tumbled across the floor, limbs flailing. Nails. Teeth. Fists. It was a blur. The pain throbbed through Eve's muscles as she blocked blow after blow. She covered her face. Covered the scars that would never heal.

But then she realised her biggest asset wasn't in the fight. It was in revealing herself.

With gritted teeth and blood soaking her chin, she stilled. Her muscles protested, barking in pain as the stranger grabbed and bit and kicked. Yet, when Eve let go, when she fought against every instinct to survive ingrained into her, forcing her arms to fall beside her.

With each breath, she braced for pain. Waiting for the shooting stars that would coat her vision. For the blackness that would take hold when her injuries became too much.

In another flash, the stranger's arm halted, nails mid-air as both of them bled. Stains covered their clothes. Dirt and mud and blood.

Eve panted. Waiting. Hoping. When a confused voice broke through the darkness.

'Eveline?'

The sea nymph blinked, their eyes wide as Eve lifted herself onto her elbows.

With every limb aching, Eve held back her laugh and spat out blood. Teeth coated in red, she breathed a sigh of relief.

'Hello Cyrene.'

Sweat trickled down Dread's back as he eyed the lineup of prisoners in front of him. The heat was stifling, causing his clothes to itch and putting his temper on edge. At least his orders had been actioned quickly. Each prisoner before him was a changeling, distinguished only by a lingering mark that claimed them at birth. Being a shifter was one thing, it was the ability to change shapes to become something else. But shifters remained human. Their blood untainted. Born into it as nature intended.

Changelings, however, were abominations. Unwanted. Most were twisted in form. Ugly, misshapen things swapped at birth by cruel fairies and creatures that lurked in the dark.

Many fled the continent, chasing whispers of a place that didn't exist. The rest – those who survived – were left to rot. Enslaved. Homeless. Hunted. So, it was no surprise to find so many in the mines. Most had been dragged in by guards or handed over by eager citizens, hungry for the clink of a few worthless medallions.

One sniffed the air with twin noses, piercings twitching as Dread passed. Others bore scales, or mottled skin. Some had extra eyes, limbs carved from wood, or features that defied nature. Each one a patchwork of strangeness.

Dread moved slowly, eyes sweeping over them, reading their movements, savouring the scent of fear. But only one changeling haunted his thoughts. The one with silver skin. The one who had shattered any hope of redemption.

He'd been chasing the rebellion for years, and that silver-skinned wraith had been a thorn in his side from the start. She had freed the prisoners from the dungeons. Taken from the mine's resources, and hidden stowaways somewhere within the city. If he could ever unlock the bone door, she would be his first target. And he would enjoy cutting her to pieces before serving her on a platter to the Queen.

He could taste it now, the Queen's hungry smile as she praised him.

Dread spat on the ground, walking down the line of changelings with heavy steps. One of them could help read the bones, could feel the magic brewing, and he had little time to find them.

He could smell urine, their terror ripe as the beasts growled around them, the sound bouncing off the cavern walls. Some of them sobbed, their broken bodies shivering. He halted near a female, and he lifted her chin. Her golden eyes were hollow. She appeared almost human, until he turned her head and found soft gills, delicately placed behind her ears. He scoffed.

'I'm looking for volunteers,' he said, letting his voice carry.

Their eyes followed him as he paced, his smile cruel and unwelcoming. 'It seems we require the talent of someone with fairy blood. Someone with the ability to read the old language.'

Most averted their gaze when he came close, as if it could hide them. He enjoyed it. Until he came across one with long talons.

Dark eyes held Dread's, strong and unyielding. Dread halted. 'I've seen you before.'

'I'm hard to kill,' the changeling replied.

Dread's lip quirked at the side. 'Is that a challenge?' The changeling didn't respond as Dread stepped closer. 'I don't like changelings. I think you're all a waste of life. And whilst you were useful,' he said, lingering on the word, 'with our new intake of dwarves, I find that even the small value you previously held for mining is diminishing.'

The changeling was quiet a moment before responding, teeth grinding, 'Then why keep us alive?'

Dread smiled. 'That's the question, isn't it?' he asked, spreading open his arms to address the line of prisoners. 'Why *do* I keep you alive?'

Some of them shuffled backwards, away from his words.

'Does he not make a statement?' Dread continued. 'If you cannot even help me with this easy task, then what's to stop me from killing every single one of you? In fact, I'll give you all ten breaths. Ten breaths for a volunteer to step forward. Ten breaths before I get the beasts to tear you all apart.'

Dread could taste the stench of fear, and he let it roll over his tongue. It was like fine dining, each course better than the last.

By the third breath, the growls from the hounds started, vicious and starved. Saliva dripped from their jaws, their claws twitching.

By the sixth breath, the guards stepped forward, their eyes glinting with hunger.

And as the last breath was taken, the tall changeling with the talons stepped forward. 'I can read the old text.'

Dread growled, pulling him forward. The changeling's

muscles went taut under the touch. 'You'd better not be lying,' Dread hissed. 'Or they'll all die.'

A flash of understanding crossed behind the changeling's eyes.

Dread released him. Turning back to the guards, he said, 'We have a volunteer.'

'And what of the rest?' one of the guards asked.

Dread waved a hand in the air. 'Whip them all.'

VIII
The Prince and the Pea

Florian shifted in his seat, the tension in the hall pressing against his ribs. Across from him, Snow pouted from her chair, throwing sharp looks at the Princess of Perridorm. He didn't know what had sparked it, only that the air had grown heavy.

Malak's shoulders were drawn tight, and Odion watched the exchange with that same calculating stillness. Florian tried to read him, to see where the prince stood in all this unrest, but there was nothing to find. At least Adanna kept her silence, hands folded neatly while the others simmered.

Unable to remain still, Florian's hand twitched on the table. His gaze roved over the food, halting on Pip who ignored them all, scoffing down his meal like he'd never eaten before. The elf smacked his lips in satisfaction as he picked up some pork, dipping it in a heavy dose of gravy.

'Well, isn't this nice,' Florian said, trying to ease the tension.

He held his glass up, ready to toast when he noted Odion's scowl pointedly facing him. Florian held his glass still, his attempt at a half smile failing as the prince's mismatched eyes glittered in distaste.

'This isn't nice,' Odion said. 'It's downright unpleasant.'

Florian placed down his glass before straightening his napkin, trying to maintain decorum. To act like a prince. But he was only met with a scowl from the rest of the group. His smile turned into an awkward grit of his teeth as he said, 'I was trying to be polite.'

Pip snorted from the end of the table.

Odion shook his head. 'Don't bother. Nobody here has a reputation for being pleasant, except maybe my sister.'

Adanna placed her hand on Odion's elbow, and shot Florian an apologetic smile. 'Forgive him, we haven't had dinner guests in a long time.'

Odion turned to his sister. 'I was only being honest.'

'You can be honest without being rude,' she hushed.

Florian sipped his drink, pretending he hadn't heard.

'Try and be polite,' she whispered to her brother. 'We are not monsters, so let's not behave like it.'

'Interesting advice, coming from a princess who controls monsters,' Snow commented from the other end of the table. Her eyes glaring daggers towards the twins.

Florian closed his eyes at the insult as Odion glared at

Snow, standing slightly from his chair. 'They are *not* monsters. They are our men.'

Flashbacks of the battle rang through Florian's ears. Empty eyes. shredded skin. And the scream that had ripped from him as Malak and Snow faced Artemis.

'Here we go,' Florian muttered to himself.

Snow couldn't resist commenting, her own body rising in defence. 'They might be your *men*,' she hissed, 'but they are still dead. It's creepy.'

Florian tried not to cringe at Snow's biting tone. He sometimes forgot he'd been the only one trained for diplomacy. For the intricacies of court. Snow never had the chance. Never had the exposure to royal life as he had. He was suddenly grateful for his horrible upbringing.

As for the twins, their story was just as isolating. Their whole family slaughtered before they could become adults. At least Adanna had the decency to pretend to be civil.

Florian opened his eyes. Snow and Odion stood, eyes blazing with challenge over the table. Florian had to reel this back somehow. To remind them of why they were here.

'What nice weather we are having,' Florian started, grappling for a topic that wouldn't end in Snow losing her temper. The weather was safe. They all knew about the weather. But it sounded pathetic even to his ears.

Snow gave him an icy stare, one that made him want to shrink under the table and hide. Since her hair had been shorn in the camp, her features had sharpened somehow. She was no longer a child, but a woman. Florian blinked. She was temperamental at best, but tonight she was a dragon. A very, very pissed off dragon.

He tried to avert his gaze, to ignore the promise of violence in whatever words she planned to throw at him later, but her stare lingered.

Adanna nudged Odion, and the prince's eyes fell on Florian and his half-upturned fork. 'The weather is nice,' she replied with a neutral tone.

Florian gave her a nod of thanks.

'*Nice.* What a boring word,' Pip retorted, his mouth full of food. 'I'm just happy we're finally eating a proper meal and that nobody is trying to kill us at the present moment. *Nice* doesn't cover that kind of joy.'

Snow turned her hateful gaze to Pip. 'That's the most positive thing I've ever heard you say.'

'Probably because you've never been around when something positive happens.'

'What's that supposed to mean?' she snarled, looking like she was about to tackle him to the ground and use her fork as a carving tool.

'Pip,' Malak warned, but it fell on deaf ears.

'It means, *Princess,*' Pip started, waving his pork at her, 'that wherever you go, destruction follows. The Queen seeking your heart. The crystal coffin and the poison. The death of the fairies and dwarves who protected you. The wood nymphs. Hansel. The Huntress. Do you see a pattern here?'

Snow's fingers twitched, gliding towards the butter knife by her plate. Her food remained untouched, when Odion spoke up. 'At least she can hold her own. What she did to save Malak was brave.'

'First you fight her and now you stick up for her?' Pip shook his head. 'This is what I get for mixing with royals.'

But even Florian was a little in awe of what she'd done. Snow had fought her way through the forest alone to only then be captured. But instead of breaking, she and Odion went straight into battle, where she picked up a sword and beat one of the Queen's best hunters, saving Malak's life in the process.

She'd already been impressive with her training while they'd travelled, but on the battlefield ... there had been no hesitation. No weakness. No mercy.

Florian watched her, his dinner going cold. He tried to take another bite, waiting for his anxiety to subside, but the food tasted like ash in his mouth. He and his companions had come here for help, and yet each royal wanted to claw each other's face off.

Thankfully, Adanna took the reins, trying to bring some semblance of peace. 'We have a lot to discuss,' she said. 'But perhaps we could at least start with a meal before we go stabbing one another?'

She grasped her brother's hand, calming him and encouraging him to take his seat. Malak mumbled something under his breath and Snow huffed.

Seeming to accept defeat, Snow picked at her potato. 'I don't see why you won't help,' she grumbled. 'You're fighting the same enemy we are. She threatens you too.'

'That is exactly why we cannot risk the resources,' Adanna replied promptly, not backing down.

Florian poked at his vegetables, his stomach churning at the thought of the dead. He felt Odion watching him, but he wasn't sure if it was curiosity or because the prince wanted to stab him too.

'I think what Snow is trying to say,' Malak intervened, 'is that you haven't shown that you're open to discussion with what's happening. Snow is right. The Queen's war affects us all. I understand you're in a tricky position. Shouldn't that mean that we pool our resources, work together?'

'There's nothing to negotiate,' Adanna replied with sad

eyes. 'We have nothing to offer you. Nothing to negotiate with.'

Florian remained silent, opting to stay out of whatever tangled mess that was brewing. He lifted a green bean covered in salt and subtly sniffed it before popping the coated bean in his mouth.

'Fairy shit,' Snow snapped.

Florian choked back his surprise with a hiccup. The vegetable lodged somewhere between his tonsils and windpipe. He squeezed his eyes shut, reaching blindly for the wine.

'I don't appreciate that language,' Adanna said, arms crossed.

'Myrenna attacked Perridorm for a reason,' Snow shot back. 'I'll bet anything it wasn't just for a silly little sword.'

Pip snorted. 'I wouldn't call a sword that raises an entire army of the dead silly or little. Particularly when that same sword helped raised the garrison that you're trying to campaign for. Rather poorly, I might add.'

'Nobody asked for your opinion!' Snow barked.

Florian felt the burn. His eyes watered. He glanced up. Odion's inimitable gaze was locked on him. The prince's dark hair curled tight to his scalp, and the umber tone of his skin caught the lantern light. He wore a navy tunic fastened with gold buttons, the colour drawing out the glint in his mismatched eyes.

'What role do you play in all this?' Odion asked, ignoring the others and the internal battle Florian was clearly losing. Odion's accent had a lilt, his syllables smooth and sharp at once. So different from the clipped tones of Bellatorre and Carnell.

Florian tried to swallow. His voice came out in a wheeze. 'I'm still trying to figure that out.'

Odion tilted his head, watching the colour rise in Florian's face.

'Snow,' Malak said, his voice a warning. 'This isn't the time.'

'He's right,' Adanna added, lifting her chin. 'Let's at least savour dessert before anymore unneeded sparring.'

Florian gagged. The bean had not given up.

He needed to regain ground. 'What's your role?' he managed to sputter at Odion.

Odion didn't blink. 'My role is to protect my sister and this kingdom. If you do not know your role, then why are you here? Is it not your army we fight on the border?'

Florian had expected this. But it still stung. His brothers were the villains. The ones who needed to be stopped. And this *cauldron damned* bean.

'It's my father's army. I'm last in line.'

Odion sneered. 'Easy words for someone avoiding blame. Are they not your people?'

Florian wanted to disappear. To fold into himself like a flower in a frost. Odion wasn't wrong. They were his people. Even if he had never ruled them. Even if he was never meant to.

'I could say the same for the dead,' Florian said, coughing. The wine was not enough. His fork shook as he set it down. He was choking. No point hiding it now.

Useless, his father's voice echoed in his skull.

His throat bobbed. He reached for water and drank, grimacing at the burn that smothered his throat. Odion watched him the whole time. By the cauldron, it burned.

As Florian's face turned crimson, Odion only blinked. Florian fought back tears, his shoulders heaving. He slapped the table once.

The room went silent. All eyes turned.

A massive cough ripped from his chest. The bean shot out and landed, slimy and withered, on the cream tablecloth.

Relief flooded through him and he gulped in air, his chest heaving as everyone just stared. Shame crawled over him, his body shaking as he broke Odion's stare. Losing whatever bet they'd silently made.

He waited for the comments. For the blistering remarks. Instead, a loud laugh broke the silence, free and full.

Florian's gaze shifted from the grimy bean to the prince. Odion's eyes sparkled with amusement, strange and bright, his pearl-white teeth flashing. 'That was the most ridiculous yet endearing thing I've ever seen.'

All eyes fell on them, the table falling silent, except for Odion's chuckle. Snow frowned from her seat, lips pressed tight, just as Odion struck the table with a bang. His rings clattered against the wood, the sound sharp and sudden.

Adanna's eyes lit up first, her face glowing as she looked at her twin brother. 'I haven't heard you laugh like that in years,' she whispered.

Florian blushed hotly, still wishing to climb under the table. Yet, Odion's strong face glowed and his skin shone a golden brown beneath the glow of the chandeliers. Florian's breath rushed out of him, a whirlwind gathering under his skin.

Odion breathed deeply, regaining his control. His mouth went back to his familiar grimace, but when he turned to the group, his beautiful eyes were bright. 'I'm going to eat now,' he stated, turning to his plate.

Adanna smiled and raised her glass. 'Enough of politics. Let's just eat and celebrate that we're alive. We can talk about miserable things tomorrow.'

Snow scowled and ate her potato with a grimace. Pip licked

clean the gravy from his meat and Malak played restlessly with his dinner. Adanna took a sip of her water and smiled at Florian.

Odion eyed Florian over his glass of wine, sipping with shuttered eyes, though Florian swore he saw the ghost of the dark prince's smile. Somehow, Florian didn't want to crawl under the table anymore.

He just wanted to make Odion laugh again.

Though the castle at Felldryn was bare, its walls draped in cobwebs and dust, Florian had been given a warm room, with clean sheets and a crackling fire.

The hearth was freshly lit as Adanna's handmaiden led Florian inside. She was a plump woman with unmarked skin, her long, ebony hair braided and strung with gold beads. Her dress shimmered silver-blue as she placed a tray of tea and biscuits on the table.

'Do you need anything else?' she asked, pausing by the door. Her gaze cut through him, quiet and sharp. She didn't use his title, and he didn't correct her.

'Ah. No, thank you,' he said. Then, awkwardly, 'Do you? Need anything else, I mean.'

He wasn't sure why he said it. He was royal. Though a lowly one by his father's standards. But something about her unsettled him, even with the kind face and polite tone.

'You could tell your brothers to stop invading our land.'

The words hit like a slap. He blinked, startled. 'I can't. They don't listen to me.'

She looked him over, unimpressed. Then sighed heavily through her nose. 'It was worth asking.'

'I would if I could,' he said quietly. 'I promise.'

She held his gaze for a moment. 'A promise is a heavy thing to offer,' she said. 'But I believe you.'

Florian gave her a nod of thanks before she left, the silence swallowing the room behind her. A set of chairs and a table sat before the fireplace, upholstered in a shade of dusted emerald green. The cushions were full, the backs tall. They reminded him of Malak, the gold thread woven into the dark green cushions much like the glint of the gold earring that Malak wore.

Moonlight spilled through the double glass doors on the other side of the room, casting pale light across the rugs and wooden floor. It was pretty, too pretty. The kind of quiet that made the skin prickle, where stillness felt like something was watching back.

He'd just slipped off his jacket when a knock startled him. He opened the door, and found Adanna on the opposite side, her wooden wheelchair parked neatly. Her dark hair had fallen free of its pins, tumbling over her shoulders in unruly curls.

His mouth went dry. 'Princess?'

'May I come in?' she asked.

She wore the same dress from dinner, soft pastel lace that cloaked most of her meek frame. The collar rose high, surrounding her neck.

Florian blinked, then stepped back to let her in. 'Of course,' he said, warmth rushing to his cheeks.

He tugged at his shirt, the wrinkles stark from where he'd been fidgeting. 'What can I help you with?'

She wheeled straight to the boiling tea and began to pour two cups. 'Sugar?' she asked.

Florian had barely closed the door before she raised a cup towards him. 'No, thank you.'

She looked so slight in the chair. So fragile. It was a wonder she could wield such power from that sword.

'Smart man,' she said, pulling him from his thoughts. 'I've always been fond of sugar. Though the healers say it isn't good for you.'

She stirred both cups, her delicate fingers lingering on the teaspoon before she nodded to the lounge and chairs. Florian sat cautiously, taking his cup with careful hands as Adanna sat before the fire.

'You're probably tired,' she began. 'So, I'll apologise first for interrupting you so late.'

Florian eyed the clock and noted it was only nine but didn't correct her. Instead, he sipped his tea. The hot liquid melted across his tongue. He hadn't had a good cup of tea in a long time – his father preferring brew – and Florian moaned at the taste.

'My brother hasn't laughed like that in a long time,' she began, swirling the tea in front of her. 'It was an unexpected delight.'

She licked her bottom lip, her eyes glassy as she looked up at him. He couldn't quite pin what the look was, but her voice had a lilt to it, as if something uncomfortable hid behind her words.

'I'm sorry,' Florian said quietly, lowering his cup. 'I didn't mean to ...'

'By the Godmother, Florian.' She laughed. 'Don't be sorry. Odion laughing is a good thing. A miracle.'

He swallowed as she set down her tea, relief shining behind her eyes. 'To see joy in his eyes was perfect. Please, do not apologise for that.'

He almost apologised again, the words pressing against his throat, but held them back.

The fire crackled softly, warmth licking at his bare feet through the plush rug. He should have dressed properly. Should have put his jacket back on. But after their walk in the garden, Florian hadn't wanted the moment to end. Adanna had enchanted him, her kindness quiet, steady, and strangely comforting.

She'd laughed at his stories, asked about the things he loved, the places he'd seen. And she'd listened, truly listened, as if each word mattered. She'd asked for another walk, after all. It had been a reprieve. A breath of peace in a world choking on war. They'd wandered through tangled paths, the garden wild and blooming, each plant bursting with colour and scent. It was a world apart from bloodshed. From the weight of Myrenna's wrath. From the eastern battlefields.

It was nice, he thought, to feel wanted.

Adanna fluffed out her skirts, the fabric whispering against her legs.

'We haven't had much joy here. Not many things we can relish and be thankful for,' she said, and sighed through her nose. 'I know you've heard the tale. The story of the fallen city in Perridorm. Defeated and demolished by the Queen. But we are more than that. We are free when others are not, despite our misery.'

'Are you free, though?' he asked, not wanting to prod too much about the battle they fought on the border.

'To an extent,' she admitted. 'While I can't officially be crowned until my twenty first birthday, the lords listen to me. I give them freedom in their regions and they heed the kingdom's overarching laws.' She paused. 'The battle remains on the border. The kingdom still remains ours. We are free.'

Florian only nodded, lifting his teacup with measured calm. He'd been about to ask more about the lords when Adanna leaned forward, her voice soft but certain.

'Do you want to know about the sword? Most people do.'

Florian was a scholar. He lived for knowledge, for the quiet thrill of discovery tucked between pages and whispered in forgotten tales. He'd heard of Perridorm, though only once. His tutors had spoken of the twins like a curse, a blight that kept aid from reaching their borders. And always, there were rumours. A wooden sword. One said to raise the dead.

In his kingdom, such stories only deepened the hatred for magic. Fuel to an already burning fire.

He'd searched for truth in the libraries of Maelstrom, hidden among dust and silence. The sword had been mentioned, buried in obscure texts, tucked away from curious eyes. He'd read in secret, while his brothers prowled the alcoves, calling his name with twisted affection. Like hunters in the woods. Florian, the boar. His brothers, the ones with knives.

Her offer was tempting and he did want to know more about the sword. When he nodded, it was slow. Deliberate. Adventure stirred in his blood. He feared it, but it called to him all the same.

He lowered his teacup, eyes steady, waiting for Adanna to speak.

The Princess clasped her hands on her lap. 'There was a little lord who ruled these lands. Young but also free spirited. He did as all little lords do and played, hoping for the best. He was our ancestor, distantly related but with potent enough blood that it carried through our veins.

'One night, as he ventured along the cliffs, he met with the lady of the stars who granted him wishes. I won't go into detail, but after some very curious wishes, he wished for a way to protect our kingdom. To slay those who dared bring horror upon these lands. His wish was granted with a sword.' She picked up a biscuit, dipped it in her tea, then took a bite.

Adanna continued. 'The sword is made only of wood. However, it's just as sharp as a blade made from witch's magic.'

Her arms trembled as she placed her cup down and used the armrests for balance as she rose. Florian darted forward but she waved him away. 'Believe it or not, I'm usually capable of walking. However, the sword takes its toll. Magic always asks a price, either from the land or the user. In this instance, I pay in blood.' There was no remorse in her voice, no pity. Only a sense of finality.

She took a few steps, her body shaking slightly as she reached behind her chair, pulling free an object in brown leather. She held her chin high as she walked over to him, laying the sword in his lap before she motioned for him to touch it.

He removed the sword from the sheath, surprised at how light it was. 'I thought it would be bigger.'

She laughed. 'You would think so. As a child I used to joke the sword could be used to cut the ham at Yulemas.'

He lifted the curious weapon before him, examining the plain wood with inquisitive eyes. There was nothing special about it. Not even a marking to show it was Perridorm's greatest weapon. The sword was bigger than a kitchen knife, but it was a far cry from the great swords of time. The ones used to defeat dragons and giants.

'Would it even cut the ham?' he asked, trailing a finger over the wood. The hilt was smooth, despite how old he guessed it was. And when he ran his fingers over the edge towards the point, the sword was blunt.

'No,' she said, her voice going quiet. 'It will not cut

anything but the skin of the descendants of the little lord. And even then, it chooses who will wield it.'

He thought of Odion's movements, his watchful eyes around his sister, and he understood. 'Odion can't use it, can he?' Florian asked, looking up at her.

She shook her head. 'No. Though he has tried.'

'But you're twins?'

'We don't understand either.' She shrugged. 'When I was a child, our parents showed the sword to us. Told us where to find it if we needed it. They'd hesitated, but they'd tested the blade on us. I could see the disappointment in my father's eyes when it cut my skin instead of my brother's. But the sword chooses. Or the lady of the stars does. We don't know.'

'So, when you cut your skin, your blood wakens the dead?'

'Almost,' she replied, taking the sword from him and wrapping it back in its leather. 'I have to let the blood run. I have to let it flow freely for the army to stay alive.'

He furrowed his brows. 'So, you bleed out until the battle is over?'

'I bleed from sunup to sundown.'

He imagined her lying on a bed, her arms slit open as blood flowed from her skin, staining the wooden sword. And Odion standing there, unable to stop the running blood.

'How have you not died?' he whispered.

'I almost have,' she said, taking back her seat. Her face scrunched as she lowered herself, her shoulders sagging back into the chair as her energy waned. 'It's a terrible balance, but my handmaiden has kept me alive. So has Odion.'

They sat in comfortable silence for a while, sipping their tea when Adanna turned towards the fire. 'What would you do to save your kingdom?'

He pondered a moment before replying. 'I'm not sure I'm

the right person to answer that. I love my people. I love my lands. But my kingdom is … confused. We have old traditions and deep-seated faiths. I don't share a love for my kingdom like you do. Snow would be better equipped.'

'Somehow, I don't believe that,' she said. 'Snow is fierce, but she is not kind.'

He imagined what Snow's reaction would be to that comment. He could picture the captured princess slicing Adanna's face for implying her lack of care. Something in his stomach twisted at the thought.

'Your heart is pure. You desire truth, and equality,' Adanna continued. 'Snow seeks something else. I'm sure of it.'

When Florian didn't reply, Adanna turned towards him. 'Can I show you something?'

'Sure,' he said, placing down his teacup.

Within minutes, they were moving through the halls, Florian trailing the steady creak of Adanna's wheels. They had taken only a few turns when they stopped before a tall, carved door. Flowers and vines twisted across the wood, rising toward a sky of etched stars. Hundreds of them – sharp, delicate, varied in shape – glimmered faintly in the low light.

He paused mid-step, lips parted.

At the centre of the carving stood a woman cloaked beneath the stars. Her hood was lowered, her chin tilted high. She looked down at them, eyes neither warm nor cold. Not unkind. But not welcoming either.

'The lady of the stars,' Adanna whispered, lifting her lantern higher. 'She's beautiful, isn't she?'

She was.

She was also terrifying.

'Do you mind?' Adanna asked. 'It's hard in the chair, and the doors are annoyingly heavy.'

Florian nodded and pressed his palms to the doors. The wood groaned as they gave way, a breath of musk and old paper spilling out. Moonlight poured through star-shaped windows along the arched ceiling, reminding him of a temple or a throne room. But there were no pilgrims here, or kings upon their thrones.

Instead, there lay books. Hundreds upon hundreds of books.

Florian's chest tightened at the sight and his feet froze. Carnell had a library of course, but it was limited. Those for the public were carefully selected, only sharing similar values of the royal family. He'd had to sneak into the restricted area a number of times to ever learn anything, and even then, they were more practical than fun.

But here, amongst the dim light of the pale moon, stood worlds and worlds of words. He'd never be able read them all in this lifetime, could never come close to it even if he tried.

Ladders attached themselves to shelves reaching as high as the ceiling, staircases wound at odd intervals, lining balconies for those books on higher shelves. The entire library was a maze and a paradise. If the Ever After turned out to be like this, then he would die a very happy man.

'When the Queen came,' Adanna began, 'she destroyed our court. She ravaged the lands and brought forth a great storm. But she did not break our knowledge.'

'It's ...' he stammered. He had no words for it. No way to explain the joy he felt.

'It's thousands of years of collections. Even our family can't count how many books lie here.' She smiled at his gaping jaw, the awe shining in his wet eyes. 'I want you to use the resources here.'

He turned to her. 'What?'

'We have hidden tomes, stories about the realm still yet to be discovered. I know that when I sleep, Odion comes in here. He reads what he can to find another way. To save me. But he cannot do it alone ... and he has been alone for far too long.'

'Odion doesn't seem like he wants company.'

'He doesn't,' Adanna replied, 'but even if you can help narrow down the work, it may help him get closer. Give him hope.'

Florian hesitated. The thought of asking Odion for help twisted in his chest. He could still picture him at the table, that sharp laugh cutting through the noise before dying on his lips. Since then, Odion's silences had said more than words ever could.

Cold. Certain. Beautiful in a way that made Florian restless.

He wasn't sure which unsettled him more. The idea of Odion's contempt, or the chance he might look at him differently. Kindly.

Adanna wheeled herself closer. 'Please, Florian,' she whispered, 'I want to help, but I see no other option. No other choice.' Gold and brown clashed in her gaze, bright with the kind of resolve that burned rather than shone. And suddenly, she did not look so small. Or weak. 'Find me an alternative to the sword and I will help your people,' she urged. 'I will help Snow's people.'

Nobody had ever asked him for anything. Let alone trusted him with something this big. 'What if Odion refuses my help?'

'Then do it anyway,' she said. 'He seems tough but he's hurting. I know he is. He's a nut you can crack. Trust me on that.'

Florian had a very vivid memory of Yulemas in Carnell when his brothers had pulled out a bowl of nuts. It had seemed like they wanted to share. Right up until Alfred grinned at him, shoved one in his mouth, and cracked Florian's jaw together breaking several teeth.

The laughter had been merciless. Accompanied by the rampant jokes of the failed Nutcracker Prince.

Useless.

Adanna squeezed his hand. Hope shining behind her beautiful, mismatched eyes.

He smiled down at her. Maybe he was still a nutcracker. Maybe this was his time to make a difference. To have an impact. To be useful.

He looked back up at the ceiling, watching the way the dust motes hovered in the filtered light.

'So,' she asked softly, 'will you help?'

'I will try,' he answered.

IX
The Scars That Bind Us

'What are you doing here?' Eve asked from the bench near the kitchen.

Cyrene and Eve looked worse for wear. Both were coated in blood, their skin nicked with cuts and bruises.

The storm was still roiling outside, but Eve had managed to light the fire again and set a few candles to retract the darkness. Her hands were sore as she mixed some salve with the help of Nona's grimoire.

Cyrene peeled off her wet clothes, her face scrunched in

pain as she left a puddle on the floor, the water always dripping from her skin. Eve tried not to gasp at the sight of her shredded scales and scars, at the mottled patches of blue and purple around her skin.

Cyrene was a mess. Broken.

Eve supposed she might look the same herself. Two females touched by the cruelties of the realm.

Cyrene looked up at her, those stubborn eyes unchangeable. 'Don't look at me like that.'

Eve tried to shrug, but it came off a little forced. 'Like what?'

'With pity,' Cyrene said. 'I'm a survivor. Like most in this realm.'

Eve looked away. Cyrene's spear lay on the floor where it had fallen. Eve's eyes lingered on the weapon, hoping the house hadn't taken offense to their sparring. That the friendly *thump* she'd come to cherish wouldn't cease after destroying most of the room. Bottles lay in broken shards across the floor. Lamps twisted and glass shattered. And the lounge ... the lounge hadn't survived the fight.

The sea nymph huffed, exhaustion settling over her shoulders as her black eyes roved over Eve, stopping on the scars that ran down her cheek. 'It looks like neither of us have escaped this realm unscathed,' she said. 'Who'd you piss off to get that scar?'

'Why does everybody always think I've pissed somebody off?'

A chuckle escaped Cyrene's lips, but there was no pity in her eyes. 'Because it's your speciality.'

Eve tried to be annoyed, but she couldn't find the energy. Cyrene lifted herself, the twitch of her brow the only sign of pain as she came to the bench. Eve pointed to the stool, a silent order to sit back down. But Cyrene ignored her, instead placing her hands on her hips in reply.

Eve sighed. 'Honestly? I was trying to help someone with some family issues.' Cyrene raised her brow and Eve held back a groan. 'Fine. It was a big bad wolf. Okay?'

'I need more context than that.'

Eve rolled her eyes, ignoring Cyrene's lingering stare. She moved her hands efficiently, collecting one of the concoctions she'd made during her time in the cottage. The clear liquid was a disinfectant. A very potent one.

Eve poured the concoction onto a cloth and raised it, wrinkling her nose at the stench. Cyrene's nose crinkled too before she nodded in approval, allowing Eve to apply the medicine to her wounds. Even with steady hands, the nymph hissed as it met split skin.

'If you must know,' Eve began, 'I dug up his wife's grave to get my belongings back.'

Cyrene snorted. Eve found herself pushing slightly harder on the wounds. The nymph hissed again and pulled back, her sharp teeth snarling.

'*Oops.*' Eve shrugged, smirking.

'What kind of person digs up a woman's grave?' Cyrene asked. 'That's a new low, even for you.'

'Other things happened, too,' Eve said defensively, but she didn't really want to justify why she'd battled a hungry wolf to save a friend. She didn't have to. She and Cyrene were already on prickly terms, and it was Eve's business, anyway. No one else's.

Still, Eve couldn't shake the timing of Cyrene's arrival. The odds of her appearing just when she was needed. It felt too precise. As if fate had a cruel sense of humour.

Eve stared at the ceiling, eyes straining to see beyond the

timber. She imagined the stars cloaked behind the roof, hidden by thick clouds and the weight of the storm.

What game are you playing? she whispered, the words silent in her mind.

Even after the Seer's death, Nona lingered. Eve felt her in the trees, in the wind, in the quiet hum of magic that threaded through the land. As though the old woman had bled into the soil itself, her spirit woven into every living thing.

It was a comfort. And a wound. Nona's eyes always watching. Waiting for her to take up the mantle she desperately desired Eve to take.

Mirrors four, of black and bone,
Of silver and gold, and night blue stone.

Eve felt the stone in her pocket now. Forever thrumming. Forever warm.

Cyrene settled back on the stool, her movements slow. 'Well, at least you didn't kill anybody this time.'

Eve went stiff. This was not a topic she wanted to cover. A conversation best left for another time.

Or never.

Eve turned away, collecting a salve she'd created days ago.

Cyrene groaned. 'You killed the wolf, didn't you?'

Eve picked up the salve, waiting for the nymph to stay still. But her eyes never left Eve's, the sharp knowing glare followed her movements like a snake in the grass.

When Eve didn't respond, Cyrene shook her head. 'You can't kill everyone, Eve. There will be nobody left otherwise.'

'Tell that to your mother,' Eve snapped, the words out before she could stop them.

She saw it immediately. The flicker of pain in Cyrene's eyes, the memory crashing over them both like a wave. Eve had never forgiven herself for what happened to Pearl, Cyrene's first love and victim to the Nysa's Queen. The way the girl had begged for death, her body broken and raw.

The Seeker shook her head, dragging herself back to the cottage. Cyrene frowned, the sea nymph remembering too.

'Don't look at me like that,' Eve said, voice sharp. 'You can't chastise me for killing when you tried to kill me yourself.'

'It was justified.'

Eve scoffed. 'Justified? So, you trying to end me is fine, but what I did wasn't?'

'It's different,' Cyrene whispered. 'Pearl didn't have to die.'

'Yes,' Eve said, sliding balm across the nymph's scales. 'Yes, she did.'

Cyrene flinched – not from the sting of the salve, but from the wound Eve had reopened. A heart torn apart the day Eve broke the bargain and took the life of the one person Cyrene had loved.

Guilt twisted inside Eve. She'd thought about Pearl's death more times than she could count. A girl lost at sea and on land. A girl with dreams as fragile as glass. Eve had been young then, barely free of the circus, when Cyrene came looking for help. She spoke of a mermaid who had bargained to become a human, a creature full of curiosity and hope. Eve took the job. She needed the coin. She wasn't known yet, and work was work.

What she hadn't expected was the bond between them. The depth of it.

What she found was a woman in a brothel, desperate and hollow, trying to reclaim something she'd lost. Her soul. Her freedom. Not to mention the fact that both Cyrene and Pearl had been royals. Eve would have been more careful had she known.

'Pearl was precious,' Cyrene whispered.

She had been. But she'd also been in agony. Trapped in a place Eve had been lucky never to see. The realm did cruel things to those who needed to survive. Pearl's once-milky skin had been torn and beaten until nothing remained but a shell.

'She was at her end,' Eve said, her voice too hard, too blunt. 'She couldn't go on. Not after the beatings. Not after the indenture. She was done, Cyrene. And I ...' she bit her lip, halting on the next words. 'I gave her peace.'

'You could have brought her to me,' Cyrene snapped. 'That's what I hired you to do.'

'She didn't want that,' Eve said quietly. 'She couldn't face you.'

Cyrene said nothing. Her eyes closed against the pain. The same argument. The same ache. It had lingered between them for years.

Yet Cyrene had visited her at the Skinny Piglet. Had cautioned Eve about the shadows, about the danger. A warning Eve had brushed off like dirt. Cyrene hadn't needed to help her. But she had.

It still gnawed at Eve.

'Who are you to judge who lives and dies?' Hansel had asked her once, the scent of pine still fresh in her memory.

She had no right. No right to deal death like it was mercy. But she had killed Pearl anyway. Her father would be disappointed. He believed that with each death you lost a piece of yourself. A portion of your soul. And when Eve had killed the mermaid, Cyrene had let herself loose.

Eve's skills in the circus had helped her, but Cyrene had been close. Close to slitting the throat of the Seeker. Of ending Eve's journey before it had even begun.

To this day, Eve didn't know why she'd stopped. Why she hadn't bitten those sharp teeth into her neck and let her die.

Instead, Cyrene had let her go.

Eve watched Cyrene now, her desperate hope of getting to Nysa scratching under her skin like a rash when the nymph met her eyes. 'I don't blame you, you know.'

Eve averted her eyes, landing on Nona's book. Focusing too hard on the scribbled text. She waited a moment before responding, her body shaking a little. 'I don't regret taking away her pain,' she ground out. 'But her death still haunts me. As it haunts you.'

Cyrene nodded. 'I see her in my dreams. In every path I follow. In each decision I make.' Cyrene took a breath. 'She's always there. Floating underneath the surface.'

Eve knew the feeling. It was the same with her father and Dante. They always hovered there on the edge of reality, urging her forward. Guiding her.

Light gleamed from the back room, the glow shimmering in blue and silver. Eve felt the thrum, the calling. Her nails dug into the table.

Cyrene didn't miss the change in her demeanour, her dark eyes following the corridor towards the back where the door was splayed open, revealing the spindle. Cyrene creased her brow. 'Did I ever tell you about a visit my grandmother had from Rumple?'

Eve's eyes darted to the nymph as Cyrene pulled back her hair and twisted it, letting a trail of water drop to the floor. 'My mother is hard, as you know. She likes to keep secrets. To collect things, and *other* prizes. She locks them away, deep below the surface inside a watery grave.'

Eve knew of her mother. Of the greed that drove her. But Cyrene's mother wasn't just a hard woman. She was a hard Queen. Brutal and well versed in magic. The ruler of the Kingdom of Nysa.

A sea witch.

Eve remained silent as Cyrene's eyes followed the glowing light. 'Well, my grandmother was worse. Not many within the realm know this, but Rumple bargained with her. Pleaded with her for a spindle that weaved dreams and thoughts,' she said. 'I was not yet born, nor even thought of, but my grandmother played with him. Kept him locked away in Nysa. And she let him fret. Let him see it and obsess.

'Rumple is known as the king of deals now, but then he was just an elf. Looking for a prize no other had obtained but her. With time, she knew she could gain from him whatever he would offer and so she bargained for the thing he treasured most. She bargained for a dream that had come true.'

Eve had never heard this story, had never even heard a whisper, and she sat carefully on the stool before Cyrene. The nymph's eyes were clear as she recalled the tale, the warning evident in her tone.

'He agreed, of course, and that night my grandmother took his whole family, including his only child. His one dream that had come alive. Do you know what she did to them?' She paused, her eyes darkening. 'She slaughtered them in front of him. In front of the whole court.'

Eve sucked in a breath, but Cyrene didn't falter. 'My grandmother skinned them like animals and then wore their flesh as a cloak to the turning of the tides celebration. Laughing in his face as she did so.

'Rumple was broken after that, something inside of him snapping as he merged his soul with the spindle. Drinking those memories in like he could replace his family with the dreams of others.'

A shiver crept up Eve's spine.

'You know the tales after that,' Cyrene said. 'That he

manipulated his way to power. That he sifted through the dreams of others. Swimming through them as if he too, could feel that delight.'

Eve had only met Rumple once, outside the Skinny Piglet after using her gift to find his spindle. Rumple's eyes had been cold, a hollowness to them she hadn't been able to pinpoint. But it had been the way he'd hungrily eyed the spindle that had thrown her off, his spindly fingers stroking it as if it lived. As if the object could *feel*.

Eve shuddered.

'The past is a hard place to live in,' Cyrene said, her voice growing heavy. 'It's like an addiction dragging you deeper and deeper until you find no beginning and no end.' Her eyes landed on Eve, her face levelling into neutrality. 'You didn't heed my warning last time, Eve, but in this I hope you will. Dream weaving is tempting, but it does you no good. No growth can come of it. No solutions. No happiness.'

Eve knew she was right. Knew that living inside another's reality was not real. Was not tangible. However, something still nudged her from deep within. An itch that couldn't quite be scratched. Her mind told her it was a fool's errand. A lie. But her heart ... her heart urged her forward, her very being pushing her towards the possibilities. Towards the safety of those memories. Towards the very things that had driven her in this world for years without collapsing.

Eve was silent a moment before answering, her eyes lingering on the doorway that beckoned her with that watery light. 'Does the past not shape who we are?'

'It does,' Cyrene replied, her voice soft. 'But the past also hinders us when we linger too long.'

'And what of the present then?'

Cyrene frowned. 'As in, dream walking?'

Eve nodded, but Cyrene gave her a hard stare. 'Dream walking is rare. Those who have tried it have failed or gone insane. Except for Rumple. It's why he holds the title of Dream Weaver. He has escaped what many have not. How?' She shrugged. 'Nobody really knows. I suspect his pain drove him somehow, kept him lucid. But that pain he felt, the pain my grandmother inflicted ... That left a mark. One Rumple still carries.'

Her eyes darkened. 'Eve? Please tell me you are not dream walking.'

Eve wanted to say no. To say yes. To say anything.

Her mouth tightened at the question. A small part of her knew the danger. Knew the risk. But the other part, the part that had fuelled her revenge for her father, wanted to prove her wrong. To show Cyrene that she was capable.

Nonetheless, the reality was, she only seen memories so far, not dreams. She'd tried it though. Played around with it enough that she'd read that particular chapter several times over.

Eve's voice was quiet as she asked, 'Would you support me if I did?'

Cyrene narrowed her eyes, her shoulders straightening. 'You ask me to be your tether?'

Eve nodded.

'To what end?'

'To find Myrenna's weakness. To find peace. To finish this.'

Cyrene eyed her carefully, the warning stare forcing Eve to shuffle on the stool. 'You have always been gifted,' Cyrene began. 'But this ... this is a risk.'

'Isn't everything?' Eve asked.

'It is.'

'Then let's take a risk,' Eve urged. 'Let me show you.' Eve's heart skipped a beat in anticipation. In hope. *Say yes.*

Cyrene eyed the door again, her scales shimmering in different shades of blue against the light. 'If this goes wrong, I cannot promise I'll save you.'

'I've been saving myself without help for years. I don't expect anyone to start now.'

'And what of your cause?' Cyrene asked. 'Your little revenge mission?'

'I can multitask,' Eve said.

Cyrene didn't push, but Eve felt the questions lingering under her stare. Finally, Cyrene took a breath. 'I can see you want this, but I can't be the one to do it.'

Something crumpled in Eve's chest. Disappointment perhaps. Or detachment. Then it was cold fury that raced down her spine.

Eve slammed the salve on the counter. 'What's the point, then?'

Cyrene blinked at her, the salve forgotten.

But even though Eve heard the poison in her tone, the anger, she couldn't help herself from speaking. *Pleading* to her. 'Myrenna has it all. The control. The scrolls. Why not take advantage of the power we have available to us? The power owed to us?'

Eve was shaking again. Tears pricked the back of her eyes as Cyrene moved from her stool and stood beside Eve. Cyrene didn't bother to touch her. To lay a reassuring hand on her arm. That wasn't their way. But she stood close enough that Eve could smell the sea. The salt and seaweed and brisk air.

'We cannot take advantage of power, Eve, because it is not owed,' Cyrene said. 'We don't use power that corrupts us. We cannot if we wish to retain our souls. That's what makes us different. Good.'

Eve's shoulders sagged. 'I think I need to sleep.'

She didn't give Cyrene time to reply before she plodded up the stairs, silently closing her bedroom door behind her. Eve stared at the blank room, the books stacked on the dresser and her clean clothes folded on the chair. And though she knew she shouldn't, she waited until Cyrene's footsteps faded for the night. When the cottage fell still, she slipped downstairs and settled before the spindle, its soft glow beckoning her in the dark.

X

The Crow and The Huntsman

They had more volunteers for training than Hansel expected. Most arriving with their own home-made weapons. He counted seven trainers in total, more than he'd planned for, and more eager than he'd imagined.

Porchid sat by the doorway, plucking invisible dust off her wings as nervous energy coursed through the room. Hansel picked up one of the wooden sticks from the neat pile beside her, gave the fairy a quick wink, and turned away.

The crowd behind him was silent, a tapestry of species and

faces. Elves amongst themselves, their skin wrinkled and paper thin, ears tapering to elegant points. Their eyes shimmered like dew in moonlight, and their clothes were a patchwork of alternating cloth. Dwarves murmured nearby, hunched and broad, their beards long and short, coloured and grey. Changelings clustered in between, no two alike. One had bark for skin and moss in their hair, another blinked with four eyes, each a different hue. A third had limbs that bent strangely, as if carved from driftwood. Their strangeness was quiet, but it clung to them like mist. Humans were scattered throughout, their expressions guarded. Some wore armour, others simple tunics, but all carried the same weariness in their eyes. They looked out of place, yet stubbornly present. Witches lingered at the edges, their presence subtle but unmistakable. Cloaks stitched with runes, fingers stained with ink and ash. Their eyes held storms, and their silence was deliberate.

Hansel felt the tension in his shoulders, the ache in his neck. He hadn't slept properly since Nona's death, and it was beginning to show. His dreams had turned cruel – Eve falling into the chasm, Myrenna locking him in her rooms, Gretel's scream swallowed by fire. And in all of them he could do nothing. He was frozen, locked by some invisible wind as all he could do was breathe and watch and wait. Over and over again.

He twisted the staff in his hands. At least he had this. Training. Fighting. Surviving. Sometimes, it was the only tether he had left. The only thing that allowed the candle of hope to burn.

At least here, he was no longer waiting. He was finally *doing* something.

With a calm breath he addressed them all. 'First and foremost, welcome.' A murmur echoed back. 'I want to thank you for coming. For wanting to survive and fight. I know that hope is hard to hold onto sometimes. But if we can at least arm you with the ability to defend yourselves in the hopes you will live, whether it is in battle or not, then that's all we can strive for. We're all here for the same things, the same dreams. So, be patient with your trainers, do not engage unless instructed and do not intentionally wound each other.'

The blank faces nodded back. Some were as young as twelve and others well within old age. He looked over them, finding Viper smirking at him from the crowd. She gave him a wink and he shook his head, quickly counting the attendees.

A woman with snow white hair and weathered skin watched him closely. Her hand grasped that of a younger child, her face stern and questioning. He gave the woman a nod before handing out some of the wooden staffs to the instructors.

Most of the trainers were dwarves, with some men scattered throughout. Either ex-soldiers or common folk. One changeling with hard grey skin and pointy ears had volunteered, claiming he had been trained by his father who was a skilled swordsman.

Piccadilly wasn't available for the first session, but even she had put her hand up to help with training. The memory of her sweeping through the bodies at The Tinder Box made him shiver. The way she had used the blades as an extension of herself, killing men with ease. She was beautiful and deadly. A dangerous combination.

He called out a few basic instructions. The instructors worked quickly, and the sounds of wood against wood soon echoed through the hall, each trainer engaging with the volunteers. They demonstrated how to stand, how to hold the right posture and the value of core strength. The session was only an hour, but it had been enough to have most of them sweating and puffing by the end.

In the next session, the stone skinned changeling – Darquin – mentioned their lack of endurance and suggested organising a route through the tunnels for them to run, to build on their stamina and hopefully their strength too.

Hansel agreed.

Soon, they cut a path through the sanctuary, arrows pointing the way in crudely drawn charcoal as the trainers took turns in leading the volunteers. On the first day there were three on the running route. But as a week passed, Hansel caught more running, more joining as they took the twisting turns of tunnels. As word spread, more joined, the voices of hope whispered along the walls. Those who ran were red faced and tired. But behind their eyes was something Hansel had not seen before. A brightness lingering beneath the surface.

It didn't last long.

The next afternoon, as he sparred with Darquin, their swords colliding with a metal clang, he felt a shift in the air. He'd ignored it at first, homing in on the changeling's sword as it swung towards him. Darquin was a gifted fighter but he tended to favour his left side. A disadvantage that played to Hansel's advantage as he dodged swiftly to the right and halted the tip of his blade at Darquin's abdomen.

Hansel grinned, winning a laugh from the changeling, his eyes bright as he shook the Huntsman's hand.

A soft applause came from the trainees before he eyed a lingering figure in the back, still as a shadow. Hansel's smile dropped as a man with deep green eyes and slicked black hair smirked at him from across the room.

Hansel tried to fight the urge to run at him, to stab his sword deep into the man's gut after what he had done at the castle. He'd left them. Handed over Hansel and Piccadilly to be locked away deep within the castle. If it hadn't been for Bjorn and Porchid, they'd most likely be dead.

As the crowd dispersed, Flynn was at his side before Hansel had wiped the sweat from his brow. He picked his shirt up from the floor as Flynn's steps fell in line with his. Hansel didn't bother trying to hide the flash of annoyance in his eyes as Flynn grinned at him.

'Don't put it back on, on my account,' he said, his arm stretching out towards a group of young women. 'I'm sure the ladies would be devastated if you covered up. Talk about a hunk right, ladies?'

The women all giggled as Hansel met their eyes, their faces turning crimson before Hansel gave them a polite nod. With flustered looks and lowered eyelashes, they scuttled away. Hansel glared at Flynn.

Flynn just shrugged. 'I'm a man of the people.'

'You're a traitor,' Hansel said flatly, laying his weapon against the wall.

Flynn clicked his tongue. 'Well, I suppose I shouldn't be surprised at the welcome. You always were a little hostile.'

Hansel chose not to bite back at the comment. He was tired after a long day. His energy was spent after his morning visiting the dwarves and checking in on their progress. That's what his days were now. Training, eating, sitting in medical, and helping Piccadilly with whatever she needed. Mostly it was the distribution of blankets and rations, but he didn't mind. It kept him busy and helped his mind from wandering into those horrible memories he liked to keep.

'Why are you here?' Hansel ground out.

'Shouldn't you be asking where I've been?'

'I take it back,' Hansel said, turning away. 'I don't care.'

Flynn showed no real surprise, only a slow blink, as Hansel strode down the corridor, leaving the soldier standing alone. Flynn caught up, his feet quiet on the stone as Hansel turned another corner, frustration evident in his heavy steps.

'I didn't leave you by choice,' Flynn started.

Hansel walked faster. His legs were far longer than Flynn's and a part of him enjoyed seeing the soldier try to keep up.

'I had no other option. It was not my intent to abandon the mission. To leave you both to the Tinker.'

Hansel's only response was a huff through his nostrils.

'I was knocked out, too, with the smoke. I was disoriented. I awoke in the eyrie with my ...' Flynn trailed off. Irking Hansel more.

Another secret. Another half-truth.

The fire in Hansel's core flared and he halted, turning to face Flynn. Hansel clenched his fists, anger like a roiling snake within him. This man had left them to die. Had flaunted his uniform with pride, dominating his power over the people.

'He's not as bad as you think,' Piccadilly had said, but everything in Hansel recoiled against him.

The huntsman's eyes were cold as they roved over the soldier before him. But he seemed different. Changed somehow. Flynn was dishevelled, his hair out of place from its normal smooth comb. His eyes were lined in dark circles and his uniform was open at the collar, where Hansel noted thin claw marks running along his throat.

'Your what?' Hansel said, not bothering to hold back the venom in his voice. 'Unless Myrenna was there herself, you're a spineless traitor.'

Flynn swallowed, his green eyes dimming.

Hansel continued. 'Does Piccadilly know you're here?'

Flynn met his eyes, the green hardening beneath the huntsman's gaze. 'She was the first person I looked for.'

'And instead, you found me?' Hansel said drily. 'Do you have any idea what you put us through?'

Hansel saw the shift in Flynn's feet, the guilt limning his eyes. 'I would never leave. You have to believe me. I was taken.'

'We all were,' Hansel said, taking a step closer to Flynn.

'You don't understand,' Flynn said, his sharp green eyes burning with ire. 'I would never leave her. Not by choice. I would never let her be harmed.' Flynn paused. 'She's all I have. She's …'

'Not yours.'

'I know,' Flynn said. 'But as long as she's alive, as long as she's safe. That's all that matters.'

'She might not welcome you after this. I sure as the cauldron don't want to.'

Flynn nodded. 'I understand. I'm used to being hated, after all.'

Hansel didn't respond. He merely looked the soldier up and down, his anger waning at the detached and beaten man before him. 'You look like you haven't eaten in days.'

'I haven't,' he replied. 'I've been hiding in the vaults.'

'The vaults?'

'I've been healing. Unable to … eat. I only managed to move this morning, after my injuries, and I headed up this way, looking for Piccadilly.'

Hansel wanted to ask more questions, to prod into whatever the soldier was hiding. But even Hansel knew a man's limits. Flynn looked as if he were about to fall flat on his face.

With a sigh, Hansel said, 'I'll go find her. The least you can do is eat and bathe. You smell like fairy shit.'

Flynn huffed a laugh.

Hansel paused. 'I still don't trust spies.'

Flynn shrugged. 'Nobody does.'

'Doc,' Piccadilly said from the doorway.

The lanterns glowed a pale yellow as Doc peered over his glasses, needle poised, thread pulling split skin together. Bonyx lay still beneath his hands, leathery skin stretched tight around the gash at his hip. His eyes flicked open when Piccadilly entered.

'I'm sorry to interrupt, but I need you,' Piccadilly said to Doc.

'Y—you look uninjured,' he replied.

She frowned at him as he continued his work, too absorbed to even look at her. The smell of spices and herbs suffocated her nose as the fire underneath the cauldron bubbled, lulling the room into a quiet harmony. A bubble popped, the hiss of water falling over the edge.

'C—could you take that off to c—cool?' Doc asked as Bonyx winced.

Piccadilly strode to the fire, snatched up a cloth from the counter, and used it to lift the cauldron from the flames. She set it down with a soft clatter just as Doc tied off the final stitch and grinned at his work. Piccadilly eyed Rabbit in the corner, his pale skin laced with sweat. His eyes jolted behind his lids, as if he too were living a nightmare. They'd used the remaining amount of Vox Leaf left to keep him alive, feeding him enough to keep his body from shutting down.

A gasp echoed from the room beyond and Bonyx's weary eyes shot to the half-closed door where Rumple stayed.

They'd enclosed the creature in the room near the infirmary after his escape. When they'd brought him here, his mind had completely been freed from any form of sanity. He'd shivered under Piccadilly's strong hands as they snuck back through the city under darkness, but as soon as the sun had shone, the lanterns and creatures risen for the dawn, something inside Rumple cracked. He'd screamed, his fists flying out, and he convulsed.

The rest of them had no idea what to do, how to react, until the calm demeanour of Doc hushed them away to his rooms, where he placed the poor creature in the dark. Though, in a far cosier set up than he'd had in the dungeons.

Rumple whispered throughout the night, his eyes wide and vacant. There had been nothing behind them, no recognition of where he was or who he was with. Despite Piccadilly's best efforts to glean information, Rumple was no longer whole.

The door creaked as a whisper seeped through the gap. Piccadilly's hand twitched towards her knives. 'I'm not injured,' she started, her eyes not leaving the ajar doorway. 'But it is about the injured.'

'*Mmm,*' Doc replied.

'I'm here for another enquiry.'

Doc monitored where she glanced, his left eyebrow raising at her concern. 'Rumple's harmless. M—more of a threat to himself than you. P—put the knife away.' He shook his head and checked his work, applying salve where required.

Piccadilly stepped forward. 'Can they be moved? The patients, that is. And if so, how quickly?'

He frowned at her, his concentration gone. 'M—moved? Where?'

'Somewhere we can fortify. Somewhere we can still hide but at least build a defence if the Queen's Guard find us.'

Doc thought for a moment, his eyes halting on Bonyx before replying. 'Are they about to f—find us?'

'They haven't yet, but they will.'

Doc seemed to understand and sighed, wiped his hands on his apron and rose. He climbed the wooden steps beside the table, each one creaking under his feet. The platform had been built for him after they arrived, letting him work without help. He preferred to be alone, and Piccadilly had done what she could to honour that.

He pushed his glasses up his nose as the steam from the cauldron fogged them and he grumbled in annoyance. 'If we are to move, I s—suppose it's a good thing I've brewed m—more popium.'

Piccadilly eyed the cauldron's contents, the thin liquid a pale watery red. It reminded her of watered-down blood and she crinkled her nose. 'I hate that stuff.'

Doc pulled out some vials from the cupboard. 'You m—might hate it. B—but a lot of creatures do not. It will save the p—patients on the journey.'

Piccadilly's brows rose. 'So, you'll go?'

'If you say we m—must go. Then we will leave. I have never doubted your judgement, P—Piccadilly. If it is unsafe, then I will move who I c—can.'

She fought back the unexpected warmth that spread through her bones at his faith. It was nice to not have to fight, to prove her worth. She was grateful to him for it.

He poked his finger in the brew, lifted it above him and dabbed some on his tongue. His mouth puckered, but he nodded, satisfied with his concoction.

She lifted her chin towards the two sick dwarves. 'Will they make it?'

Doc didn't need to ask who she spoke about as he replied, 'They might. With s—some help.'

Bonyx was at least on the mend, his old bones sturdier than they looked. He'd been the most coherent. Outlining his journey with the accuracy only a storyteller could give. He'd managed to begin walking again, barely, even if he relied heavily on his cane to do so.

Bonyx was an asset, and without Beetle, she knew the dwarves needed him to survive. Needed them both to survive.

Rabbit was her real concern. The small dwarf coughed from the corner, his breath wheezing as another nightmare took hold.

'We still haven't heard from Bryn,' she said. 'I managed to send a scouting group out for more Vox leaf, but the flower is still missing. Just like him.'

Bonyx looked up at the name, his frown deepening at the news. 'He is strong,' the old dwarf said. 'Sturdier than you think.'

'You all seem to be sturdier than I think.'

He winked at her. 'If even half the tales are true, we are indestructible.'

Rabbit wheezed again, the grin dying on Piccadilly's lips.

Doc remained silent as he gathered up more herbs and dropped them into a new cauldron with boiled water. His fingers were nimble as he spooned the concoction into a bowl and fed it to Rabbit. The dwarf's mouth barely opened.

Doc furrowed his brows. 'Without B—Bryn's return. I c—cannot say whether Rabbit will s—survive. He is weak.'

Bonyx stood, his cane creaking at the weight. 'Such negativity for one in the healing arts.'

'What are you d— doing?!' Doc cried. 'I only just s— stitched you. You'll tear your s—sutures!'

Bonyx just smiled. His feet shuffled on the dirty stone floor with slow, jolted movements. Piccadilly ran forward but he waved her away, focusing on Doc. 'Hush, you old elf. I'll only be moving a moment. Grab that chair, would you?' He indicated to Piccadilly.

She hurried to the chair by the wall, pulling it quickly across the room as Bonyx pointed to the spot beside Rabbit.

Bonyx scrunched his face as he sat, his bones creaking with the cane. His clothes had been cleaned, the cloth and leather removed of the bloodstains from when he'd arrived. He may have been ancient, but at least he'd been in a better condition than his imprisoned comrades.

Piccadilly took the cane, placing it beside the chair as Bonyx took Rabbit's hand. Rabbit's eyes fluttered in response, but he remained unconscious.

Bonyx gave Doc a cheeky grin. 'See? I'm perfectly still.'

Doc just grumbled and hauled away his instruments.

'Rabbit will recover,' Bonyx said to Piccadilly. He ran his thumb over Rabbit's hand. 'You talk of the sturdiness of dwarves. Of how you see miracles. Then this too, will be another miracle. Bryn will gather what he needs. However, he may not be able to do it alone.'

The clank of jars filled the room as Doc glared at the dwarf. Piccadilly tried to hide her smile, but Doc caught that too and she knew he was resisting the urge to throw something at the both of them.

'He doesn't like nonsense,' she whispered to Bonyx.

'Is it nonsense if it's true?'

Piccadilly leaned down. 'What do you mean, Bryn can't do it alone?'

Bonyx wiped the sweat from Rabbit's brow, dabbing the cloth with soft, careful movements. There was a stab in her heart at the touch, at the sincerity and love behind it. It didn't bring jealousy, no, but something far deeper. A longing that had been wedged between her heart for the entirety of her life.

'Doc advised the flower was near the mines. If Bryn has not returned, then I would say he has been taken. Or he has entered them himself.'

'That would be suicide,' she said.

'Perhaps,' Bonyx replied. 'Yet, it is also loyalty. And love.'

Love. Peace. Hope. Words whispered in the darkest parts of this rebellion. For the future they may one day see.

If we don't all die first.

Another whisper melted through the doorway of Rumple's room, and Bonyx's eyes softened towards it. Something behind them reflected understanding. Or sorrow. She didn't know which.

'I hear Hansel has been training volunteers?' he asked, pulling her attention back.

She nodded.

'I also hear Zacariah wishes to free the mines?'

She nodded again.

'From what I've gathered, you plan on moving us elsewhere. To another sanctuary?'

She gazed down at him; her mouth unmoving as he smiled again.

'So many different paths,' he mused. 'But not so different. Bryn is in the mines, and so is whatever weapon the Queen seeks. You are out of options and allies, but perhaps, your answer lies not in one place but multiple. Nona always said paths never ran the same way. Choices are made up of many journeys. All of ours led us here.'

Piccadilly didn't ask who Nona was, she didn't need to. Hansel and Viper had told her everything about the Seer. About the old woman's words and warnings. But whenever she heard about her, she'd heard half-truths. Feeling the lingering absence of some part of the story, of some element neither of them had chosen to share.

'I suppose,' she said.

'In the meantime, what will you do?' he asked.

'I'll need to think on it. Meditate maybe,' she replied. 'And you?'

He looked down at Rabbit, ignoring Doc's clamouring in the background. 'I think I might tell Rabbit a story.'

Hansel found Piccadilly near the new training area, her casual attire swapped for fighting leathers. She moved across the floor like water over stone, each step even, silent. Her hair streamed behind her, silver catching the lantern light.

Eyes closed, she turned with the ease of someone lost in the rhythm. Not performing, not thinking. Just moving. Her breath steady. Her limbs sure. As if the routine was stitched into her bones.

Hansel leaned against the doorway, arms folded. He didn't speak. Didn't dare. He watched the way her back curved with each shift, the flick of her wrists, the quiet strength behind every motion.

Changelings had always been despised, most of them called ugly, or abominations. They were the result of some fairies playing tricks on human children. Some assumed they'd been swapped at birth. Others believed it was a fairy's blessing turned into a curse. As if the hybrid could never be anything but disgusting.

Piccadilly's skin caught the glow of the fire, silver and smooth. Her hair, the colour of moonlight, flowed down her back in loose waves. Her eyes, when they opened, held the night. Not the shadows of the forest, but the sky between stars. Deep. Infinite.

He didn't know how long he watched her. Only that she didn't falter. Didn't stumble. The air seemed to hold its breath with her.

He blinked as she turned and her swords halted, her breaths deep. When she cracked an eye open, she said, 'Are you standing there to be creepy, or did you actually need me?'

He laughed. 'I'm not creepy.'

She looked him up and down, lingering on his warm golden-brown eyes before shrugging. 'Standing by the doorway in silence, unannounced and watching as I meditate. Looks creepy to me.'

'Thank you for the lesson,' he drawled, as she placed her weapons into the halter on her back.

Hair stuck to her forehead in curls and sweat gleamed on her shining skin. 'What is it?'

His face was grave as he said, 'Flynn's back.'

'When?' she asked.

'A few hours ago. I've sent Porchid with him to get cleaned up. He said something about being unable to eat in the vaults. He's been there for days, though how he got inside I'm still trying to work out.'

Piccadilly licked her lips and grabbed a flask of water. 'We'll need to schedule a meeting. I've been working on some things. If he's back, we can call the council. Plan out the next steps.'

Hansel frowned. She'd gone stiff, the tension evident in her straight shoulders and tight lips.

'Why was he in the tunnels, Piccadilly? How did he get there? Why aren't you mad at him for the stunt he pulled at the castle?'

She didn't face him as she lifted her shirt over her head to replace it with a clean one. She wore a bandeau that covered her chest but Hansel turned away anyway to give her some privacy.

'You demand so many secrets, yet you won't share yours,' Piccadilly said, as he turned back around. She tied her hair back. 'If we're asking questions, then who is Nona, really? Why is she important in this war when I've never heard of her before? What is it you know that I don't?'

His lips thinned.

He and Viper had decided to keep the prophecy hidden. Should news of the Seeker being a saviour reach the wrong ears, she'd have a bigger target on her back and he wasn't prepared to let that happen. Myrenna still searched for her and Snow, along with her murders, and if the prophecy was known, how many others would want a piece of her?

He still wanted to keep Eve safe. At least while he couldn't help her.

Piccadilly stared at him defiantly, waiting for his response, but he wasn't sure what to say.

'I think it's about time we stopped keeping secrets, don't you?' Piccadilly asked.

It was too reminiscent of the Briar Rose when Eve had said, *'A truth for a truth.'*

Some terrified part of him wanted to run, to keep Eve's fate a secret. He wanted to hold some things close to him, and only him. But as he looked at Piccadilly, at her earnest and angry eyes. He only saw hurt.

If they were fighting for a world where peace existed, then they couldn't start with secrets. They would have to trust one another.

And he did trust her.

So why is it so difficult?

She waited, unmoving as he sighed.

'Okay,' Hansel agreed. 'No more secrets.'

Silence echoed through the stone halls, broken only by the low crackle of firelight glowing orange beside the cauldron. Bonyx shifted on the bed, eyes wide and unblinking. His neck gave a soft crack, his body aching from the too-soft pillows and the mattress that swallowed him whole.

Sleep had eluded him since waking. Not once had he closed his eyes and drifted fully. He missed the grotto, the scratch of grass beneath his bedroll, the scent of wildflowers curling through the air. But it wasn't comfort he longed for. It was distance. Distance from the softness that reminded him of the dungeon. Of nights spent on mouldy hay, pressed against cold stone, waiting for the next scream.

The bed creaked again as he turned. Behind him, Rabbit's breath came even and steady. A small mercy. The young dwarf's skin still bore the bruised hues of trauma, but the stories Bonyx had shared earlier seemed to have settled him. Tales of old battles, of enchanted rivers and foolish kings. Anything to distract from the pain.

Bonyx stared at the ceiling, the flickering fire casting shadows across the beams. He didn't know if sleep would ever come again. But for now, Rabbit breathed. And that was enough.

He'd told two stories tonight. More than he usually told, but one had been Rabbit's favourite. The one about the War of Thorns and a sleeping princess.

The other had been his own. The one where he waded through dreams to reach Nona. Outlining a prophecy and the beginning of their world.

The bed creaked again as Bonyx rolled to his other side. Strength had come back into his bones at the Doc's care, his old body more receptive than he'd thought. But it still didn't stop his churning thoughts. Or the grief that coated his bones. His dreams had been broken, sifting through real and false scenarios. Nona had been prominent in most. Her grey eyes and tempting voice piercing through the haze. Incense and tobacco from her pipe ripe with every visit.

He missed her visits. Missed the way they swapped stories and played cards. She had always been a constant for him. Appearing when he was a younger dwarf, still strong and wild and fierce.

'You have the voice of the stars,' she'd said upon their first meeting.

'I don't think the stars have a voice,' he'd replied.

She'd only smiled at him, pouring a cup of tea, and pointed to a painting hanging by the rear of the tent. It was a field of green rolling hills, the stars glittering above the grass, and in the centre lay a small red flower, barely blooming before the full moon.

'If they did,' she'd mused, *'what do you think they would say?'*

He'd thought it an odd question at the time. Something

playful and challenging. He'd learnt later that nothing Nona said was random. Every word had a meaning. A price.

'I think they would tell us stories,' he'd joked.

Nona sipped her tea, her eyes assessing him over the porcelain cup. The bottom was rimmed in gold, matching her jewelled fingers and earrings. *'Would you tell me a story?'* she'd asked.

Bonyx had been confused, a little taken aback at the beauty and the sharpness behind her gaze. *'I don't know any.'*

'Would you like to?'

And from the moment Bonyx had nodded yes, she'd become his muse. His tome of words.

He'd always told stories since then, mostly repeating ones she'd shared, and others that he'd grown up with about dwarven history. Even some that he'd seen in his dreams.

You have the voice of the stars.

He wondered what the stars thought of him now. What would they say about the war they found themselves in and the deaths that reverberated across the plains of this world.

In the end, he supposed, it didn't matter what the stars thought. Only what those who had been chosen managed to save.

XI

The Riddle and The Crow

An hour after Erick had been taken, Bryn crept through the tunnels, his axe gripped tight in clammy hands. The guards were few. Their mutters drifted through the gloom, restless and sharp. Most had been called away, leaving only the discontented behind. One lit a pipe, the scent sweet and cloying. Bryn's nose twitched as he risked a glance around the next bend.

He kept to the walls, steps light, heart thudding with each

unknown turn. His breath was shallow, his grip slickening with each shuffle of the axe. The pipe smoker bent over his flint again. Bryn moved, silent, across a junction of tunnels.

Shadows clung to the walls like webs, and he swore they shifted as he passed. In the distance, screams ripped through the compound, setting him more on edge.

He waited, listening for a shout. A footstep. A command to halt. But the tunnel held its breath.

Bryn skirted the main paths, and slipped into shadow each time a noise stirred the air. Sweat clung to his brow, breath shallow, heart thudding like a drum against his throat. He moved with care, winding further into the mine's twisting arteries.

At last, he emerged onto a ledge that hung above the central pit. Stone pillars rose at intervals, locking the tiers in place like ribs in a giant's chest. Far above, sunlight poured through a jagged wound in the rock, slicing the gloom into shards of gold and grey. Miners moved below, axes swinging into the stone. The thuds echoed. A few paused to glance up, but none spoke. None dared.

Bryn flattened himself against the rock, edging along the pillar's shadow. Voices rose from the pit, murmured and slow, paired with the shuffle of feet and iron chains. He peered over the ledge. The prisoners looked tiny from here. Like insects. A nest without order.

Blood hounds paced among the guards, their growls bouncing off the cavern walls. At the rear, changelings limped along, their limbs heavy with chains. The iron links clinked as they moved, their steps uneven, their eyes downcast.

A man stood by the back wall, elevated on a platform. His fingers brushed the coils of his whip as if to clean it.

Bryn's stomach turned.

A memory surged, unbidden. One of torn skin and blood soaking rock. A dwarf's broken body, where the lashes buried deep. His eyes rolling white before Erick and Bryn had tried to save him.

Bryn shuddered and turned his face away.

He moved along the ledge, quick and quiet, avoiding the shafts of light. One by one, he searched the faces below. But there were no claws. No talons. No sign of Erick.

'Where are you?' he whispered in the dark.

Screams rose as the first lash struck. Bryn flinched. The metallic sting of blood thickened the air, curling in his nose. His eyes watered as he slipped through the shadows.

He dodged some prisoners hauling rock, aiming to somehow get a closer look at what was happening in the pit. Most didn't look at him at all. Blank faces, eyes glazed, too far gone to care.

He whispered apologies. But his words fell like dust, unheard. That was what it was like here. Hollow. Hopeless.

His grip faltered, sweat slicking the handle of his axe. The swallow in his throat caught as he moved along the edge of the divide. He veered into another tunnel, crossing a narrow platform.

The deeper he went, the warmer the air grew. Heat hung thick, clinging to his skin. At the entrance to the eastern tunnels, he paused, licking his dry lips. Something felt off. The air was heavier. Not blood. Not exactly. Something older. Older than pain. It tasted like magic, bitter and stale, like the ancient dark beneath Parador.

Bryn crouched in the shadows as a line of dwarves approached, flanked by soldiers. He counted under his breath.

When the guard glanced away, he stepped in line. Lowered his axe. Let his arm hang slack. His steps became slow, dragging, like the others.

No one noticed.

At the next passage, he peeled away and pressed himself into the shadows once more. His breath came shallow, chest tight. He wiped his brow and winced as another splinter bit into his palm.

Good. The pain grounded him.

The tunnel narrowed, walls closing in like a throat. Cracks veined the stone, offering fleeting glimpses into the chamber beyond.

Bryn moved slowly. Quietly. The air here was thicker, more alive. Magic pulsed through it, deep and relentless, a rhythm that beat against his skin, sank into his bones, clawed at the edges of his thoughts.

His shoulders sagged beneath its weight. It felt like drowning. Too deep now to rise.

Whatever this magic was, whatever the Queen sought, it was wrong.

Unnatural.

Strange.

Voices echoed from below. Orders barked. Whimpers. The heavy tread of boots on stone. They drifted up the shaft, reaching Bryn where he stood, spine pressed to cold rock.

He edged forward, breath held and peered down.

Then he saw it. A door. Made entirely of bone.

It wasn't large, but the bones were etched with intricate carvings. Symbols twisted across the pale surface, curling and clawing deep into the ivory, as if carved by hands that had bled to finish the work.

Bryn's fingers trembled. He knew that kind of work. The quiet reverence of a maker. The focus. The sweat. The soul poured into every carving.

He had shaped beauty once. The crystal coffin, clear as starlight, had been his masterpiece. But this ... This had not been made with love. It stank of suffering. Of warning. Of death.

A shiver crawled up his spine.

Below, a small group clustered at its base. Among them, he saw talons. Erick. Dragged by the man from the tower. The Crow.

Bryn slipped back into shadow, pressing himself flat against the stone. His breath came fast. Magic clung to him, cold and sharp, needling beneath his skin.

Erick had been right.

Bryn swallowed the lump in his throat. Fear clawed inside him, but he forced it down, deep into his chest where it couldn't reach his limbs. He breathed through his nose. Counted. Steadied himself. Then he turned to look again.

The bone door waited below.

Dread stood in the cavern and shoved the changeling forward, enjoying every minute of control. The creature was just as tall as Dread. His eyes asked for a fight, demanded it. Dread just grinned. If he was being honest with himself, he was itching for a fight too. One with bloodied fists and screaming lungs.

But it would be all too easy to cave in. Especially after his stint in the Silver City. Dread needed redemption. A way to break the door.

To win back his Queen.

Biting back the urge, Dread clenched his fists. His eyes simmered with hate as he shoved the changeling forward again.

'Decipher it,' he ordered flatly.

The hot air covered Dread's skin like damp towel, and he tried to shake it off. He cracked his neck in discomfort. The bone door vibrated before everyone present, calling them.

The eldest dwarf, who had helped decipher the door, stepped forward and assessed the changeling. 'We can only guess at these three,' he said, his wrinkled finger pointing to some of the carved symbols. 'Witch. Bone. Key.'

Erick didn't move. Didn't whisper a word as the old dwarf frowned towards the bones.

'Can you read the rest?'

The changeling studied the markings, eyes narrowed, brow drawn tight. He stayed still, and Dread nudged him again. A low growl rumbled in the changeling's throat, raw and rising.

Let him seethe, Dread thought. *I'll gut him regardless.*

Erick dropped to his knees, reaching for the doorway. Dread struck his arm aside. 'It's fragile. Don't touch it.'

The changeling's glare was sharp enough to cut. 'It's a warning. And instructions.'

Dread caught the edge in his voice and let it slide. The older dwarf stepped closer, voice rough. 'Explain.'

Erick stayed silent. Dread's boot found his ribs.

This time he did growl. Loudly.

'Answer him,' Dread ordered.

Erick shuffled on his knees. 'You're right about the bone and the key,' he said, voice low. 'but this symbol here isn't *witch*. It can easily be mistaken because of the slightly curved top but it's not a sharp edge, its blunt. Meaning, it actually says *witchling.*'

Not a grown witch. But the child of one. Witchlings were coveted. Rare and powerful despite the most witches being women. Covens protected them at all costs.

'And what of the other symbols?' the dwarf asked, his curiosity peaking.

Dread stepped around the bone door's edge, eyeing the curves of the old language. The way they interlaced in smooth lines and harsh edges.

'Why don't we just break through it?' Dread interrupted. 'Why do we need a key?'

Erick shook his head. 'If you don't enter the correct way, it may disappear. This door is a protection mechanism of some kind. Made of strong magic. If we just destroy the door then it may not open to wherever it goes.'

Dread grunted, sniffing the thick air around him.

'What does the rest say?' the dwarf asked.

Something snaked across Dread's skin. A warning. Or fear? He was starting to get impatient. The echoing click of time ticked against his mind.

Erick shook his head again. 'It's hard to make out in some places, the words faded ... but from what I gather, it reads: *Black glass and boned frames, a depth so dark it withers flames. Beware the song from faded tomes, made with a key of witchling bones.*'

Dread froze, the throb behind his eyes made him blink. Once. Then twice. Magic this heavy make him sluggish, volatile. 'And what *exactly* does that mean?' he asked.

The changeling frowned. '*It means* her Majesty is playing with some very dangerous, very *old* magic.'

Dread growled at the tone. His hand shot out, his fingers

tightening around the changeling's neck, crushing his windpipe.

Erick's eyes remained defiant.

'You will not question her. Do you understand?'

The rush of blood bubbled under Erick's skin, brown turning to a deeper red as a choke escaped him. Dread smiled, the dry gasps like a siren song, calling sailors to their deaths.

Erick lashed out, his talons cutting into Dread's skin, drawing blood from his calloused hands.

A call broke out from above. 'No!'

Dread's eyes snapped to the ledge above. Where a dwarf stood, his shoulders heaving.

There was nothing special about him. Nothing unique. His shirt was frayed, stained in blood and dirt like every other prisoner. Hair grazed his chin, neater than the others and not as matted.

He looks familiar.

Pain stabbed behind Dread's eyes. His vision blurred at the edges, the throb in his skull sharp and erratic.

'No!' the dwarf shouted again, arms raised. 'Let him go!'

Dread's grip faltered. Heat surged behind his eyes, a blinding pressure that forced him to release Erick. Blood rushed back to the changeling's face as Dread blinked through the pounding ache. This magic would break him. If not his body, then his mind.

He staggered back with a snarl, rubbing at his temples in tight, trembling circles.

The dwarf swallowed, voice thin. 'You need him.'

The hounds beside Dread growled, their bodies taut with the urge to lunge. Dread didn't bother to mask his irritation.

'I only need his knowledge,' he snapped. 'As long as he's relevant, he's useful.'

He flicked his hand. The beasts surged forward.

Some scaled the walls with such speed that Dread raised an eyebrow. Impressive. Almost.

The dwarf braced himself, pickaxe clenched, muscles coiled. It didn't matter. One hound struck from the right, sending the weapon clattering across the stone.

A cry tore from the dwarf's throat as the vicious creature dragged him down into the pit. Dread met them at the slope near the entrance, his gaze cold. The hound dropped the dwarf at his feet. He lay panting, arms curled protectively around his ribs, dust clinging to his skin.

Dread frowned, taking the dwarf in. Smooth complexion. Young. His hands, though, were long-fingered. A craftsman's hands. Delicate. Precise.

Then the dwarf looked up. His brown eyes locked onto Dread's, wide and wild. Fear shimmered beneath the surface, but there was something else too.

Defiance.

Then it clicked. Dread had been sitting in his tower, his body too broken to move. He'd watched the latest round of lashing from his window of recruits who had tried to flee. There had been blood and fire. And behind it all, standing with that same look of defiance had been this dwarf. Watching. Never looking away.

'I know you,' Dread said, tilting his head.

With a gulp, the dwarf shuffled back, his nails biting into the dirt. 'I know you, too.'

Dread's lip curled.

Fate played funny games.

The dwarf tried to swat away a barely controlled hound. Dread's fist clenched, the swing sure and true, before it smashed into the prisoner's face. Bone cracked against skin, the dwarf's body flailing as he fell onto the ramp.

He is small, Dread reminded himself. *Inconsequential.*

In two strides Dread leaned over him. He yanked the dwarf's hair back and the creature let out a small moan. Blood covered his chin, his long lashes brushed his cheek.

'I should just kill you now,' Dread growled.

'No,' the changeling said from behind him.

Dread sneered, turning his chin an inch as he said, 'That word has been used too many times today.'

Dread pulled free a dark blade, holding it against the dwarf's throat. The cold edge drew blood as the dwarf swallowed. The changeling didn't back away. Didn't falter as he took a step forward.

Was that concern in his eyes? Or was Dread so sick with magic he'd missed it.

'He can make the key,' Erick said. 'Nobody else can. Only he has the skill for it.'

The dwarf's wide eyes stared at the changeling in horror.

'Only he can do it,' Erick said again.

A second turned into a minute as the dwarf swallowed. Blood dribbled down his neck. 'I can do it,' he whispered.

Dread breathed through his nose, the beasts and men silent beside them as he tilted his head. Considering. Contemplating.

The slender fingers of the dwarf lifted and shivered before the blade as Dread made his decision. He pulled back the steel and slammed the dwarf's head down. Blood seeped into the wood and dirt.

Dread's voice was rough as he said, 'Take them to the tower. They'll no longer be staying with the others.' He spat on the ground and turned to Erick with lethal calm. 'He'd better be able to make that key,' Dread said, 'or I'll kill every single changeling. I will make it my personal goal to cut down every last one of you.'

Erick didn't move, didn't breathe as Dread curled his lip. 'You have three days to make me a key.'

Erick swallowed, his voice barely a rasp as he asked, 'With what bones?'

Dread gave him a wicked grin. 'Leave the bones to me.'

XII
The Witchling

The little girl crouched in the alcove of a narrow tunnel, her breath shallow, her brow slick with sweat. Around her, the coven fanned out, each witch hacking at the walls with steady rhythm. Bones clattered to the ground, mingling with loose dirt and the stench of old death.

She no longer flinched at the screams that echoed through the mines, nor at the screeches and growls of the beasts beyond. Once, she'd covered her ears. Now she just waited for the quiet to come back. Dead bodies had become familiar shapes in the dark. Screams had replaced bedtime songs.

Twelve witches worked around her, their axes rising and falling in grim cadence. With every few strikes, one or two glanced her way. She was meant to stay hidden. Folded into shadow. Forgotten.

The witches didn't make her work, despite her protests. Even now, they looked at her with anxious eyes.

She huffed in the dark. She was seven, almost grown she liked to think. A growing witch. And when she was twelve, the same number as the coven, she would become a woman. She thought that was silly, that a number could decide when someone stopped being a child. But rules were rules. The coven had been adamant, reminding her to stay hidden. To stay safe.

But safe was boring. Monotonous.

The witches snuck her extra rations when they could. Entertained her when nobody else was around. But with the guards who marched past every few minutes, clanking and shouting, they had little time to spare. Which meant she spent most of her days alone.

She was special. A witchling. A precious thing. She knew the coven meant well. Their only wish was to keep her alive. Most days, she did what they said. She had learnt to swallow her magic. To stay silent when the soldiers passed. She wasn't the only child in the mines. Others had come and gone, most of them fading within weeks. She had learnt not to ask their names. The coven had warned her against attachment.

Still, sometimes she whispered names to herself anyway, just to hear a friendly sound.

The image of the dying dwarf in the sleeping cabin lingered in her thoughts. Maleny had gripped her hand so tightly it had cut off the blood. Her voice had been hollow when she told him there was no hope left. The witchling had bitten her lip until it bled, because crying would wake the guards. Death was ordinary here. Friendship was not. She had learnt that the hard way.

The witchling peered from her hiding place as her coven heaved into the rock. Footsteps echoed along the stone, purple and red uniforms kicking up dust. Their eyes were cruel, bored, scanning the witches as they passed. Sometimes they struck them. Sometimes they took them.

She would wait, watching the darkness swallow her sisters. And when they returned, their eyes were hollow. Bleak. She hated those moments.

She tried to remember the world outside. No sun lived here. No green grass that tickled her ankles, no smell of rain, no warm wind that made her dance. She should have been practising her magic. She should have been chasing frogs and hiding in haystacks. But not here.

Not with so many enemies.

Not with so much death.

She twitched inside the alcove and clutched her little stone deer tighter. It had been kind of the dwarf to gift it to her, to offer a friend while she hid in the dark. Her finger traced the smooth curves of the carving, pretending it could breathe. Pretending it could talk back. It made her brave.

She knew she shouldn't, but the urge was stronger than caution. Magic slipped from her fingers, brushing against one of the malnourished witches nearby.

Maleny, the coven's leader, turned. Her eyes locked onto the girl's, defiant and unyielding. A warning. First and final.

The girl recoiled, drawing her power back and hugging the carving to her chest. The heat in the tunnel pressed against her skin, and she wiped her brow just as Maleny froze, her gaze fixed on the mouth of the passageway.

Bootsteps thudded against the packed earth.

The girl pushed herself deeper into the hole. The rock scratched along her clothes like claws trying to hold her still. The coven grew still as a light pierced the dimness. The witches blinked, forming a protective wall, when a large man entered, followed by a changeling with talons. She held her deer close. Held her breath. Held her magic.

The coven will protect me. They promised.

She had to keep still. To stay silent. To pray like Maleny had taught her, to the Godmother and Stars.

'Where is she?' The voice rumbled through the tunnel, low and jagged.

The witchling froze. She shut her eyes as metal scraped against the air, sharp and deliberate. Maleny hissed somewhere in the dark, her whisper slicing through the silence as the coven shifted. A wall forming against the chaos.

'I know she's here,' the voice said. 'Give her over. Or we kill your coven.'

The witchling shivered. Magic stirred around her, faint and fractured, stifled by the weight of stone and the dark power that clung to the mine. Still, the coven was stronger together.

She curled into a ball, clutching the stone deer tight against her chest. Its edges dug into her skin as more metal rang out, echoing through the tunnel like a warning.

'Traitor,' Maleny spat, but the girl had no idea who it was directed at.

Silence.

A breath.

Then the screams began.

From where she hid, she could only see shadows, the

tunnel alight with shouts and steel. Shadows flickered against the pale light from a lone lantern, a terrible shadow-play, witches and beasts dancing to screams. There was fire, then an explosion, the walls shuddering. Then silence again.

The little girl held back her wince at the thump of something rolling.

Dust tickled her nose as she finally blinked open her eyes. One look towards the small entrance of her hiding spot in the rock. That was all it took before she saw Maleny's head on the ground, her vacant eyes staring deep into the little witchling's soul. And before the witchling could blink, two large hands pulled her by her hair and tore it from her skull.

She screamed. But it was for nothing.

The witchling's magic sputtered out. Doused like a small flame as she was dragged by the man with long dark hair. The one who shifted, who followed the Queen around.

And as the ground bit into her bare legs, the rocks tearing at her skin, she choked back a sob. Her deer slipped from her hand, landing face-down in the dirt beside her coven's broken bodies.

XIII
The Voice of The Stars

Florian slipped through the halls of the library, the morning light glinting through the star shaped windows in the ceiling. Even now, the room stole his breath. The smell of parchment and ancient bindings lingered. The towering shelves, their spines heavy with the weight of time and knowledge. Even just the sheer size of the room had him smiling like it was his birthday.

Every corner presented a new discovery, a new room or alcove or row of books. He'd been lost multiple times at this stage, but it still couldn't halt the warmth he felt from just existing here.

While Adanna had mentioned a librarian – Petrella – Florian had yet to see a single soul among the twisting corridors of books.

Sunlight spilled through the great glass windows, casting shifting patterns across the stone floor. In the centre of the library stood a circular desk surrounded by shelves, likely holding the catalogue.

He'd spent hours here yesterday. Started with the basics. Books on elemental theory. Foundational magical laws. Diagrams, charts, annotations scrawled by scholars with impossible names.

His arms ached beneath the weight of today's haul. He shuffled to a thick table of murky, knotted wood and set the tomes down with a thud. Then he checked his list. He needed more.

If he was to uncover what Odion hadn't, he'd need every scrap of knowledge this place could give him. This time, he'd search for bloodlines. Family records. But those were near the back.

As he moved deeper into the stacks, the light thinned. The shelves grew taller, narrower, the spines more frayed. Scrolls appeared among the books, wrapped in brittle twine. The scent changed, too. Still paper, but older. Fungal at the edges.

Florian paused. The air was colder here, the shadows dragging at his boots. Goosebumps prickled along his arms.

Something shifted. A breath. A whisper. Not words, just the sense that something else was breathing in the dark.

He blinked. The letters on the books grew harder to read, half-swallowed by the gloom. He reached out, letting his fingers graze the shelf edge, feeling for the cold metal of a lantern bracket. They were usually there. Hooks screwed into the wood, meant for hanging glass-encased lanterns. Finding none, he reached into his bag with a shaking hand and pulled free a candelabra he'd taken from his room. It felt oversized in his grip, awkward and too grand for what he needed.

He struck a match, trying to keep his fingers steady. The flame flickered and his heartbeat followed. It took everything in him not to flee.

There is nothing to fear in the dark.

With a swallow, he tried again, the wick crackling as it shot to life in his fingers. With quick work, the candelabra was lit and Florian finally took a breath.

He turned, the cold melting away as he raised the light. The shelves loomed above him, the scrolls well-kept and cared for.

'Hello?' he whispered.

But nothing whispered back.

Useless.

Florian chastised himself for his vivid imagination and checked the catalogue card. He was close now, only another corner or two. As he rounded more shelves, the tomes grew thicker.

Something sparkled ahead in a small flash of silver. He slowed his steps, pausing to see what it was. Chains. He lifted the light, trailing along the shelves when more appeared, wrapped around scrolls and books and shelves. It resembled something akin to metal ivy and he leaned in to see the titles. They were hazy.

With careful fingers, he reached out and touched one of the looped chains and hissed as a spark shot free, singeing his fingers.

'I wouldn't do that,' said a cranky voice from the shadows.

Florian squeaked and jumped back, only to touch another

chain eliciting a shock through his back. He almost dropped the candelabra, his fingers barely let it go before an old, gnarled hand caught it.

He held back another scream as angry gold eyes stared back at him. 'Are you trying to set my library on fire?'

Florian was frozen.

The woman placed her free hand on her hip and tapped her foot against the hard floor. 'If you hadn't noticed, this place is full of *paper*. Why do you think there are no open flames here?'

'I'm sorry,' he stammered.

'Sorry? What a silly word. Meaningless and daft.' Her sharp eyes looked him up and down. 'I suppose you're the prince from afar? You look like one. Soft and pampered.'

He ignored the jibe. 'I'm helping Adanna.'

'Then you're in the wrong section,' she replied. 'Give me the catalogue card.'

She yanked it from his grip with a grunt. 'You're about three shelves out. I'll show you.'

Though her personality was the size of a giant, she was tiny. Her long white hair was braided back in a tight bun. She wore a loose black dress – half the reason why Florian hadn't seen her coming in these unlit halls.

'Are you Petrella?' he asked.

She halted in front of him, her chin pushing out in pride as she said, 'I'm Petrella. And I'm the librarian. The keeper of these books. So, don't set them on fire. Or I'll be setting *you* on fire.'

He tried to keep up with her short legs as she gruffed at the catalogue and turned into a stack further down. She lifted the candles and pointed to some books on a higher shelf. 'Here is where the bloodlines and family history is kept. But you won't find what you're looking for here, Odion has already tried.'

'Perhaps a fresh set of eyes might help?' Florian asked, his nose tingling from the dust.

Petrella narrowed her eyes. 'You sneeze on my books, boy, and you'll never set foot in this library again.'

With a grimace Florian held back the tickle behind his nose and gave her a nod.

'Collect them and go,' she said, finding a lantern on a nearby hook. She plucked it down and opened the lantern's glass door, using the candelabra to light the new candle inside. Shadows caressed her face as she replaced the candelabra's light with the lanterns, glaring towards Florian the whole time. 'And don't leave a mess.'

With the shake of her head, she slipped away, leaving Florian to gather the books on his own. He held back a sneeze, breaths stuttering as he collected what he could.

When he finally made it back to the table, he ran to the exit and released a huge sneeze in the hall. His nose ran and he used his handkerchief to clean his face.

Returning to the books he'd collected, Florian peeled open the first cover. The book revealed a family tree, tracing back to the little lord who'd established the current line. Florian tried to concentrate. His eyes skirted over names and places but he couldn't help but think about the chains latched onto those lost books.

He eyed the dark corridor, waiting for Petrella to tell him off again. She never came.

An hour slipped by while he worked, notes taking shape across the page. But as the night deepened, something stirred in the quiet, a faint hum. Calling out his name to come see.

A fractured whisper broke through the silence of the night as Bonyx shuffled on his bed inside the infirmary. His eyes drifted to the half-closed door of the healer's room. The infirmary was split into smaller alcoves, based off the main hall. With everyone asleep, this room only held the two dwarves, nobody else brave enough to sleep beside their neighbour in the adjoining one, where Rumple lived.

Rumple was an elf, once. Bonyx knew that, but still, it didn't elicit any kind of imagery to the voice he'd heard in the castle's dungeons. People in the Sanctuary had whispered about him. About how he was more monster than creature. More criminal than hero.

Since the rescue, Doc had tried to coax Rumple out of the dark, even so much as returning the spindle to him – though Piccadilly had been against the idea. She'd been adamant Rumple's mind wasn't ready for it. With the power the spindle wielded, they couldn't be certain they weren't freeing some sort of doom amongst the dreams and nightmares of the realm.

Bonyx had tried to reassure them. To tell them Rumple wasn't what he seemed.

'*He grows more sickly without the spindle,*' Bonyx had muttered.

The Doc had shushed him with some kind of painkiller.

He remembered the drug filling his veins, like he'd dived into cool water on a hot summer's day.

'*He cannot be whole with a piece of him missing,*' Bonyx had croaked. And as Bonyx had drifted back into a dreamless sleep, he'd mumbled, *'She is his as he is hers.'*

When he'd finally woken again, it had been to Piccadilly's grim stare and the Doc's unwavering one.

'He's a liability,' she'd said.

'He has influence,' Doc had replied. *'P—perhaps he is more v—valuable than we think.'*

That had been days ago. Despite receiving the spindle, Rumple had refused to leave the chamber. Refused to walk into the light, even with his beloved spindle returned to him.

Another whisper came from the adjoining room. Soft and soothing. Bonyx sat up at the sound. His knees cracked under him as he gripped his cane with strong fingers. He understood what it was like to be left in the dark. To feel as if a piece of you could be held in someone else's hands. Or, in Rumple's case, by something else.

You have the voice of the stars.

The door creaked open, cutting through the shadows as Bonyx stepped inside and spotted Rumple huddled in the corner. Silence hung heavy in the room, thick and unmoving. Rumple shrank further back, black eyes glinting as Bonyx paused in the doorway.

Bonyx made no sound as he shuffled forward, leaning against the far wall before easing himself to the ground. The others had spread hay across the stone floor to soften their bedding, and Bonyx caught its scent. Dry and clean, nothing like the rot of the dungeons.

Rumple stared from the corner. His skin was grey and creased, ears long and pointed. The spindle rested in his bony grip, the wood worn smooth where his fingers curled tight.

'I couldn't sleep,' Bonyx said as he placed his cane beside him. 'I noticed you couldn't either.'

Rumple narrowed his eyes, the spindle pressed against his chest.

'I thought we might stay awake together,' Bonyx offered.

Rumple looked him over, his eyes halting on the cane, before he said, 'You are the storyteller.'

Bonyx nodded, trying to keep calm though he felt a raging storm brew inside him. He hadn't spoken to Rumple since the castle. Hadn't heard anything from him since the hushed whispers they'd given each other in the dark. To hear him speak now … was more than Bonyx had expected.

He tried to stay still for fear the creature would run, and opted for a modest smile, his voice placid. 'I am a storyteller. I wouldn't say I'm *the* storyteller.'

Rumple looked at him curiously, his deep black eyes holding nothing and everything at once.

Bonyx wondered if that's what living an age did to you. What it did to those who had seen the changes in the world and outlived them.

Bonyx was old, almost one hundred and forty – if he remembered correctly. Dwarves lived long lives, some as old as two hundred. But Rumple's age was another matter. The creature could be five hundred for all he knew.

Rumple blinked twice, as if he was unsure of how to respond. 'I knew of another storyteller once. One who held all the secrets of the realm.'

Now it was Bonyx's turn to blink. 'As did I.'

Rumple nodded and his fingers loosened from the spindle just a fraction. 'She was the maker of the realm. One of the four.' Gentle, careful words. 'She had eyes the colour of doves.'

Something tightened around Bonyx's heart, stealing his breath. 'I used to hear her, too, her voice lighter than the *others*,' Rumple continued. 'She was a song on the wind. A whisperer of dreams.'

Bonyx closed his eyes, remembering those unfaltering hands. The way she laughed at his curiosity like a young child who chased a butterfly. Her name escaped his lips in a whisper, 'Nona.'

Rumple's pointed ears twitched at the name.

They sat in silence for a while after that, two lost souls in the dark, dreaming of other things and other stories. Bonyx blinked drowsily, his eyes bleary with sleep and his body finally giving into much needed rest, when Rumple hissed. The hard sound shattered the silence as the creature pushed himself deeper into the dark.

'What is it my friend?' Bonyx asked.

'She is not the only voice I hear.'

Bonyx swallowed. 'Who do you hear?'

Rumple shot towards him, his hands gripping Bonyx's shirt. 'I hear *her.*'

Rumple twitched. A flutter of his eyelashes told Bonyx he was only living half in this world. Only half aware of the shaking fingers latched onto an old dwarf's shirt.

'I hear the Queen above the others,' Rumple mumbled. 'I hear her mirror. It whispers across my bones.'

Bonyx's mouth went dry as words tumbled from Rumple's mouth.

'It seeps through the cracks in the world. The watchful eye. And amongst the silence, when I push it away, I hear all of them. Her crows. Her soldiers. Her slaves.'

Bonyx rested his hands over Rumple's, his weathered palms almost covering them entirely.

Rumple loosed a shuddered breath. 'They are like drums,'

he continued, 'beating against the black abyss. Begging for a way to get in. To seek out those who are *weak.*'

Bonyx swallowed. His hands were sweaty.

Rumple's ears twitched, his head lolling towards whatever it was he heard. 'I even hear them now. Closer ... closer,' he whispered.

And in the dark, where the shadows crawled along the stone, Bonyx heard it too. The beat of feet against granite. The steady thrum of bodies. A vibration rippled through the room, barely a whisper, but enough for Bonyx to still. 'What is that?'

Rumple's head whipped towards him, his unhinged grin widening. 'They've come.'

'Who?'

Rumple twisted his neck, his twitch more noticeable with every shake. 'The Queen's army.'

'Have you seen the books with chains?' Florian casually asked Adanna as they walked through the gardens.

'Books with chains?' she asked, frowning at him. 'What in the cauldron are you talking about?'

The sun peeked from behind white fluffy clouds, bathing the unruly garden in a golden glow. They'd stopped beside a pond where a statue stood of a small boy on a horse, his stone face stern and unyielding.

Florian stared at the still, black water, the pumps long dry. 'I saw the books yesterday,' he said. 'Hidden deep within the library.'

Her voice was sweet. 'The library is massive and endless.' Her smile faltered at his frown, and she gave his hand a squeeze. 'If what you're saying is true, then Petrella should know. She lives there.'

'Petrella terrifies me,' he admitted.

'She terrifies everyone.' Adanna laughed. 'I can raise an army of the dead and yet that old hag gives me nightmares.'

Florian laughed. At least he wasn't alone in that. 'She knows about them,' he said.

'How can you be so sure?'

'Because she caught me in the stacks after discovering them. She hushed me away from there so quickly I had no time to think.'

'Mmm,' Adanna mused, plucking a flower from its stem. 'If you're too afraid of Petrella, I'd suggest speaking with Odion. He's spent years in that library trying to find a way to end the curse, or at least tweak it. If anyone would know, he would.'

Florian's cheeks heated at the thought and Adanna didn't miss it.

'Or are you afraid of him too?' she asked.

'A little.'

She sniffed the flower, plucked a petal, and smiled at him playfully. 'How about we let the flower decide for us, then?'

He turned towards her, her eyes sparkling as she pulled another petal free. 'Talk to Odion.'

Florian held back a groan.

Another petal fell to the ground. 'Don't talk to Odion.'

She continued on, pulling petals free and switching between the two answers as Florian laughed.

When only one petal remained, Adanna smiled up at him, as if she knew something he didn't. 'Talk to Odion. There you have it, Prince. The answer you have been seeking from an oracle flower.'

'An oracle flower?'

She waved her hand at him. 'I can't be responsible for everything. Nor can I see everything. Sometimes, I need an oracle flower to help me when I'm confused.'

He laughed again. 'You're a Seer and you use petals to make big decisions?'

She shrugged. 'Sometimes you have to get creative when you need an answer.'

She threw the stem away as she looked up towards the palace, the two towers gleaming high above them. 'He looks hard,' she said softly, 'but on the inside he's melted butter.'

Florian suspected she was right, but it didn't ease the churning of his insides every time he thought of the prince.

The prince, who now took long strides towards them.

'Speaking of,' Adanna winked, wheeling herself forward.

Odion's brow furrowed at the sight of them, his gait purposeful. Florian gulped under his piercing gaze, but his feet remained firmly planted on the stone path.

'There's a problem,' Odion said, his voice laced with venom.

'What kind of problem?' Adanna asked, carefully.

'The feral princess has stolen my horse.'

Adanna snorted. 'I'm surprised you aren't out chasing after her.'

'I wanted to,' Odion replied, 'but I know you have a policy against killing our allies.'

Adanna watched her brother prudently, something passing between them in silent conversation. She turned to Florian. 'Does your princess have a habit of taking things without asking?'

Florian wanted to correct her and say that Snow wasn't his princess, but he knew it would only sound weak. Instead, he replied, 'She can be reckless and a little rash. If she's been locked up for a few days then she would need freedom. She's been imprisoned all her life. Not to mention, we just rescued her from a war camp.'

Adanna nodded in understanding. Turning to her brother, she said, 'I'll speak with Malak. Would you help Florian? He needs help with some research.'

Odion eyed the floppy haired prince, the contempt clear on his face, before he turned back to his sister. 'Do I have to?'

'I'm going to pretend you didn't ask that.'

As Adanna wheeled away, leaving them alone, something in Florian's gut lurched. He remembered the salty bean and choking at dinner, and heat laced his cheeks at the thought.

Florian attempted a smile, but it came out awkward and forced.

'What do you want?' Odion asked, his voice flat and cold. 'A nanny?'

Florian wanted to curl into himself. *Perhaps facing Petrella would be better than this?*

Instead, he stood taller, hiding his trembling fingers behind his back. 'I was hoping you could tell me about the books with the chains.'

It took everything in Florian to stand still, but his legs twitched at Odion's frown, longing to run far away from this place. From this confrontation.

'You've been lurking in my library.'

'I wouldn't say I've been *lurking*.'

'What else would you call it? Sneaking? Spying? Intruding?'

Florian's cheeks still burned, the flush refusing to fade. 'I'm trying to help with your sister's curse.'

'If you really want to help,' Odion said. 'Then stay out of it.'

'But I—'

'What?' he snapped. 'Want to feel useful?'

Florian's lips thinned.

'Stay away from our business. If you want to help, then *back off*.'

The surly prince turned away, leaving Florian speechless and a little confused.

Within moments, Odion was out of view and Florian stood, dazed. He sat by the fountain, a faint tremor running through his legs. He wondered where he'd gone wrong. Perhaps he had been lurking? It did feel a little like he was sneaking around, even if Adanna had given him permission. Without Odion's approval and Petrella's grumbles, he still felt like a stranger.

He supposed he was, especially since it was his kingdom attacking the borders. But he didn't want to be a part of this war. Didn't want to take responsibility for decisions he had no control over. He only ever wanted to help, to be useful.

He looked towards the glass towers at the top of the castle, both tips piercing the clear blue sky and sighed. He wondered if his father and brothers knew what they were doing. He didn't wish for them to win but he also didn't wish for them to die, no matter how badly they behaved.

He stared at the fountain's statue, the grim face of the little lord gazing straight towards north. 'What would you do?' Florian asked him, quietly.

There was no response. Florian sighed, wishing that Odion would help but also praying he wouldn't. He didn't quite know how to behave around him or why Odion seemed to hate him on sight.

'I don't suppose you know how to open the chained books?' he asked, speaking to the statue like the little lord could help as easily as Adanna's oracle flower.

He rubbed his eyes, wishing he could find something other than dead ends. The books remained a mystery, but there was still no guarantee they could help. He didn't even know what information they held, he just assumed they were dangerous, considering how they were protected.

Even Adanna had no idea they existed, though she hadn't been able to explore as she once had, her time now spent either in her chair or bed rest. It just surprised Florian that Odion hadn't spoken to her about it. Maybe he'd already looked into the chained books and found it a lost cause?

Without Odion's help, Florian was starting from the beginning.

Useless, his father's voice echoed.

Even Odion thought so.

Florian stood and dusted himself off, biting back the sting of tears. Even unruly, the gardens were nice. Filled with colour and a vibrancy he hadn't seen in a while. Maelstrom was greyer, the smog and depression stifling.

The marble statue loomed above him and he took a closer look. The little lord was carved in beautiful detail, and each curve and muscle in the horse's body engraved with precision. The little lord's hair was windswept, his proud shoulders strong. Along his back he wore the wooden sword, the scabbard plain but neat. Florian circled to take a closer look; it was just like the real one Adanna had shown him in his rooms.

He was just about to turn away when something glinted. Not the horse, nor the sword, but something smaller.

He squinted but was too far away to tell. Checking the perimeter to make sure he wasn't being watched, he stepped into the black, murky water of the fountain. He tried not to think too much about his wet feet as he touched the horse's neck for balance. He leaned in and looked at the little lord's hands. They were tiny, each fingernail carved and smoothed. The statue's hand was clutched around a point, the shape resembling a quill. Though it seemed to be missing the feather usually attached to the back, leaving only the miniscule point without the other end.

Every other section of the statue was immaculate. Every other point untouched. Except for this.

How curious.

Departing the black water, Florian went straight for the library, a trail of wet footsteps left in his wake. A new fervour had come over him, something that tugged him back towards the stacks. He left his tomes forgotten, left the librarian to silently wander the halls, and tried to ignore the sting of Odion's words.

And as he picked up a book of Perridorm's fables, he lost himself in the tale of the little lord.

XIV
The Threads of Dreams

The world inside the spindle collided around Eve, as if it were a living rainbow, where colours shifted and blended like magic. Dream weaving felt like your world was underwater. Manipulated and foggy, like swimming with your eyes open.

She gripped the dream book with tight fingers as she waded through what she called 'The Theatre'. Pictures and memory swam past her, captured moments in time where it played live for her to watch. All of them were happening now. Fresh and pure and beating.

As she walked, some called to her, echoing like a song, or what Eve supposed was a lullaby. It reminded her of seeing a play on stage, of the actors ready to deliver their lines. Ready to tell a story.

Except this was something more. Something alive. It was hundreds of plays. Hundreds of performances. Hundreds of actors living in their imaginations and improvising.

Each dream thrummed, buzzing around her in all their glorious light. She could feel the dreamers' emotions. Their happiness, their sorrow, their anger, their anxiety. It scratched against her bones like the sharp claws of a wolf. Gnawing at her to see, to touch, to smell.

Eve plucked at a dream here and there, grasping at them like pieces of string. Without a solid tether she was walking a dangerous line. The dream book recommended someone who was awake. Someone who could guide and break through the fog when the weaver became lost.

But it had only been a recommendation.

Rumple was proof it was possible.

So, Eve had tied a rope, found in one of the suitcases of lost creatures she'd uncovered over the last few weeks. One end was bound to the door, the other wrapped neatly around her wrist as she wandered further into the images.

She'd decided to start small. To walk through a dream of someone she knew, someone she trusted. To dive into Myrenna's thoughts was a suicide mission. Myrenna held considerable magic, and after her own experiments on the spindle, Eve wasn't sure how much the Queen had learnt about the art. Or how much she had done herself.

She tested her knot again, tugging the rope to ensure it was tight. When she was satisfied, she plucked through the images.

Intent. The book said it was all about intent.

Intent was the anchor. The reins on the proverbial horse.

Eve closed her eyes and let the dreams float over her as she pictured Porchid. Her bright wings and blue hair. Her changing lights and swift moods.

The pictures shifted around her. Some held laughter, with scattered wings and firelight. Others played music filled with energy and joy. Some held screams.

Torn skin and ripped wings. Fairy dust crushed into powder. Wings on a rich suit at a ball. Fairies locked in jars, their light shut away in a glass cage, displayed as a lantern along city walls. She saw a warehouse stacked with fairies. Hundreds of them chained along shelves as a man wandered past with a clipboard.

Eve frowned, sifting through them all. Rearranging them like a puzzle.

'*Intent,*' she whispered.

She thought of Porchid's broken body by the creek. Her dimmed light in the Dark Forest as Eve picked her up. She remembered the blushing pink of her skin in Roserock, her lovesick gaze following Hansel. Porchid's squeals in the snow as Eve landed on her, where tiny fists pounded at her side.

A thread appeared before her, the colour brighter than the rest, and Eve pulled. A vibration rippled down its length when an image appeared: one of a grotto with a crystal coffin.

Eve followed the thread, her rope going taut behind her as she reached out. Her fingers tingled as they grazed the image, shining like emerald water before her body was pulled, twisting on itself.

The familiar sensation of falling up and down at the same time brought bile to her throat. She closed her eyes and barely held the sickness in before she hit solid ground.

Eve's eyes adjusted as the hazy dream formed around her.

Fairies flew in colour, their wings bright and patterned against the lush greenery.

Porchid sat by a dwarf, his gilded hair falling over his eyes. He pushed it from his forehead and frowned at the splay of cards before him. Porchid tinkled as she pointed to another card, and the dwarf swiped her away. She huffed, but her skin glowed in a warm yellow.

Eve choked back a sob as a twig snapped under her step. Porchid's muscles went rigid at the sound. With a slow turn, Porchid's dark eyes met Eve's and ... faltered.

Eve couldn't move, didn't dare to as the fairy disappeared behind the dwarf's back. He shimmered as Porchid touched him, his form bending with the light like the rest of the dream.

'Porchid?' Eve whispered.

The fairy peeked from behind the dwarf's back, nostrils flared as she assessed the intruder of her dream. Her eyes were still dark, staring at Eve with unfamiliarity.

Something icy pierced Eve's heart. A shard breaking through the barrier and bringing forth blood.

Afraid. That's what Eve felt. Afraid that the dream would fade. That Porchid would leave her. That this fragile world would shatter. A world she should be able to alter according to the book.

The rope went taut as she stepped forward then halted amongst the moss lined trees. She couldn't risk the rope being severed. 'It's me, Porchid. It's Eveline.'

The fairy blinked. Once. Twice.

Porchid carefully flew closer, her light blazing in the forest. The other fairies were gone, the dwarf distracted. Until it felt as if it was just the two of them, standing alone. Eve reached out her fingers and Porchid sniffed them. No doubt smelling the blood still covering Eve's clothes. She wrinkled her face in disgust and Eve choked on a laugh.

Forever the judgmental fairy.

The dream shifted, the world blurring at the edges. Voices echoed from far away. Grunts and yawns stretched across the sky.

Porchid blinked again, a yawn escaping her lips. She was waking up.

Panic sluiced through Eve. 'Porchid. It's a dream. I'm in your dream.'

The fairy looked towards the dwarf, who ignored them both, eyeing the cards before him. Eve didn't recognise him, but he looked to be a mix between Beetle and the dwarf with the kohl liner.

Bronson. She remembered.

The air shifted as the trees moved. Cold wind blew through the grotto like ice hardening on snow. Eve shivered, the cards in front of the dwarf floating along the forest floor. Three landed before her, tarot cards of sorts. One of a tent, shrouded in shadows. Another with a dark monster. And the last, with a cauldron.

Darkness spread as a stranger broke through the trees, a whimper escaping Porchid's lips. His jacket was deep brown, weathered and brutal like the black eyes that stared back at them. His smile was rotten, teeth missing and crusted in yellow film.

The dwarf shimmered, a wall of white pillars and a silver changeling visible through his form before he turned to dust.

Is that where Porchid is now?

The stranger cooed at Porchid, offering a small, shiny trinket. The fairy hovered close, eyes bright with curiosity, while

Eve's gaze caught on the knife at the stranger's hip. An odd, curved blade with ribbed edges.

A wing cutter.

Eve cried out, but she was too late.

The stranger materialised beside the fairy, seizing her fluttering body in his heavy hands. Porchid's light flared white and the forest crumbled to dust, reshaping into a creek lined with barren trees. Eve ran forward, cold biting into her skin, until the rope snapped taut around her wrist.

She couldn't reach Porchid. Couldn't help. The rope's coarse fibres bit at her skin. The tether might have been her lifeline, but it was Porchid's doom.

It is only a dream, her mind echoed.

But it felt so real. The grass under her feet. The nip of the wind. The smell of blood.

The stranger's pack dropped, and the flap fell open. Eve held back bile at the sight of severed wings. Bloodied and shredded and dull. Porchid shrieked as the stranger pulled on her wings, his grin eager.

Eve pulled free her knife and halted, her fingers twitching as the blade hovered above the rope. *It is only a dream.*

The sawing started, Porchid's wings falling to the ground beneath her. Eve's mouth went dry, yet still her knife hovered.

If only she could change the dream. Change the scenery. Stop the nightmare. Her gaze darted to the book clutched in her other hand, she'd almost forgotten it was there. Maybe it held something. Maybe it could help. She tore it open, flipping through the pages with trembling fingers until she found the one she wanted.

She focused on the stranger, willing him away. Imagining him turning to dust and carried off by the wind. A strange sensation tingled across her skin. The stranger melted into dust. Eve fell to her knees, her strength slipping away.

It seemed dream weaving demanded a price.

It is only a dream.

Yet, Porchid's body bled out. Seeping into the cold hard ground as the stream beside her trickled. Eve's eyes watered.

It is only a dream.

In the real world, Porchid had her wings. She'd escaped the wing cutter's knife. Eve had found her. But as the vision faded, Porchid's whimper rammed into Eve's chest like a wound and her knife lowered an inch.

Until the dream went black.

Eve was hurled back into the cottage, her body striking the floorboards hard. Pain shot through her limbs, leaving her shaking. The room spun. Cold air seeped through the cracks in the walls, rattling the shutters as she clutched at the floorboards. Bile rose in her throat, and she vomited, the sound echoing in the small space. When it was done, she wiped her mouth on her sleeve and lay there, panting in the dark, the scent of ash and sweat thick around her.

Still holding onto that leatherbound book, Eve looked up at the shimmering lights of the tapestry. And swore the spindle was laughing at her.

Bryn stood in the pit, the damp air thick against his skin. From the shelves of rock above, the recruits watched, wide-eyed, silent, waiting. Their stares pressed down on him like the weight of the mine itself. He could hear their breathing. Feel their fear.

Erick stood to his left, shoulders rigid, jaw tight enough to crack. Bryn had always admired how the changeling hid his fear, but today that stillness felt unnatural, forced.

Across from them, Dread basked in the attention. His grin split his face wide, arms raised like a victor before the crowd. Down here, among stone and darkness, the shifter ruled. He was a god. A king of the underground. And he revelled in it.

He prowled around the witchling girl, each step deliberate, savouring the moment.

The girl was held fast by a guard, his face blank, unmoved by her struggle. Bryn guessed she was no older than seven. Maybe eight. A child.

His heart thundered in his chest, terror sinking into his bones. She sobbed, the sound garbled and raw, as the guard dragged her closer. Blood bloomed across his arms where her broken nails raked his skin, desperate and defiant.

No, no, no.

He'd never thought they'd find her. Not after the coven had hidden her so well. Not after he'd handed her that carved deer only days ago. Where were the others? Where was her protection?

The girl was pale, her blinking eyes wet with tears. Her brown dress hung in tatters, one shoe missing. Her fingers trembled so violently it took everything in Bryn not to break cover. Not to run to her.

They were going to take her bones. *A little girl's bones.* And he would be the one to carve them.

His hands already felt dirty. Coated in blood he'd never be able to wash off. He couldn't.

He wouldn't.

Bryn took a step forward, but Erick's sharp look stopped him mid-stride. He froze, mouth dry, as Dread drew his sword, the metal whispering from its sheath. His black eyes gleamed with a hungry anticipation. This was wrong. Everything about this was *wrong*. Whippings were one thing; the cold murder of a child was another.

Dread paced, his eyes roving the crowd, waiting to put on a show.

The changelings stood in chains on the other side of the pit, crowded together and bloody. Bryn caught the flick of Erick's eyes toward them. It was subtle, but not enough to escape Dread. The shifter's grin sharpened, his head tilting like a predator scenting fear. 'I was going to do the honours,' he said, voice laced with challenge, 'but I find I have a better idea.'

The crowd was silent.

Sweat trickled down Bryn's back at Dread's words. The shifter moved closer to Erick's ear. A slight flinch was Erick's only sign of discomfort. Both Bryn and Dread caught it, but where Bryn shook, Dread smiled – a cold, deadly thing.

'As the one who deciphered the symbols *and* who found our witchling,' Dread said, 'I'm giving you an opportunity. You have responsibility over the key, after all – you and your dwarven friend.' Dread's eyes flashed towards Bryn with cool promise. 'So ... you will also be the one to kill her.'

Erick swallowed, shaking his head. 'She's ... she's only a child.'

'She's exactly what we need,' the shifter drawled. 'Do you want to reconsider your answer?'

Erick's eyes met Bryn's, then drifted to the clustered group of changelings.

'What is one child's life over your own kind?' Dread

continued. 'What is the price you would place on their existence?'

Bryn's hands were clammy, his thoughts clouded as Dread leaned in closer, his breath lacing with Erick's. 'What is the price of everyone's lives here? One child, or a massacre? Choose.'

Choose. The word sliced through him. Around the pit, faces watched in silence, wide-eyed, terrified, waiting. It was the same look Rabbit had worn when they'd discovered the Queen had destroyed the Peaks of Carfell. He could hear the laughter that once filled the colony halls, smell the smoke and oil that clung to their skin after work. His family. His kin. All gone because someone else had chosen violence.

Bile crept up Bryn's throat as Erick lifted his talons. His face twisted, the kind of pain that carved itself into bone. Bryn saw the tremor in his hands, the flicker of hesitation in his eyes, a storm breaking behind them. For a heartbeat, Erick looked ready to shatter, torn between duty and mercy, between saving many and damning one.

And Bryn knew that war. He'd fought it once, too. If it were him standing there, if it were Rabbit on his knees and the Seven behind him, Bryn knew what he would have done.

And he would never have forgiven himself for it.

As the sickening realisation ran through Bryn, Erick shot him a pleading glance. His talons gleamed, his shoulders shook.

It had only been a blink.

A breath.

But with his eyes closed, Erick sliced his talons across the little girl's neck.

The silence that followed carved itself into Bryn's memory, broken only by the wet, choking sound that would echo in his mind for the rest of his life.

XV
The Fall of The Futile

Bonyx threw open the door to the Doc's laboratory, cane steady in his hand as he hurried along the halls. His breath hitched, his eyes wild as he followed the dim lights along the alcoves of the walls. The whitewashed edges of the Sanctuary felt too bright, too smooth, as he stumbled past the sleeping bodies.

He'd never left Doc's chambers, never seen the full bellied ceiling or the mass of creatures gathered about. But he had no time to think, to ponder or wonder about this many creatures surviving. Living.

Pain shot through his body. He was still weak. Still a liability. Even though he knew it, he did not falter. He looked for his kin, for Bjorn's deep snores or Hansel's steady breath, as he eyed trolls and fairies and changelings.

Humans mixed with elves, and gnomes slept beside goblins. It was a wonder he never knew he'd feel. A sight he never believed possible. But there was no time.

The Queen's men come for us.

How long did they have? A day? An hour? Bonyx didn't know. He only knew he had to warn someone. Tell someone what was coming. *Who* was coming.

His foot hit a sprawled leg, and someone barked expletives at him. With apologetic hands he kept weaving through the throng, avoiding limbs where he could and staring into any face he might recognise.

Rumple had remained in the dark room, and Bonyx had run.

'*It's too late,*' Rumple had whispered, despair and loathing coating his tone.

But Bonyx wasn't done. He wouldn't give up. Not when they still had the six. Not when most of them survived.

The prophecy lingered in his mind. Nona's voice whispering against his skin in that misty tent, her eyes heavy with sorrow. She had *known*. Though most would, he couldn't bring himself to hate her for it. Her gifts were both blessing and curse.

The Weaver.

The Creator.

The Destroyer.

The Grimm.

Pushing aside the memories, he blinked against the dim light, his old sight failing him, when a snore rose above the rest. Louder and gruffer.

Bjorn.

He pressed on his cane harder, his knuckles paling as he limped through makeshift curtains and the maze of groups. A cropped beard came into view, fat hands and dirty hair outlined in the low light. Bonyx's breath hitched, relief a sweet taste in his mouth.

Bjorn slept beside Zacariah and Hansel, the three of them sprawled along their bedrolls, so unaware of the danger.

Faster. He had to move *faster.*

With a crack of Bonyx's cane, Bjorn sputtered awake. The old dwarf leaned close, fingers clutching Bjorn's shirt, breath coming quick with urgency.

'We must leave,' Bonyx warned. 'The Queen's men are coming.'

Bjorn blinked up at him, confusion softening into realisation. He turned, smacking Hansel's chest. 'Wake up, you fool,' he hissed. 'We have to find Piccadilly.'

To Bonyx's relief, the Huntsman sat up straight, eyes alert. 'What's happened?'

Bonyx gripped Hansel's arm. 'The Queen's men are coming. We must leave. *Now.*'

'I'll find Piccadilly,' he said grabbing his weapon, before deftly moving through the crowd.

Alone, Bonyx turned to Bjorn. 'Wake Zacariah, warn the others.'

'What about Rabbit?' Bjorn asked. 'We can't leave Rabbit.'

'We won't,' Bonyx replied, holding out his hand. 'I'll get him.'

Hansel sprinted towards Piccadilly's chambers. He tore around the corner, one hand slapping the wall to keep his balance, boots pounding against the stone. Bonyx's warning still rang in his ears, sharp with panic. Then, turning the final bend, Hansel jerked to a stop, breath caught, heart hammering, at what lay ahead.

Flynn paced outside Piccadilly's door, dragging his fingers through his already wild hair. At the sound of Hansel's boots, he looked up, his face tightening into a scowl.

'We have to move,' Hansel said, striding towards the door. Piccadilly needed waking – she'd warned him she slept deep, often lost to dark dreams. He'd never asked about them. Her eyes carried enough ghosts to know the kind of sleep that left you breathless. He had his own. He didn't need hers.

He was nearly at the door when Flynn stepped in front of him. 'What are you doing here?' he hissed.

Hansel bit back the urge to shove him. 'I could ask you the same.'

'Don't talk down to me.'

'Why not, when it's so easy?' Hansel smirked, towering over him.

'She's asleep.'

'Then it's time she woke up.' Hansel shoved past and hammered his fist against the door. The wood shuddered under the force, echoing down the corridor. No answer.

He turned to Flynn. 'Have you seen her?'

Flynn's glare was sharp. 'Not yet.'

Hansel struck the door again, harder this time. The sound cracked through the corridor, but still no reply came from within. He shot Flynn a look, then braced his shoulder and shoved. The old wood groaned under his weight, bolts straining until the hinges tore loose and the door crashed inward, splintering across the stone.

He stumbled into the dark. The air inside was close, heavy with smoke and iron. Silver flickered in the gloom, then movement. Before he could draw breath, Piccadilly was there, twin blades flashing up to his throat, her eyes sharp and wild, catching the faint light like a predator's.

'Hansel?' she said. Her gaze flicked to his right. 'Flynn.' She lowered the blades at once, regret flickering across her face before wariness settled in. 'What in the Godmother's name are you doing?' She tilted her head, hair spilling over bare skin.

Flynn stiffened.

'I'm sorry,' Hansel said. 'I did knock—'

'Barely,' Flynn muttered.

'There's an emergency.'

'What happened?' Piccadilly said, moving towards the bed.

'He's an idiot, that's what,' Flynn snapped. 'Breaking down doors in the middle of the night. And I'm the one nobody trusts?'

Piccadilly strapped on her curved blades, tightening the belt at her waist as Hansel stepped forward.

'I came to warn you,' Hansel said. 'Rumple—'

An explosion tore through the Sanctuary. The ground shook, a crack slicing from floor to ceiling.

Piccadilly froze. 'They've found us?'

'They've found us.'

Piccadilly was already moving, blades flashing as she spun toward the tunnel. Hansel fell in step behind her, boots pounding against the stone. Another blast rippled through the walls, showering them with dust.

'Where are they coming in?' she called over her shoulder, eyes darting through the gloom.

'The sound's coming from the cellars,' Hansel said, keeping pace beside her.

'How many?' Flynn demanded, his voice finally sharp with focus. 'Have the others been woken? We need to evacuate.'

Hansel tried to recall what he could. Piccadilly stayed focused and listened while Flynn rattled off evacuation plans like he'd written them himself. She led them deeper into the tunnels, dust thickening in the air from the explosion.

'The children and weaker species will split,' Flynn said, keeping pace with Hansel. 'Some through the western tunnels and others heading north. A few of the newer recruits can guide them.'

Slipping through the city unnoticed would be near impossible. The rebellion's numbers were too great. Over a thousand. But the old Commander had prepared.

Piccadilly nodded along with Flynn, and took over with clear, concise instructions. 'Both exits lead to sprawling tunnel networks. The northern route cuts into the sewers near the city's edge, towards the mountains. The western path leads to Silver Lake. Not all can swim, so boats have been hidden along the shore.' She paused. 'Though, with raiders and thieves, it's hard to know how many remain.'

'The dwarves are waking the others now,' Hansel said. 'They're dividing them into groups. Some will fight. Buy time.'

'Time,' Piccadilly echoed, brow furrowed.

She stopped abruptly and spun, Flynn colliding into Hansel. Hansel raised an eyebrow, but Flynn refused to meet his gaze.

'Can you buy me some time, too?' she asked.

Hansel opened his mouth, but Flynn cut in. 'No.'

Piccadilly stepped forward, her hand resting on Flynn's forearm. He softened slightly, though his jaw still clenched.

'I have maps in the Commander's office,' she said, turning to Hansel. 'Contacts. Safe houses.'

Hansel's eyes widened. 'Isn't that next to the cellar?'

'It is.'

'It could be half gone already!' Flynn said.

'Or it might not be. I can't risk leaving it.'

'Piccadilly,' Hansel began, but she raised her blades.

Another boom echoed, followed by a scream from below.

'You get them out,' she said. 'I'll protect our secrets.'

Flynn sighed. 'You heard her,' he muttered. 'Time to prove your usefulness.'

They split, vanishing into the dark. Leaving Hansel alone and conflicted.

Myrenna cracked her neck, bracing for the sting that always came when her magic stirred. Each day it returned a little more, trickling through her veins like melting snow.

Her prison had been emptied of maidens, their fresh hearts feeding the dark pulse in her chest. She stood on the parapet below the castle's aerie, a narrow ledge of pale stone slick with rain, the wind clawing at her loose pants. Far below, the city stretched before her, the lights from the fire fairies' lanterns flickering like stars across the empty streets. From here, she could see the curated gardens, where the maze stretched into the dark, the hedges reaching out like long limbs. The view did little to ease her rage, but at least her strength had returned.

The throne room had since been scrubbed clean, the stench of blood replaced with beeswax and lavender. Seamstresses scurried about like anxious mice, draping the windows with absurdly lavish curtains, a riot of crimson velvet stitched with gold thread, heavy enough to drown a man if pulled down. Each fold shimmered faintly when the light hit, the silk lining soft as skin. It was all *so much*. Flowers embroidered into flowers, silks layered upon silks, a dizzying spectacle of excess. All for a stupid Summer Ball.

Myrenna pressed her fingers to her temple, feeling the pulse of a headache rise. The very thought of all that velvet made her teeth ache. What use were curtains when the world outside still burned?

Still, the twelve princes would attend, and she would welcome them with food and drink and women. It was tiresome but a necessity. The ball was how she could woo in the nobles. The city folk.

The mirror had suggested she invite some of the lesser classes and have a competition to give those in the lower reaches something to dream about. She was still contemplating it. She wasn't in the business of matchmaking, after all.

Her murders cawed in the distance, and she held back her growl. Rage pooled in her stomach as she thought of Dread and Trik. The brothers who had ruined her. Her chess pieces that had gone rogue.

Dread. Who so carelessly *burnt* her city. Who had threatened her control. Who had freed her prisoners.

She'd believed Trik was better. That was why she'd placed him at the border, handed him command of her army. He had strength. He made sharper decisions.

Or so she'd thought.

Then the message came. Snow had been captured, only to escape. Myrenna's rage had been instant and searing. It clawed up her throat, burned behind her eyes, and threatened to split her in two.

But she didn't scream. She didn't lash out. She swallowed it. Let it coil deep inside her, tight and venomous. Rage was a weapon, and she knew how to wield it.

She didn't make rash decisions. She crafted plans like spells: layered, precise, and unbreakable. And her plans for the mines and Perridorm had taken years to shape. She wasn't about to watch them unravel because of incompetence.

Her time of staying away was over.

If something needed doing, she would do it herself.

And this time, she wouldn't be forgiving.

She would start with the mines, and when she was done, she would go to the border where the battle unfolded. At least she knew where Snow was. That was more than she had before.

Myrenna began her shift, letting each crack of pain fuel her rage.

When she rained down fire on the kingdom of Perridorm with her men in tow, they would be begging in their own blood.

XVI
The Imps and The Coffee Pot

Dread stood in his tower, his arms clasped behind his back as the sun began to set over the mines. The day had been hot, the air heavy with the promise of summer's suffocating grip. Soon the heat would crawl down into the tunnels, thickening the air until even the guards struggled to breathe.

He imagined the Silver City preparing for Myrenna's solstice ball. Velvet and silk draped from her halls, jewels polished to outshine the stars. The ball was always held on the longest day of the year. Even after he burnt a portion of the city to the ground, the ball would hold royals from Carnell and nearly all the lords and ladies. With most of the twelve princes attending, the women of the Silver City would soon forget the horrors with the hopes of snagging a prince.

Flashy dresses and poised grins. He ground his teeth. It was when he would have to face the Queen, too. Unless she called on him first. He just hoped he had something to show her before then. Because if he didn't, she'd have his head.

His main guards stood at the open door to his study, outlining the latest rotations and food rations. Dread tried to hide his boredom and feigned interest where he could. Outbreaks had been non-existent since the witchling's public execution, most prisoners resigning themselves to their fate.

It was a small win, but it was something finally going in his favour. And yet, he couldn't stop thinking about the bone door. Couldn't stop seeing the witchling's blood. Or the sharp talons of the changeling.

He dreamt of the changeling's eyes, the sagging shoulders and absolute silence as something broke within every being in that pit.

Since then, his men had cleaned and cut the body apart, ensuring to dry out the witchling's bones. The dwarf had been issued the best tools possible, the lock had been measured, giving him ample information on what shape the key would take.

The horizon glowed orange, and the black shape of a bird flew through the skies. Dread frowned. A lone crow.

Dread held his hand up and the guard ceased his report.

'How much stardust do we have,' Dread asked, his eyes not leaving the lone bird flying towards his tower.

'The raiders have backed off – either in hiding or dead, Sir.

Our stocks are the highest they've been in a while. We'll have plenty to expand with after we open the eastern door.'

Dread nodded, before turning around. 'Good, but we won't be expanding after we open the door.'

'Sir?'

'We won't need it. We'll have what the Queen wants. Your new orders are to place stardust in and around the mines. Find the weakest points. Spread them wide. I want each bottle hidden. I want them loaded. And I want every single bottle ready to go as soon as I open that door.'

The soldier swallowed. 'Will there be an evacuation, Sir?'

'You'll wait for my orders. Just be ready.'

With a sharp nod, the soldier left, and Dread looked back out the window. The crow was closer now, its wings almost touching the northern black walls.

With a low growl, Dread left his tower chamber and climbed the winding stair. He took the steps two at a time, the air growing hotter as he ascended. At the top, he pushed open the heavy door leading to the parapet, its hinges groaning in protest.

The dry wind lifted his hair and his nose stung from sulphur. There was only one crow who would dare visit him unannounced. And it wasn't Flynn.

The dying sun behind Trik illuminated his shadow. The crow glided in on his wings and shifted as his feet hit the floor. Dread braced himself for the rage, for the anger he knew was coming from his escapade in the city. Instead, his brother met him with frantic eyes.

Trik breathed heavily, his energy waned from the flight, and he clasped onto Dread's hand before embracing him. 'Thank the cauldron you're alive.'

'Alive?' Dread asked, confused.

'I messed up, brother,' Trik said. 'I don't know if she'll forgive me. Or if she'll let me live. I *really* messed up.'

Dread frowned. He took hold of his brother's shoulder. 'What are you talking about?'

Trik looked up at him.

Though Trik wasn't slight by any means, he was leaner than Dread, more on the side of their mother. Like Flynn. Dread's stature had come from their father. A powerful shifter who could turn into a bear.

'I had her,' Trik said, swallowing. 'I had Snow.'

Dread stepped back. 'What?'

'I had her, and I lost her. And then the dead came. It was so fast. It happened so fast.'

Dread wasn't the only one in trouble now. 'Does Myrenna know?'

Trik panted. 'If she did, I'd be dead. Or you'd be dead. When you hadn't responded to my messages in a few days, I'd expected the worst. I had to fly here to see. To know.'

Dread eyed the wall, of the mines where his soldiers stood at attention.

'Follow me,' Dread said, pulling Trik along. 'It's too public here.'

His brother was ragged, deep circles shadowed his eyes and specs of hair grew back in patches on his scalp. Trik never left his head unshaved. It was always crisp. Shaved daily and with a precision only his brother could attain. Dread frowned in concern.

Guards dodged them as they took to the rocky hallways towards Dread's quarters. This section of the tower was off limits to anyone without Dread's specific commands. It held three doorways just to enter: one for the main door, the second to his living quarters, and the third to his bedroom.

Each door had been warded against spells, thanks to Myrenna who liked to keep her property safe from anyone but her.

They entered the chambers and Dread shut the door behind him, lighting the lanterns in quick, succinct movements. Trik faltered as he entered.

The room was large, segregated into his main living quarters, his bathroom, and his dressing area. A double poster bed stood against the back wall, and on the opposite side was a long dining table, a seating area, and a fireplace, flanked by a soft lounge.

Dread went straight to the cabinet and pulled out a bottle of rum. He yanked the cork free with a pop before he took a swig. This wasn't the night for glasses.

'They killed her,' Trik whispered.

Dread spun around. Trik was a mess, his eyes were glassy, his uniform rumpled.

'Snow is dead?' Dread asked.

His brother met Dread's eyes. 'Not Snow. Artemis.'

Dread handed him the bottle. 'Tell me everything.'

Trik took a swig and coughed. Dread started a fire, the heat prickling his face as Trik told him what happened.

When his brother finished, Dread rubbed his brow. 'If it's any consolation,' he started, 'I burnt down half the city and let the rebellion free her most prized prisoners. Including killing her Tinker.'

Trik's jaw dropped. 'You bloody what?'

Dread clenched his fists. 'I also let them take the spindle. And the worst of it was that Flynn was involved. I fought him, brother, and he almost killed me.'

And yet Myrenna had not come.

Dread didn't feel fear often. But he felt it now.

Myrenna did not linger. She was a tornado. Destructive and fast. It was a part of why he loved her.

Trik's eyes went dark. 'Is that why you've been avoiding me?'

'I thought you'd be mad.'

'You fought our brother.' Trik seethed. 'How could you think I wouldn't be? Is he alive? Does Myrenna know? By the Cauldron, Dread, we are screwed. We are so *screwed.*'

'There's still time.' Dread said, snatching the bottle from Trik. 'Flynn lives, but I'll kill him if I have a chance.'

He held his hand up as Trik tried to bite back a retort. 'I won't have it brother. I won't be chastised, and you won't change my mind. He's ruined us already. He's with the rebellion. He's chosen his side. But we still have a choice. We still have a chance.'

'When Myrenna comes—'

'She will be furious,' Dread said, handing the bottle back to his brother. 'But we don't know how much she knows yet. She was away before I left. She'd taken a Nightkiss flower, so it'll depend on when she gets her magic back. Our only way out now is to prove our loyalty. To give her something she needs.'

'The army is barely holding on at the border,' Trik said. 'I have nothing left to give that I haven't already.'

'We have the bone door,' Dread said. 'I have a key being made now. Whatever she's looking for, it lies beyond that door. If we get that for her, if we provide her with the one desire she has spent years looking for, then we have a chance.'

'A chance at what?' Trik asked.

Dread stopped pacing and slowly turned. 'A chance at happy ever after.'

Eve didn't sleep that night. She stared at the ceiling as her clothing stuck to her from perspiration. The bed was lumpy, poking and prodding her, reminding her of her failures. The dream still felt real and tangible in her mind: the wicked man crumbling into dust in front of her, Porchid bloodied and beaten in the dirt.

She squeezed her eyes shut, willing away the nightmare with each dry gasp. She clenched her hands, her nails biting at her calloused palms.

It was no wonder Rumple had gone insane without a tether. If this was what dream walking felt like, he was more powerful than they knew.

Except, Myrenna had known. Or had at least guessed. The Queen was always one step in front, one countermove ahead. As if she had been playing this game for a millennium.

Eve focused on the feeling of her hands, of the sharp bites of pain. It was over. The dream was gone. Porchid was safe with Hansel. She had to hope so at least. Hope they hadn't been caught in the war that was brewing. In the death that would soon come.

After Eve had fallen to the floor, vomit soaking into her knees, she'd run from the watchful gaze of the tapestry straight to the bathroom. From there, her stomach had churned. She'd washed herself twice since then, trying to scrub away the blood and memory of Porchid.

The dream book had advised nothing about her energy waning. On how the change in the dreamscape sucked you dry when you tried to manipulate it. She lifted her red hands in the tub's water, checking for any changes, any drops of blood. But she'd scrubbed them raw, dripping rivulets of soapy water in the candlelight. A *thump* had echoed, replacing her clothes again, as they always did, before she'd finally fallen into bed.

She couldn't remember when dawn broke over the horizon, the pale-yellow glow seeping through the windows.

Sounds came from the lower floor. Eve supposed Cyrene was poking into things she shouldn't. Making a mess or cleaning up the one they'd left after the fight. She didn't know, and she couldn't bring herself to care.

The nymph had been right. Had seen the danger and the torment the spindle wound bring. Instead, Eve had not heeded the warning, choosing to throw herself into chaos as always.

The creak of the door was the only giveaway that someone had arrived. Eve only blinked at the ceiling. The sound of a tray hit the surface on the bedside table and Eve's eyes darted to the steaming pot of hot tea and breakfast. The smell of eggs and bacon tickled her nostrils, making her mouth water.

It hurt to turn her head, to look towards Cyrene's red hair and scaled blue skin. But when Eve had expected a lashing, the nymph just looked at her with sad eyes.

'Somehow I knew you'd ignore me,' Cyrene said quietly. 'Yet I also didn't stop you. I suppose it's both of us who made mistakes.'

Eve didn't reply as the nymph poured the tea into the cups. Another *thump* echoed throughout the room, leaving a pot of coffee.

'It seems they know what you like,' she said, reaching over for the new pot.

Eve's mouth was dry, her throat sore as Cyrene handed her the warm cup. Tea was probably the better option, but she could never turn down a cup of coffee. The bean was hard to obtain and since arriving here she'd had her fill.

Eve lifted the cup to her cracked lips, the liquid sliding down her throat like honey, waking her from the inside out. When she finally felt like she could speak, she turned to Cyrene and rasped, 'Who?'

Cyrene raised her brow and Eve rolled her eyes. She hated that look. The one where people stared at you like an idiot.

'The imps,' Cyrene replied.

A giggle sounded at the name. Soft and childlike.

Eve jolted up and her body groaned at the movement. She held back a wince, before her eyes fell on the coffee pot. 'Don't make me ask it.'

To her credit, Cyrene didn't laugh. She lowered her teacup and stared Eve in the eyes.

'House imps,' Cyrene started, 'usually live in older abodes and can be quite mischievous. They either help or hinder you depending on their judgement of the occupant. If they have been supplying you with coffee then they like you. Which is a miracle in itself.'

Eve frowned, ignoring the dig. 'So, the house isn't enchanted?' she asked. 'It's the imps that have been providing the clean clothes and tidying up?'

Cyrene did laugh then, her voice ringing throughout the room. She sounded like a siren, almost captivating as Eve sat perfectly still. She worried if she moved, she would run straight to the bathroom and lock herself in. Heat crept up her cheeks, blooming along her tanned skin.

Cyrene waved her hand, her red nails chipped. 'I wondered at the sign on the door. Why someone would call it the *Cottage of Convenience*. Though, in a realm full of magic, I suppose a living house wouldn't be *too* farfetched.'

'I'm glad you think it's funny,' Eve huffed, trying to not throw her coffee at the nymph.

'Don't be embarrassed. They aren't as common as they used to be,' Cyrene said, reaching for the food. She handed Eve a plate, the bacon extra crispy just as she liked it. 'Imps are a rare breed now. Most occupants treated them as pests when they didn't comply, using spells and poison to kill them or send them off where they couldn't survive.'

Eve took a bite of the bacon, and salivated at the salty taste. 'Why would people want to get rid of them?' she asked between bites. Energy slowly returned to her body. 'They've been very accommodating to me. Though they didn't cook me eggs and bacon. How did you even get this?'

Cyrene shrugged. 'There's chickens out the back, and the bacon was in the root cellar.'

Eve pretended she'd known the cottage had a root cellar and let Cyrene continue.

'As for the imps. You've been lucky. Usually, they're temperamental. If they don't like the owner, they aren't as hospitable. They make a mess, or steal your shoelaces, or leave rocks in your bed. That kind of thing.'

Eve thought about all the little wondrous things that had appeared, or been helpful in her time here and smiled softly.

They sat in silence a while before Eve whispered, 'I'm sorry.'

Cyrene's ear twitched. She never missed anything. 'I'm going to accept that apology with grace, but just so you know, I *really* want to bathe in that apology. I want to mount it on a wall for the realm to see. An apology from Eveline Rafter, the Seeker.'

'If you wanted to do that gracefully, you ruined it.'

Cyrene winked at her. 'I know, but you're fun to poke fun at.'

At that, Eve snorted. 'I don't think anybody has ever said that. I don't have a reputation for being *fun*.'

'No,' Cyrene said, her voice turning serious. 'You have a reputation of finding things that are lost and returning them. You have a reputation of being moody and selfish. But you still bring joy to people. You still help them somehow. That's more than many others in this dark place can claim.'

Eve stopped eating. She didn't know what to say.

Cyrene stood and collected the plates, placing them neatly back on the tray. 'We are traumatised you and I, but we are not broken. We keep going everyday despite our pain. And it is enough.'

Some part of Eve cracked at the words, warming a deep cold place within her. Words were a powerful thing. Her father had lived by them. In each tale he told, or each moral he'd ingrained within her.

Cyrene wandered to the door with the tray and paused upon the threshold. 'We have sat in the shadows for long enough. When you're ready, come downstairs and you'll tell me what you're really doing here. Then, and only then, will I help you. Because if we don't lift each other up, nobody else will.'

With that, the door clicked shut, and a fresh towel was placed at the end of her bed with another soft *thump*.

Though Eve's body protested, and her heart was shattered and worn, she pulled herself into the bathroom and entered the steaming tub.

For the first time in a long time, Eve wanted to try. And she wanted to try today.

XVII
The Magic of Brittle Bones

Bryn sat in a damp room, far below the sharp black walls of the mines. His hands shook as he stared at the parchment he'd drawn with diagrams from his assessment of the lock. He'd never carved a key before, but he had always been gifted at forming shapes. At making something from nothing.

He'd spent at least two hours sketching the diagram, his every movement being watched by the guards. He tried to concentrate but his thoughts ventured towards the bone door and what surrounded it: white flowers, the bulbs full and pale.

Dread had not been the only thing to shake him that day.

It was the same flower Doc had drawn for him. The same flower that had placed him in this predicament. The same flower that could save Rabbit.

It had happened too fast. After admitting he could make the bone key, the guards had swept down on him and Erick, dragging them away before he'd had the chance to see the flowers up close. For now, his only chance at getting one was to create a key. One that would open the bone door.

He shuddered at the thought.

Erick sat on the floor in silence. He hadn't spoken a single word since the witchling's execution. Bryn hadn't known how to communicate with him and if he was being honest, he didn't know where to start. He was still shaken too. His conscience stained with guilt and a black mark that could never be fully removed.

Everything about this place pained him, each moment filling with more heartbreak. More grief. More desperation.

The lock rattled as the door opened, and two guards entered. One looked to be in his mid-twenties, his messy brown hair knotted in a bun at the nape of his neck. The other lugged in a bag made of twine, his face etched with lines. The contents rattled as the older guard placed it down and glared at them both before leaving. The younger one remained at the door and nodded to the bag. 'There are your bones.'

Bryn's thoughts ran wild.

Will pieces of the witchling still be left? Will I know it is her?

With trembling hands, Bryn loosened the drawstrings. The fabric stuck to his fingers, damp with sweat. He peeled it open.

Inside lay a skull. Small. Fragile. The pale bone glimmered faintly in the dim light, fine as porcelain. Brown stains clung to the edges, sunk deep into the grooves.

His breath hitched. The room tilted.

A broken sound tore from his throat as he stumbled back, the bag slipping from his grasp. He reached the far wall before his knees gave way, and his stomach heaved, spilling what little he'd eaten onto the cold stone.

'At least it's almost over,' he whispered. Then he vomited again.

'You're a fool if you think it's over,' Erick mumbled from the corner.

He was right. The bones were only the start. Once Bryn made the key, they would unlock the door. Unlock whatever *evil* was lurking inside. And give Myrenna exactly what she wanted.

'Erick,' Bryn whispered.

'What did you expect me to do?' Erick asked, his voice laced with guilt. 'The witchling would have died anyway. I had to save them.'

Bryn chugged from the rim of a water jug, spilling it into his beard. With small gasps he turned to his friend. 'I don't think it's me you're trying to convince.'

Erick's shoulders sagged, his eyes glassy. 'Would you have done it?'

Bryn paused. 'I would do anything for the Seven.'

Bryn placed the water jug down and leaned his head back, staring at the black stone ceiling above him. From the way this place had been built, it was as if they hated light. Onyx walls surrounded them, depthless and hopeless. He'd lost track of time, trapped in this obsidian cell.

Bryn closed his eyes, seeing a vision of Rabbit's sick and dying form. How long would the young dwarf have now? Had somebody else been sent to find what he needed? If Bryn didn't return, would Bjorn take up the cause?

If Bjorn survived.

'Why did you choose me?' Bryn asked, turning to his companion. 'After a whole year of being here, why choose me after being alone for so long?'

Erick rubbed his eyes. 'At first I didn't know. I'd been alone for so long and seen so many die that I avoided most who came. But when you stood in the crowd near that whipping post and stared Dread in the eyes, you surprised me. You had spirit. It was a spirit not broken easily. I thought, maybe, maybe you could return some of mine.'

Erick had always seemed impenetrable down here. He had endured a year. He was still strong in Bryn's eyes. A survivor.

Bryn's heart cracked and he stood, eyeing the bones of the child. He couldn't stay here. He would die if he did. Rabbit would die if he did. He didn't know how to stop it. To end the horror that existed here. At least he knew where to begin.

'I'll make the key,' Bryn said, picking up the girl's skull, 'but I don't want to be here when whatever is behind that door comes out. I came here for one thing, and I need your help to get it.'

Erick eyed him from the ground. 'What do you need?'

'I need the flowers surrounding the door, so I'll open it. But whilst that happens, I need you to organise a riot. A big one.'

Erick shook his head. 'It's been done before. They'll all die.'

'Some will,' Bryn said, 'but not all. Which is better than our odds now.'

Murder.

Bryn placed some of the stronger bones near his carving instruments, sorting them into pieces that would suit the shape of a key. Hating himself for it.

'Something terrible is about to happen. Something I don't

think anyone in this mine can survive. Brufell said back in the grotto that war is coming'—Bryn swallowed—'and I think it starts with the death here. With *whatever* we unleash from that door.'

'What are you suggesting?' Erick asked.

'I'm suggesting that most of the guards will be at the bone door. They'll be distracted, forgetting those who linger here. There are a lot of tunnels. A lot of us wielding makeshift weapons.'

Erick shook his head. 'The recruits won't do it. Too many attempts have failed.'

'Only because pockets of them tried. When only a few try, they will be defeated. But together? There's more of us than there are of them. This is our chance. And who better to convince them than the changeling who has survived? Who has been a constant as their world crumbled. They know you.'

'They know I'm a murderer,' Erick said, his brows creasing.

'Only so you could save your kin. You still spared them and survived in the face of death. They will follow you.'

Erick looked unsure. 'How do you know?'

Bryn gave him a smile and picked up the carving knife. 'Because, if it were me, I would follow you anywhere.'

Nearly a full day had passed since Trik's sudden arrival, and Dread had spent it in silence. Pacing the caverns, inspecting the stardust placements, keeping his thoughts to himself. Towards the late afternoon, Dread stopped in on his brother. His room had been cleaned, Trik's notorious habit of order winning out despite his grief. His brother's arm laid over his face, his breathing steady despite spending the night on the couch. Dread changed and ate dinner. More salty meat with bread. More of the same dreary monotony.

The fire crackled as he ate in silence, his mind roaming to Myrenna as it always did. Trik shuffled on the lounge, and an empty glass fell from his hand to the floor with a thump.

Dread looked at him.

I could wake him. See how he's feeling.

But the whisky bottle had been drained, and Dread doubted the company would soothe him.

The only thing that would was finding the object behind the bone door.

Myrenna was still quiet, but that wasn't a good thing. She could be ice when she needed to be, and the silence from her unnerved him.

Three days Dread had given the dwarf to carve the key. Only two remained.

Time pressed upon him, constricted and restraining. He could feel it in his shoulders, in the tightness of his replies to his men. It wouldn't be long until the time came for him to face his mistakes.

Dread fidgeted and cracked his knuckles, his leg bouncing as he sat watching his brother. He needed to move, do something. Anything to quiet his thoughts. Dread lunged to his feet and strode for the exit, knowing the only cure was to seek out the bone door. Gain a progress report.

The forges still burned, flickering orange light against the now deserted rock. The prisoners were usually collected after dusk and taken to the decrepit huts sprawled near the furthest wall of the mines.

The guards on duty were hunched and tired, just like the

prisoners. He knew they needed rest, but there was too much at stake already. Too much hanging by the smallest of threads. Dread hated this place. He hated the dreary setting, the constant death. The misery and defeat that sunk into the walls. If his orders had been followed, the stardust should be lining every corner, and he couldn't say he was sorry to see it go when the time came. It just depended on that bone door. On finding what Myrenna needed. And getting it before she came to kill them both.

Trik, he thought, *I've never seen him like that. So unhinged. I didn't think he had it in him. Not over a woman. And Artemis, of all people.*

He'd never liked Artemis.

The Huntress had been carved from the same feral nature as the beasts she hunted. She'd never liked to be wrong and when Myrenna had chosen Hansel as her huntsman, Artemis had never forgotten it. Her loathing had made her more even more unlikeable.

At least to most.

The dark irony was, their mutual hate of Hansel was really the only thing that kept Dread and her civil to one another.

Dread knew Trik had been partial to her. That they tumbled in the sheets and worked together, but he couldn't fathom the idea that Trik may have cared about her. May have even loved her. He never considered that, after her death, something would break inside his brother.

And all because of Snow.

Perridorm may have an army of the dead, but their princess's strength was dwindling. It had been for some time. It was only a matter of when whatever magic she used failed her and left her kingdom ripe for the taking.

Snow couldn't hide anymore. Couldn't flee. She was trapped.

It was the one bright spot in Dread's day.

The platform creaked beneath his weight, the scent of magic sharp and metallic in the back of his throat. Candle stubs smouldered in their holders, casting faint halos that clung to the air like ghosts. Petals shimmered in the dim glow around the door, their pale colours unnaturally vivid, as if fed by something other than light. Ahead, the bone door loomed. Pale, smooth, and cold as judgement.

All it took to open was a key. A small bone key. It seemed too easy. Too simple.

The door glowed, the ivory laughing at him. The magic thrummed here. Like a living, beating thing buried beneath the earth. Dread's fingers traced the edge of a femur, the structure fragile under his touch.

The key was easy. The inside was not.

He had no doubt what lay within would bring death. Would they survive it? Or would they bring forth a curse that even his Queen could not face?

Years he had been searching, and he was so close. It was too late to back out now. Yet he was conflicted. If it came to Myrenna or him, it would always be the same answer. The same choice.

Myrenna.

Forever and foremost.

It was an obsession, a dangerous one. But she called to his very being. Cruel or not, she was something spectacular, and he was grateful to just be with her.

The silence broke as a horn blew in the distance, its echo barely louder than a breath where Dread stood.

Dread ran through the tunnels, his boots kicking up dust.

He dodged guards and pillars and pulled himself up the wooden lift with every ounce of his energy. His muscles burned as he reached the top and pushed his feet forward.

The warning of horns meant only one thing.

Myrenna.

Had she heard his thoughts? Known his worry? He couldn't think, he could only run. She would expect him to greet her. To be ready for her arrival.

But he wasn't.

The key was not yet made. Trik had abandoned his post. And Dread was filthy.

His breaths were strained as he reached the eastern tower, the sun setting low. Black ash flew in a cloud across the sky, taking the shape of a large bird. Amethyst eyes pierced him from afar.

He stilled.

The ash cloud broke and Dread's chest ached. The cloud moulded into the lean figure of a dark and beautiful woman. Her wild onyx hair whipped around her as she formed, strong and lovely. The stars twinkled above them, the night bright and piercing. Her steps did not falter as she landed with fierce grace.

She was night. And power. And beauty.

Her eyes sparkled as the ash disappeared, and just as Dread went to bow, he saw the glint of a golden hilt.

The Queen stabbed him in the stomach.

XVIII
The Fading of Hope

The Sanctuary's walls shook as blow after blow cracked along its skin. Hansel ran towards the main area, screams echoing along the halls. Fear gnawed his insides as his feet flew across the ground.

Piccadilly had left him. Had left her people so she could run towards the mighty explosions raking through this place. Despite the danger, she had to keep that information safe. Had to save those who weren't here.

But he still felt rage.

Secrets. The thing that seemed to always tear them apart.

A truth for a truth. Eve's words echoed as he pushed himself forward.

He reached the balcony, the banister cracked and warped from the explosions. Creatures ran in mayhem below, parents collected children, and trolls roared towards the rafters. Hansel tried to find the dwarves, but in the chaos, it was hard to tell who was who.

Chaos was dangerous. Chaos would kill them all.

Swearing under his breath, he took two steps at a time down the stairwell, his breathing rough. Bodies pushed against him, the screams rang out like a choir amongst the high stone roof. Blood stained the floor, bright and thick against the whitewashed walls.

Soldiers piled in from the right, the door to the cellar broken on both sides. They pushed through the crowd, grabbing and slashing whoever crossed their paths. Hansel released his axe, his grip firm as he pushed through the crowd.

He should shout orders. Give some direction to the burning anarchy that churned around him. But even if he did, nobody would hear him. When you weren't trained, a sword and blood were the only things that controlled you.

As did fear.

He needed his trained comrades – people, dwarves, changelings, brought together to fight, to defend their stronghold.

As if the cauldron had heard his plea, he saw his trained warriors. Lined like a shield against those who fled. A reprieve amongst the onslaught of soldiers breaking through a broken doorway. Waves of soldiers came, clad in purple and red. The colours of Bellatorre.

Fear pierced Hansel's heart.

A flicker of light shot through the mayhem. Porchid zipped through the throng, her pale glow trembling, eyes wide with fear. She flew in frantic movements, and her tiny form fired into his shoulder with a light thump.

'I need you to do me a favour,' he said to the fairy.

She swallowed and her body shivered as the crowd bellowed around him.

She can be brave, he thought. He'd seen that bravery in Parador. Seen it when she'd stood up for Eve or tackled the castle with Bjorn. She could do this. She just needed to believe in herself.

'Porchid,' he said again, and she lifted her panicked eyes to him. 'You can do this. You can save them. I need you to rally the other fairies, to show them the escape tunnels. They can lead the rebels out. Rally everyone to safety.'

Hansel side-stepped as a recruit shot past him and screamed, her voice piercing his ears. He pressed himself against the wall and raised Porchid up before him. 'I know this is scary, but I can't do this alone. Will you help me?'

She twinkled in a way that let him know she was swearing in fairy tongue, but she didn't back down. Her frown deepened, shoulders squared as her gaze followed the other frenzied fairies. 'You can do this,' Hansel repeated. 'Do it for me. For the others. For all of us who fight.'

She licked her lips, then flew to his face to kiss him on his cheek. Her light glowed white, her usual colour for fear, but there was a stern determination too.

Hansel moved as soon as she flew away, her high squeal rallying the fairies and survivors. He fixed his gaze on the line of soldiers crashing into the barrier of bodies, their ferocity shaking the air. Metal rang against metal, each strike quick and vicious.

Hansel didn't hesitate. He lifted his axe and charged, bellowing as he tore through the crowd.

Steel met steel. He cut down an unwary queen's guard, then twisted left, his blade slicing cleanly through another. Blood slicked the stone, but his footing held firm, his stance unyielding amid the chaos.

Blood sprayed as his axe tore through another soldier's uniform, splitting him open from gut to spine. A wet, choking sound escaped the man's throat, hatred still burning in his eyes even as they dulled. Before the body hit the ground, Hansel swung again, the blade cutting clean through his neck.He didn't have time to blink, to watch the life leave the soldier's eyes, as another shouted at him and charged.

Hansel went into that cool calm place he always did when in battle where his instincts took over and demanded blood. His moves were swift, his legs sturdy as his axe turned into an extension of himself. He sliced through uniform after uniform, draining blood from every soldier within his reach.

Sweat beaded his brow and his muscles clenched. He was steel and fire. Death and life.

His axe slashed skin, the enemies' swords falling before they could swoop. He danced in blood and chaos. He could feel the gore along his skin, his clothes, his hair.

The line of rebels held firm. Each one pivoted around the blows from the queen's men. But more and more guards crawled through the darkness. The line began to break, pushing the rebellion further and further back.

With a cry, one of the dwarves fell, his sword skittering across the stone. Four soldiers descended on him, blades flashing, eyes bright with triumph. Then an arrow punched through one soldier's eye, and he collapsed like a felled tree. Hansel's gaze snapped to the balcony where Flynn stood, bow drawn, another arrow already notched. Their eyes met, and Flynn's lips moved in warning, but a soldier had already broken through.

Steel gleamed against candlelight – a soldier rising up – and before Hansel could blink, something solid smacked into him. Hansel fell, his axe skittering across the ground. Hansel's hands slid under him on the blood-soaked floor as he tried to get up and failed. The soldier advanced, delighting in his glory as a cry came from the left.

Darquin, the stone-skinned changeling, ran forward like a beast; his sword raised. And with only a breath, the soldier's head spurted blood, then thumped on the floor.

Hansel braved a look behind him and found the threat to the rebellion had lessened. Most would be in the tunnels by now. Attempting to cross the dangerous path ahead of them.

Time. It was everything and nothing. It was the only thing they had. Without this rebellion, Snow didn't have a chance. None of them did.

With a grip of Darquin's hand, Hansel was up again. The changeling nodded and ran back into the fray.

More of the rebels ran, and a woman screamed. Before Hansel could react, her throat was slit.

I will not let these people die.

Hansel put another soldier down with a throat punch and picked up his axe in a firm grip.

Eve had told him he had a hero complex. But what Hansel really had was a wanting. A wanting for something more. For something better. A purpose. And as that kindle of flame burned inside him, that growing light of hope, he swung, promising death to those who tried to blink it out.

Snow barrelled through the trees, the black horse strong between her thighs. She squealed as the wind lashed along her skin, the sun warming her shoulders. Grass scattered across the plains and wildflowers bloomed as they blurred into colour.

She felt like wind. And fire. And flight.

Snow pulled the reins and brought the horse to a trot back out into the open fields. She sucked in a breath, the beast doing the same. The forest lay to her left, the old trees twisted and gnarled. Uninviting and shady.

With a crack, she stretched out her back. It had been some time since she had ridden this fiercely, and even with her training, her body would feel it tomorrow. Just like her feet did from being barefoot on that battlefield. Though, the pain from riding was welcome, one that greeted freedom instead of death.

She spun in the saddle, and groaned at the movement, the castle sparking in the distance. Felldryn's crowning glory – the shining glass towers – peaked high into the cloudy sky. They glimmered against the light. A beacon to all the people below.

She tilted her head, imagining its glossy surface slick with blood. Even something as clear as the towers could be stained by her stepmother's wrath. She pictured Myrenna soaring through the sky, her army close behind, darkness swallowing the land. She saw the dead, scattered across the halls like discarded dolls.

Back in Bellatorre, after her father's death, Myrenna still visited her. Snow had been a child then, woken at strange hours to meet her stepmother's whims. She remembered the Queen's voice, low and silken, whispering details of conquest in the dark.

Snow had longed to be included. When Myrenna left without her, sometimes for weeks, she'd felt forgotten. Her father was gone, and all she'd wanted was for the baker's girl who once held his hand to return.

But that woman had vanished long before that night.

Snow remembered every visit. The way the Queen entered her room without a knock, performing warmth like a stage role. She would speak of her day, of bloodshed and bridal offerings as though they were weather reports. As though eating hearts was no different than eating porridge.

One night stood above the rest. Snow had curled into herself, her nightgown clinging to her skin, as Myrenna stepped inside. The Queen hadn't even bothered to wash. Blood gleamed on her brow, dried brown across the bodice of her gown.

Myrenna had smelt of metal and smoke and lavender. Her amethyst eyes were bright as she told Snow of the butchering. Of the crimes against the kingdom. And as the Queen had sat beside her, she had whispered in Snow's ear, '*Your time will also come.*'

Snow shuffled on the saddle.

Ten years it had been, and yet the Queen still clawed her insides. Threatening to find a crack. To shatter her.

A buzzing sounded in her ears and Snow stared at the fields surrounding her. Farms dotted along the landscape, smoke from the chimneys of cottages misting towards the sky. The city lay far away, nothing but a speck on the horizon. And yet, it still looked like a cage. As any castle or town did now, she supposed.

After her run-in with the wood nymphs, she didn't like the forest either.

Something had changed in her the day the crystal coffin shattered. Now, she couldn't get enough space. Enough freedom. As if she would never again be able to breathe between the walls of a building. She would forever be reaching for the sky.

The horse trotted along the grass and Snow imagined Odion's face when he realized she'd taken his horse. He would be furious, no doubt he would act like a stubborn arse about it. She didn't care. The thought made her smile.

She had originally tried for Adanna's horse, but the animal had looked old. Soft-spirited. A horse to match the weak princess in her hideous chair. Snow needed a steed with fire. Something with burning energy and an attitude. So, when she had seen Odion's midnight horse, the very same from the battlefields, she couldn't resist.

Ride, the voices inside her screamed.

And so, she did.

A shout echoed from the plains and Snow turned. Malak rode a horse in the distance, the animal far larger than her own. She supposed no other horse would hold him, though the mount looked beaten. Weathered and tired from the troll's weight. She twisted the stallion around and met him halfway.

'Malak!' she cried, laughing at the sight of the poor horse.

Malak looked unnerved, but his eyes gave away his relief. 'I've been looking for you everywhere,' he said. 'Why in the realm would you steal Odion's horse?'

She trotted around him. 'I wanted to go for a ride.'

'You do realize they have other horses.'

'Yes, but where is the fun in that?'

Malak just shook his head. 'You know you haven't fully recovered yet? To steal a horse and go riding without the healer's okay is reckless.'

'I feel just fine,' Snow said, holding back the venom in her voice.

He sighed, as if he'd expected no other response. 'I suppose you want me to stop worrying? Stop caring?'

'I want you to stop acting like I'm ten years old. I'm a woman. And a princess. I survived battle. I'm alive. So, let me act like it.'

Snow expected him to correct her, to find some other sort of logic to explain why she should stay indoors, but instead he softened. His eyes became apologetic. 'You're right. I'm sorry.'

She raised her brow, barely containing the smugness that crossed her face. 'Could you say that again? The part where I'm right.'

'I said it once,' Malak replied. 'That's all you get.'

She chuckled. 'Once is enough.'

He laughed too and lifted his face to the sky. 'It's beautiful out here.'

'Why do you think I ran away?'

Malak's smile faltered as he turned to her. 'Is that what you're doing?' he asked. 'Running away?'

Snow watched him cautiously, choosing her words with care. She knew she wanted to get out. To seek something that made her feel free.

At the time, she'd felt like she never wanted to return. But where would she run to? The rebellion waited for her, Myrenna sat on her throne, Hansel was still missing, maybe even dead. Given those reasons, she had every right to want to run away. But Snow didn't want to run away.

She wanted a throne.

She wanted her kingdom.

She wanted Hansel.

And she wanted Myrenna dead. Preferably by her own hand.

The thought of spilling the Queen's blood by her own blade sent a thrill through her. Seeing Artemis die had been a vicious delight. To see Myrenna's own head get detached was a drug Snow didn't know she needed until that day on the battlefield.

Snow gave Malak a smirk. 'I'm not running away. I know exactly what I need to do.' She halted her horse beside him. 'I need to eat, and your poor horse needs to rest. You're a heavy bastard.'

Malak laughed and tapped the horse's neck. 'He's holding up okay. I didn't bring food.'

'I did,' she replied, with a cheeky shrug. 'I packed a *whole* picnic.'

Malak narrowed his eyes. 'Just for you?'

'I expected company, so I packed accordingly.'

'Of course, you did,' he said. 'You knew we'd come after you.'

She gave him a grin that said she knew more than she was letting on, but he let her lead him towards the edge of the forest anyway.

With a few quick movements, Snow hauled a blanket out of her pack and laid it carefully on the grass before she pulled out some smaller bags. Within moments, the rug was layered with breads, cheeses, fruits, and wine. The spread was more than enough to feed them both.

Snow was smug as she sat down, waving her arm over the generous lunch.

'How did you know it would be me that followed?' he asked, selecting an apple.

'It's always you that follows,' Snow said as she cut into the cheese. 'Adanna can't ride in her condition, and she wouldn't have let Odion leave for fear he'd ruin whatever hope of an alliance we have. Pip would laugh if I was eaten so he wouldn't care.' She popped the cheese in her mouth. 'That left you.'

'Florian would have ridden out.'

She nodded. 'He would have, but only at your request. He's like a puppy, tripping over his own feet, except he sneezes instead of drools.'

Malak was serious as he turned to her. 'He saved your life, you know. With the wood nymphs.'

Snow didn't respond, instead opting to shove more cheese into her mouth.

'He also ran into that battle for you,' he continued. 'He saved Pip's flute. He's betraying his family by siding with us. And even after all the goading, he's still trying to build a relationship with Perridorm. To help us save this realm.'

He's still a fool, she wanted to say.

'I think you should give him a chance,' Malak said, swallowing the whole apple core.

'A chance for what?' she asked, mouth full of cheese.

'A chance to be a part of change. Kindness costs nothing.'

'Kindness costs *everything,*' she replied darkly.

Concern reflected in Malak's eyes. 'Are you okay?'

'Why wouldn't I be?'

His food was left forgotten as he said, 'You've been different since we left the grotto. Since you were on your own. Since Hansel ... I'm worried about you.'

She waved away his concerns and plucked a grape, tossing it into her mouth. 'You need to stop worrying. I'm fine.'

They didn't say much after that. Snow laid back and watched the fluffy clouds pass over. One looked like a crown, another like a sword.

'I miss Hansel too,' Malak said a while later. 'He's my best friend.'

Snow sat up and looped her arms around her knees as she asked, 'Malak?'

'Yes?'

'I want you to know something.' Snow's voice faltered, the words catching like a snagged thread. For a heartbeat, only the soft rustle of her skirts filled the space. Then she went on, quieter now. 'I appreciate you and everything you do. I know I push your buttons; I push everyone's buttons.'

He chuckled.

'But I genuinely want to help. I'm no longer the trapped little girl in the castle. I'm a woman.'

He sighed. 'Snow, I know you feel—'

'You don't know how I feel. Nobody does.'

He was silent, staring at her with new intensity. No, staring at her shorn hair. She cringed.

'I know you're trying to understand,' she said.

'What happened to you?' he asked. 'In the camp?'

The voices in her mind hissed at the question and she recoiled, swallowing a too large bite of cheese. Her fingers trailed her hair on instinct, stopping at the ends too soon. Trik had taken her hair and tortured her. He'd enjoyed every minute, too. She'd heard the proof in his tone as he'd whispered to her when he'd cut her skin. When she'd been shut in that horrid cage.

'I survived,' Snow said. 'That's all that matters.'

'Is it?' he asked. 'Some pain is short lived, some pain is not.

It can linger after an experience. Change pieces of who you are without you trying or knowing.'

'What would you know about it?' she snapped.

He didn't falter as he said, 'I know what it is like to carry burdens and carry pain. I've carried it my whole life. Whilst the harsh words or isolation were temporary. Pain lingers. I feel it in my heart, like it's burrowed there.'

She rubbed her neck and sighed. Malak had known hardships. She knew it. But they were different hardships. Different pains. He couldn't understand hers, no matter how hard he tried.

'I've been poisoned and kidnapped,' Snow bit back. 'I've been a prisoner, a princess, a girl. I was tortured in that camp. Beaten and bruised. They put me in a cage. The hounds came, sniffing for food. For *me*. Trik would visit every few hours with the Huntress, and the guards would jeer, tell me how pretty I was. Except, it never felt like a compliment.'

Malak sucked in his breath.

She continued, 'But I'm alive now. I have purpose. I have a kingdom, and I have Hansel.'

'You have me, too,' he said quietly.

She laughed offhandedly. 'And you.'

She picked at the grass.

'I have something to tell you,' Malak said. 'Adanna said she'd been in contact with the rebellion. That Hansel was there with the others. All of them helping. Preparing the survivors for battle, for us to arrive.'

Snow embraced the troll and squealed. 'I knew he was alive!'

Relief flooded her, pure and true.

'That's not all,' he said. 'That stranger in the Skinny Piglet was right. Hansel and the others may be with the rebellion, but we can't meet them with nothing. They are low on resources and allies. We don't have enough to face Myrenna. We need another army. We need Perridorm.'

'Why are you trying to convince me?' Snow snapped, pulling away. 'It's Adanna who knocked us back before we'd even said hello.'

Snow imagined them all happy inside the rebellion. Laughing over brew whilst she was here, arguing with a damaged princess and her broken kingdom. Then the unbidden thought of Eve crossed her mind. Was she there with them? With Hansel? Stealing kisses in the night?

Thief, the voices echoed. *He is yours. She's a thief.*

'Adanna is scared,' Malak said. 'She doesn't know how to help when her kingdom is at risk.'

'Is the Seeker with Hansel?'

Malak frowned at Snow's demand. 'I don't know. Nothing was mentioned in the letters, but we're not talking about that.'

She's a thief.

'Snow?' he asked, carefully.

But Snow's mind was on Hansel and Eve. Alone. Together. She didn't care about Adanna or her stupid curse. Didn't care about the rebellion's training. All she cared about was him. And the crown that was promised to her.

Take it back. Take back what is yours.

'We've wasted enough time already,' she said, packing up the food. 'Either Adanna helps us, or she doesn't. Why don't we just take what we need and go?'

'Take what we need?' Malak repeated.

An idea formed in her head. Pieces floating into place. 'If Perridorm won't choose to help, why don't we just *make* them?'

'I don't understand.'

'Don't be an idiot, Malak. There's so much more at stake here. Myrenna is already looking for us, her murders are too. If we want something to happen, we must make it happen.'

Malak's frown deepened the more she spoke. 'You can't just take what isn't yours.'

'They have power here. Magic,' she said, 'The sword—'

'Can't be used by anyone else but Adanna,' he interrupted. 'They're at war. Our only option is to help them win.'

'What is it you want, Malak?' she asked, ignoring his ultimatum. 'After all this is done, what is it you *truly* want?'

'I want you to be on the throne, to be happy.'

She scoffed at his words. 'I don't mean what I want. I'm asking what *you* want. What do *you* wish for?'

He pondered for a moment before he took a deep breath. 'I want equal rights. I want different species to live in peace. I want to be free and happy. I want to live out my days with my two favourite people. You and Hansel.'

'Good,' she said, smirking. 'So do I.' She paused. 'Malak, do you trust me?'

Malak swallowed. 'Of course, I do.'

'Then trust me in this,' she replied. 'I have an idea. One that will help us and stop wasting time. I want what you want, but we have to work together to do it.'

'Why do I feel like you're about to convince me to do something wrong?'

Her lip quirked, but she didn't respond. She could already feel him caving.

Malak tapped his fingers on his knees. He gave her a considered nod. 'You know I'll be by your side. Just tell me what I need to do.'

Something wicked and thrilling ran through Snow's blood

at the words. She could see it now. The throne. The sword. The people on their knees. And Hansel by her side.

Stones that paved the way to the new path she would forge.

Yes, the voices echoed inside her. *Take it.*

And she would. Starting with the wooden sword.

XIX
The Betrayal of Brothers

Trik blinked open his groggy eyes as soon as the horn blared. The fire burned low and something about the night had stilled.

His head throbbed as he sat up and he immediately regretted the amount of drink he'd consumed the night before. But it was the only way to silence the dreams, the only way to quiet Artemis's haunting figure whenever he closed his eyes. Even now he could hear her sharp laugh, the way her cruel smile and auburn hair had lured him through the maze at the castle. He'd dreamt of her pale skin, the scars that lined her body in untold stories. He sometimes smelt her and the sound of her aching breath as they intertwined their bodies.

The relationship was never meant to go for as long as it did, had never meant to be anything else but a convenience. Then one year had turned to two, and then more came. She had been his solace in a vile and lonely place. A calamity but also a safe space.

Something in his world had shifted when she'd died. Her corpse bloody and battered amongst the fields of the dead. He hadn't said anything when he'd found her. Had only blinked at the finality of it. And in front of his men, he'd laid her upon the burning pyres without an inch of emotion.

Afterwards he had mourned. The chasm inside his soul opened with each shaky breath, her face in every dream, in every memory.

She was everywhere.

And nowhere.

The complete silence and *aloneness* consumed him. Before he could do something erratic, he sought out the only person he could trust.

His brother.

So, when he was alone again. He poured another glass, then another. At the time it felt right. Perhaps if he drank enough, he could forget her for a while. Forget the danger he was now in for coming here.

The horn blared again as he picked up his sword and dashed through the corridors, reaching a winding stairwell. The air echoed across the black stone, singing a silent song as he ascended the stairs, taking two at a time.

He didn't know where he was going exactly, and his pounding headache didn't help, but he followed his instincts, reaching the top in mere minutes. As the cool air brushed along his cheeks a cloud of ash broke, changing into a glorious and beautiful woman. His heart ceased as Dread's large figure bowed. Ever her faithful servant.

And as the Queen landed, her eyes never left Dread, even as a golden hilt glinted against the night.

Searing pain coursed through Dread's abdomen as the knife twisted in his gut. His eyes never left Myrenna's as she thrusted it in. Again. And again.

The blade was frozen against the heat of his blood. Myrenna sneered, her eyes cold and cruel. Pain ebbed through him, lacing his skin with fire.

I deserve this.

He deserved this moment where she pierced his flesh, the same way she pierced his heart, day after day. Her beauty hurt more than the disappointment flashing behind her eyes. Dread fell to one knee, blood dripping onto stone.

A scream tore across the balcony. Dread's head snapped toward the doorway. A figure filled the frame. Trik. His brother stood frozen, sword slack at his side, eyes wide and unfocused. The stench of whisky clung to him as he stumbled forward, dishevelled and still half drunk.

Myrenna whirled around, her arm raised. With the flick of her wrist, Trik's knee snapped under him. He screamed in agony as another crack ripped through the night, crushing his other knee before he collapsed. Trik's voice was hoarse. 'Don't hurt him.'

Myrenna sneered at him, her steps harsh and sure.

'Leaving your post, *General*?' she seethed. 'I'd like to say I'm not surprised, but betrayal seems to run in your bloodline.'

Dread flinched at the tone.

'I don't like being lied to,' she said, lowering her voice.

Sweat glistened on Trik's brow. Dread tried to move but he stumbled. He pulled the knife free, wincing in pain. Blood flowed freely from his wound and his fingers were slick with it. His gaze fell on his brother, his breaths shallow as Trik's legs split in ways they shouldn't.

Why was he here? Why would the idiot come at this moment?

Myrenna was on a rampage. Her anger was cold and cruel. But it was deserved.

He deserved it. They both did.

Trik wheezed as the Queen came closer. 'I'm sorry, my Queen,' Trik stammered, lowering his head. 'I didn't know—'

'Didn't know what?' she spat. 'That I would be arriving?'

They *hadn't* known she was arriving. If they had, Trik wouldn't have been here. Dread would have been prepared. Been ready to greet her. To kneel.

Myrenna had come unannounced on purpose.

Anger flickered behind her irises, a promise of punishment. Dread shivered. He knew there was no point in fighting. No point in arguing. Trik had lost her most prized possession. Her only chance at immortality. And in the process, their enemies had killed his Queen's huntress.

Trik shrieked as she snapped his elbow. It was a broken, hollow sound.

Dread bit on his lip, blood dripping from his mouth.

Myrenna's teeth flashed as she looked at them both. 'Explain yourselves.'

Trik trembled on the stone, Myrenna's hand raised, waiting.

Waiting for Dread, he realised. 'Your Highness,' he said from behind her. 'I know you're angry.'

'You know *nothing*,' she hissed, twisting around. 'Otherwise, you wouldn't have ruined my city.'

Dread twitched as she stalked towards him.

'You wouldn't have killed my Tinker, or let Rumple escape with the spindle.'

'But Snow—' Dread started.

'*Snow!*' she screeched, turning back to Trik.

Dread realised his mistake too late.

'Snow was in *your* hands. She was *there.* In your fingertips and you. *Just. Let. Her. Go.*'

Trik winced as Myrenna twisted her wrist, his other elbow snapping. 'I should kill you! You should be *begging* for forgiveness.'

Trik wavered, his eyes blinking in and out of pain.

Dread stepped forward, his head bowed. He dropped to his knees before her, his bloodied hand reaching out. He knew what he looked like. A pathetic worm. But he would kneel for her. He would beg if that's what she wished.

'You should kill me,' he breathed. His energy waned as blood dripped from his wounds faster than he could heal. 'Yet I beg for your patience. We have good news. News of the weapon you seek.'

She froze, her amethyst eyes assessing. 'Well, isn't that *convenient*. I arrive without notice and threaten to kill you both and now you have something to report.'

Dread swallowed, his eyes flicking to Trik. The pain burned through him, each cut to his stomach crying out for help.

Dread's voice wavered. 'Your arrival is destined by the fates. I was about to contact you, to ask for you to come.'

He held firm. He would not show weakness. Would not show defeat.

Her eyes narrowed. 'Were you now?'

He swallowed. It was getting harder to talk. 'We have found a door. One made of bones. I'm having the key made as we speak.'

Her foot tapped the stone beneath her, and her hair was wild and free around her high cheekbones.

By the cauldron, she's beautiful.

Trik's eyes rolled to the back of his head. Dread pressed his hand against his gut, blood soaking his fingers. The golden knife was tiny in his large hand. Myrenna's amethyst eyes were cruel as she flicked her wrist again. Bones cracked like fireworks as Trik's limbs snapped back into place.

He screamed again and Dread tried to ignore it. Tried to ignore the throb in his chest. The blood that pumped through his veins and the pain lacing his core. Gasping, Trik's nails clung to the black stone, his body trembling.

Myrenna leered at them, silent. But that was all he needed. Dread loosed the breath he'd been holding. She'd pieced Trik back together at least. If only for a moment.

'Show me,' she demanded, turning to Dread. 'If you're lying, I'll do more than snap your brother's bones. I'll use yours and your brother's bones as finery. You'd make a divine corset.'

Dread nodded and stood. His shirt was sticky and wet, but the wound had begun to clot thanks to his shifting abilities. He was dizzy, but he remained upright.

Trik panted on the ground and Myrenna pushed him with

her boot. 'You were supposed to be the smart brother, and yet you made the biggest mistake of all.'

Dread tried not to flinch, and failed. The Queen's sneer cut sharper than any blade, her disgust almost tangible. With a flick of her raven hair, she turned from him and descended the stairs.

Trik looked up at his brother, his eyes pleading. Dread paused for a moment, only letting his weakness for his brother peek through a crack for a split second before he left him alone and bloody on the floor.

XX

The Confessions of a Commander

Piccadilly rushed towards the sounds of explosions. Her swords sliced the air, chaos ringing throughout the cold tunnels. Her hair flew unbound and free. She wished she'd had time to braid it.

As she veered closer to the cellar's entrance, a shout rang out and four guards emerged. Their uniforms were coated in dust and torn from the debris and stardust they'd used.

She didn't have long. All she needed to do was to secure the documents. Their hope for survival. With Hansel fighting the soldiers below, giving the rebels time to flee, this was all she could offer. All she could do. She had failed as Commander. But at least she could offer them this.

Protection.

She gave the soldiers a wink before she sprinted around the corner, her feet silent along the floor. Heavy steps followed, racing from behind as if she were prey for a hunting party.

The walls turned rockier as she ran, transforming from smooth stone to ruin. It broke her heart to see the Sanctuary this way, damaged and splintered.

Just like the rebellion.

Her breath was heavy as she turned down a hallway and pivoted around another corner. This time, she halted. She held her blades at the ready, easing her breaths as she counted the feet barrelling after her.

One. Two. Three. Four.

The first soldier appeared and, before he could blink, she was upon him. She danced like starlight and cut through flesh with an ease her mother would have been proud of.

As she sliced through the second and third soldier, she whirled on the last, the one who had yelled. His eyes went wide, desperately looking for a doorway, an escape.

She smelt his fear. Sweat covered his uniform, and she released a low growl.

He dropped to his knees with raised hands and pleaded. 'I don't want to do this.'

His body shook as she approached. 'Why come for us, then, destroy our sanctuary, why kill us?' she asked, her voice dripping poison.

'I was ordered.'

Her steps lingered, drifting over the stone in silence. She knew what she looked like. Death incarnate.

When others had hated her kind, her mother had embraced her. Protecting her when all others posed a threat. Her mother, who had stood before the raiders that attacked their home with only a stick to protect herself. She, who had let the raiders take her if only to spare her daughter.

The man's eyes widened, his throat bobbing. *'Please,'* he whispered.

'Is that what the others said to you?' she asked quietly, her voice dark and low. 'Did you give them mercy when they pleaded with you. Begged you for their lives?'

Tears streaked down his cheeks, his hair greasy and limp.

Pathetic.

'Please,' he begged again.

Before her better judgement could take over, Piccadilly swung, her blade meeting his neck.

His head fell with silence. Something hollow and merciless taking hold.

Blood roared in her ears. Her heart thrummed along her skin, as if it beat to the sound of death.

She wanted to embrace it, to become someone powerful, someone feared. But as she lowered her bloodied blades, there was no satisfaction. No joy.

There was only silence.

And a hollow pit in her heart.

Florian tentatively knocked on Pip's door, the smell of tobacco floating from beneath. Even in a castle, the elf never left his pipe behind.

'What is it?' a gruff voice answered.

'Shouldn't you be asking who is it, instead of what is it?' Florian said as he entered.

'That would imply I'm getting a visitor for the sake of just visiting. I asked *what* because someone always comes for something.'

The elf sat in an armchair by the window. The cool breeze wafted through, but it barely hid the smell of smoke. Florian wrinkled his nose as the elf raised his brow. 'So, *what* is the reason for your visit?'

Florian's cheeks burned. He had come here to seek help, not just to visit. And now, staring at the elf holding his pipe in front of him, he wondered if he'd always feel like a chastised child. Never quite meeting the expectations of others.

'Do I need a reason to visit?'

Pip grunted at him. 'Everybody has a reason to visit, even if it is only for a conversation. Though, the Prince seems to be the only one calling for a conversation.'

'Odion?' Florian asked, walking towards the desk. It was littered with books, scrolls, and ink marks etched into the paper.

'Don't be a ninny. What other prince would there be?'

'Um ... me?' he squeaked.

Pip rolled his eyes, but didn't respond.

Florian turned the pages, the scrawled notes detailing past magical artefacts and their effects. Florian was used to Pip calling him 'ninny,' but at least it was no longer said with venom. After the wood nymphs, it was a nickname, said with more affection than Florian felt he deserved.

He'd only spoken to the nymphs after all, ensuring to agree to their request. To stop hurting the forests and ask permission before collecting any wood they needed. Adanna had already said she'd found the request reasonable, agreeing that if they were to win, she would work with the nymphs on a viable solution.

'I didn't pick the Prince as someone who enjoyed a conversation,' Florian said. 'Let alone visiting people for the sake of being social.'

'Then you have him picked wrong,' Pip said, taking another puff. Florian's nose twitched at the smell, but he pulled out the desk chair and took a seat.

'He's quite interesting, actually,' Pip continued. 'Knows his stuff. But he's also straight to the point.'

'So, you like him because he's blunt?' Florian asked.

'More or less. It's a rare trait these days.' Pip shrugged, watching Florian's foot twitch. 'I see the powders have worked? You're not as red or snivelly.'

It was true, Florian wasn't as bad as he once had been. His allergic reactions were only mildly uncomfortable thanks to the tea leaves the elf had given him.

Pip had been one of the first friends he'd met on this journey. When Florian had been caged upon a giant's shelf, the elf a housekeeper of some sort.

Florian had vomited all over himself at the sight of the giant's cooking the villagers, and Pip had been the only one to know what the giants were like. It was an experience Florian hoped to never repeat.

If it hadn't been for Eveline, Porchid, and Hansel, he would have been eaten, and Pip would still be a slave.

'I've been taking the herbs with my breakfast every morning,' Florian replied. 'Thank you.'

Pip rested his pipe on his knee. 'Now that the pleasantries are done, you can ask what it is you want to ask.'

Florian didn't quite know what to do with his hands. His

hat had been traded to a wood nymph, so his usual habit of fiddling with the feather was no longer an option. Instead, he wiped his sweaty hands on his pants. 'Have you ever heard of any magical objects, other than the wooden sword?'

Pip shrugged. 'I know of many magical objects. I know of cauldrons and pens and books and cups. Be specific.'

Florian tried not to squirm under the sarcasm. 'I meant any magical objects related to the sword, specific to Perridorm.'

'Not really, no. Perridorm likes its secrets.'

'Odion hasn't said anything about it?'

'Why would he?'

Florian bit the inside of his cheek. 'What about books covered in chains?'

Pip puffed his pipe, leaning against the windowsill. 'You don't mean like an illustration on a cover, do you?'

'No,' Florian said. 'I mean physical chains, locked around books and scrolls.'

'Interesting concept,' Pip said, 'but not unheard of.'

Florian perked up at the words. He'd expected to be shut down immediately, just as he had with Odion. But after floundering in his rooms, Florian figured that if anybody had come across something similar. It would have been the elf.

Pip doused his pipe and jumped off the seat by the window. He opened a wooden cabinet by the side wall, pulling free a bottle of dark liquor. He shook the bottle before offering some to Florian. The prince shook his head as Pip shrugged and found a glass.

'When I worked with Rumple,' Pip said, 'we went to a village called Arrow's Den, in the north of Perridorm. It lies on the intersection of the Shadow Forest and the Dark Forest. The people there are mostly known for their lumber and for all the strange things that happen there. Serves them right for building on the edge of not one, but two magical forests.'

Florian's backside had gone numb on the hard seat so he moved to one of the lounges. He still had a full view of Pip, but the old elf wasn't staring at him, he was staring at a lone bird jumping in the tree outside.

'We were still building Rumple's empire at that stage. Looking for children to call and manipulate with his spindle. We wanted future spies. Allies to grow up knowing us, trusting us. It's why I used the flute. To call them to me.

'But when we arrived at Arrow's Den, the children had all gone missing the night before. Vanished before the villagers' eyes.'

Florian tried to imagine Pip and Rumple in their prime, two elves wandering through villages playing with music and magic. It unnerved him. Especially the part about luring children.

Pip swirled the liquor in his glass as he said, 'Initially, we decided that we wanted nothing to do with it. It was too hard a task, but the more villagers Rumple spoke to, the more he wanted to find out. He said to me, "If children can go missing here, then why not somewhere else?" At the time, I thought him insane, but Rumple never did anything without cause.

'He knew that if something was amiss in Arrow's Den, then something amiss could happen elsewhere. He always protected his assets.'

Pip took a swig of the liquor, his cheeks turning red. 'It turns out, there was a local witch in town, a woman who lived within the Shadow Forest and visited villagers surrounding the forest. She'd been seen in Wolf's Den, Arrow's Den, and even Roserock. Each tale about her was different, slightly obscured by whatever terror she'd caused. But the one thing they had in

common was the missing children, and her name, *Baba Yaga.*'
Pip shook his head.

Florian crossed one leg over the other. He wished he'd asked for a glass of liquor now. He'd heard of the witch from his old nanny, a woman who hated magic. She'd told him about a witch who stole children and ate them, insinuating that if Florian didn't do better, he'd be in her clutches. To hear she was real raised goosebumps on his skin.

'We ended up heading deep into the forest,' Pip continued, 'very close to the area where we met the wood nymphs. It's where most of my knowledge about them comes from. It's why I could point them out.'

Pip shuffled in his seat, turning to meet Florian's eyes.

'When we finally found the witch's cottage, it was surrounded by a fence of bones. I remember the wallpaper, stretched thin and full of veins.'

Florian gagged, but Pip ignored him and pursed his lips. 'It was human skin. Worst of all, she thought it was marvellous!'

Pip swallowed another glass. 'Rumple convinced her to have tea with us, using the spindle as a lure. I followed, of course – I never left Rumple's side – but it still made me sick. I remember clutching my pipe tightly, having it as near to me as possible should the worst happen. Surprisingly, she was pleasant enough.

'She was very interested in the spindle. In swapping stories. I suppose when you're alone that long, you'd crave any kind of company. Even from two old elves.

'I don't remember much of the conversation, but I do remember she had stacks on stacks of books. All lining every corner of her home. On shelves, on tables, on floors. The interesting part was that one corner was different. It had chains all over it. Some shelves completely covered in silver chains and other books individually constrained.'

'And?' Florian asked.

Pip twirled his glass. 'And when I asked about them, she said it was because they were enchanted and old. Older than the creatures who roam this realm. Alive or too powerful to open without proper precautions. By that point though, she had lost interest in me. Rumple made a deal with her that day. For every village we visited, we would send one child to her cottage each month. She agreed.

'So, we did, for years. Rumple got his dreams and spies. The witch got her child.'

'You can't be serious?' Florian asked. 'You *gave* her children?'

Pip shrugged again. 'We didn't know what she did with them. I suppose she either ate them or used them as decorations. Who knows? I got out of there as fast as I could.'

'You said the children you and Rumple used to lure always came back.' Florian breathed. 'Unharmed.'

'I didn't lie,' Pip said, frowning at the prince. 'Most of them did, but far fewer were harmed after making that bargain. Trust me on that.'

Florian scratched his neck, envisioning the children leaving home, only to be swept away by the evil clutches of a witch.

'I thought you were here about the books,' Pip said dryly. 'Not to judge my past discretions.'

'I was,' Florian stammered. 'I mean, I am. I was taken by surprise.'

'Why are you asking about enchanted objects and chained books anyway?' Pip asked, his eyes narrowing. 'Odion never mentioned either of them.'

'Odion wasn't overly forthcoming when I asked him about it.'

'Maybe he doesn't like you.'

'Most people don't,' Florian said a little sadly.

Pip raised his eyebrow, his eyes looming over the glass. He sighed, before he placed it down. 'I think you are far more liked than you give yourself credit for. You may look useless from the outside, but you're far from it. Even I'll admit to that mistake.'

Pip wasn't one to concede when he was wrong. It threw Florian a bit.

The elf gave him a wink. 'Even one as omnipotent as I can make mistakes. Remember the giant debacle?'

Florian smiled at the memory, Pip's arrogance having been his biggest downfall.

'So, what are you going to do with these chained books?' Pip asked, returning to his drink.

'I'm not sure.'

'Want some advice?' he asked. 'Not that anybody ever listens.'

Florian nodded.

'Talk to Odion.'

Something tightened in Florian's stomach at the thought, especially after their last encounter. The Prince seemed to be the only one in on the secret and, despite Florian's fear, he was far easier to talk to than the librarian.

'We judged you wrongly,' Pip said. 'Try not to do the same with the Prince.'

When Florian had left, he wandered the halls of the castle, pondering Pip's words. He supposed he could try again – he was used to rejection, after all. But something about the permanent grimace on the Prince's face unnerved him. That, and the blades he wore at all hours of the day.

The Prince looked at Florian like he was food. As if he imagined cutting him into tiny pieces and spreading him out on a cheese platter.

He shook his head and turned back to the window. The sky glowed orange over the horizon, shining through the glass like a warm fire. It was as if the castle held onto the light, clutching it tightly in case it disappeared.

Curiosity got the better of him and Florian made his way up the stairs, passing a number of housekeepers and onlookers. He noticed they didn't shy from him like they did in Maelstrom. Most of them actually smiled as he passed or gave a small wave, none concerned about his status or reason for being here.

Again, he felt that warm glow of being noticed. Of being acknowledged.

It was nice.

Pip's story rang through him as his breath grew heavier with each step. The staircase was steeper than he'd expected. He wondered if he'd really changed. If, somehow, away from his family, he'd become a better man. Maybe he had. Maybe he'd finally found a way to be useful. To bloom beyond the walls that once held him small.

He had always secretly known who he was, but it had never stopped him from trying to be like his brothers. Or to prove himself to his father. Since being free he'd felt like a weight had been lifted, like he'd spread some invisible wings and finally learnt to fly or to jump.

Maybe he was used to being terrified. Used to being the last to be chosen. Used to being the sick one. Or the embarrassing one. The useless one.

The night he had chosen to run, he had attended a family dinner. It was a normal night, except he'd had a strange sensation that he needed to leave. As if a thread in the universe had tugged him and pulled him towards the giants. It had been so out of character for him. Reflecting now, he supposed something larger was guiding him. Bringing him here to the twins.

He reached the top step and opened the wooden door softly, the light momentarily blinding as he stepped outside. When he turned, he stood on a huge balcony. It was made of glass and marble, the colours a living rainbow.

He smelt the ocean air and walked to the edge. It overlooked the cliffs. The water spread out in an endless blue, touching the sky in a glittering display. Warm light wrapped around his fingers, covering them in burning orange and shades of gold. He let out a laugh and turned towards the glass towers above him. They were massive. Both reaching far into the sky and shining blood orange.

It left him breathless.

The grey stones of Maelstrom had nothing on this palace. Nothing on this kingdom. He wanted to miss home, but found he couldn't.

Florian closed his eyes, breathing in the salty air. Letting it float over him with an ease he'd never encountered. As the sun paled behind the water's edge, disappearing into its depths, stars began to dot the sky.

He wasn't sure how long he stood there, seeing the world fall to sleep, but he knew when he wasn't alone.

Quiet footsteps walked over marble, and a deep voice broke the silence. 'What are you doing here?'

Odion emerged from around the corner, dressed in his black tunic. It was unbuttoned at the top, showing lean collarbones and a muscular chest, the edges of his tattoo visible. Florian's mouth went dry. Odion's eyes were cold, his arms crossed against his broad chest waiting for an answer.

Florian tried to remember his laugh. Tried to focus on the warm side of him he'd glimpsed at dinner. It made it a little easier to speak, but it was like speaking underwater as he murmured, 'I wanted to see the sunset.'

Odion's response was a frown. 'You can't be here.'

'Why not?'

The moon shone a brilliant white, leaving the balcony in a pale silver glow. It made Odion's skin seem richer. As if he could blend into the sky and take those stars for himself.

Odion looked back at the prince, his eyes burning with something Florian hadn't noticed earlier. 'This is a private balcony.'

Florian frowned. 'There was no sign to indicate that.'

'Get out,' Odion said darkly, pointing to the nearest door.

Florian's cheeks flushed. He knew Odion was defensive, but he didn't expect the look of rage in his eyes or the burning hatred that reverberated through his body. Florian wanted to protest and found he couldn't. Fear froze him to the spot.

With a growl, Odion wrapped his calloused fingers around Florian's arm. The grip was hard, and the heat of his skin burned through Florian's sleeve. Florian barely had time to blink before Odion shoved him back in the tower stairwell.

The marks on his arm from where the prince had touched went cold. Florian turned, ready to speak, but the door slammed in his face. The echo shuddered through the corridor, leaving him standing in the dark, cold and utterly alone.

XXI
The Roaring of Blood

Rubble sprawled across the ruined Sanctuary, jagged stones jutting from the floor where the stardust had ripped the foundations apart. Smoke coiled through the air, thick with the scent of ash and crushed mortar. The great arches that once crowned the ceiling were cracked, threatening to break. Piccadilly sprinted through the wreckage, boots slipping on the loose rock, lungs burning. The explosions had stopped, but the air still trembled with the memory of them and she ran, every muscle screaming for her to keep moving. Her blades still dripped blood, though she'd half-attempted to wipe them clean on her pants.

'*Please,*' the guard had begged.

Yet, she'd given him no mercy.

When she finally reached the entrance to the cellars, her breath was laboured and sweat stained her shirt. The doors lay shattered, the casks of wine broken and crushed. Liquid soaked into the dirt, leaving dark stains.

The room was empty and silent, a stark contrast to the screams ringing out in the tunnels.

Perhaps the rebellion had been lucky, that the guards had been solely focused on the bloodshed and not the intel the rebellion kept.

She followed the side wall, dodging a few corpses as she looked for the familiar doorway to the commander's old office.

The Commander had never been one for elegance, opting to give what he could to the rebellion. He could have taken a bigger room upstairs but had instead chosen the tiny room behind the cellar. He'd said it suited him. Close to wine, private enough to not be bothered, and that it fit his purpose just fine. She'd always preferred the apartment she'd stolen from Hansel for similar reasons. Plus, it was bigger.

Piccadilly wanted to smile at the memory. To remember all the good times and mourn this safe place of theirs.

But she couldn't.

Not with them under attack. Not when the memory of the Commander's empty, dead eyes stared back at her every time she tried to sleep.

She kicked a glass bottle, long empty, and reached the study door. It lay half-broken, barely attached to the hinges. The door creaked as she pushed it open. She swore under her breath.

Half-burnt papers were scattered across the floor. Books lay cracked open, spilled ink bleeding into the normally clean ground. The once decorated shelves were empty of their belongings.

Something in Piccadilly's heart twisted, a fist closing over what hope she'd held a moment ago. She began to open drawers, fitfully circulating the room for anything of importance. But every inch of the room had been searched, each corner touched and split and violated.

She moved aside the broken desk chair and crouched under the table. She scanned the tattered wood, her deft fingers trailing against its worn surface until she found what she was looking for.

A latch.

She let out a sigh of relief as a hidden drawer opened with a click, revealing a stash of papers. Red ribbon held together small scrolls, the handwriting still fresh despite the owner's absence. With quick fingers, she tucked each one into her pockets, only lingering a moment on the neatly wrapped leather journal left at the bottom.

The door creaked behind her, and she was up in a flash, her swords free.

Silence met her like an old friend as her ears twitched. Waiting. Hoping.

But nothing.

Nothing.

The screams were gone, the banging and war cries all but forgotten.

Hansel.

She shoved the journal into her pocket and ran.

Piccadilly flew through the twisting tunnels with a grace that only few could claim. The closer she came to the halls, the screams came back. She'd barely reached the balcony when Hansel shouted. 'Stay in formation!'

He was not a Huntsman. He was a soldier.

He shouted more orders, and the others followed suit. Metal clanged against metal, the sound ricocheting around the room. Hansel stood with only five others, the Queen's men outnumbering them in a blur of purple and red.

By the cauldron.

Bodies lay strewn across the stone floor, tangled in death. Some wore the patchwork armour of the rebellion, scraps of leather, rusted metal, tattered cloaks soaked in blood. Others bore the polished uniforms of Myrenna's soldiers, now stained and shredded, their insignias barely visible beneath the carnage.

Limbs twisted at unnatural angles. Eyes stared blankly, mouths frozen mid-scream. One rebel lay curled around another, as if shielding them from the final blow. A soldier's helmet had rolled across the floor, revealing a face caved in, jaw slack and bruised.

The air reeked of iron and ash.

Brutal heartache built in her chest.

These soldiers had served Myrenna. The Evil Queen who knew nothing of creation – only destruction. Only control.

And now, the cost of her ambition lay in broken bodies and blood-slick stone.

She who only destroyed. Who let them violate, and pillage, and burn.

Myrenna was not here. The Queen didn't work that way, opting instead to have others slay for her. Yet it was still these men under her command. These men who followed her. These soldiers who killed her people.

Myrenna's time was coming. Piccadilly felt it deep within her bones. And with a roar from the balcony, she jumped.

She sailed through the air, wind lashing through her hair before she dropped and rolled against the hard ground, avoiding debris and bodies. Her knees buckled, but she kept moving, her body arching in a smooth turn as she unleashed herself. Her swords slashed the enemies' skin, blood spurted from wounds. Screams raced along her bones as her feet pounded along the floor.

She was death. She was wind. She was steel.

Piccadilly didn't have time to look up, to see Hansel cry out as the enemy surged forward. All lay forgotten in this place she had delved into. Dug somewhere deep within her soul. She thought of the pain. Of the terror. Of each family begging for safety.

She gnashed her teeth as a soldier charged from the fray. She dipped, the soldier's sword barely missing her neck, and she rose up again and swung. Pain lashed her arm as she sliced his chest, his sword cutting into her exposed arm in the same moment.

But it didn't hinder her. It drove her.

One stab, for all the jibes and exclusion. Another neck sliced, for all the death and calamity and lies. A deep wound, for all the hurt. And the pity.

She didn't stop.

As one more came, two more fell. Her blades were a ghost and siren song amongst the dark. And when the last soldier fell, her vision blackened with blood, Piccadilly growled.

She had awoken an animal inside her.

A figure moved in front of her. She whirled, turning to arc her sword when the terrified eyes of Darquin came into focus. One of her kind. One of the rebellion.

A friend, something deep inside her said.

Spots crawled along her vision as she blinked, frozen. Her teeth bared.

'They're all gone,' the changeling, Darquin, said.

She could smell his fear. His caution. As if she were some wild beast.

She settled, the room becoming clearer. The stench of dust, and blood, and sweat crept through her nostrils.

None moved.

She brought her hand to her chest and felt the slow pulse of her heart as it calmed, falling into an even rhythm.

It was done.

'Hansel,' she choked.

Her throat was raw. She didn't know how much she had screamed, or roared, or raged. But it was done. And she was here.

Alive.

Darquin pointed toward a shattered doorway where Hansel lay sprawled across the floor. Blood soaked his shirt, his hair wild and matted. Her boots slid across stone as she ran to him. His breath was irregular but at least he was alive. She swallowed, observing a wound along his stomach.

His eyelids fluttered, his forehead covered in sweat as he said, 'Hey.'

She let out a sob. 'You're alive.'

'Barely,' he whispered as blood dribbled down his chin.

He removed his hand from his stomach and revealed blood.

So much blood.

'Staunch the wound,' Piccadilly ordered.

She ran towards the infirmary, dodging bodies and debris. Barrelling through the door, she shot straight for Doc's rooms. Papers lay scattered, bottles broken and empty. The fire was still burning, slowly dying in the shadowed room as Piccadilly narrowed onto Doc's shelves. She smashed through jars, reading each symbol and tag with panicked eyes.

The top shelf lay mostly empty, but with each halting breath, with each gasp of Hansel's wheezing pain she was hyper aware of what was at stake. She could feel paper and the burning fires. The names of the dead scrawled on the tiny slips as they blackened to ash. She refused to believe Hansel would be one of those names.

Her eyes landed on a concoction of honey and a halopod. Piccadilly snatched the jar, the glass cool against her skin. She grabbed bandages, soaking them quickly in the honey before stockpiling whatever ingredients she could think of, and ran back to Hansel.

Darquin squatted next to Hansel, his hands pressed firmly on the Huntsman's wounds. Hopefully, it was enough.

Piccadilly prepared the medicine, trying to still her shaking hands. 'How many?' she asked.

Darquin didn't hesitate. 'One hundred and twenty-four.'

She'd had one thousand in her care. One thousand souls of desperation and hunger. And one hundred and twenty-four of them were gone.

'Children?' she asked, checking Hansel's wound.

'Six,' he sighed, moving out of her way.

That's something. 'And the survivors?'

'Most escaped through the northern tunnels,' Darquin replied, readying the bandages. 'Roughly three hundred went to the lake.'

Her hands worked quickly, covering Hansel's wound with proficient care. It was deep, but she didn't think the cut had hit an organ. He could survive this.

'And how many boats?'

At that, Darquin stilled.

When she peered up at him, he licked his lips. 'Unknown.'

She gave him a nod. Boats were always the hardest to keep stock of as people within the city walls stole them to fish or pilfer. Her friends along the barges had warned her as much.

The northern tunnels were always safer, a clean break towards the mountains. She hoped they'd made it in time. She'd only just made the decision to move them to the Peaks of Carfell, to have them hide within the dwarven mines. And only a few of them knew the exact location. How many of the rebellion were now left on their own, vying for escape without a destination?

She had to move, *now*.

'Flynn and the fairies are leading the escapees through the northern tunnels, but I think the other group by the lake are alone,' Darquin said.

She already knew what came next. Her first course would be towards the Silver Lake – that's where she was most likely to find people stranded. Some could fight, at least, thanks to Hansel and the others, but most ... most were still weak. Unaware of what war could bring.

Hansel shivered as his hand rested on her forearm. 'Better,' he whispered.

She gave him a tight smile.

She wasn't good at coating things in sugar, in making something unpleasant seem the opposite. But she tried. At least for him she would try.

They had to move, to chase the creatures who had escaped. But something inside Piccadilly couldn't leave. Not without Hansel. Somehow, he had become integral.

He was stubborn. Annoyingly so. But he was also funny and bright.

She placed an arm under his neck, looping her other arm around his back and lifted him.

Heavy bastard.

Piccadilly groaned as Darquin wrapped the bandage, his movements sure and precise.

Hansel gasped. 'That hurts.'

'Yes, of course it does,' Piccadilly retorted. 'That's what getting stabbed feels like.'

He groaned, his face going grey. Too close to the shade of the stone changeling wrapping him. His eyes fluttered.

'Don't die on me,' Piccadilly growled.

The corner of his mouth lifted up at the comment. 'And what if I did?'

'Then I'd kill you again,' she said flatly, watching as the bandage was tightened.

His breath was shallow, his chest barely moving. She lowered him back to the floor but didn't let go of his neck as she leaned in towards him. 'I mean it, Hansel. You don't get to just leave. You have more to do, more to see.'

His head flopped to the side as he looked up at her. 'If I live,' he said roughly, 'will I be stuck with you?'

She lifted his head. 'Yes. You are stuck with me, and I'm stuck with you. The only way we win this war is with you. You are not allowed to die. You hear me? I order you not to.'

'I don't want to die either,' he breathed. 'I'm pretty stubborn.'

She laughed. 'Good.'

He groaned as she and Darquin lifted him. Darquin taking the brunt of his weight. She'd forgotten how tall Hansel was, his shoulders almost larger than the creature made of stone.

Piccadilly gripped Hansel's chin. 'You will make it through this,' she said, forcing command into her voice. 'You will survive. And when this is over. You and I will figure out what comes next.'

His eyes pierced hers, pain laced behind those beautiful irises of his.

'I don't have many friends left. I can't do this without you,' she whispered.

He gave her a smile, his dimple playing along his cheek. 'I'll live.'

For now, that was enough.

She released her hold and nodded to Darquin. 'We need to save the others. Feed him this,' she said, handing over a halo-pod. 'Watch him, and punch him if he starts to pass out.'

She created a path for them, outlining orders, some part of her awakening at the authority. Hansel's steps were sluggish as they moved, reaching a doorway towards the back.

Licking her lips, she pointed to the tunnels. 'Let's get ourselves a boat.'

XXII

The Key of Witchling Bone

Cyrene kept her face unreadable as Eve spoke, recounting the last few weeks. Eve knew she'd been reckless, her decisions laced with foolishness, but Cyrene only listened. No scolding. No sigh of disappointment. Just a quiet, steady nod.

Then Cyrene began her own story.

She spoke of being captured, dragged into a fighting pit beneath the Silver City, her freedom stripped and sold. She told Eve about the sea's call, how it had grown quieter with every fight, every breath. About a golden dwarf who'd given her life so Cyrene could escape.

Eve's hands tightened in her lap.

But it wasn't until Cyrene mentioned the rebellion – and Hansel – that Eve stilled completely.

'How is Hansel?' Eve asked, her voice choking on his name.

'He's infatuated by you,' Cyrene scoffed. 'His taste in women is questionable.'

Eve didn't bite back, though she wanted to. She'd left the part out about him and the Queen. Of the many countless nights Myrenna had swept him into her room against his will.

It was Hansel's secret to tell. Not hers. If she could do anything right, just one thing, it would be this. To protect what little he had left.

'Is he—'

'Happy?' Cyrene asked gently. 'Alive?'

Eve nodded, the motion small, tight. The memory of their kiss rose unbidden, soft and perfect, like sunlight through leaves. It caught in her throat. She swallowed it down.

Cyrene's hand found her arm, a quiet comfort. 'He's doing the best he can,' she said. 'Like the rest of us.'

Eve was glad. Or she told herself she was. But the ache didn't ease. It pressed against her ribs, a reminder of everything unsaid. Of the fight. Of the silence that followed.

She blinked, forcing herself back to the moment. 'Can you get me to Nysa?' she asked, voice clipped.

Cyrene frowned, picking at her nails. 'I can get you to Nysa, but I can't promise you my mother will help. She's—'

'A bit of a bitch?' Eve interjected.

Cyrene laughed. 'You could say that. Though I wouldn't be throwing around comments like those in front of her.'

'So, your relationship with your mother is still rocky?' Eve asked, sweeping her hair back into a bun.

'The relationship's not rocky. It's more like a tidal wave waiting to breach a city.' Cyrene sighed. 'She's difficult to work with, but she's not impossible.'

'Any suggestions?'

Cyrene thought for a moment. 'Do you have something to offer her?'

'Something to offer her?'

'Yes. Do you have something to trade? Something to entice her to give you the mirror.'

'I don't suppose she would just hand it over?'

Cyrene rolled her eyes. 'Don't be daft. Even you don't believe that.'

Eve didn't, but she was also hopelessly lost on what she could trade. Not many things she owned held value, at least not to anyone else. They were priceless tools filled with grief and memory.

'I've checked the cottage and it doesn't have much to offer,' Eve replied. 'The only thing of value is the spindle and the tapestry.'

'Don't you dare let her near that thing,' Cyrene warned. She stood from her seat and paced the worn floors of the living room, her scales shimming a soft blue.

'She values things that hurt people, doesn't she?' Eve asked, watching Cyrene's ruby hair ripple behind her. 'Things that you wouldn't expect. Like a voice, or Rumple's true dream?'

Cyrene paused and narrowed her eyes. 'What are you implying?'

'I'm implying that I offer her something of value to me, something I will greatly miss.'

'You don't know what you're saying,' Cyrene said, coming

towards her. 'My mother has a way of taking something vital from you.'

Eve sat still, her eyes locking with the nymph's. An ache opened somewhere in her chest at the friendship that had somehow been rekindled.

'Whatever you offer may not be enough,' Cyrene said, her voice soft. 'She will still require a token for her time. For you to even see her. Without a gift, you won't even make it to the castle.'

'You mentioned a while ago that whispers had reached Nysa. Whispers of dark things even she was concerned about.'

Cyrene paused. 'She'll never admit it, but we've heard things. Sound travels through water, sailors like to tell stories and gossip. Some of the merfolk have even commented, but my mother won't meet with the Merking, not without an advantage. Plus, she won't acknowledge that something is changing.'

'What happened?' Eve asked, tapping the cushion beside her.

Cyrene sighed, but plopped down beside her, picking up a strand of her hair. Her lean fingers tugged at a split end. 'Something changed in the water. A vibration or thrumming of sorts. It started when the mines were opened. When the Queen cracked open the soil. We think it rippled somehow.'

Cyrene turned to Eve. 'It was small at first, but we feel it. Underneath the surface, it hums. As if something has been awakened that has been sleeping for too long. It's one of the reasons I came back to the land, to find out what it was.'

Eve knew Myrenna wasn't just mining. She was looking for something. Something that would give her more power than she already held.

'*You and I are after the same thing,*' the Queen had said.

Realisation crawled over Eve's skin at the memory. At the

emotion behind those words. Eve had only sought one thing: to destroy the sisters Grimm and avenge her father.

She shook her head as Cyrene waited for her to respond, but something cold and oily curled in Eve's gut. 'She's looking for a mirror.'

A vision of Nona flashed across her mind, of a woman cracking open the earth and throwing down a mirror.

A Grimm's Mirror.

Myrenna had been desperate for the grimoire. Had been frantic to use its secrets. So much so, that she had made herself mortal to reach it. The only thing that confused Eve was the Grimms. They'd given Myrenna power. Had given her the gilded mirror that hung so brightly in her throne room. So, why would she want to kill the Grimms? What price had she promised? What cost were the Grimms asking for? And was Myrenna's time to pay rapidly approaching?

'I think we are having two different conversations right now,' Cyrene sighed.

Eve shook her head. 'No. The ripple, the hum you talk about,' Eve said, her voice coming out faster than she could think. 'It's relevant. Think about it. The mines. The strange things happening. The shift. The Queen isn't looking for jewels, she's looking for a weapon.' Her foot tapped below her. 'She's hunting for one of the other mirrors.'

'How do you know?'

'Nona,' Eve said. 'Nona showed me. She hid her mirror away, deep beneath the soil of a battlefield of some kind, I just never put it together. It can't be anything else. Myrenna wants to destroy the Grimms. To do that, she needs more magic. Each mirror holds immense power. Myrenna already has the gilded mirror, and we've seen what she can do with it. Imagine if she had two? Or all of them? She needs the mirrors. To defeat the Grimms.'

'Didn't you just destroy one of the mirrors?'

Eve nodded and her hand grazed her pocket. 'I did, but it also isn't wholly gone. The mirror's power still lingers. Sort of.'

She licked her lips, her hands shaking lightly as she pulled free the blue stone. The silver veins swelled inside, and Cyrene quickly backed away.

'What is that?' she asked, a bit too sharply.

'It's a magic gem. Hansel found it for me in Parador. I thought the stone just had basic magical properties but when Rapunzel's mirror smashed, the stone's power or whatever it was got stuck inside. And then I remembered the prophecy.'

'What prophecy?'

'Mirrors four, of black and bone. Of Silver and gold and night blue stone,' Eve said, repeating Nona's words.

'At the dawn of light with powers three, a soul will tear and hearts will see.

'A gift for giving at the aftermath, or a land in ruin of pain and wrath.

'When one will stray, another shall gain, And in blood and loss they will be slain.

'When betrayal and love finally mix, Hearts will shatter as seven become six,

'Wood from a tree that's existed an age, and mirrors of glass in a watery cage,

'The theft of a gem and its keeper's revenge, an obsidian cauldron and the price to avenge.

'Shadows of memory death will reap, but an act of love will wake her from sleep.'

Eve was breathless as she clutched Cyrene's hand.

'You just happen to know that whole thing off by heart?' the nymph asked sceptically.

'Don't you see?' Eve said, 'I've found the gem and faced the keepers, the wraiths in Parador. Malak woke Snow with his sacrifice because he loves her. I met travellers with an ancient wooden vargo from a magic tree. I fell in love with Hansel despite our secrets.

'I was meant to find the stone. Meant to use it to collect the mirrors and stop Myrenna. I always thought my goals were different. That revenge was my only path, but now I'm starting to think fate has played me. That I was always on this journey; regardless of my own goals, they align. *The price to avenge.*'

'I'm trying to follow along here,' Cyrene said, her eyes warily judging the stone. 'But you're speaking all over the place.'

Eve tried to slow down her heart, to take a gentle breath, but it was too real. Too much. At least, for the first time in her life, something started to make sense.

'All I have ever wanted to do is seek revenge for my father's death,' Eve continued. 'To destroy the Grimms and take from them what they took from me. If Myrenna has the same goal, and she's figured out the mirrors will do it, then she's done what I could not do. She has a mirror, and so do I. But she's about to find another. And the fourth mirror ... that mirror lies with your mother.'

'Mirrors of glass in a watery cage,' Cyrene repeated.

That's why the cottage had brought her here. That's why Eve had ended up finding a home, why she had run into Cyrene. A fate so strong that even the stars could not stop it.

I never even had a choice. Never stood a chance at carving my own path.

'Can I point out something?' Cyrene said. 'Because

bursting your bubble seems to be my new characteristic, but I think you're missing the point where the prophecy is about saving the realm. Not destroying it. Though it does sound all doom and gloom. You and Myrenna might have the same goal, but you didn't ravage kingdoms to do it.'

'I can't explain it, Cyrene. I'm right. I know it.'

Cyrene sighed. 'Even if you are, my mother won't hand over something that powerful without a harsh price. She drives a hard bargain.'

'I know you mentioned the tapestry wasn't an option,' Eve said, 'but what if we only gave her a small piece. A little section of the thread, something with only a tiny scrap of power.'

'That would get you an audience and a short window to live before she drowned you,' Cyrene said. 'You would still have to give something up. Offer her another treasure if she's to give you the mirror.'

'If this is what the fates foretold and it's what I was trained by Nona to do, then I have little choice. I've always had no choice.'

'And you truly believe in this? That this is the right path? To destroying Myrenna and stopping the war and fixing whatever magic is going crazy?' Cyrene asked.

'I do.'

Cyrene stared at the gem. 'Then I suppose we need a plan.'

'What do you suggest?'

Cyrene crossed her arms. 'I can get you in. It's getting you out that's the problem. I'll be risking everything. My court, my family and potentially my future crown.'

Eve rolled her eyes. 'All things you care deeply about.'

Cyrene smacked Eve's arm.

Eve turned over the stone and flashed Cyrene a wicked

grin. 'So, what do you say, *princess?* Will you fight the monarchy with me?'

Cyrene laughed but echoed her smile. 'It would be my pleasure.'

Bryn was gentle with the bone, his hands steady against the dying light of the candle. The tools he'd been provided were the best quality he'd ever used. Sharp and light, easy to grip and smooth. It pained him to enjoy using them.

Despite his steady hands, some of the bones had cracked under his guidance. He was on his third now, and it looked promising, the bone holding together better than the last two. Diagrams and sketches were spread out before him, the lock drawn in precise lines across the parchment.

He lifted the partially carved key to the light to inspect it. The problem was the key's shaft was cut into four teeth. The lock itself was a complex mechanism and it had taken some care to get the diagram right. No normal carver could accomplish this, and as he broke another bone, he wondered if he too were not equipped to create such a thing.

Erick slept by the back wall, his breathing uneven. He'd done little else since they'd been moved down here. Whatever fight he'd clung to had gone quiet after the death of the witchling.

Bryn watched Erick for a moment. He wanted to help, but the weight of the key left minimal room for anything else. He stayed polite, spoke gently, even shared what slow progress he made. But Erick barely heard him. His eyes stayed hollow. It worried the dwarf more than he cared to admit.

Footsteps echoed down the stone stairwell, and Bryn flinched. Voices followed.

He had three days to produce a key. Two had already slipped through his fingers.

There was no time for sleep. Not now.

He set the carved bone onto the table, hands slick. He wiped them on a cloth. The echo of boots grew louder. Bryn darted to Erick and shook him awake. The changeling stirred, lids dragging open, confusion swimming in his gaze.

A key slid into the lock.

It took some urging, but Erick was standing by the time the door cracked open, ready to greet whatever guard wanted to spit at them tonight. To Bryn's surprise, it wasn't a guard that entered, but Dread.

Bryn straightened and felt Erick do the same. The shifter looked them up and down but said nothing as he stood to the side. Dread lowered his gaze, clasping his arms behind his back.

Bryn went to speak, but the air in the room grew heavy. The whisper of boots glided across stone just beyond the doorway, and he smelt perfume with a hint of lavender.

He saw raven hair first, wild and free around a young woman's shoulders. Her cheeks were pink, as if the wind had kissed her face. But that wasn't what made Bryn almost piss himself. It was the amethyst eyes. The thrum of power. And the cool sweet kiss of death that lingered in her presence.

He clenched his fists and tried to remember how to breathe.

She was here. Here with him.

She who massacred his people. Who had enslaved the

Princess. Who had imprisoned a kingdom and created this hollow place.

The Sorceress.

The Demon.

The Evil Queen.

She didn't smile as she entered. Didn't even look at him as she stepped over the threshold. She moved like a snake, smooth and precise. Bryn tried to swallow, but he was frozen, staring at the witch queen who had single handedly thrown his life into turmoil.

He could hear the scream of the witchling. See the crystal coffin hidden in the grotto. He could feel the devastation from the empty mines in Carfell. His cousins slaughtered and enslaved.

Dead.

Erick didn't move beside him, his breaths just as shallow, as the Queen of Bellatorre soaked up every essence of hope they had clung to.

Her manicured nails scraped along the stone doorway, a shrill rasp that split the silence. The sound trailed after her as she moved to the table where the half-finished key and parchment waited. Myrenna shuffled through the contents, her eyes cold and assessing.

Bryn tried not to flinch as she picked up the makeshift key. It was so delicate, so slight. He prayed to the Godmother it didn't break. He expected a smile at his progress. A hint of emotion. But got nothing as she tilted her head and slowly turned to look at him.

Her voice was silky when she spoke. 'You do realise,' she began, piercing her eyes into Bryn, 'that we are in this predicament because of you?'

His mouth went dry, unable to answer.

She turned to Dread. Her voice was like ice. 'We are relying on a *dwarf* to carve the bone of a witchling to enter a magical doorway. We are relying on this *thing* to unlock one of the greatest possessions the realm has ever seen.' Her voice went dark as she said, 'A dwarf with no magical skill or importance.'

Dread swallowed, and Bryn tasted the fear in the room. It clung to his tongue like iron and ash, sharp and metallic, the kind of fear that numbed the throat and froze the breath in his chest. None of them moved as she circled the room, her cape whispering along stone.

'A dwarf and a changeling,' she mused. Sweat beaded on Bryn's back, the venom in her voice disquieting as she paused. 'When we had the Tinker who could have carved *anything*. Who could have *created anything*!'

The last words were heated, rage lacing every syllable, and Bryn tried not to wince.

Her chest rose and fell, her cheeks flushed.

Bryn chanced a look at Dread, whose face had paled. The guardian and king of the mines looked small next to his Queen. His shirt was covered in blood, his knuckles white, stained in splotches of red. And if Bryn was terrified, Dread was a ghost.

She turned to Bryn, her eyes savage. 'You have one day, dwarf. *One day*,' she seethed, her voice turning to a deadly whisper. 'Or I'll slaughter every single creature in this mine.'

With a sharp turn she stormed towards Dread, her palm smacking across his cheek. The sound ricocheted off the walls and he winced. Her chest heaved, but she exited without another word, leaving Bryn to stare at Dread with panicked eyes.

Dread's nostrils flared, his eyes locking onto Bryn. 'One day, dwarf. A mere twenty-four hours. Or you die.' He slammed the door shut, locking it behind him.

One day was all Bryn had. One day to carve an impossible key with little to no light. One day to organise a riot. One day to collect the flower he needed.

And one day to hopefully free them all.

The wind howled, tearing at Eve's hair and stinging her eyes with salt. She lifted an arm to shield her face, squinting toward the dark outline moving ahead. Cyrene was already halfway down the slope, her cloak snapping in the gale as she led the way to the beach. The weather hadn't eased in days, and Eve couldn't shake the thought that the Godmother was toying with her. Waves crashed onto the shore, angry and wild, their spray soaking her clothes as if warning her to turn back.

Cyrene's face was cool, giving nothing away about how she felt as they scrambled over the rocks and sand.

Something nibbled under Eve's skin, warning her to tread carefully. As Cyrene navigated the pass, Eve turned back behind her. The cottage stood on the edge of the cliff, its smoke curling from the chimney. Even amongst the howl of the wind, Eve swore she could hear the whispers of the spindle, begging her to come back. To tread through their stories once again. Her hand reached inside her pocket, the stone warm and sure. And beside it, something smooth and soft.

She pulled it free, the wind attempting to tug it from her grasp. It glittered even now, the light flickering across the threading, shimmering pictures of many places and things. Even detached, a piece of the spindle's dream tapestry was thriving. Alive.

Cyrene barked something at her, but she missed it over the sound of the crashing waves and howling wind.

The sea nymph had already reached the sand, having climbed past the heavy wall of rock. Eve quickly tucked the material back into her pocket, straightened her spine and met Cyrene by the receding waterline.

The nymph frowned towards the distance, her eyes slightly hollow as she took Eve's hand. Eve only squeezed back, unsure how else to respond.

Cyrene had been honest about her terror in re-entering her kingdom. She'd left without permission. Without good-byes. According to her, that was a betrayal of her kingdom.

After the rebellion had freed Rumple, and with the Queen close to finding her treasure, Cyrene unfortunately didn't have the option to avoid home.

Cyrene had also told her how to enter Nysa, and it was disgusting.

The night before, Cyrene had peeled off parts of her scales like shells from the surface of her skin. Cyrene had gritted her teeth at the pain, and Eve had almost vomited at the smell of fish and decay and blood.

'If you want to get into Nysa and not drown, you'll need these.' she'd said as she'd handed over the scales.

They were slimy in Eve's palm, the edges bloodied and sharp. She couldn't stop staring at Cyrene's legs, where the torn flesh glistened in the cold air, skin raw where the scales had once been.The nymph had only shrugged. 'Most of them will grow back. Others will never return from my scarring.'

From her time in the soldier's fighting pits.

Hansel had saved Cyrene. Just as he'd saved Eve. Always there when you needed him.

Eve remembered her last words to him, the vile and selfish

thoughts she'd held about him. She'd been cynical and blunt, brushing away his hopes as if he were a fly buzzing around her on a hot summer's day. She regretted those words now. Regretted the way she held back, assuming they'd had all the time in the world to sort everything out.

Come with me.

Somehow, despite his promise, she couldn't let her past prejudices go. Couldn't let go of that fear. Or hate. She should have cherished those moments. Held them close and spent more time with him. She should have let herself open up. Let in happiness.

Sometimes, when she closed her eyes, she saw him standing there. His palm open and welcoming. And her, drifting away.

He had been an impossible dream. But one she wanted badly.

'Do you have the scales?' Cyrene asked, holding out her hand to Eve on the beach. Eve ran her thumb over the scales, waiting for Cyrene to give her a signal.

The nymph stared across the water; her eyes lost as if she could see the rocky black towers Eve could not. The Seeker shuffled on her feet, anticipation and anxiety running through her veins like a drug.

She was to face the Queen of Nysa. The Sea Witch. She was to collect the Grimm's mirror. To survive breathing underwater.

With a swallow, Cyrene took Eve's hands. 'This will be a *little* painful,' she warned.

The nymph placed the two scales over the Seeker's eyes. Eve went to hold them in place but was swatted away by Cyrene's hands. 'Let them do it.'

Eve felt a bit ridiculous and leaned her head back before the scales could fall. The last thing she needed was sand in her eyes.

Cyrene whispered, so soft that Eve couldn't make them out. The scales shifted, moulding over her eyelids like skin. She tried to squeeze her eyes shut and found they couldn't move as the scales grew tighter. The sharp edges dug into her skin. Crawling under it as if it wanted a piece of her. All of her.

Pain shot through her spine like white fire, racing through her veins as a scream tore through her throat. Sand hit her knees as she fell and the scales stretched. Digging and digging beneath her skin. They crawled under her cheeks, extending, and pulling. It sliced under her neck, her hands clawing against the movement under her skin.

Eve choked.

Get it out. Make it stop.

She'd never felt anything like it. As if a thousand ants crawled under her skin, biting, and chewing and tearing.

Air burned her throat, and Cyrene's voice died out as fast as it had begun.

She landed on her shoulder, her body convulsing. Consuming her. The scales stretched further, covering her collarbones, piercing through bone. Her vision blackened with each rip, each tear.

It was a thousand shards of glass. A thousand cold nights. A thousand knives nicking at her skin. And though she felt like she was dying, her life seeping away with every inch, she also felt *remade*.

She gagged on the sand, Cyrene's words never missing a beat. And when the pain covered her whole body, crawling to the ends of her toes, it stilled.

Then something inside Eve broke. She couldn't breathe.

She could feel the sand, hear the surf, taste the air. But ... It burned.

Strong hands lifted her up and dragged her across the

beach. Eve blinked in the light, her vision hazy and too bright. The wind burned like acid, blazing and melting away whatever was left inside her. Her body felt too tight. Too new.

She was floppy.

Like a fish.

Perhaps, she was a fish.

In a world full of magic, it was possible, but even this seemed ridiculous.

She lifted her hand in front of her, and a tingling sensation rippled along her arm as cool liquid wrapped around her torso. The hands let her go and sunk her deep into the freezing waters.

Except, it wasn't cold.

Eve kept staring at her hand, at the skin that was now not skin. It had a shiny texture, with a gloss of blue. It felt rough to the touch. Spiky almost.

Eve held her breath and the waves caught her, clinging so tightly they threw her deeper into the ocean.

She tumbled and twisted. Losing sight of whether she was up or down when Cyrene appeared before her, hair flowing freely. The sea nymph gripped her arm, steadying Eve as her body adjusted to the change from the scales. The water accentuated the beauty Cyrene already had. But her eyes were not kind. She frowned as her voice came out in a garble.

Muted.

Hollow.

Drowned.

Eve choked, her chest bursting. She couldn't hold it. She struggled to swim, attempting to pull herself towards the surface but Cyrene grabbed her and held her, pinning her under the water. Letting Eve's lungs expand. Letting her wide eyes panic.

When Eve couldn't hold her breath anymore, she opened her mouth, bubbles loosing under the surface. Water flowed into her lungs, full and viscous. She let out a cry. Waiting for death. Waiting for the cold watery grave to embrace her.

It didn't.

The water felt like air. It soaked into her skin with a tickle and her lungs cried in joy. She gulped. More and more, her body shivering as Cyrene grabbed her and pulled her towards calmer water.

'Breathe,' the nymph yelled. 'By the Godmother, Eveline, *breathe.*'

Eve did, but it felt heavy. Like it was mid-summer and the humidity was unbearable. She faltered on her next breath as Cyrene coaxed her, her vision becoming clearer. The nymph floated and her scales shimmered amongst the light filtering through the surface. Her eyes, normally dark, shone a strange shade of pearl.

Eve's chest calmed, her breaths steadier as Cyrene let out a sigh. 'Thank the cauldron,' she said. 'I thought you'd suffocate.'

'I thought I'd drown,' Eve said.

'The scales work the opposite. Air drowns you, not water.'

Something like cold rage creeped up Eve's spine. She whirled on Cyrene. 'You said it would be a *little painful.*'

Cyrene backed away. 'Did I or did I not get you underwater? You are here, and you are breathing. A *thank you* would not go astray.'

But Eve wasn't thanking her. Not after whatever fairy shit that was. She could still feel the stabbing pains of the scales, reaching into her, *underneath her skin,* as if they would tear her apart.

Her feet floated, the water now flowing through her lungs

more evenly. Her heart drummed in her chest, but she was alive.

Not drowning.

Cyrene had kept her promise.

'Specifics would have been nice,' Eve retorted. The nymph rolled her eyes. 'How long will this last?'

'Only a day or so,' Cyrene replied. 'I've never tested the scales to their full length, so I can't be sure.'

Great. 'Will it be enough?'

'It'll have to be,' Cyrene said, pulling Eve's hand towards the open water. 'My mother would have already sensed you. We have to move.'

The water glided over Eve's skin, cool and soothing. As they swam, Eve's anger ebbed away. She focused on her surroundings. Everything looked different under the surface. New and untouched and magical.

After a while, something inside her bloomed. She was breathing *underwater.*

Cyrene's grip stayed firm as she pulled Eve along. Eve's eyes widened as the world shifted around her. Coral burst with colour, weaving through rocks in shades of orange, violet and blue. A turtle glided past on her right, its head dipping politely towards Cyrene. Light filtered through the surface above, still grey from the storm, but shimmering as it touched the sand and the flickering bodies of fish.

The deeper they swam, the clearer the water became. She had always imagined Nysa as cold and dark. Beautiful, perhaps, but silent and heavy. That was how the old stories told it, a kingdom of deep pressure and forgotten songs, nothing like the warm pearl gardens in the kingdom of the merfolk.

Eve let out a muffled cry that turned into laughter.

Cyrene rolled her eyes, but didn't bother hiding the curve of her mouth.

The grotto had been lovely. Safe. A quiet place untouched by ruin. But this ... This was something else. A garden of the sea, wide and alive, cradled in quiet peace.

Fish darted through her hair, lifting it in soft tendrils behind her. She grinned, full and helpless, another laugh bursting free even as she swallowed water in the process.

She didn't care. Nothing could ruin this.

'You're acting like an idiot,' Cyrene hissed, eyes alert.

'Look at the turtle!'

Cyrene dragged her hand down her face as she mumbled, 'It's the same every time.'

Eve wasn't deterred. Whatever pain she'd suffered, whatever the transformation had done, it had been worth it. For this.

'Why go to land when you have this?' Eve murmured.

She tried to pull away to explore, but Cyrene grasped her wrist tightly. 'Enjoy it while you can, not all of the ocean is this beautiful.'

Something like sorrow touched Cyrene's face and Eve was reminded of Pearl. Of the mermaid who swam the seas and found treasures beneath. Of a red headed nymph following her every whim.

'Is this where you grew up?' Eve asked, slowing down. 'Where you and Pearl—'

'No,' Cyrene said, a bit sharply. 'Sorry,' she sighed. 'It was further west from here. Closer to the border of the undersea kingdoms.'

Eve didn't ask more questions. If it had been her, she wouldn't have wanted someone to press. Instead, she reached out her hand as a pod of dolphins swam past, clicking their voices in welcome.

'Do all of them know you?' Eve asked, noting the fish halting and some of the sharks avoiding their path.

'It's my mother's domain,' Cyrene said. 'They know who rules here. Who feeds them and keeps them safe.'

An eel slid under a rock, his yellow eyes following their movements as they swam deeper. Sand turned to rock; coral turned to clumps of seaweed. And where it had been shallow, Eve noticed the deeper shades of blue and then caverns dipping in and out of the ground.

She wondered how much of it had been explored. How much had been seen, even by those who dwelled here.

A vibration rippled through the water and Cyrene froze, halting them both. Cyrene looked down, her brows knitted, her jaw tight. 'My mother,' she said quietly, 'hides many things in dark places.'

Cyrene's gaze hovered over a sliver in the shadows: claws grinding against rock before they disappeared again.

'But even though she has rules here, there are still creatures more powerful than her. Ones who keep to themselves because they wish to. Not because they are afraid.'

'What's down there?' Eve whispered.

'Something far more ancient than even the Grimms.' A horn blew and Cyrene's head whipped around. 'They've seen us.'

As if summoned, two sea nymphs appeared from the gloom, both male and both snarling. Their eyes locked onto Cyrene first and Eve took note of how different they were from humans. Their braids coiled tight in their hair and they moved without a ripple, a stillness that belonged only to those born of the sea. Each held a spear, but neither was the same. One had coral spiralling along the shaft, sharp and jagged. The other was wound in seaweed and metal, with shell and wood bound at the base. They looked mismatched. Crafted with whatever was at hand. But there was purpose in them. Intention.

They halted when they saw Cyrene, but one of them let his gaze drift. He took in Eve with a flick of his eyes. His lip twitched. No words came.

The other bowed. 'Princess,' he said. 'Welcome home.'

Cyrene gave a nod. Her shoulders didn't soften.

No fanfare. No ceremony. But it was enough. Without a word, Cyrene pulled Eve close again, her fingers firm around her wrist. Her voice barely moved the water between them. 'Tread carefully.'

'You mean swim carefully?' Eve whispered.

Cyrene didn't answer. Just grimaced.

The guards turned and began to lead the way. Cyrene didn't release her grip. Her fingers only tightened as they moved.

The water darkened as the two of them descended. The bright shimmer of coral and sand gave way to deeper blue, then near-black. Shapes moved far below, vague and slow.

And then it appeared. A castle, carved from the rock bed, rising out of the shadows like a thing grown instead of built.

Eve slid her hand into her pocket. Her thumb found the soft threads of the dream tapestry. She pressed into the fabric, grounding herself.

She would not falter. She would hope. Like Hansel hoped.

She pictured his crooked grin and almost smiled.

One of the guards turned. 'The Queen is expecting you.'

'Of course, she is,' Cyrene murmured. Then, quietly, she let go of Eve's arm.

XXIII

The Princess and the Pawn

Princess Snow crept through the halls of Felldryn castle, her steps light despite the bandages still wrapped along her feet. Patches of sweat lingered along the sleeves of her shirt, the cotton sticking to her as she entered the Royal halls. The air was humid, stuffy despite the late spring breeze.

The only heat she didn't feel was the space at the nape of her neck, where her hair used to be. She'd tried to pretend her short hair didn't bother her, but it was impossible to forget. The worst was when she brushed it, habit still expecting the phantom strands to fall to her waist and always abruptly ending.

She'd loved her hair. It was part of who she was and how the realm described her. She was delicate. Beautiful.

Lips of ruby rose. Skin as white as snow. And hair as black as a raven.

Except hair was a relative term now. Trik had hacked it well, leaving uneven layers and longer strands. The healer had helped, attempting to even out the strands before that awkward dinner, but still, it only passed her ears, and when she went to touch ... She grew angry.

Everything was slowly being taken from her. Hacked away just like her hair.

Take it, the voices whispered. *Claim it. Power.*

She would take what she deserved.

Malak had kept true to his word after the picnic, distracting Adanna with a political debate in the parlour. He hadn't pried into Snow's plans, though he'd wanted to, and trusted she would do the right thing.

In truth, she was a tad guilty about it, but not enough to change her mind. Malak was a gentle giant with a strong moral compass. She had no need for either trait. Not when her kingdom was on the line.

She'd followed Odion before, watching as he rode away with a stern face on that black steed of his. Pip sat in his bedroom, doing whatever it was Pip did, and Florian was in the library. Leaving her alone.

She knew the story of the wooden sword. She'd been told the tale by Myrenna many times. It was a gift and a curse. Leaving a young princess bleeding to raise the dead.

But it also left a kingdom without support. Without power.

She had to see the fabled weapon. To feel what kind of power it held, and whether it was possible to manipulate. She needed something, *anything,* to help her cause. With the rebellion being so far, and her current group so small, she needed any kind of leverage she could find to win back her crown. To defeat Myrenna.

Power against power. It was the only way to win.

The doors to Adanna's rooms were a creamy white, lined in deep blue. The hall was silent, except for the whisper of air escaping through open windows. With quick fingers, she pulled out the silver pen from her pocket. The one she always carried with her. It was an odd contraption, most people assuming it was useless. With quill and ink still a staple for writing, most thought her pen an oddity. In fact, she distinctly remembered her tutor calling it *'an abomination to the skill of calligraphy.'*

But Snow's mother had loved it. So much so, that her mother had even ridden to the village of the inventor who had created it. Best of all, he'd been so enamoured by her visit that he'd made one just for her. Filled with little surprises.

Like the latch it held, revealing a hidden lockpick.

She'd tried to pick the lock on the cage in the camp, after Trik had shut her away. But even with an open door, the drop was too far. She'd been weak, inefficient. Surrounded by guards.

Here, inside a castle, she was in her element.

Snow smiled at the contraption, the steel cool on her fingers, and placed it into Adanna's door. A few tries and the door creaked open.

Snow entered Adanna's quarters with quiet steps, careful as she shut the door behind her. She took a breath, her heart racing as she looked around the room. She'd snuck around before, hiding between the walls of the Silver City's castle. But here she had no tunnels. No secret passageways. No backup plans.

Here, she was exposed.

Yes, the voices inside her echoed. Urging her. Caressing her.

She'd learned to embrace the voices. To listen to them in the quiet confines of the night. They'd helped her when she'd been alone. Had listened to her when her insecurities flared.

The chamber was plain for a princess. The walls bare except for a tapestry outlining a young boy under the stars and a white pathway leading to a cliff.

She glanced about the room, and lifted the tapestry to see if it held what she hoped would be a hidden door. She was met with only brick. Undeterred, she turned towards the study area. Bowls lined a table, with linen folded neatly upon its surface. The bed was made with perfect lines and in the middle sat a doll, tattered and worn.

Well, that's a little creepy.

A modest trunk lay near the window, the outside stained from age, and Snow walked towards it. Just as her fingers grazed the worn lock, the door opened behind her.

Snow whirled, about to flee, when she was met with Adanna's handmaiden.

Laurie?

She was a stout, curvy woman with dark brown eyes. Her hair was braided, folded back into a high round bun.

Snow's mouth went dry.

'You're not as stealthy as you think you are,' Laurie said, hands on hips. 'You've done nothing but prowl and sook since being here.'

'So, you followed me?' Snow asked.

'Of course, I followed you,' Laurie replied, shutting the

door behind her. 'You're not the first one to search for the sword and you won't be the last.'

'Who said I'm looking for the sword?'

She is only a maid, the voices whispered. *She means nothing.*

Snow rolled her shoulders and stood taller, pushing back the flush that spread up her neck at being caught.

'If you're not looking for the sword, then what are you looking for?' the woman asked with a raised brow.

'What if I was just curious?' Snow said, trying to reel back some control. She took a step backwards, trailing her finger along the desk. 'It's always good to know your opponent.'

'Are we opponents?' Laurie asked.

'Are we not?'

'Curiosity is a dangerous game,' Laurie warned. 'If we are not opponents, then there should be no need to lie.'

Snow sighed, holding back the roll of her eyes as she turned to the woman, her mouth pouting.

Lies help us, the voices whispered. *Lies save us.*

Snow pushed them to the back of her mind.

'I know nothing about your kingdom. Except for the whispers or what my stepmother has told me,' Snow replied. 'I know little about Odion or Adanna, and I know even less about the sword. I wanted to know more.'

And she did. She'd at least been honest about that.

Snow turned back to the table, eyeing the litter of papers and letters addressed to someone named Piccadilly.

'Why did you assume I was going for the sword?' Snow asked again, stalling for time.

Laurie took a few steps and halted in the middle of the room. She eyed Snow's trailing finger as if she were staining the wood with blood. 'What is it you want, Princess?'

Snow shrugged, noting the change in topic. 'An alliance. I've been honest about that since the beginning.'

'And what could you offer us?'

Snow was taken aback by the question. It was one thing to be asked by the twins, but it was entirely different coming from the help. 'What do you mean?'

'Adanna has an army she commands. One used with the sword. One that could help you overthrow your stepmother. What do you offer? What do you bring to the table should you win the crown?'

She asked a lot of questions for a handmaid.

'Peace?' Snow answered.

'Why do you say peace like a question?'

Ugh. What is it with this woman? 'I don't,' Snow snapped. 'I say it because that's what we fight for.'

Laurie remained silent, sucking her teeth a moment before she met Snow's eyes. 'Is that what you fight for? Peace? Or is it something else?' When Snow didn't reply, Laurie ran her hands down her apron. Something Snow also did when she was nervous. When her palms were clammy.

Snow's lip quirked at the side.

Nervous little mousey, the voices said. *Nervous little maid.*

'What do you think I fight for?' Snow asked. Now it was Laurie's turn to be surprised. She frowned as Snow turned towards her, moving closer on silent feet. 'Be honest. We're trying to be friends here, after all.'

Laurie swallowed. 'I've heard stories about you too, you know. The princess locked in the dark after her father died.'

Snow tried not to flinch at the mention of her father, her fingers tapping the side of her leg.

'I think you have people who believe in you,' Laurie continued. 'Not because they've met you, or seen you. But because your father was kind. And so was your mother. I met them once. The king and queen. They visited here before you were born.'

Snow's nostrils flared at the mention of her parents.

'Your mother was a beauty, just as you are,' Laurie said. 'It was sad how she died. How the sickness took her.'

'Do you have a point?'

Laurie didn't falter at the venom in Snow's voice. 'When your parents were here for an alliance, they were honest. They were open about what they fought for and the future they were building. I saw the hope they held. A hope in building a better world. One they wanted to build for you. The result of that alliance was Wolf's Den. The trade city near the border and the large road between the capitals.'

Something cold lined Snow's stomach, a dread of what words came next.

Laurie stepped forward again, her eyes unblinking. 'My *point*, princess, is that I think you fight for you. I think you tell yourself it is for your people. That it's for peace. But nothing I have seen you do shows that. You have been nothing but rude and selfish. You take what is not yours and you demand as if you deserve it. You may have been locked away, but it does not excuse bad behaviour. Especially when your parents would have taught you better.'

A *crack* rang through the room as Snow slapped Laurie. 'If you were my handmaiden,' Snow seethed, 'I would have—'

'What?' Laurie whispered, eyes defiant. 'Killed me? Imprisoned me? Hurt me?'

Snow blinked at the clear outline of her hand on the Laurie's face, bruised red.

'You think you are different from the Evil Queen, but from what I see, you are just the same.'

'Take that back!' Snow growled.

Laurie only smiled. 'Monsters breed monsters.'

A pit of fury opened inside Snow, a moment frozen in time as it pulled her under. This woman knew nothing. Understood *nothing*.

Snow was a saviour. A hero. She would win the day. She would have her kingdom. And crown. And Hansel. Always Hansel.

Mine, the voices whispered. *Mine.*

'You want to know what I fight for?' Snow asked, the voices inside her building in unison. 'I fight for *my* crown. For revenge against my stepmother.' Her hand closed around Laurie's throat and the woman struggled. But Snow held firm, some dark part of her clawing towards the surface. 'I fight for what is *owed* to me. For what I deserve. I fight for *love*.'

Laurie's eyes were wide as she tried to push Snow back and failed miserably. 'I feel sorry for you,' Laurie choked, her face reddening. 'You did deserve more, but now you fight for the wrong things.'

Her nails dug into Snow's arm, biting at her skin. Snow was too angry to care. The voices too loud—

Yes. Yes. Yes.

Laurie fumbled as Snow gripped tighter, right into the jugular. Exactly where Malak had taught her to aim.

Snow smiled, the voices singing inside her. 'How would you know what is right?' Snow asked. 'How could you possibly understand?'

Laurie's eyes were bloodshot, red-rimmed against her mottled skin. Snow embraced the onslaught of noise. Embraced the blitz of voices—

Yes.

Yes.

Yes.

She held Laurie's life in her hands. Like a dove whose wings were pinned. With only a crack, Snow could break her. Could turn her to ashes without anyone knowing.

Snow was not alone. She was not weak. She was a princess. A future queen.

And as Laurie collapsed, the life leaving her eyes, Snow blinked.

Her fingers loosened, releasing Laurie into a sagging heap on the floor. Snow squatted next to Laurie, pushing back the riot of noise in her head.

Snow gripped Laurie's skull, her fingers shaking. 'I could have killed you, but I didn't.'

Laurie blinked up at the princess, her chest heaving.

'Unlike Myrenna, I'm not a tyrant. Nor do I want war. You asked me what I want?' Snow paused. 'I want my kingdom back. And I will hurt anybody that gets in the way of me and my people. Do you understand?

'You will not say anything to anyone about today, especially not your princess. You will not speak about finding me here. Or that you accused me of lying. You will return to your duties, and we will forget this encounter ever happened.'

Laurie's mouth thinned at the words, her eyes blazing with hate.

But Snow wasn't done. She stood, cracking her shoulders. 'And one last thing. If you ever corner me again, I will find your children and your husband. Then I will cut them, with my very pointy, very sharp axes. You will have nothing left of them but their pieces. And when I'm done, you will also be gone. Leaving Adanna alone and vulnerable in her creaky wooden chair.'

Snow left the woman wheezing, but before she reached the

door, she noted a light cloth on the side table. As she flipped it over, she smiled, seeing the wooden sword lying in plain sight.

Her fingers trailed over the wood. And felt nothing.

It did not cut her. Or feed her. Or fill her with power.

It was feeble, just like its owner.

Laurie watched from the floor, her shoulders hunched as Snow turned back to her. 'I don't need your sword to win this war,' she said. 'I just need Myrenna's heart.'

XXIV
The Gilded Wall

Hansel was in a bad state. His legs barely worked, and his breathing was shallow and uneven. No matter how many times Piccadilly adjusted her hold, he slumped against her, his frame too large for her slender build. Still, she bore his weight, though there was a guilt that ate him for it.

Hansel, Piccadilly, and Darquin moved under the cover of darkness, slipping through narrow paths until the lake stretched before them. A sheet of still water mirrored the sky, the stars trembling with every ripple. The air smelt of salt and weeds, cool against the heat clinging to their skin.

Hansel stirred. His eyelids flickered, and he lifted his head just enough to notice the shapes gathered along the shoreline. In another life, it could have been romantic. Moonlight catching on the water, stars open and luminous above. But blood clung to his tunic, and pain pooled in his gut. Every movement carved new fire through his chest. The beauty did little to soften the ache.

Piccadilly shifted his arm and passed him to Darquin, his skin rough and uneven, snagging the cloth at Hansel's side. There were no boats waiting, no signs of life beyond those who had escaped the tunnels.

Behind them, the Silver City loomed. Towers stretched high into the night, their gleam catching in gilded reflections. From a distance, the city looked majestic. Golden. Imposing. But up close, its secrets peeled through. Paint flaked in brittle patches. Gold faded to rust.

Once Hansel was settled, Piccadilly moved through the shadows, her voice rising here and there. A question. A name. She checked wounds, counted the frightened, and knelt beside a girl whose hands trembled with fear.

They had little. Scraps of food. A few water skins. A sack of healing salve that would not last the night.

The silver changeling moved among them, speaking soft comforts. She bent to whisper over a babe. Touched a shoulder. Tucked a blanket tighter around a child.

Every glance she met returned the same expression: terror, laced with something like hope.

He remembered her on the podium, voice rising like a thread of silk through the air. A song for the dead. A lullaby for those left behind. It was the same now.

Not a warrior. Not a commander.

She had suffered, just like the rest of them, but she hadn't crumbled under the weight of it. She had met it head on. Worn it like a badge. Every ounce of respect she held, she had earned. Not through fear. Through will.

He admired her for that. The way she moved among people and let them decide. The way she led without lifting her voice. Without raising a weapon.

Never demanding. Never afraid.

Pain gnawed at him as he stood, each step hard and unwieldy, but though his body threatened to fold, he kept moving. A grunt escaped his lips, the only sign of how deep the wound still cut.

Darquin held him upright, one arm beneath Hansel's shoulder. Dark eyes glanced down, taking stock of his dried blood. The wound had clotted but it had drained something vital from him.

Ahead, the mountains stood in silhouette, jagged against the sky. The lake lay silent, no boats in sight. Lanterns flickered along the tops of the city walls, the last of the guards now visible, their outlines sharp against the soft glow.

Piccadilly rejoined them, brushing windblown hair from her face. 'Most of the boats were taken early,' she said, glancing at the grey stretch of shore. She gestured north. 'There should be a cave not far from here. With luck, a few smaller boats will still be there. But it's a hike. Can you make it?'

Her eyes met Hansel's, and he gave her a slow, deliberate nod.

'How many survivors?' asked Darquin.

'About forty,' she said. 'The others made it out earlier. The youngest and weakest were first to go.'

Hansel winced as he shifted his weight. Sand gave beneath his feet, tugging at his wound with each step.

'Can they fight?' he asked, voice tight.

'Some,' Piccadilly answered. 'Not all.'

Hansel looked out over the group. Forty seemed small until you imagined hiding them. Then it felt enormous. Too many bodies. Too many eyes.

His gaze found a woman he recognised. Pale hair flowing down her back in a grey thread. She had attended that first session of training. She stood alone now, the child she'd held before nowhere in sight.

'I'll go ahead,' Piccadilly said, breaking his thought. She stepped back, her focus already turning north. 'I'll find whoever's still waiting and meet you at the cave.'

'How will we know we've found it?' Darquin asked.

'Once you cross those skirting rocks over there, you'll see it,' she said, pointing to the north. 'It's tucked away. The tide is coming in fast, so we have to move.'

A voice rang out across the sand, followed by the darting figure of a child. The bells of the city rang in a high chorus piercing through the night, crushing any hope of stealth.

We've been seen.

'Cauldron help us,' Piccadilly said.

Hansel knew those bells, knew the alarm that rang with it. It had been the same one that had rung when the fires had started. When the golden dwarf had made her sacrifice upon a podium inside the Tinder Box.

Shouts rang out, the soldier's lanterns gathering above them.

'You go,' Hansel ground out. 'You're fast. Get them to safety.'

She gave him a tight nod, warrior to warrior. Gone was

their moment in the Sanctuary. Gone were the soft-spoken words of worry.

'The cave is further up that way,' she said. 'Meet me there as soon as you can.'

Darquin grunted under Hansel's weight, his neck twisting to where Piccadilly had pointed.

'I can stand on my own,' Hansel said. 'You should go and gather the others.'

The changeling hesitated, but Hansel felt the vibration through his body. The urge to help. Hansel knew the feeling well. It had fuelled him through many battles. With a clipped nod, the changeling lifted Hansel's arm, letting go slowly. Hansel swayed, but not enough to topple over.

With quick steps Darquin ran to the others, giving directions. The bells chimed, piercing through the night. Hansel gritted his teeth. They didn't have long before they were found. Not with the lanterns and weapons coming their way. Their only reprieve now was the darkness. And even that wouldn't last long.

He shuffled forward, pain rippling through every step. He'd insisted he could walk without help. Now, he wasn't so sure.

Was this how it would end? Bleeding out by the city he both loved and resented.

He tried to focus. He hadn't seen Porchid since the blasts, since her kaleidoscope wings had warned the others. He hoped she was safe. Eve would kill him if she wasn't.

The cave was still far. Treacherous terrain lay between him and safety. His adrenaline was thinning, the Halopod and medicine barely holding him together. His vision blurred. Shadows warped with vertigo. He imagined Eve, what she'd say if she saw him like this. She would've tried to carry him first, her small frame laughably incapable. She barely reached his chest. He loved that about her. That fire. That defiance. Like she knew the realm would only listen if she fought to be heard.

He stopped.

A figure stood ahead, faint at first. Then sharper, shaped by moonlight.

His breath caught.

No mistaking her. Not in this realm, not even in the Ever After.

Gilded brown hair. Tanned skin kissed by the night. That half-smile that always knew more than it let on.

He blinked.

'Eve?' he whispered.

She stood on the shore, her smile coaxing him forward.

No words. She didn't need them. He understood well enough. *Keep moving. Keep walking.*

Refugees passed him, clasping loved ones, Darquin urging them on. No one seemed to see her. No one but him.

Even in a vision, she was lovely. A thorn-covered rose. Fierce, wild, unforgettable. Her long hair was in a loose braid, the small whisps tickling her cheeks. Eve brushed her hand along his and he swore he felt the shadow of a touch. He stumbled forward, following her steps as she guided him onwards. Her eyes never left his.

Come on, you slowpoke.

'I'm coming,' he wheezed, pain throbbing along his gut.

While the sand had been challenging enough to walk on, the rocks proved trickier. Jagged edges cut into his boots with each step. He laid a hand on the outcrop, heaving himself over with stilted gasps. Another few creatures passed him, one stopping to reach out a hand, but Hansel shook his head. He couldn't accept the help, not when the bells chimed in the distance and the gates of the wall creaked open.

More shouts echoed along the shoreline as Hansel urged the creature to go, to leave him. They ran off with a sad smile, leaving the Huntsman grunting as he climbed over another boulder.

Eve jumped from rock to rock, the waves hissing against stone as the alarm grew distant. When he'd made it over the ridge, he shook. His eyes watered but Eve was already in front of him and pointed to a cave. The opening was narrow, hidden behind the vast network of rocks and sand, but big enough that it would fit him.

He choked on a laugh at having made it this far, when Eve's hand brushed his again. He paused. Darquin caught up, lifting Hansel's arm over his neck. 'That's everyone,' he said. 'It's just you now.'

Shouts rang out, echoing across the shore as the glow of lanterns spread out along the beach.

'They're coming,' Hansel said through gritted teeth. 'Keep moving. I'll catch up.'

Hansel waved the changeling away, his hand clutching his stomach as he moved again. Eve remained silent, observing him in a way that unravelled him.

It wasn't until Piccadilly broke through the entrance that he halted again. She glowed in the night; her long silver hair stained with black smudges.

One made of starlight, and the other of gold. Two sides of a similar medallion.

He blinked, trying to erase the memory.

Eve frowned. Her eyes questioning. She circled Piccadilly, a golden knife twisting in her hand.

He tried to focus, to ward off whatever magic this was but failed miserably.

Piccadilly frowned at him. 'Are you okay?'

He watched them both. Eve tilted her head again. *Are you?*

A lantern pierced the rock above them and a soldier cried out.

The Queen's men were moving too fast.

With one swift pull, both of Piccadilly's blades were free, her eyes challenging. 'Get to the boat,' she ordered.

Screams echoed from the cave as creatures pushed the boats out, the waves lapping against the entrance. They were only modest, made of simple wood with long paddles. They would have to be enough.

He tried to stand taller, but Piccadilly growled at him. 'Don't be a fool. Get to the boats and send the ones who can fight.'

He begrudgingly obeyed, his wound throbbing.

But Eve didn't move.

Not as Piccadilly whistled, pulling their attention away from the boats. Not as the changeling released herself on the guards, her blades cutting through skin like butter, other rebels following suit.

Grunts and screams. Blood spurted from wounds. Words flew in cruel and bitter voices. But when Piccadilly reached the last two soldiers, one broke free and ran towards the gilded wall.

One of the other rebels tried to follow but Piccadilly pulled him back. 'This is our chance. He'll bring back more. Get in the boats.'

They didn't argue.

The vision of Eve watched as Piccadilly placed herself under Hansel's arm.

'Don't argue with me,' Piccadilly snapped before Hansel could protest.

As they climbed through the cave, Hansel saw that there were two boats left, the creatures clamouring into them as more shouts rang out. More soldiers responding to the call.

I want to find you, he thought as Eve watched silently from the rock.

His energy waned and Piccadilly pulled him towards a boat. With a heave from the remaining survivors, the boat was pushed out. He leaned into Piccadilly, the soldiers' lanterns breaking over the rocks.

The boat swayed, the current strong.

Hansel licked his lips, his tongue meeting dry, cracked skin. Eve stood on the shore, growing smaller and smaller the further they sailed away.

Piccadilly pulled Hansel closer, securing him as they bobbed along the waves. Her hands were cold against his hot skin as she checked his wound, the sound of her voice buzzing in his ears. And as guards finally broke over the ridge, reaching the entrance to the cave, Hansel's boat slowly floated away. Leaving the ghost of Eve alone on the shore.

XXV
The Little Lord's Gift

Florian scanned through the tomes spread out before him. He'd gone back to researching the tales and myths surrounding the wooden sword after his chat with Pip. Mostly, he'd found nothing, the information more of a children's tale than actual fact. It seemed to centre on a lord who had struck a bargain with the Lady of the Stars. But there was no evidence to support the story was true. Most actual magic was granted by the Grimms and their cauldron. It was how everyone had come to be, how so many creatures roamed this land. But it confused

Florian that there would be another entity who was able to give or create magic.

However, if the older tales were true, the stars had been the ones to gift the cauldron to the original fairy in the first place. Creating children who then became the Grimms. Each version of the tale varied slightly, but they held common traits. The stars being the givers, and the lord taking his gifts.

He knew the twins held the sword, but he'd seen or heard nothing about the other prizes the prince had received: the horse and the quill.

Supposedly, the tutor of the boy had taken them, but when Florian asked Adanna about it, she'd stated the only truth to that story was the sword and the celebration they did each year. A celebration that ceased the day Myrenna had come when she'd slaughtered most of the court.

Florian rubbed his eyes as they drooped, the words on the books beginning to blur. He'd spent his days walking with Adanna through the gardens, or in the library. He'd successfully dodged Odion, averting his gaze at the dinners and staying away from his quarters. Mostly, the prince kept to himself, choosing to ride and train alone.

Whenever Florian asked about him, Adanna would laugh and remind him that her brother was a mystery even to her. She didn't like to talk about the family much – though, she still encouraged him to try with her brother – and Florian found himself talking about his days in Maelstrom instead.

As Florian closed his book, he noticed the lanterns had dimmed. He supposed he should sleep.

The chair creaked as he stood, the clock chiming eleven. Silence crept in, thick and steady. Enveloping the room in a way that made the hairs on his arms rise.

He rubbed his eyes, suddenly aware of the weight of something unseen. Shadows shifted between the stacks, deep, unmoving, until a whisper slipped across the floor.

The library was empty. Only the characters on the page to keep him company.

Lantern in hand, he moved carefully, drawn by the whispers that slithered low, soft and coaxing. His fingers trembled, the flame flickering against the shelves that loomed like sleeping giants.

The whispers grew louder as he reached the back of the library, the gloom grasping at his ankles. Before him, silver chains looped across worn scrolls and yellowed parchment.

His neck prickled and he gulped hard. Fear had ruled him for most of his life. It had kept him behind walls, out of the sun, away from danger. What if he got hurt? What if his allergies flared? Pitiful thoughts, maybe, but anxiety didn't care for logic.

He thought of Adanna. Of how telling his story out loud had shifted something inside him. Of the battles he'd survived. The kingdoms he'd crossed.

He clenched the lantern tighter.

'Breathe,' he whispered to himself. 'Be brave.' He stepped forward. 'It is your mind playing tricks. Fear rearing its ugly head.'

He didn't want to be afraid anymore. Didn't want to hide in the shadows as history passed him. So, as the cold feeling of terror covered his skin, Florian ignored it.

He lifted the lantern, roving the light over the scrolls as he tried to piece together how they were organised. That was when he glimpsed a pale flicker darting round the corner, barely more than a silhouette. His lantern cast long shadows across the dusty walls, and for a breathless moment, he thought it was a ghost.

'Hello?' Florian called out.

When nobody replied, he followed, veering around the corner as the whispers started up again. The figure moved like smoke, silent and swift, their edges blurred by the gloom.

But as he stepped closer, the illusion broke.

Mismatched eyes blinked in the dark and before Florian knew it, he was on the ground, the lantern rolling across the floor. The flame licked the glass, the small window of the lantern opening to the air.

Florian's neck twisted at an odd angle as a hand pinned him down, cracking his spine. He groaned as a heavy body pressed into him. Solid and strong.

'What are *you* doing here?' a rough voice hissed.

Florian knew that voice.

'What are you doing here?' he grunted at Odion.

The prince's hands pushed him down, digging into the soft bit of his neck, and he choked. Florian struggled. His back hurt, the floor harder than rock, but the real fear was the dim light beside him, the flame licking along the glass so close to the papers.

'The lantern,' Florian rasped. 'The flame.'

Air filled his lungs as Odion released him. The fire flickered along the open glass panel, touching the stone floor. Too close to a scroll, too close to parchment.

Petrella will be livid.

Darkness consumed them as Odion doused the flame with his fingers. Florian tried to reorientate himself when rough hands hoisted him up.

'You can't use light here,' Odion growled. 'She'll see us.'

Florian's eyes adjusted as the prince gripped him by the elbow and hauled him through the stacks of shelves. 'You don't belong here.'

At the hiss in his voice, Florian pulled away, and his spine hit a bookcase. But his voice was firm as he said, 'I might not belong here, but neither do you. You warned me against these books, so why are you here?'

He didn't feel brave. Not exactly. But something about the dark and hiding behind the shadows made him feel stronger. Odion's glare had been set into his mind, but without the visual, Florian said his words with courage and defiance.

Odion was silent a moment before he replied, his voice only a few pixies away, 'I'm the prince. I don't have to explain myself to you.'

A flicker of light stirred ahead. In one swift motion, Odion caught Florian by the collar and dragged him down. Florian landed hard, breath knocked from him as Odion pressed close.

Something whistled through the dark.

Petrella. It had to be.

'If that's the case,' Florian breathed, 'why are we hiding from her?'

Odion didn't answer. He just shifted them deeper into the shelves, his grip firm, his silence sharp.

The lantern light dimmed to nothing.

Odion's chest moved against Florian's back, steady, unbothered. He smelled of metal and oranges, strange and sharp, but not unpleasant. The scent clung to the folds of his shirt, to the heat in the space between them.

Florian didn't dare move. The shadows pressed in, thick with dust and secrets.

'If you must know,' Odion whispered, watching the light snake between shelves, 'I'm not allowed here either.'

'Why don't you just order her?' Florian said. 'If I recall, you were very adamant about your position as a prince minutes ago.'

'You're a prince too,' Odion murmured. 'Would you give Petrella an order?'

Florian imagined trying to tell the woman what to do and his stomach twisted. 'I find her to be ...'

'Frightening?'

'And then some.'

Florian felt Odion shake his head before the prince let go, the sudden space between them cooler.

'That's why you don't give Petrella orders. Petrella gives you orders. Especially when it comes to her books.'

'Are you scared of her?' Florian asked, glancing up as the light shifted.

'I wouldn't say scared,' he replied. 'I'm *cautious*.'

'You literally hid on the floor like a petrified child when she came past.'

'Fine,' Odion hissed. 'She's terrifying. Are you satisfied?'

Florian was grateful his smug smile was hidden. But he *was* satisfied. The thought of silent, tough Odion hiding from a woman barely six pixies tall made him grin. Fear affected everyone, and it was nice to see Odion wasn't immune to it.

As they both stood, Florian stared at the chains in the dark, the shapes taking form as his eyes finally adjusted.

'Why are you here, Fabian?' Odion asked, pushing past him. 'Snooping through people's homes isn't exactly an endearing quality.'

Neither was choking on a bean, but Odion had used the word endearing then. Florian tried not to reflect on it too much as he replied, 'It's Florian, actually.'

But the prince didn't reply, instead assessing the shelves. He twisted around the corner to where the scrolls grew older, more decayed.

'Okay then,' Florian stammered. 'You're probably going to

think I'm crazy, but I was on my way to bed when I heard whispers from the stacks. And I, um … followed them.'

Odion paused, his beautiful eyes narrowing on Florian. 'I think anyone from Carnell is crazy. Superstitious, magic-hating folk that they are. But you're not crazy for the whispers … They're why I'm here too.'

'Oh,' Florian replied. 'Well maybe we could work together, then? Help each other go through the scrolls. Double the eyes, double the information.'

He cringed at the last few words. He sounded pathetic, but having Odion talk to him without a threat made him stumble.

Odion halted. 'First of all, I don't work well with others. Secondly, I don't know you. And last of all, we aren't even looking for the same thing.'

Florian ignored the jibe. 'I thought Adanna said you were also researching the sword? On how to help spread its power so she doesn't have to do it alone.'

'I don't have time for this,' Odion mumbled.

He loomed over Florian, eyes sharp as flint. His breath brushed Florian's cheek, warm and close. Every part of him tensed. 'Get out and leave me alone,' Odion warned.

He stood barely a pixie's width away, his mouth hovering an inch from Florian's. The nearness crackled. Florian's lungs hitched, his heart thudding too fast in his chest. Could Odion feel it? Or was Florian the only one suffocating in silence?

By the cauldron, he is beautiful.

'Why won't you let me help?'

Odion didn't falter as he replied, 'I don't want your help. We're not looking for the same thing.'

'But I—'

'Stop that,' the prince hissed, grabbing Florian's shirt.

'Stop what?'

'Stop following me and trying to help. I don't want it.'

Florian shook his head. He didn't understand the prince or the hostility. But it was Odion's next words that felt like a stab to the gut.

'I don't want your interference and I sure as the cauldron don't need you here.' His voice was rough, cruel. The prince's eyes turned to ice as he said, 'You are useless to me.'

Useless.

The word that had irrevocably crushed him his entire life.

Florian's entire world froze, his gulp a loud drum in his ears as Odion pushed away. He didn't move as Odion left, disappearing into the dark stacks as if Florian never existed.

Useless.

One word. And all of Florian's bravery dissipated.

XXVI

The Wrath of a Queen

Dread hissed through his teeth as Trik pulled the thread taut, stitching his skin where Myrenna's knife had split it. Trik's face had lost all colour, his hands steady, eyes locked on the wound. Dread focused on breathing, counting each one.

Water sloshed in the bathing room, lavender curling into the air while flames crackled in the hearth. Myrenna's presence filled the space, even if she was out of sight.

Whenever she visited the mines, she took his rooms. They were the best, after all. He didn't mind. Normally, he bunked with the soldiers, but tonight she'd told them both to stay. To wait.

It was both terrifying and strangely thrilling.

The firelight danced across the stone walls. Dread heard the shift of water again, imagined skin slick with lavender soap, and his breath caught. Trik raised an eyebrow, the thread still in hand, his patience fraying.

He said nothing. The pain had dulled after one of Trik's concoctions. Something Myrenna hadn't approved of. She'd wanted him to feel every moment. It was why she'd made him follow her to the room with the dwarf and the unfinished key. Why she'd made him stand there, silent, bleeding, while she inspected progress on the key.

It was never just punishment. It was a lesson. A quiet warning. And Dread knew it wasn't over. Not yet.

Dread eyed the golden knife on the small table as Trik tugged again, the skin going taut. The hilt glittered against the firelight as if it were laughing at him. When Trik did one last pull, Dread released a groan.

Trik frowned, finally finishing. 'Eleven wounds,' he said quietly, tying the thread.

'Eleven wounds well deserved.'

Trik smoothly cut the thread and packed up the medicine box. The stitching wasn't neat, it was a soldier's work, but it did the job just the same. It stopped the bleeding, which was all Dread needed.

Dread lay on the floor, shirtless, his torso covered in bruises. He didn't want to move. Not yet. Not when he could just pretend for a little longer that he wasn't in this mess. That the love of his life bathed a few metres away not to torture him, but to love him.

Trik slumped on the couch, his eyes roving over his brother's bruises. 'Sometimes I wonder about you.'

'Wonder what?' Dread said.

'I wonder if you were always this way.'

Dread locked eyes on his brother.

Trik leaned forward. His elbows rested his knees, his fingers interlaced as if he were about to tell a great secret. 'I sometimes wonder if you were always a masochist,' he shook his head. 'You took beatings as a child. You always found trouble. And you always took the punishment, even if it wasn't your fault.'

Dread stayed silent, but Trik continued. 'You always said Flynn was the troublemaker. That he ruined things. But you do too, and you always liked it. The punishment. The pain. You've never done anything different.'

Trik sighed, rubbing his fingers along his temples.

'I thought Artemis enjoyed violence, but you ... you always embraced it. Like you believe you deserve it now.'

'He does deserve it,' a cold voice said from the doorway.

Trik's shoulders went rigid.

The Queen stood in an open robe, her wet hair dripping rivulets down her skin. Dread sat up, pain shooting through him at the jolt. But the ache was numbed as he saw her perfect, unscarred skin.

She is a Goddess. Built and brewed by the cauldron itself.

'You do too,' she said looking down at Trik. 'Don't think I've forgotten about your grievances.'

His brother flinched, but Dread didn't move. Couldn't.

Myrenna twisted her wet hair, running her fingers over it as it dried from her magic. 'As for Artemis,' the Queen continued, 'she deserved that death. She was killed because she was weak and blinded.'

Trik clenched his fists. Dread caught the movement, the way his brother's rage simmered just under the surface. But any kind of brotherhood was drowned out by his own heart roaring in his ears.

'Artemis was rash. She was distasteful. Petulant. Savage,' Myrenna said. Her hair was dry now, shining, and perfect under the firelight. 'She was also a liability. She never followed orders the right way, never displayed any talent for anything other than hunting and even then, she had half the talent Hansel possessed. She was abysmal at hiding her feelings. Her temper controlled her.'

Trik closed his eyes and Dread watched them both, waiting for the stardust to blow. They were both angry, icy rage brimming under blunt words. The room was a taut rope, ready to snap.

'At least Hansel had the dignity to know his place,' Myrenna said. 'He knew how to follow orders.'

Dread hated when she mentioned Hansel. Hated that he still crossed her thoughts.

But she was in a robe. She was wet.

He was at a loss for words. Utterly and forever devoted to her.

Masochist or not. Dread would always choose her. Again, and again.

'So, Hansel was pliable, and Artemis was not?' Trik ground out, the words thick with disdain.

Dread turned sharply, eyes wide, but Trik didn't spare him a glance. His focus was fixed on Myrenna.

She didn't flinch. Her ever-present smirk curled like a blade, all mockery and promise. She wore her beauty like armour, but the edge beneath it was sharp. Violent in its silence.

Something had cracked in Trik after Artemis. Dread didn't

know what, not yet. But whatever it was, it had weight. Enough to shift things. Enough to matter.

Love ruins us all, he thought.

Myrenna strode across the room, slow and sure, her amethyst eyes colder than stone. 'Hansel was raw,' she said, voice low. 'Untouched. Unused. He could be moulded. Twisted.' She stopped just before Trik, tilting her head to one side. She traced her finger slowly down the line of his cheek, soft and deliberate.

Trik sat frozen, the only sign of life in the slow rise and fall of his chest. Fear was etched into his stillness.

His loyalty had never been born from admiration like Dread's. It was survival. The need to protect their brothers. In his youth, he had been greedy, taking whatever Myrenna offered. Riches, women, blood. He had drunk deep from that cup. Until Artemis.

Myrenna's smile turned sultry as her robe slipped off her shoulders. It fell to the floor with a faint thud. Dread felt his heart stop.

The Queen's fingers trailed Trik's skin, lining his scars, and bruises, and torn flesh. She flashed her white teeth, her nails shooting out so fast that Dread barely had time to blink before her hand sunk into Trik's chest.

He cried out, but she held firm, squeezing his beating heart.

Trik gasped, his face paling.

Dread's breath halted as Myrenna pulled Trik closer, massaging her fingers inside his chest. Her voice was low when she spoke, almost too quiet for Dread to hear. 'Hansel was soft clay, ready to be moulded,' she murmured. 'Artemis was already set in her ways when she came to me.'

'She loved you,' Trik rasped.

Myrenna laughed, but there was no warmth to it. 'She didn't love me. She loved what I could do for her. It wasn't *loyalty*. It was greed.' Her other hand stroked his face. 'Your loyalty is much the same, is it not? Tell me you haven't thought about killing me?'

Trik gulped, his eyes flicking to his brother.

'Tell me you haven't thought about it, not even once?'

Trik winced. But Myrenna wasn't one to wait. She growled, her grip tightening on Trik's heart. Then he howled.

'Tell me you never whispered it under those sheets of yours,' she seethed. 'That you never dreamed of who you could kill together. Be honest. I might even let you live.'

Trik lowered his lashes and choked out his confession. 'I have.'

'*I know you have,*' she fumed, but her hand loosened. 'At least we can be honest here. I'm a woman of my word, after all.'

She released him with a snap and Trik screamed. Blood poured down his chest, his shirt torn from where her hand had been.

The air felt thick, as if time moved in slow motion. Trik swayed and fell to the floor. Dread waited for the wave of the Queen's bloodied hand before he ran to his brother's side. He placed pressure on the wound, holding black the blood until Trik's healing ability could kick in.

At least she let him keep his heart. She was merciful.

Myrenna brushed her hair aside as she strode toward his bed. 'The unfortunate thing in all of this,' she said, 'is that I'm yet to receive the apology I deserve.'

Even Dread squeezed his eyes shut at that. He'd expected this reaction, the violence that came next, but that didn't make it any easier.

She laid back on the sheets, bare under the flickering

candlelight, but Dread's gaze stayed fixed on Trik. On the wound bleeding slowly through his chest. This was his brother. His comrade. His family.

Yet she was his Queen. His dream. His world.

Before Dread could move, Myrenna flicked her wrist. The skin along Trik's chest stitched together with unsettling ease. The pink flesh tightened, unmarked. Dread took a step back, eyes wide.

Trik's shoulders heaved, ragged breaths filling the silence. At least he was alive. For now.

Dread turned toward the bed, catching Myrenna's smirk as she ordered, 'Stand before me.'

Like a puppet, he obeyed. Trik lingered a moment longer before following suit.

'Have I not been kind to you?' she asked. Both brothers remained silent. 'Have I not been a merciful Queen?'

She clicked her fingers. A silky nightgown flickered over her, and she swept her hair aside, spreading it across the pillows like a dream he'd often had.

'The mirror drivels on about a lot of things,' she said, eyes sharp on them both, 'with its rhymes, warnings, and stories. Though I've proved it wrong before, it was not wrong about the both of you. Or your *traitorous* brother.'

Flynn.

Trik's jaw twitched. Dread's palms went clammy.

She clicked her fingers again. A glass appeared, filling itself with wine. Myrenna took a leisurely sip.

'Do you know what I'm looking for in these mines?' she asked. 'What I plan to do?'

Dread shook his head. Trik didn't move. His eyes stayed fixed on the carpet as if some secret lay woven there.

'I'm here to find the mirror's sibling,' Myrenna said, licking her lips, the wine leaving a bright stain. 'To bring them together. Like some kind of family reunion.'

'Why?' Trik asked, his teeth grinding together.

'Why do you think I look for its sibling?' she asked.

He shrugged. 'Power, I assume.'

'Of course. That's obvious. What else?'

'You want to rule?'

'I already rule.'

'But you don't rule the whole realm, only a kingdom.'

Myrenna smiled. 'Good little shifter. Who does rule the realm?'

Dread put up his hand, but Myrenna ignored him. He felt like a child at school vying for attention. Trik's frown deepened. 'The royalty—'

'Wrong,' she answered. 'Try again.'

He paused. 'The Grimms?'

She smirked, showing those brilliant white teeth of hers.

Trik took a hesitant step back. 'But that's ...'

'Impossible?' she interrupted.

'No,' Trik replied, 'It's crazy.'

She shrugged. 'I've been called worse.'

'The Grimms can't be killed.'

'Your lack of faith in me is annoying and petulant,' Myrenna hissed. She leaned forward on the mattress, her glass floating mid-air. The way she slinked towards them reminded Dread of a predator. Graceful, calculating, dangerous. She paused at the edge of the bed. 'I'm tired of this. I want my apologies.'

'I'm sorry,' they both said in unison.

She grinned again. 'Shall we start, then?'

Dread held his breath, blinking back whatever pain he

expected to come. Instead, Myrenna turned to Trik. 'I want you to shift.'

Trik didn't move.

Her eyes glittered with cold, calculating menace. They both knew the rules: to earn back her trust, they had to obey.

Trik hesitated, wrestling with uncertainty, then nodded. He began to shift.

Dread heard the familiar crack of bones, skin twisting as Trik morphed into a large black crow. Inky feathers drifted to the carpet.

Myrenna gave an approving nod. 'Now shift back.'

Trik obeyed. But just as his feathers started to shed, Myrenna flicked her wrist, freezing him mid-shift.

Trik's agonised scream tore through the room, a raw arrow straight to Dread's heart.

Shifting was brutal. Magic forced the body into unnatural shapes. Some, like Dread and his brothers, were born for it. Others, like the Queen, wielded a harsher magic with no relief from pain, no poppy or potion to dull the torment.

Dread stared at his tortured brother, silent, praying to whatever gods might listen.

Trik's eyes were wild with agony, bones bent and skin stretched thin. Then Myrenna released him.

He collapsed, gasping as his human form struggled back. When he was whole again, Myrenna laughed cruelly, and took a slow sip of wine. 'Again.'

Trik's eyes locked onto Dread's, pleading. *Help me.*

But Dread didn't move. Couldn't.

This was his Queen.

He deserves this, he told himself. *We both do.*

Trik turned to the Queen, her cheeks faintly flushed. 'Don't make me ask again,' she warned.

He breathed deep and shifted again, louder cracking this time. Wings unfurled, feathers sprouting from his back. Then she froze him once more.

Dread twitched at the bone's sharp sounds, but remained still.

Myrenna released Trik as he took full shape, a black crow, then floated a grape from the side table, eyes bright with cruel amusement. 'Again.'

And again.

And again.

Each time, Trik obeyed without fail. And Dread did not stop her.

Bryn didn't know when he'd last slept or ate. All he knew was the key. His fingers were steady as he shaved off tiny amounts of bone, shaping the ridges and edges. His thumb caressed its underside, feeling the indents and curves as if he stroked a lover. It was perfection.

Almost.

It was nearly a match to the sketches scattered before him. The lines shaped to fit the keyhole within the bone door.

One day they had given him.

And his time was up.

As he smoothed out the last section, he didn't need to look at the diagram to know the key was finished. Because something in his blood recognised it. Welcomed it.

Erick sniffled in the dark, his even breath breaking as he snored. Bryn was used to those sounds now. Used to the quiet with only his thoughts to keep him company. Erick hadn't been himself and Bryn wanted to give him time to grieve. Though he knew that kind of memory would never be forgotten.

He and Erick had talked throughout the night, uncovering a makeshift plan for when they were free of this chamber. Erick was sceptical, but that was expected considering how long he'd survived in this place. His eyes remained hollow, unsure, but Bryn had faith in him. You didn't survive this long without resilience. Without grit. And Erick had those qualities mastered.

He lifted his hands, trying to catch the minimal light he had left glowing from his lantern. The key was so delicate, fine enough that it could break with only a whisper.

Yet power reverberated through it.

Bryn felt it in his fingers. The way the warmth lingered at his touch. He couldn't explain what he had crafted. How he had made this.

All Bryn needed now was Erick's talons. The tools were spectacular, but even with his full kit, none of them held the sharp edges the changeling's talons possessed. They were the only thing that could create the point he desperately needed.

Holding the key up carefully in his hands, he pushed on Erick's chest. 'Erick,' he whispered.

Erick opened his groggy eyes, his bags darker than the day before. He looked rotten, as if death had dragged out a piece of his soul and left a shell behind. His dark eyes pierced Bryn but there was nothing behind them. Not anymore.

Bryn pushed away the thoughts as he squatted next to the cot, waiting for his friend to focus. 'It's done,' Bryn whispered. 'I've finished. Well ... almost.'

Erick sat up slowly and stopped when he saw the tiny key

in Bryn's hand. His friend swallowed and wrapped his arms around himself. 'Almost?'

'I just need you to sharpen the last point,' Bryn said. 'It's too fine for my tools and your talons should do the job.'

Bryn had expected compliance, so when Erick shook his head, he was confused.

'No,' his friend said. 'That's not a good idea. My hands are too shaky, not like yours. It'll crumble under my touch.'

Bryn pushed the key forward. 'I trust you.'

A thin sheen of sweat clung to Erick's brow as he stared at the key. He shuffled back, shoulders tense. Bryn pushed it closer and Erick flinched.

'Please,' Bryn urged. But Erick stayed frozen, as if the key were diseased, ugly. 'It doesn't need much. Just a touch-up to fix the symmetry.'

Erick recoiled. 'I can't. I can't touch it.'

He bit his lip before adding, 'You don't have to touch it.' Erick's body sagged, breaths heavy. 'But I'll still need your talons.'

Erick frowned but Bryn caught his hand before he could pull away, wrapping his fingers around one of Erick's sharp metallic nails.

'You don't have to touch it. I'll use the talon as a tool. Otherwise, we'll never get out of here.'

Erick trembled but gave a grim nod.

Bryn tried to offer a soothing smile. 'It will be quick.'

The changeling closed his eyes as Bryn took the talon and began sharpening the final point. He was so close to finishing it now.

'How do you do it?' Erick asked.

'How do I touch the bone?' Bryn clarified.

'Yes.'

Bryn eased his breath. One wrong move, one jolt, and the whole thing would shatter. 'It's strange,' he said. 'When I create ... whatever it is ... something comes alive. It makes me feel warm. Whether it's a coffin, a hairpin, or a home, it just feels right. An object isn't made for good or bad. It just is. And it's always mine.'

His fingers itched to shape, carve, build. It was in his blood, alive from the day he was born. While Bryn had never known his father, Bonyx had told him stories. How he couldn't keep Bryn still, how he always had something in hand, adding, changing.

The thought made him smile.

Erick kept his breath steady, but Bryn felt the shudder running through him as he carved. Each touch raised the hairs on Erick's arms, waking his fear. The work had to be precise. Delicate. A shave here, a touch there.

Bryn was about to speak when Erick whispered, 'I see her when I sleep.'

Bryn didn't need to ask who.

'I see her in the tunnels. Shivering in an alcove with her doll.'

Bryn kept the changeling's hand steady, the talons trimming off the slightest bit of bone. Bryn could see the point now, the tip beginning to curve in just the right way.

Almost there.

'A year I have survived, Bryn,' Erick continued as the dwarf worked. 'A year I have watched creatures come and go. Yet, I have never seen a witchling. Never seen a coven still intact. Not down here.'

Bryn let him ramble. The words a distant blur as the bone thrummed, beating under his skin.

Almost.

'My sins have been great over the years,' Erick said, 'yet never have they been as great as what I did to that little girl.'

Bryn scarcely heard Erick's voice as the final thin layer shed from the tip. It glowed, a light sheen sparking at its finish. Bryn dropped Erick's hand and gasped.

It was complete.

The key was complete.

'Bryn,' Erick said from behind him, but the dwarf didn't move. Didn't hear as the thrum of magic weaved through his soul.

In the old histories, dwarves had once built great things. Tunnels and homes and jewellery. Only a rare few could mould magic and shape it into something beautiful and alive. He thought he'd almost done it with the coffin. The crystal plucked from the mountains itself. But even the crystal coffin had nothing on *this*.

'Bryn,' Erick said again, his voice firmer.

The dwarf's ear twitched but he barely registered as two strong hands gripped his shoulders. 'Bryn? Did you hear what I said?'

Bryn blinked, pulling away for a moment at the terrified look on Erick's face. 'Umm,' Bryn stammered. 'Sure.'

Erick frowned, his eyebrows deepening as his head flicked between Bryn and the key. 'I said that shouldn't exist.' His eyes turned cold, full of fear. 'That *thing* should not exist.'

Bryn clutched the key to his chest, pulling his shoulders out of Ericks grip. 'I made it. How could you say that?'

Erick shook his head. 'Do you see this?' Erick said, pointing to his heart. 'This feels magic. My heart feels magic. It follows it. It tells me what kind of intentions it has. What kind of power it has. It's how I found the witchling. It's how I've survived this long. And that'—he paused, pointing to the key

—'That is unnatural. Something made that should never have been.'

'Like the bone door,' Bryn murmured.

'Exactly like the bone door,' Erick said. 'Bryn, I can't do this.'

Bryn pressed the key against his chest, feeling it hum beneath his fingers.

'Do what?' he whispered.

'Our plan.'

Erick paced, restless. 'I'm sorry. I know we had a plan, but after the witchling ... I can't do it. Too many risks. I can't kill anyone else. I won't be responsible.'

Bryn's throat tightened. He saw again the girl's gurgling, remembered a night beneath the stars, the pact with the Seven, Brufell's warning about sacrifices to come.

'What are you saying?' Bryn's voice grew sharp. 'Our plan was to save everyone. To free them.'

'At what cost?' Erick's voice was low, heavy.

A chill crept along Bryn's skin. 'You didn't contact anyone.'

Erick shook his head. Bryn's lips parted in a horrified whisper. 'You've left us to die.' He held the key out before him, a strange mix of death and life, delicate but powerful.

'There's only one option left,' Erick said, stopping in front of the dwarf. 'One way to end this.'

Bryn stepped back, the key thrumming in his hand.

'We have to destroy it.'

Bryn shook his head, bitterness rising. 'Why in the cauldron would we do that? It's our saviour, our way through the door.'

'A door that should never be unlocked.'

'I need that flower, Erick. I need to escape. My cousin—'

'Is already dead if you open that door.'

Erick's steps were slow but sure as he closed the gap. The weight of his resolve pressed down. '*Please*, you have to listen to me, Bryn.'

'No.' Bryn backed behind the desk, jaw clenched tight. 'No. Not after everything.'

Sadness pooled in Erick's eyes. 'Please don't make me fight you.'

Bryn was in despair. There was truth to Erick's words. That the door was a curse. But it was also his only chance to save Rabbit. To be rid of this terrible place. War was coming whether they opened that cursed door or not. And he didn't want to be here when whatever magic lay behind that door broke out along the realm.

If Erick hadn't told his contacts, then there would be no riot. No distraction. The only thing Bryn had now was his wits. Something inside him chilled at the thought of doing this alone, of his friend backing out, but it wasn't Erick's fault. It was his fear. And his guilt. Two feelings Bryn understood well.

What his friend did not understand was that sacrifices had to be made. That the realm did not bend to the wishes of one creature. He hated himself for it. But family came first. The Seven always came first. Erick had taken a witchling to save his people. Killed her for them.

Bryn would do the same for the Seven.

The dwarf gulped. 'I can't give you the key.'

Erick looked taller than normal, his strong shoulders and dark skin terrifying in the shadows. Bryn felt like one of the wagons Erick would have raided before he'd been banished here. A shadow crawling from the brush before your throat was slit.

'*Please,*' Erick begged.

Bryn shook his head. He wouldn't do it. Not after every-thing. Not after all the plans. All the suffering.

And within a moment, despite the pain, or the lives they'd saved, or the grief, or the bonds formed, something vital shat-tered between them. A fragile trust, broken with only a few short words.

Erick dived across the table, smashing bottles as Bryn's tools clattered to the floor. Paper and scrolls whipped through the air while Bryn leapt, barely dodging Erick's sharp talons. Clutching the bone key, he willed it to stay whole as he sprinted to the other side of the room.

Bryn overturned the cot, the legs scraping against the stone as he heaved it upright, using it as a barrier.

His breathe came in ragged bursts, heart hammering as Erick lunged. Bryn pulled with everything he had, muscles straining, desperate to keep the key out of the changeling's reach. Erick growled, low and guttural, and the cot slammed between them with a jarring crack. The impact sent both the key and the dwarf skidding across the floor.

Bryn scrambled upright, boots slipping, and darted for the table. He barely made it halfway before a hand yanked him back by the collar, choking the breath from his lungs. He twisted, flailing, and found himself face to face with Erick.

The changeling's expression was wild, eyes wide and plead-ing. Not angry. Not cruel.

Desperate.

Hopeless, Bryn gripped the key tight.

'Rabbit,' he muttered.

He tried to pull free, but Erick's arms locked around his wrists. They staggered, struggling, each fighting for the key. Erick clawed to shake it free, but Bryn held firm.

Erick's tone was pleading. 'Destroy it.'

But Bryn couldn't. Wouldn't.

Then Bryn's foot caught on a loose stone. He fell with a scream. The key slipped from his grasp, soaring through the air. It cut through the space like a shooting star. Like a wish cast out and forgotten before it reached the sky.

The magic left the dwarf. The cold pierced deep into his bones.

It's going to shatter. All of it. Each fragile bone.

And as Bryn's hip snapped on the floor, the door to the room flew open. The key froze mid-air.

She stood like the Queen of Death, ready to rage and bring wrath down on all who lived.

Myrenna.

Her hand was raised, the amethyst colour of her eyes bright as she watched them scrabble helplessly on the floor.

Bryn didn't know if he was relieved, or terrified.

With sure steps, Myrenna entered and plucked the key from the air. She twisted it between her fingers, a smug smile playing on her lips before she wrapped it tightly in her palm.

'*No,*' Erick whispered.

Bryn was frozen. The air seemed to vanish, hope burning to ash right before his eyes.

'Lucky I arrived on time,' Myrenna said. 'Otherwise, you wouldn't still be breathing.'

She lifted Erick into the air with a flick of her wrist.

He hovered, suspended between floor and ceiling, limbs flailing in slow motion. The magic held him like a snare, invisible but unyielding.

Myrenna turned to Bryn, her gaze sliding over him with a flicker of pleasant surprise. Her voice curled like smoke. 'Thank you, Dwarf.'

He swallowed hard, throat tight, as she turned back to

Erick. The smile faded from her lips, replaced by something colder.

Erick clawed at his throat, eyes bulging as invisible pressure crushed his lungs. The Queen's hold didn't falter.

Bryn moved to help, arm half-lifted, then stopped. His body refused to obey. Eyes wide with horror, Bryn realised he was frozen, locked in place by a force he couldn't see, couldn't fight.

He could only watch.

Myrenna lifted the key again and drifted towards Erick as if time belonged to her. 'Even I have to admit I can be unfair. Sometimes I'm even a little judgemental.' She paused. 'The mirror likes to remind me of that all too often.'

Erick's skin flushed crimson as he lingered there, feet twitching.

'But rarely have I been so wrong that I'm actually pleased by the outcome.'

Dread entered then. His skin was sallow and blotchy, the same haunted look Bryn had seen in Erick earlier.

'I've heard tales of the great dwarven makers, but never have I seen it,' Myrenna said, lifting the key before her like a trophy. 'To truly witness it is incredible. You're like a rare collector's item, creating more collector's items. It's fascinating.'

Dread tried to remain still, but Bryn caught the flicker of uncertainty in his eyes, drawn to the key the Queen held.

'I may keep you around,' she said to Bryn, eyes sharp and cruel. 'As for you,' she said, turning to Erick, 'you're the bone I'm going to use to build my new crown. With my new Maker.'

New Maker.

A Queen's Maker.

The Queen's Maker.

The thought hit him like a slap to the face. Bryn couldn't do it. Wouldn't do it. But his words and body failed him.

Erick's legs jerked uncontrollably, spasming like a marionette with tangled strings. Bryn's stomach turned. The tremors weren't natural. They were too sharp, too sudden. Bryn's boots scraped against the floor, trying to move, to help, but his body refused.

Erick's eyes bulged, the whites streaked with crimson veins that crept outward like cracks in glass. Each twitch drew another thread of red, until his irises looked drowned in blood.

The Queen's wrist turned, slow and deliberate.

Erick convulsed.

Bryn felt the pressure in his own chest, as if the invisible grip around Erick's throat reached for him too. He couldn't breathe. Couldn't speak. Could only watch as the Queen stood poised, her fingers dancing like a conductor's, pulling life from a body that had no defence.

Erick tilted his gaze towards Bryn. The dwarf had expected disappointment. Anger. Maybe, even hatred. But as they locked eyes, he only saw pain, and regret.

Bryn understood every silent word because his own eyes told the same story.

Forgive me. I'm sorry.

Sorry for not listening to his friend. Sorry for not trusting his judgement. Sorry for the unspoken words. For the betrayal.

Bryn choked on the weight of it, his body thrashing in the deep hold of invisible hands.

Erick's body went limp.

A cold claw scraped beneath Bryn's skin at the sight of Erick's vacant eyes, the light gone from them. As Myrenna released her grip, a surge rose from the well within him, raw and blistering. Grief twisted with fury, a storm of anguish and rage that had nowhere to go but out. It tore through him, burning away the last fragile thread of hope.

A howl burst from his throat, wild and vengeful, shattering the silence like glass against stone.

Myrenna sneered, lifting the key before him so he could see. So he could watch. And as he crumbled, she kept smiling as if she'd unlocked the entire realm.

For all Bryn knew, she might have.

He crawled forward, latching his hands onto Erick's talons. The body was still warm.

The Queen paused at the threshold. 'Welcome to the court, dwarf.'

The words rang in silence as Bryn held the corpse of his only friend in the mines.

XXVII
The Song of a Tomb

The water should have chilled Eve to the bone. But in this new skin, she was remade. Built for conditions that would normally kill her.

The black walls of Nysa rose from the depths of the sea towards the watery surface, looming over them. Her body followed its own instructions, adjusting where it needed to. She could even see in the dark as she and Cyrene followed two of the queen's soldiers.

Cyrene's shoulders were straight, her head held high as

nymphs of all shapes and sizes swam by. Some nodded towards her in recognition, others kept their heads down, but most watched her with wary eyes.

Eve kept quiet, attempting to adjust to her new body as the black rock glittered. She felt like herself but didn't. Her skin stretched tight, as though she'd been crammed into a space too small, like jam forced into a jar, the lid twisted down until there was no room left to breathe.

As they swam, a tall gate shimmered in the distance, carved deep into the rock like a wound. Its bars were made of shell and coral, jagged and cruel, reminding Eve of sea-swept thorns, beautiful, but meant to pierce.

When they reached the watery keep, the guards led them through narrow corridors where the walls seemed to drink the light. Murk clung to every surface, thick and oppressive. Small fish darted along the edges, glowing faintly in a sheen of ghostly white. The only living light in this forsaken place.

Eve slowed as a pale fish drifted past. It hovered near the wall, translucent as glass. She could see everything inside it: the lattice of veins, the fragile bones, the swollen belly that bulged unnaturally, like a woman heavy with child. Something about it unsettled her. It didn't blink. It didn't breathe.

She reached out, drawn by a strange compulsion.

The fish snapped. Its teeth flashed, jagged and needle-like, striking the water with a hiss.

Cyrene yanked her back, grip tight around her arm. 'Don't touch anything,' she hissed, voice low and sharp.

Eve's heart thudded. Her skin prickled with unease. She glanced back at the fish, now gliding away like nothing had happened.

'What was that?' she asked, her voice barely above a whisper.

'One of the Queen's pets,' Cyrene replied flatly. 'They also double as lights.'

Dotted glows drifted through the halls, their movements slow and fluid, like breath in water. Eve swallowed hard. They were everywhere.

Ahead, Cyrene's hair shimmered dark red, strands catching the light like embers. She surged forward, her webbed feet slicing cleanly through the current. Eve followed, the tunnel winding upward, leading them toward clearer waters.

The floor was a tapestry of life. Flowers, coral, and seaweed tangled together, pooling over every inch like a forgotten garden. Eve brushed her fingers along the seagrass, startled by its slick, almost oily texture. It clung to her skin, then slipped away.

This place was suffocating. Heavy. Yet here and there, it bloomed. Pockets of colour burst through the gloom like cracks in a wall, sunlight leaking into the deep. Beautiful in its own deadly way.

At the top of the tunnel, Cyrene tore through a sheet of kelp, parting it like a curtain. Eve swam through – and froze.

Four yellow eyes stared back.

Eels. Grinning. Their teeth were blackened, jagged like broken glass. Their skin vomit green, slick with patches of black that clung like oil. They hovered just beyond the kelp, watching. Like Rapunzel's shadows.

Eve tried not to squirm as they swam close, the hum of electricity buzzing from their slick, mottled black hides.

'*Human,*' they hissed.

A spark shot out, aiming for Eve's heart just as Cyrene swatted one of them away. 'Leave her alone.' Her voice was hard. Commanding.

Eve felt a shiver stroke her skin as they said, *'Precious treasure. Filthy skin.'*

Eve wanted to swim away, to thrash toward the surface where she knew there'd be light. She already missed the sun.

Cyrene's mouth pressed into a grim line.

Eve had once been on the other side of that hatred —had nearly been killed by it— but something in the nymph's mood now offered a strange kind of comfort. Gently, Eve placed a hand on Cyrene's arm, a quiet gesture of calm, as the nymph continued to glare at the eels.

'I said get away from her,' Cyrene said coldly, 'or I'll have your precious skin for dinner.'

The eels were hesitant, but they obeyed, swimming away slowly as if they'd lost their curiosity.

Eve knew better.

'Don't mind them,' Cyrene said, turning back to Eve. 'They have nothing else to look at in their boring lives.'

'What are they?' Eve asked.

'Electric eels,' Cyrene said with disgust. 'Horrible things. Normally they live out near the dark crevices, but those two are my mother's advisors. She likes to keep them close. In a kingdom located underwater, their electricity is useful.'

One of the eels twisted around a courtier, who jumped as they neared. Their snickers echoed.

'They seem charming,' Eve drawled.

'If you think they're charming, wait till you meet my mother.'

Eve snorted. 'Can't wait.'

Cyrene gave her a grateful smile.

When they entered through the kelp doorway, trumpets rang out at their arrival. The throne room was almost full, overflowing with sea-nymphs decorated in their best finery, drinking from goblets made of sea glass. Their hair was woven into braids, tied back with shells in every variation and colour.

Drifting from the ceiling in an assortment of banners, were ribbons of flowers bound together. Shades of green, blue, and yellow stitched with accuracy. The courtiers moved in small groups, their outfits different but the same. Some barely covered the creature's scales and others wore heavy sets, almost like a suit of armour.

Eve didn't know where to look first. At the high tables filled with fish food, or at the soaring ceiling that opened towards the sky, the setting sun hazy behind the surface of the sea.

As the trumpets ceased, the courtiers gazes roved over Cyrene with contempt. The guards remained unmoved, their eyes cold and hollow.

Despite the uninviting welcome, it was the podium where Eve's eyes lingered. The Queen of Nysa lounged on her throne, her gold and red hair burning bright against the crown atop her head. Her eyes were emerald, but her scales shimmered a deep blue. Just like Cyrene's.

Eve could see the resemblance. The upturned eyes, the full mouth, the pointed chin. But where they shared features, they did not share the same presence. The Queen was something else entirely. Her eyes held no warmth, only calculation. She was lean where Cyrene was curved; raw-boned, with sharply angled shoulders and a neck that seemed too long, too poised.

The throne was a feat on its own, too, climbing halfway up the rock, melted, and moulded into the stone as if it had grown from the very walls. The cushions were made of woven seaweed, cleverly sculpted into the seat in a way that Eve suspected stopped the sharp pieces from piercing her backside.

The Queen's crown was made of sea glass, its points

veering towards the sky, entwined with black rock to match her kingdom. It reminded Eve of sharp teeth.

Better to eat humans with.

Eve held back her shiver. At least mermaids had human teeth. And kind smiles. None of that existed here.

Cyrene grabbed Eve's hand and gave it a firm squeeze. Eve's other fingers twitched at her side, resting lightly on the golden hilt of her knife.

Then Cyrene stepped forward.

The room fell silent. Courtiers stilled like statues, eyes greedily fixed on the unfolding scene, each one bracing for the storm they sensed was coming.

'They're all gossips,' Cyrene had grumbled in the cottage. *'The lot of them are only there to please my mother. Grovelling, selfish creatures.'*

Eve had only laughed, imagining the vicious creatures fighting over a little attention. It had seemed silly then. Yet, standing in the throne room now under their watchful eyes, Eve understood. She wasn't laughing anymore.

The Queen lifted the corner of her mouth at her daughter's arrival, stroking the neck of one of her eel advisors as her daughter approached. Cyrene bowed gracefully, her red hair sailing behind her like gleaming fire as she said, 'My Queen.'

'Daughter,' the sea witch replied. 'How lovely of you to come home.'

Eve heard the warning, the underlying threat lacing the dark words.

Cyrene smiled softly. 'I will always return home. Nysa is my heart.'

The Queen sneered at the comment. Her nose twitched before she eyed Eve. 'What is this *thing* you brought with you?'

Cyrene waved Eve forward.

Eve bowed, though it was far less graceful than she'd have liked.

'Introducing Eveline Rafter,' Cyrene said. 'The Realm's Seeker.'

At the mention of her name, the Queen assessed Eve with mild curiosity. 'Is she a gift for your penance? Or have you brought home a stray?'

Sea Nymphs and their possessions. Collectors. Thieves. Hoarders.

Irritation bubbled under her skin and Eve tried to rein herself in. This reminded her of Maelstrom. Of the insolence and threats made to Porchid and herself. Hansel's words had been smooth that day, his sway with compliments getting them out of there alive. Including saving Eve from being arrested.

Somehow, Eve thought compliments wouldn't cut it here. Where the prince in Maelstrom enjoyed them, the Queen of Nysa was the type to kill you for it. She was a woman who already knew her value. Her power.

'We bring you another gift,' Cyrene said. 'The Seeker has brought you magic.'

The throne room was silent, but Eve heard the breaths, the unspoken anticipation for an answer.

The Queen narrowed her eyes. 'What kind of magic?'

'Dream magic.'

The Queen laughed and something oily crept up Eve's spine. The courtiers laughed with her and the rumble echoed throughout the room. Even the eels seemed to smile. Eve remained frozen, trying to remember how to breathe.

The Queen lifted her hand to silence them. 'How quaint. A gift and a fond memory. You do know me well, daughter.'

Cyrene bowed again as the Queen stood, gliding towards Eve. 'Show me,' she commanded.

The stone went warm in Eve's pocket. Its thrum a reminder of what she had come for. Of what she had to lose.

With steady fingers, Eve lifted out the small piece of tapestry. Even underwater its light wasn't dimmed, its shimmering images bright.

'I always wondered what Rumple would create with what I gave him,' the Queen mused, pulling the piece out of Eve's hands. Her eyes sparkled at the marvel of it. Of how it glimmered, illustrating snippets of dreams. 'Where is the rest?'

'This is all we have,' Cyrene answered. 'A token stolen from some raiders in the north of Bellatorre.'

The lie rolled off Cyrene's tongue with ease. Her finger trailed down Cyrene's cheek as she purred, 'My little liar.'

Cyrene flinched, but the Queen disregarded her. She lifted the piece of woven dreams before her and peered at it, her thumb sliding over the silky material. With a click of her fingers, a guard rushed over and she handed them the cloth. 'I expected something grander for your return, but this will do,' she said, turning back towards her daughter. 'I'm fair with my bargains, after all. Your pet shall not die today.'

Relief flooded through Eve's veins as the courtiers whispered. Eve expected the Queen to look away and return to watching the room but her eyes remained on Eve. 'I could fix that for you, you know.'

Eve didn't have to ask what she meant, her gaze was too piercing, too pointed on her scar to not notice.

'All for a price of course,' the Queen said. Her voice was saccharine, sugared with a promise of smooth skin.

Eve went to answer when Cyrene halted her, bowing to her mother. 'Thank you, my Queen. But the Seeker has no other bargains at this time.'

The Queen narrowed her eyes at her daughter. Then she

waved them away, forgotten the moment the band began to play. Notes drifted through the water like silk, rising from the coral instruments below the throne, each one pulsing with bioluminescent light.

Cyrene gripped Eve's elbow and leaned in, her breath warm on Eve's ear as she said, 'Never ask her for more than one thing at a time. Today was a small win. We will try for another bargain tomorrow.'

But Eve's scar tingled and time pressed on her. The prophecy echoed its infuriating words as she looked over her shoulder. The Queen spoke to a courtier, his face alight with attention, and Eve met the yellow eyes of her eels. Electricity sparked along their bodies, flashing white and gold. Their sharp teeth glinted as they grinned.

Eve turned back to Cyrene. 'What is the likelihood of me surviving here?'

'Uplifting answer, or the truth?' Cyrene asked, pulling them towards a table laden with food.

'The truth. Though uplifting would be nice.'

'The truth is,' she said, 'your chance of surviving this kingdom is slim. The uplifting part is that you got through the encounter with my mother unscathed. So, you still have a chance.'

Chances. Hope. Fate. Why was it that Eve was always plagued by those three things?

She found herself scowling as Cyrene lifted one of the delicacies. Raw fish dotted in some kind of herb. They were cut into small pieces across the plate, but it didn't make it any more appetising.

'This is actually a really good dish,' Cyrene said. 'It also won't make your human stomach explode like some of these other delicacies.'

She eyed the tables where plates upon plates sat on layered tiers. Most of it was raw food, fish and oysters and pale meat that Eve didn't want to ask about. Others were salads made of sea kelp and seaweed, and the rest Eve couldn't begin to guess at.

Cyrene shoved a plate forward. 'You'll like it.'

Eve grunted but obliged, her stomach betraying her despite the disgust at the spread before her. She lifted the meat to her mouth and began to chew.

The flavour hit her instantly, coating her tongue in salt and seaweed. The fish wasn't tough, and the bite sized portion was small enough that she swallowed it before she wanted to spew. It wasn't the taste so much that made her stomach churn, but the texture.

Flabby and slimy.

Cyrene lifted her brow. 'The verdict?'

Eve smacked her lips. 'If this food is all you eat, I now understand why sea nymphs are cranky all the time.'

Cyrene laughed. 'Come on, you sook,' she said, pulling on Eve's arm. 'Let's find something you will like.'

As Cyrene dragged Eve through each tasting platter, naming strange meat, Eve felt a prickle on her neck. She turned, her eyes lifting slowly back to the podium, where the Queen of Nysa watched from her throne.

XXVIII

The Black Doorway

Dread woke to find Myrenna gone, her lavender scent already faded in the pale light of morning. He rubbed the sleep from his eyes and glanced toward the hearth, where Trik still lay curled on the rug. He hadn't moved since the night before, when his wheezing had finally given way to sleep.

Dread moved quietly as he washed and dressed, careful not to wake him. Comfort never came naturally between them. It wasn't their way. Affection was something traded in drinks or women. Rarely in words. Even now, Dread hesitated, staring down at his brother's sleeping form, uncertain whether to leave or stay.

Eventually, he crouched and shook Trik's shoulder.

Trik flinched at his touch, as if burned. He looked like a broken stag, tortured and left for the wolves.

'Trik?' Dread whispered.

His brother's eyes opened slowly, hardening the moment they found Dread's. He didn't speak, but he didn't have to.

Traitor. Liar. Monster.

Dread exhaled through his nose and shook his head. 'We deserved it, brother. You'll forgive me.'

Trik said nothing at first, only watched with hollow eyes as Dread strapped his sword to his hip.

'I won't, you know,' Trik said, low enough that Dread almost missed it.

The words landed like a blade.

Trik's voice was rough, unused. 'I won't forgive you. Not for this.'

Dread didn't answer. He closed the door behind him, heart twinging with something that might have been guilt, or sorrow, or both.

Forgiven or not, what was done was done. He still worried for Trik. For the loss of Artemis. For what last night had carved out of him. Myrenna had been cruel. But they had earned it.

Hadn't they?

Trik had lost Snow. Dread had burned her city. They were lucky to be breathing.

His brother would forgive him. He had to.

The night before came back in flashes as he walked towards the lift, the smell of sulphur and ash burning his nose. Dread had just watched, helpless as Trik screamed. Myrenna had laughed, sharp and delighted, while Trik's body twisted, broke, and was remade before their eyes. Laughed as Dread clenched his fists, nails biting into flesh, blood slick and hot between his fingers. Ordered Trik when to shift. When to breathe. When to dance.

Dread traced the scabbed lines across his palm, his calloused fingers brushing over the torn skin. The marks were fresh, raw and swollen, his nails having carved deeper than he'd meant. His hands throbbed, but he kept touching them, as if the pain might anchor him to the moment.

A reminder.

The screams of the recruits rang along the dirt walls. Something inside Dread compared them to his brother's. Of Trik's pleading voice, his wheezing promises and weak apologies. What Dread had hated the most, was the final breath. The choked, cracked sound that had come from his brother's mouth when Myrenna had finally broken him. Begging like one of the hungry, dirty children on the streets of the Silver City.

And yet, Dread still couldn't fault her for it.

We deserved it.

He shook his head as he veered towards the eastern tunnels. He had to be composed when he found Myrenna. Calm, and ready. She would expect nothing less.

He would need to act as if last night had not altered his entire perception on everything. He still believed in her. Still loved her. He was just off kilter. That's all. Torn between the love of the greatest woman to ever live and his brother.

The lift jolted as his heavy boots hit the wooden floor. He ignored the growling beasts prowling along the caverns as it lowered. Ignored the clang of metal on rock from the pickaxes and the forging fires littering the alcoves. A buzzing noise echoed through his ears, drowning out everything except for his beating heart. He didn't need to ask where Myrenna was. He already knew.

She was at the bone door.

The memory clawed at him, her eyes fixed on the key, bright with hunger. The tomb had pulsed with heavy magic, thick in the air, alive and watching. And her voice, smooth and certain, had curled around him like a snare.

She'd smiled like she had already won.

Perhaps she had.

He didn't know. He wasn't privy to all her secrets. The Tinker had reminded him of that.

He straightened his shirt as he reached the bottom, and sniffed the air. He waited for the stench of fear, of the quiet stillness that came with the door's presence, but he was met with silence. Something in the air had changed. A steady thrum vibrated from the deep.

He frowned, passing recruits who stood frozen, soulless and mute. He spat on the ground, trying to let it roll off him. He would not be unravelled, unnerved. He was a Crow. The *Queen's* shifter.

A soft weeping echoed up ahead, chased by the Queen's purring voice.

Dread turned the corner and saw the dwarf – the Maker – trembling before the door. His hair matted. His eyes vacant.

Death did that to people, he supposed.

Others watched, soldiers and dwarves alike. Waiting for Myrenna's move.

She turned as he approached, lashes lowering like a veil. A smile curled across her lips, slow and sultry. 'What *delicious* timing,' she said, plucking the key from her pocket. 'I'm *absolutely ravenous* to open this door.'

Shit.

The Queen was still bloodthirsty.

'I've just heard some news that I must attend to, so I was going to give one of these dwarves the opportunity to open the door, but I find myself reconsidering,' she mused.

Terror gripped Dread, colder than anything he had felt in years. It sliced through his bones as the door pulsed, the heavy magic pressing down on him like wet stone. It clung to his skin, thick and sticky, whispering threats he could not name.

Myrenna stood unfazed. Her smirk was sharp, deliberate, the kind that invited defiance just so she could enjoy crushing it. She wanted him to refuse. To test her rule. Just so she could play.

But he would not give her the pleasure. He had sworn to serve.

He bowed low, avoiding her gaze. 'Would you like me to open it first?'

She clicked her tongue, her voice smooth as silk. 'I always knew you'd be useful one day.'

Dread clenched his fist at the insult.

The outline of her shoes came into view first, polished obsidian leather, sharp at the toe, glinting with flecks of garnet. They tapped against the stone, soft and precise, a sound too delicate for the weight they carried.

Her gown trailed behind her like spilled ink. Midnight velvet hugged her frame, embroidered with gold thread that shimmered like firelight. The bodice was sculpted with curling thorns and serpents, stitched so finely they seemed to move. Sleeves of sheer black silk floated at her wrists, trailing like smoke. Pearls and rubies clung to the fabric, catching the light with every step.

She reached out, her nail hooking beneath Dread's chin,

lifting his face with cruel precision. It was lacquered black, tipped in gold, and cold against his skin.

She held up the key.

Hunger burned in her eyes. Not for food. Not for power alone. But for control. For the moment when he would break.

Her smile was slow. Measured. 'Be a good little Crow and open it for me.'

Dread opened his palm and the Queen placed the key there as if it were made of glass. The dwarf who had forged it followed with dead eyes, his rage a quiet, festering thing. Normally, Dread would have enjoyed that. Played with it. But today, it turned his stomach. They had no idea what lay behind the door. No sense of the magic sealed within, bound by spells older than memory.

He knelt before the bone, the carvings slick with age and power. The key felt too small for his thick fingers.

Myrenna purred behind him. 'Go on.'

He gulped.

He was a warrior. A brother. A shifter.

He would not break. He would not bend. And he sure as the cauldron wasn't going to die.

Dread slid the key into the lock, holding back his surprise at the perfect fit. With a small twist, it clicked. The door hissed open, a sharp exhale of ancient air escaping the seal.

The cavern was silent.

Stale air wrinkled Dread's nose as a sound, as quiet as the spring breeze, whispered through the gap. He leaned in. It was a song. Something faint and mysterious, crawling through the darkness. Dread called over one of the dwarves, who helped him pull back the door. Half of it crumbled at their touch, but the words, the old language, remained intact.

A steep set of stairs twisted their way into the shadows,

disappearing into a black curtain of mist. The echo of the song lingered towards them.

Myrenna's eyes were cool and calculated as she stared at the darkness, but even she didn't utter a word.

With a sharp intake of breath, Dread twisted to a guard who handed him one of the fairy lanterns. The small creature inside thrashed around, her yellow glow paling as she eyed the shadows.

Without another word, Dread took the first step, the song unhindered despite his presence. Magic pressed on him. The horrible headache was coming back. And with slow, careful steps, Dread entered the bone door.

XXIX
The Watery Grave

If Eve had a medallion for each person she wanted to stab in this kingdom, she would be a very rich woman.

The first night in the hall was horrible, filled with chatter and curious glares. Eve found herself constantly lifting her chin in an attempt to glare them all away. It was safe to say, she failed.

Eyes followed her like prey, itching and hungry. Some even went so far as touching her like she was some pet they could pat. Cyrene had tried to control it, distracting them with words and politics, but even that barely held back Eve's temper.

As another member of the court floated by, Eve twisted her head to Cyrene. 'How long do we have to stay?'

Cyrene's plastered smile never wavered. 'Until the Queen decides she's tired.'

'And then we'll corner her, right?'

Cyrene whirled on Eve, her eyes fierce. 'Have you heard nothing I've said these last few days?'

'Calm down. I was only making a joke.'

Her eyes darkened. 'Well, make it *funny* next time.'

Before Eve could respond, a stranger's voice broke through the crowd. 'I like hearing a good joke.'

Cyrene groaned as a male sea nymph glided toward them. His scales shimmered blue like the others, but carried a hint of red, like sunset light caught on the sea. He took her hand and kissed her knuckles with practiced ease.

Cyrene rolled her eyes.

'Forgive me for intruding,' he said. 'I couldn't resist meeting your friend.'

Cyrene pulled back her hand, barely containing her grimace. 'This is Eveline,' she said, and waved. 'Eveline, meet Edmar.'

Eve raised her brow at the name.

'It means wealthy sea.' He smiled. 'My parents also liked jokes.'

'They liked flashing their position,' Cyrene retorted. 'Edmar is from one of the most influential families in Nysa. They own a great deal of the treasure trove the Queen uses.'

He gave Eve a cheeky smile. 'She's missing the part where I'm also her betrothed.'

Eve's mouth shaped into an *Oh* and Cyrene growled. 'He really does like jokes because that's the biggest one of all.'

At that, he laughed out loud, his golden tunic gleaming with each ripple of movement. He was tall, his eyes the colour of deep-sea water, and his cheekbones sharp as carved stone. His hair was braided and drawn back, threaded with rings of gold and diamonds.

Cyrene's glare was in full force. Her arms were crossed tight over her chest. 'Don't you have someone else to annoy?'

'I only wanted to meet the famous Seeker,' he said, turning his gaze to Eve. He took her hand and brushed his lips against her knuckles. 'It's a pleasure. I've heard many stories.'

Eve pressed her lips together. She wasn't used to this kind of attention, and offered a stiff nod in response.

Cyrene stepped between them, her eyes darkening. 'Don't think I've forgotten what you did.'

'Should a mother not know where her child has gone?' he asked, shrugging his shoulders.

'Not when her mother is the Queen.'

'Oh, come on, Cyrene,' he replied. 'You can't hold that against me. I have a duty.'

'A duty?' Cyrene scoffed. 'A duty to whom? You? Because it certainly wasn't for your future wife.'

'Cyrene, I—'

The trumpets blared, and the room stilled, halting Edmar mid-sentence.

'I wonder who this is,' he asked as a group of creatures entered.

The eels swam in slow circles, their yellow eyes hungry as they hauled in a chained mermaid. The Queen's glass was refilled by a smaller nymph, her eyebrow twitching just enough to betray a flicker of displeasure as the mermaid was dragged across the sandstone floor.

Eve held back a gasp.

He was beautiful.

His pointed ears peeked through thick locks of long black hair. Bruises stained his skin, some fresh and raw, others faded to a pale pink. Eve's eyes traced down to his tail, massive and shimmering in shades of pearl and green. The fin at the end rippled behind him like a wave caught in slow motion.

The room fell silent, courtiers watching as the chains scraped along the floor. The Queen rose, lifting her glass. The courtiers mirrored her, their movements echoing through the hall.

Eve gripped Cyrene's arm and squeezed tight. Cyrene's glare warned her to stay quiet as the Queen stepped down from her throne.

'Prince Mizu,' the Queen greeted, voice smooth. 'We welcome you.'

The prince did not lift his gaze. There was tension in his shoulders, his jaw clenched and breaths shallow. When he finally looked up, his eyes burned dark with hatred.

'*Majot,*' he spat.

The crowd gasped but the Queen laughed. 'Even you can be more creative than that,' she said. '*Witch*. Spoken like it's an insult.'

Laughter rippled through the courtiers as she raised her glass again, turning to face them. 'Prince Mizu was found on the borders, sneaking where he shouldn't. Tell me, what is the punishment for crossing the sea borders?'

A courtier shot a hand into the air, eyes bright with zeal. 'Death!'

The Queen nodded, her approval clear, and the courtier was slapped on the back by his companions.

'Death is the penalty,' she said, 'but I find myself in a good mood. A giving mood. A reason to celebrate the return of my *loyal* daughter.'

Cyrene cringed but Eve gripped her arm tighter. Together. They would get through this together.

The crowd murmured as the merman was brought forward. The chains left a foul taste in Eve's mouth, her palms sweaty even underwater.

His eyes lifted to the audience, slowly raking over them with hate before they halted. Lingering on Eve.

He frowned, something like surprise crossing his features.

It was gone as soon as it had come and they pushed him before the throne.

'Though you have crossed into our borders, I will offer you a bargain,' the Queen said. 'You're clearly looking for something. Perhaps I may be able to give it to you ... for a price.'

The prince's head peered up at her, his dark hair like liquid night. He licked his lips. 'How do I know this is not a trick?'

His accent was heavy, but his words were clear as the Queen feigned hurt, her hand on her chest. 'First he calls me a Majot, and now he deems to call me a liar?'

'Kill him!' a courtier called.

'Feed him to the sea monsters!' another yelled.

The crowd roared at the insult and the Queen hushed them with her hand. 'Do you hear that, Prince?' she asked. 'The cries for your demise? I'm offering you an alternative. A deal. Fair and honest.'

Eve looked towards Cyrene but her dark eyes remained steady.

'How about it?' the Queen asked.

'*Firl chi hai mele.*' he whispered.

'What did he say?' Eve asked.

Cyrene leaned in closer. 'He says, "Father, forgive me."'

The Queen's eels sparked, causing the prince to flinch. With a quiet breath, he nodded. Conceding to bargain.

'Good,' she said. 'What is it you wish to trade for? Your life?'

But the prince shook his head. 'We want what is ours. What was entrusted to us. The *Morei.*'

Cyrene stilled.

Even the Queen did, her cold eyes assessing him. 'The Morei,' she said quietly, 'is ours. It was given to us by the Gods of this realm. The Grimms themselves.'

By the cauldron, Eve thought, *he is asking for the mirror.*

At least it was confirmed it was still here, but from the tone of Cyrene's mother's voice, she wasn't keen on parting with it. They'd have to re-evaluate their position. From the look on Cyrene's face, the sea nymph knew it too.

The Queen laughed cruelly. 'Even if I did bargain with you for the Morei, you have no way of taking it to Teal Cove if you're dead.'

Prince Mizu smiled. 'Why not bargain for both? For my life and the Morei.'

The Queen stared down at him, pondering a moment before answering. 'If you are willing to pay a heavy price, then I'm willing to listen.'

He nodded. 'Then let us bargain, Majot.'

The water rippled as the crowd floated back, the stone floor splitting open with a slow, grinding groan. From the dark chasm emerged a twisted black cauldron, its shape coiling like writhing tentacles. Deep green spots glowed along its surface, the sea glass shimmering like scales under the flickering light.

The room thrummed with power, the taste of magic sharp and bitter on Eve's tongue. It was wrong, something unnatural.

Smoke curled from the cauldron's depths, weaving through the air as whispers rose among the courtiers. The energy buzzed, thick and expectant, like the calm before a storm.

'And what will you offer me?' the Queen asked.

He was quiet a moment. 'The Grimm who told us the story,' he said, raising his voice so the crowd could hear. 'We are only its temporary keepers until its rightful owner comes to claim it.'

'Nobody has come to claim it,' the Queen spat.

He smiled. 'They will. The waters whisper.'

The Queen's nostrils flared. 'So, what is your bargain, then?'

'My bargain,' he replied, 'is for you to release the Morei. In return, my king and I offer you a prince.'

The Queen laughed. 'A marriage proposal?'

The crowd snickered and Cyrene frowned.

'I knew what I was doing when I crossed the borders,' the prince said. 'I come here to offer an alliance. To marry your only daughter.'

The crowd turned on Cyrene, and Eve wanted to shrink under their glares. The courtiers would have gossip for weeks.

'What need do I have for an alliance?' the Queen sneered.

Mizu smiled, though there was no warmth in it. 'War is coming. The land dwellers prove more powerful by the day. Long have our kingdoms been at war. Darkness flows from the land. Old magic brews and it affects us all. But we may survive. Together.'

The Queen barely twitched at the words, at the reminder of what was to come.

War. Magic. Death. It was why Eve needed the mirror so much. Why she had so little room to move.

'What makes you think you are worthy of her?' the Queen asked.

'I'm strong,' he said. 'A warrior amongst my kind.'

'Would you prove it?' she asked, intrigue filling her voice.

He nodded. '*Hyn.* Yes.'

The Queen pondered a moment. 'Then you would be willing to take the trial. To test your skills amongst this court?'

He nodded, though Eve saw a flinch of uncertainty behind his eyes.

'This has been an interesting day,' the Queen said. 'I shall think on it.'

As the guards dragged Mizu away, his gaze swept the crowd once more. It caught on Eve and Cyrene, and held. Was it possible he knew who she was? What she was after? The timing was too coincidental. *Too close.*

Cyrene moved nearer to Eve, her body warming the Seeker amongst the chilled waters. The eels twirled around the Queen, whispering in her ear as she drank the last dregs of her wine.

Her face was steel as she said, 'I find I'm tired. The party is over.'

Cyrene pulled Eve's arm, tugging her out with the crowd. Some of the courtiers lingered behind, but most shuffled out without another word.

When Eve made it back into open water, she let out a breath she hadn't realised she'd been holding. The heavy cloak of fear the queen wielded seemed to lift here, replaced by whispered gossip drifting in small groups as the courtiers peeled away towards their homes.

Eve's mind spun, unsure how to make sense of what she'd just witnessed. She glanced at Cyrene, who watched the crowd with thinly veiled contempt. The nymph's calm was unsettling.

'What just happened in there?' Eve asked.

Cyrene shook her head. 'Not here.'

She grabbed Eve's hand and pulled her through the throng of sea creatures going about their day. Once they reached open water, the city unfolded around them, vibrant and sprawling beneath the castle's shadow. Towers of coral spiralled upward, their surfaces encrusted with glowing barnacles and fluttering sea fans. Bioluminescent lanterns hung from kelp-strung arches, casting soft light over bustling plazas where nymphs bartered shells and traded stories. Schools of fish darted between the buildings like streaks of colour, weaving through the currents with ease.

As they passed through the neighbourhoods, Eve watched the inhabitants. Some tended to seagrass in their front lawns, others planted flowers that swayed gently with the tide. The farther they swam from the castle, the more the homes thinned out. The rock-shaped dwellings spread wider, each one nestled into the ocean floor with quiet solitude. Two sea nymphs slipped inside a spiral carved from tourmaline, while another glided into a flat dwelling wrapped in seaweed. Pearls and shells adorned each home, their designs as varied as the nymphs who lived within. With tidy gardens and winding stone paths, even Eve had to admit that it looked like a nice place to live.

But the farther they went, the more desolate the sea floor became. The rocks gave way to a wide granite gorge, where a solitary home clung to the edge, carved from the same stone.

'You know Edmar is following us, right?' Eve said, catching sight of shimmering scales trailing behind.

'He does that,' Cyrene replied, sliding a hand over the stone door.

From the outside, the door looked plain, but inside Eve gasped.

The room bloomed with colour. Reds, purples, yellows, and pinks softened the stone in the form of pillows, rugs, and blossoms. Cyrene had planted flowers and coral that thrived on the walls, breathing life into the space. Bright curtains caught stray light, chasing away the darkness that tried to settle in the corners.

'I didn't pick you for a colour girl.' Eve said, trailing a hand over the nearest curtain.

'Anything to piss off my mother,' Cyrene said as she drifted onto a plush couch.

Eve peered through the curtain, Edmar becoming clearer through the hazy depths. 'Can I ask why it's next to a giant chasm?'

'It was the furthest place I was allowed from the castle. It's also private.'

She looked tired, dark circles beginning to rim under her eyes.

'Will your mother make you do it?' Eve asked. 'Marry the prince, that is?'

'She almost made me marry Edmar,' she replied. 'His family won't be happy about this. The Queen will have to rectify it somehow if she does agree. But even she can't deny the benefits. If we marry, the prince's loyalty is sworn to Nysa. He'll have secrets about the merkingdom. Numbers of armies and what treasures they hold. It's too tempting for her.'

'Is it tempting for you?'

Cyrene rubbed her temples. 'I always expected to be in an advantageous marriage. It's how my mother came to power. She was from a good family, and my father who was a prince at the time fell in love with her. Though they suspect she created a love potion to do it.'

Eve snorted. 'She sounds like Myrenna.'

'All tyrants are the same.'

The door groaned as Edmar entered, his brows furrowed. 'Are you going to do it?'

'It's not up to me,' Cyrene replied. 'You know that already.'

'Do you not think it's cruel?' he asked. 'To even consider the marriage? You already loved a mermaid, and she was a princess. Why did the king not offer it then?'

Cyrene flinched, but Eve intervened. 'Perhaps we shouldn't talk about that.'

'Perhaps we should,' he said. 'He made a bargain about this ridiculous Morei, whatever that is. But I think Prince Mizu might be very interested in who killed his sister.'

Eve spun around, her blade free and steady at Edmar's throat. 'Are you threatening me?'

'Do I even have to, human? You're chum in a kingdom of sharks.'

'Put it down, Eve,' Cyrene said. 'Edmar isn't going to say anything. It doesn't reward him in any way to share it.'

'It is useful information though,' he said, smirking at Eve.

She lowered her knife, keeping it ready in her hand. The thought of stabbing him felt nice, the knife itching for blood.

'Always a gossip,' Cyrene moaned.

'What do we do now?' Eve asked.

'Any plan we had of asking my mother about the mirror is

gone. Now it's just navigating how we get our hands on it if the Queen agrees.'

'Can't we just make our own bargain?' Eve said.

Edmar laughed. 'Two bargains in twenty-four hours for the same object? The Queen will have an aneurysm.'

'Why are you even here?' Eve asked.

'Because he's nosy,' Cyrene said, inspecting her nails.

'It's true. I'm nosy. Why do you want it anyway? The Morei.'

Cyrene ignored him and turned to Eve. 'If I know my mother, a few things are going to happen and they are going to happen very quickly.' Eve nodded as Cyrene listed them off on her red nails. 'Firstly, she will call me to her rooms to discuss the terms. Outlining the proposal and what I have to do. She'll then try and turn it into a lesson somehow.

'Secondly, she will make the bargain, and the prince will have to do a trial. She'll make it public. A way to prove his worth. You'll see how bloodthirsty we nymphs can be when that happens.' Cyrene frowned. 'She'll lock him away until the ceremony is organised. Probably beneath the keep.

'Thirdly, she will want to put her power on display. Show how fair and just she can be. Including inviting the Merking himself to watch his son. If he fails, he dies on fair grounds. When a bargain is made, he won't be the property of Teal Cove. If he lives, she'll take him away as soon as we're married. She'll then be free to use him however she wants, at least until she kills him.'

'Why would she kill him if he survives?' Eve asked.

'Are all humans this dumb?' Edmar asked. 'The Queen won't trust a mer in her kingdom. She'll kill him once she gets what she wants, and the King of the merpeople won't be able to do anything about it.'

'So, you'd end up marrying Edmar anyway?' Eve asked, realising the Queen's play.

'That's correct,' he replied.

'No wonder you're not phased,' Eve said to him. 'You and your family get more power and the wedding still goes through.'

'Now you're following, little girl.'

Eve bit back her retort.

Cyrene said, 'Our option for a bargain is over. We cannot ask for the mirror now. Not after the prince has. She'll know something is wrong. She keeps it for fear of what's coming. She believes it's our only protection. She'll follow through on her bargain with Prince Mizu. She thinks she's already won. Nobody has asked for the mirror in centuries. She didn't believe anybody ever would. She gets a prince, keeps the mirror and doesn't break the alliance in a way the merking could retaliate.'

'Does the merking know she'll kill his son?' Eve asked.

'I was wondering the same thing.' Cyrene said. 'Unless they truly do expect an alliance and Teal Cove is just as worried about Myrenna's power as Nysa is.'

'It could also be a ploy just to get the mirror,' Edmar said. 'Perhaps they don't expect a marriage at all.'

Cyrene shrugged. 'Maybe.'

Edmar walked towards the window, eyeing the waters outside. 'There're too many variables. I don't like it.'

'We don't have any options except for one,' Cyrene replied. She turned to Eve, waiting for her put the pieces together.

'You want me to find it,' Eve replied.

Cyrene nodded. 'You're the only who can.'

'Can't we just make a bargain after the wedding? She'll have to give it to me then.'

'She won't,' Cyrene said. 'She'll put a loophole in the contract.' Cyrene let the words sink in as she swam to Eve and gripped her hands. 'What is your gift telling you?'

Eve met Cyrene's dark eyes. If she was honest, her gift had been tugging at her since she arrived, pulling her towards the depths of the chasm. The same black river that cut through the kingdom's floor. She'd felt it the moment she arrived. The dark creature with claws watching her.

She just hoped that wasn't where the mirror was.

'It's telling me I'm an idiot.'

Edmar growled quietly from the window. 'The guards have arrived already.'

'Why are you even helping?' Cyrene hissed at him.

'Because I owe you one,' he replied. 'If we are to be wed, I don't want that seething hate aimed at me for the rest of our long lives.'

'That's probably the most honest thing you've said all day,' Cyrene said.

'I can still be charming,' he said, winking at her.

She rolled her eyes. 'Okay, Eve, we don't have much time. The trial will probably be slated for a couple of days. I'll need to give you more scales between now and then.'

Eve held back a shiver at the memory. 'I think I'd rather peel my nails off than go through that again.'

'You're always so dramatic.'

'Coming from the nymph who targeted me in a tavern and warned me of dark things coming.'

'Can the bickering be postponed?' Edmar said. 'Do we have a plan or not?'

Cyrene nodded. 'Eveline, I need you to find the mirror and steal it. The Queen will organise for the prince to do something

– collect an item or battle in the arena. It'll be the event of the year.'

'And a perfect distraction,' Edmar chimed in.

'Exactly,' Cyrene said. 'Perhaps this is a blessing from Godmother. While Mizu is competing in the trials, you'll already be searching for the mirror.'

'I'll what?' Eve said, stepping back.

'It'll most likely be in the treasure trove,' Edmar said.

'Agreed,' Cyrene replied.

Eve blanched. 'How in the realm am I supposed to get into a treasure trove?'

Cyrene waved away her concerns. 'Like Nysa. Getting in isn't the problem. It's getting out.'

'This sounds like a really bad idea,' Eve said. 'One where I'll become a floating corpse.'

'What if it doesn't work?' Edmar asked. 'It's protected by the drakon.'

Eve threw up her hands. 'What's a drakon?'

'A sea monster,' Edmar replied. 'Kind of like a sea dragon except longer and more vicious.' He shivered. 'It's horrible.'

'Great.' Eve said flatly, but they had both forgotten her, lost in their own conversation.

'It will work,' Cyrene said to Edmar. 'Eve's too stubborn for it not to.'

A knock at the door alerted them to the guard's presence.

'One moment!' Cyrene called. 'You've got this,' she said to Eve. 'If anybody can do it, it's you.'

Eve's mouth went dry. Words stuck in her throat.

With a kiss on Eve's cheek, Cyrene waved to Edmar. He opened the door and let the guards in. They were just as terrifying as before.

Cyrene gave them both a final wave, stopping on the

threshold for a moment to stare down Edmar. 'One single bruise on her and you'll receive tenfold of it.'

He nodded and she left, closing the door quietly behind her. Eve watched from the window as Cyrene and the guards shadows faded into the blur of the ocean.

'This feels like I've signed up for a lot of responsibility,' Edmar said.

Eve groaned. 'And I've signed up to go to my funeral early.'

'It's fine,' Edmar said, though he didn't sound convincing. 'You just have to find the mirror amongst thousands of years' worth of collections, face a giant sea monster, and sneak out of this kingdom without getting any of us caught or killed.'

'I'm dead,' Eve said.

'If you fail,' Edmar replied, 'we all are.'

XXX
The Pouting Princess

Snow tapped her foot on the wooden floor as Malak hosted another sparring lesson. This time he was covering defence, a topic Snow dreaded. She always preferred the attack, striking before her enemy could. She attempted to feign interest but failed miserably as he demonstrated another blocking motion.

They were inside one of the forgotten rooms in the castle, the dust covered floor making her nose twitch with every breath.

'Snow?' Malak asked. 'Are you even paying attention?'

She wasn't. Snow couldn't care less about any of it. But Malak did, which had been enough of an incentive for her to at least attend. She owed him for distracting Adanna, after all.

In truth, her mind was far away from the lesson, lingering over the encounter with Laurie. Pondering over the sword lying under the cloak on the side table. The sword still interested her, even though she couldn't use it. The sword was power, and Snow didn't like that it worked in the hands of someone so fragile.

Since she'd been caught that day, she'd been on high alert, watching the royal twins carefully. Odion seemed to disappear randomly, and Florian kept to the library. They had dinners, most of them uncomfortable, where Adanna usually started some incessant conversation about irrelevant topics whilst Pip shoved his face full of food.

It infuriated Snow. All this sitting. And waiting. And moaning.

She wanted action. To fight.

Malak waved a hand in front of her face to get her attention. *'Hellloooo?'* he called.

She swatted him away. 'Why are we even bothering?' she asked, throwing her sword on the ground. 'This is pointless. Why are we even still here? They won't help us.'

He frowned. 'Where is this coming from?'

'Ugh,' she groaned, crossing her arms. 'What are we even doing? My stepmother continues to be a tyrant. There's a war happening, and I have people who *actually* want me there, waiting for me. Instead, we are here'—she raised her arms and turned—'in a place where we aren't even wanted. Why aren't we with Hansel and the rebellion?'

'We came here to find allies. To rally an army.'

'BUT THEY WON'T HELP US.'

Malak lowered his sword, his eyes softening. 'Politics takes time. So does building relationships. We weren't always friends, remember? You used to throw apples at me when I wasn't looking.'

She shrugged. 'I'd never seen a troll before. Your point?'

He took a few steps forward. 'You've also never seen another kingdom before, or seen magic other than Myrenna's. To be a good ruler, you have to understand the realm and the bigger picture. It's not just you who has been locked inside the walls. We've all been locked away. Either through words, or lack of work, or no food. A cage doesn't have to be physical to have the same impact.'

Snow pouted. 'There *has* to be a quicker way. A better way.'

'You'll find, Princess, that the hardest things we do are often the most rewarding.'

'Can we at least ease off the training, then?' she asked. 'We both know I'm good with a sword.'

'You still have a lot to learn.'

'I know enough,' she gritted.

'Snow,' he replied. 'We never stop learning. It's one of the most wonderful things about life. You can never know enough. You are being hunted, not just by those brandishing weapons but by beasts. One of these lessons could save you.'

With a dramatic sigh she picked up her sword. '*Fine,*' she ground out. 'But let's at least make it fun. Want to make a bet?'

He narrowed his eyes, but a smile played on his lips, and she cracked her neck. Malak may be intelligent and kind, but he was also a troll and some deep instinct in him never wavered when there was a challenge. It was why she'd stopped throwing apples at him.

'I bet I can beat you,' she said.

He laughed, twisting his sword in his hand. 'Your arrogance always astounds me.'

'My arrogance is one of my best traits.'

'What do I win when I knock you on your backside?' he asked.

'My undivided attention?'

He laughed. 'You know that's not enough.'

'I will make you another picnic,' she replied, batting her eyelashes.

Malak licked his lips, hesitating. 'How about, if I win, you sit down with Adanna and work out a deal? A way to get along and work together.'

She groaned. Of course he would bargain for something practical and boring.

'And if you win,' he continued, 'we'll never have a slow lesson again. Only duels to keep up our fitness and stay on our toes. What do you say?'

It sounded tempting, but it also wasn't adequate. Even if she did win, Malak would always turn it into a lesson. That wasn't sweet enough for her tastes.

'How about ...' she said, tapping her lips with her finger. 'If I win, no more lessons *and* I get to see Adanna slice herself with that ugly wooden sword?'

Malak blanched but Snow shrugged, her sword held high. 'I'd like to see how this dead army thing works. Don't you?'

Before Malak could respond, a knock came from the open doorway. Adanna sat in her chair, Laurie pushing her from behind as she wheeled carefully into the room. Laurie's gaze latched onto Snow, her body on high alert. Snow pointed the sword and gave Laurie a challenging smirk.

'Interesting that I should be included in this bet,' Adanna said as they entered, 'considering I'm not the one duelling.'

'I apologise,' Malak replied.

But Snow hissed at him. 'It's only a bit of fun, Malak. The princess isn't offended. She's curious.'

She'd seen courtiers like Adanna before. People in Bellatorre who pretended to be polished when they had darkness lingering inside. Snow felt it in Adanna too. That monster. Nobody who could bleed and raise an army like that was ever wholly good. Snow wanted to exploit that darkness. 'Tell me I'm wrong, Princess.'

'You're not,' Adanna replied with a modest smile. 'I am curious. It is a flaw of mine.'

'One of many,' Snow murmured under her breath.

Malak shot her a look of warning, and she stuck out her tongue.

'I haven't been able to duel in a long time, but I've always enjoyed watching Odion,' the Princess said. 'I'll place a wager on Snow.'

Laurie scowled but Adanna ignored her, making herself comfortable by the side wall.

Snow turned to Malak. 'Looks like the Princess agrees. Do you?'

Malak spread out his feet, rolling his shoulders back as a wide grin spread along his cheeks. 'You'll need the Fairy Godmother when we're done.'

Snow grinned back. 'You'll need a new attitude. Cause I'm about to crush it.'

Snow's fingers twitched on her sword, her body vibrating. She was ready for a proper fight. To release the writhing energy hiding beneath her skin from being so stagnant.

Adanna raised her hand.

Snow and Malak stood opposite each other, blades lifted,

feet braced on the worn stone floor. The air in the old castle room felt heavy, thick with dust and memory.

The silence stretched.

Snow's grip tightened. Malak's breath slowed. The room seeming to hold its breath with him.

Then Adanna dropped her hand.

Malak moved first. His sword clashed against Snow's as she met him head on. He was quick, faster than she'd expected for his size, but not unpredictable. Snow knew his tricks, the way he shuffled his feet, and she'd prepared to use it to her advantage.

As Malak swung again, aiming for her exposed abdomen, Snow rolled. Her feet were nimble as she swung up, metal ringing against metal. He blocked her strike and twisted, his blade whirling back towards her.

He was like a tornado, wiping away every attack she launched within seconds. His blows met hers, steady and unyielding, as if he anticipated every move.

When a blow rocked her sword, she stumbled back, creating space between them. Her heart thrummed, ignited, alive.

She charged. Malak raised his sword just as she ducked, aiming for his thigh. The troll missed by a breath. A roar broke free as her weapon snagged his skin. Blood sprayed, running down Malak's leg like crimson paint.

'Perhaps using real swords wasn't the greatest idea,' Laurie commented from the sidelines, but Adanna didn't respond, her eyes wide.

'Malak insists on using real weapons to train,' Snow said, hunger in her voice. 'Perhaps, he might learn from one of his own lessons.'

She felt free. A spark flared inside her, sharp and electric, stirred awake by the sight of blood. She twirled her sword. A challenge and a threat. 'You say this isn't a game. Then *show* me it isn't.'

She saw the war in Malak. The rational side of him fighting against the brutality that was ingrained in his genetics.

He growled. Within a flash, he swung. His sword rose high, clashing against hers. Snow's arm shook on impact.

She stepped back, pushing against the onslaught. She dipped, then swung again, missing him.

She dodged his next swing, diving low as he turned. Their blades met with another clash. Pain vibrated through her spine as the weapon collided, pressing against her bones. A low snarl escaped Snow's lips.

She stepped back and swivelled. Managed to swing in an upward motion as rage filled her core.

Do it, the voices whispered. *Cut him.*

She could smell the blood on his leg. Smell the metal and the sweat. But as she arched her arm, she left herself open.

The hilt of Malak's sword shot out, smashing against her jaw. Her teeth clacked, hot pain firing through her jaw as she fell. Her sword clattered to the ground. Leaving her vulnerable, and metaphorically dead.

She groaned as she twisted, and was met with cold, hard metal. The sword a pixie away from her throat.

Malak's breath was ragged, his eyes fierce as he snapped, 'That was foolish.'

Snow barely heard Adanna's claps in the background. She only heard the beating heart in her chest. The buzzing that came with the anger threatening to break the surface.

Kill him, her mind whispered. *Kill him.*

Malak dropped his sword on the ground. 'I win, but if you find no value in my lessons then I find no value in teaching them. Whatever is going on with you, fix it. Because it's starting to get on my nerves.'

Snow was left panting on the ground as he walked away, her ears ringing. Even though Malak had won, he'd looked upset. Angry even.

'I suppose you'll have more free time,' Adanna said, wheeling over.

Snow stood, reining back the shriek she wanted to unleash at losing.

'It looks like we finally found something in common, Princess.' Adanna said.

'And what is that?' Snow seethed.

'We both lost.'

Snow looked to the back wall and found Laurie smiling. The wench held up five medallions as if she were a queen.

Snow wanted to scream.

'How angry was she?' Florian asked Adanna later that evening.

They meandered through the gardens again, the sunset falling low over the cloudless sky. Adanna had been in a good mood all day, despite her supposed loss as Florian wheeled her chair.

'The cauldron wouldn't have stood against that anger,' Adanna laughed. 'I thought my head was going to get chopped off. I'm lucky her sword was several pixies away.'

Florian laughed with her as he pushed her along the path. Whilst he enjoyed the story, he was grateful he hadn't been there for Snow's wrath. 'What about Malak?'

'Malak is okay, though a little wounded.'

'You said he'd only received a leg injury?'

'He did,' she replied. 'I'm talking about wounds of the heart. Snow pushed him too hard today, further than I think she's ever done. He was very upset.'

'I don't think I've ever seen Malak upset,' Florian replied. 'His feathers aren't ruffled easily.'

Adanna nodded. 'He's very diplomatic in that sense.'

They passed by the rose garden, the half buds barely blooming. Adanna signalled him to stop, her delicate hands pausing before the thorns. The garden was built into a huge trellis, the vines and roses twisting through the gaps like an impenetrable wall. Florian thought it was beautiful and menacing. A bit like Myrenna and the Seeker. And Odion.

'Do you think she'll be a good queen?' Adanna asked casually, pulling some snippers from a hidden pocket on her chair. Her hands were smooth as she clipped a rose free and lifted it in front of her to inspect its petals.

'Snow?' he asked.

She took a sniff, her eyes closing at the sweet scent. 'Yes.'

He wasn't sure how to answer. Snow was headstrong and a little reckless. She could be abrupt at times, but she'd also been lonely.

'She would do the best she could,' he replied. 'Whether she would be a good queen is hard to say. She hasn't had it easy.'

From the sigh through Adanna's nose, he knew he hadn't given the answer she'd wanted.

'None of us have it easy, Florian. The realm is cruel.'

'And Myrenna even more so,' he replied.

With the change in topic, Florian felt the conversation turning into something dark, but just as he went to speak again, Adanna beat him to it.

'How goes the research, then?' she asked, pointing him to a larger bush ahead. 'Odion doesn't like to share his findings with me. He worries he'll disappoint me.'

Florian worried about that too. 'It's slow,' he replied. 'Your brother has years on me for this search. It would be easier if I knew what I was looking for.'

'*Mmm,*' she replied, placing another rose in her lap. 'The sword appears in many of our tales. Sometimes, I worry that Odion searches for the wrong things. He's bent on finding a way to share the burden. To somehow use the sword together. I fear there is no other way but this way. Where I do it alone.'

'I'm looking for that, too,' Florian replied, 'but I'm also thinking there might be more to it.'

'How do you mean?'

'Well, the tale of the little lord mentions two other objects that came to life, much like the sword. He had a quill and a horse.'

'They've been lost for generations.'

'Surely they couldn't have gone far,' Florian said, walking to the front of her chair. 'The tutor or advisor took them. Depending on what tale you read, it varies, but it's all the same. They can't have left the castle, and if Odion cannot use the sword perhaps he could use the other objects.'

Adanna bit her lip. 'The reason why I said they were lost or didn't exist is because we used to look for them. The quill and the horse. Odion and I did treasure hunts as children, drawing maps and flying through the castle like one of the adventurers from our library.'

She hissed as a thorn caught her skin, a drop of blood welling red against her slim finger. Instinct pulled him forward, but she raised a hand before he could reach her.

'Don't fret. I'm used to bleeding.'

He watched as she brought her finger to her lips, calm as ever, as though pain had long since become familiar.

Her eyes drifted across the garden, pausing on each bloom with a kind of distant hope before landing back on him. 'I know you're trying, but I don't think the objects are the way forward. We've scoured the castle and found nothing. Odion knows it, too.'

The words sat heavy between them. Florian wanted to argue, but deep down, he felt it too. The echoing absence where answers should have been. He'd had this conversation with her before, yet it still didn't lessen his scepticism. There were too many links to the tale. Too many stories twisted over many generations.

'Why do I get the feeling Odion knows more about this than he lets on?'

Adanna gave him a smile. 'Because he probably does.'

'Does it not annoy you?'

'Not as much as it used to. I keep secrets from him all the same.' Adanna gripped his hand, her thumb running over a small scar from his run-in with the wood nymphs. 'Florian,' she said, her voice quiet. 'I need to tell you something, but you cannot tell Odion.'

Her hands were smooth, the skin paper thin. The grip was strong but careful.

He nodded.

'My visions have shown me shadows and blood. Betrayal and bargains. Every time it's a torrent of violence and I can't control them.' She licked her lips, eyeing the prince with a creased brow. 'What I see most frequently is another storm. One made of purple clouds and crackling thunder. It's the same dream that rocked my sleep before Myrenna came that night. Before she ...' her voice cracked. 'I cannot give you a time of when it will come. A day. Possibly a year. But it comes all the same. The Queen will return, and without an alternative option she will wipe us out, and with it, our army. If Odion were to know, he would fret, lock me away and hide me before they could touch me. I can't leave my kingdom alone. I would never forgive myself if I did.'

'What can we do?'

'I need you to keep searching. To find another way to protect us. If we can save this kingdom, maybe we can help save yours.'

'Then you give me your blessing to look for the other objects?'

'I think it's futile,' she said, 'but if that is where your heart leads you, then I give you my blessing.'

This was worse than Florian had expected. With Snow here, they were a target. They all knew it, especially Adanna, and she'd let them stay anyway.

Adanna scanned the sky. 'We don't have a choice. If you don't find another way. Then I'm afraid this will be the end of us.'

The words were flat, as if she stated a known fact. Still, it didn't ease the seed of fear in Florian's heart.

XXXI
The Fear Behind The Glass

The song from the bone door echoed from within the depths, snaking across Dread's skin in warning. His headache was back, throbbing against his skull with each whisper of whatever lurked behind the door. He could feel the eyes of his guards above him. The dwarves holding their breath. Myrenna pacing above as he moved down the bone steps towards the looming door.

A curtain of black mist rippled before him, thick and slow.

It wasn't just fog. It felt like a threshold. Like something watching.

His fingers hovered before the mist, hesitating, before he pushed them through. Cold. Not painful. But wrong. Like the air itself recoiled from his touch.

He pulled back.

The mist clung to his skin, dripping through the air in slow, deliberate strands. Beside him, a fairy shivered inside the lantern he held, her weeping form a distant haze.

Dread stared into the black.

It will be worse for you if you don't go, he thought. Worse still for Trik.

He could do this. He'd been in battle. Had murdered dozens of creatures. He was a shifter. A killer. A crow.

This was his path to redemption. To Myrenna's forgiveness.

With one last look behind him, and a heavy breath, he took the final step and crossed the threshold. The lantern rattled in his hand as the fairy screamed. A fog of obsidian wrapped around him, blocking everything out. Something cold slivered over his body, like ice and death before he stood on the other side.

In complete darkness.

He held up the lantern but found it snuffed out. With a shake, he raised it high, only to see the fairy frozen, her skin a pale grey.

Dead.

The eerie song echoed, luring him onward. It was closer now, the muffled sound intensifying. His heart thrummed, steady and loud, beating against the cloak of magic that veiled the chamber. Each step forward was silent, deliberate.

The ground was solid beneath his feet, but there was a mist

coating the surface, shifting with each step. When Dread turned around, the door he'd come through was nowhere to be found.

He carefully placed the lantern on the ground and released his sword. This place was empty. A void full of nothing except for the song, the tune alluring and translucent.

Black glass and boned frames,
A depth so dark, it withers flames.
Beware the song from faded tomes,
With a key of witchling bones.

With the abyss spread before him, he had no idea where to go. This place had no map to lead the way. No tale to help him navigate. So, he did the only thing he could: he followed the song.

He knew the warning said to beware, but everything about this shrieked of death. And darkness. And hopelessness. It almost made the forges in the mines seem homely.

At least his sword still worked. He'd sharpened it only yesterday, the blade ready to cut through bone.

He thought of Myrenna. Of her vengeful eyes as he'd entered.

Will she wait for me?

It was a pointless thought.

All that mattered was retrieving the mirror. If he could bring her the mirror, then all would be well. It would go back to the way it was. But if he surfaced without it, last night's torture with Trik would look like child's play. He feared to entertain the thought.

A flicker of light loomed ahead, glowing pearlescent white. Glass shimmered against the shadows and formed a mirror. His steps faltered as he reached shallow water, the ground turning into a pool. The pebbles beneath were slippery and uneven.

Black glass and boned frames.

The song was louder now, reaching a long note as the sound of a woman's voice held. Something about it unnerved him, reminding him of shaiths and spirits. Two things he despised.

A depth so dark, it withers flames.

The glow deepened as Dread approached, casting long, pale reflections across the water. The pool stretched wider than he'd first thought, its surface still as glass, broken only by the faint ripple of his steps.

At its centre stood the mirror.

It rose from a square podium of stone, half-submerged in the shallow water. The base was rough, chipped by time, but the object it held was anything but crude.

The mirror's frame was a lattice of bone, aged, yellowed, and meticulously arranged. Each piece had been chosen with care. A femur jutted from one side, thick and solid. A line of delicate toe bones curled along the base like ornamentation. Ribs, vertebrae, finger joints, all woven together in a grim mosaic. But where the masterpiece laid was in a skull protruding from its very peak.

The skull was massive. Far too large for any human. Troll, perhaps. Or something older. Something forgotten. Whorls and swirls were carved into its face, etched deep into the bone. Not just symbols, but language. Pictures. Stories. They spiralled across the brow and down the cheekbones, a map of meaning that Dread couldn't decipher but felt in his bones.

As he got closer Dread noted how the frame twisted, melding into the mirror's surface, like a mirage or reflection. It pulsed with the same magic that leaked through his dreams, through the mines. The headache was worse here, piercing his skull like a thousand needles.

He peered around the mirror's side and was met with the same inky black air. The only light shone from the bone mirror's frame, illuminating a petite body walking inside the mirror's glass surface.

It was a shadow, crawling from the mist until it broadened and grew. He was met with himself.

Dread frowned.

His long hair dark hair was brown, his thick eyebrows lower than he remembered. His eyes were a little hollow, his skin sallow. Dread backed away a step, his hand gripping his sword, thinking of how he could claim the mirror.

The reflection rippled.

A dry cough escaped the skull's mouth, brittle and hollow. The sound echoed through the chamber, bouncing off the black fog like a warning.

Then came the laughter.

It rang out in a jagged circle, sharp and distant, as if pulled from somewhere deep beneath the water. The skull's jaw cracked open with a brittle snap. Dust burst from its chipped teeth, drifting into the air like ash.

'*Shifter,*' it whispered.

Dread wanted to run, his head pounding. This felt off. Wrong.

He tried to reel in his fear, to squash it back into the box inside him, but his body wouldn't obey. There was a tremor in his hands, his sword unsteady in his grip. Dread tried to stand tall, lifting his shoulders as if he were meeting an enemy on the battlefield. He could not come back empty handed. He would not.

Dread met the hollow eyes of the skull and asked, 'What are you?'

The skull clacked its teeth, and Dread swore he felt it smile. *'I am fear.'*

Dread smelt the tang of metal, the magic reaching out towards him, stroking his skin. 'And how do I claim you?'

'Do you wish to claim fear?'

'I wish to claim the mirror.'

The mirror laughed. *'I smell it on you, shifter. That fear. To claim me, you must take it, and to take it, you must claim it within your very soul.'*

Dread did not like the sound of that. 'How do I claim fear?'

A flicker passed behind the glass, a ripple that disturbed the reflection. Dread watched as his face paled and shifted, replaced by a woman cloaked in shadow and beauty. Her hair was dark as ink, her eyes a piercing amethyst that caught the light like cut gems. She lifted a single finger and traced it along the other side of the glass, slow and deliberate, as if drawing a mark only he could see. *'You must take it.'*

Dread frowned. 'I don't understand.'

The skull clacked his teeth again. *'Take it.'*

Myrenna tilted her head behind the glass, her black nightgown barely covering her porcelain skin.

'I do not fear Myrenna,' Dread said. 'I love her.'

'Can fear and love not hold hands?' the woman in the mirror's glass asked.

Behind her, Trik's reflection emerged from the darkness and grasped Myrenna's hand. She stroked his face, her nails clawing down the side of his smooth cheek.

'What game is this?' Dread demanded.

But the skull remained silent as the reflection spoke. *'Am I not what lingers behind those eyes of yours? Am I not of your dreams and nightmares, Crow?'*

Trik remained still and Myrenna smiled, her eyes wicked and cruel.

'You're not real.'

'I'm as real as anything in this realm,' she laughed. *'We are all shaped by magic.'*

He gulped and held up his sword, steadying his feet. She took a step closer, her body almost piercing the glass. Her eyes might have been the same colour as Myrenna's, but something about them was off kilter, like a lullaby sung in a language he didn't recognise. Familiar in shape, but not in sound.

As he took a step back, water sloshed against his boots. He could feel it lapping through the leather, soaking his feet. 'Just tell me what I need to do to claim you.'

'Why does your Queen not come to claim me?' the woman in the mirror asked. *'When she has my sibling already in her keep. Are you not here for her?'*

His hands were clammy, but he could feel Myrenna's expectations. The years of waiting, of yearning building outside these walls.

Redemption, his mind echoed.

The woman smirked, her eyes turning upwards towards the skull. *'What will we do with him, Master?'*

'Take it,' the skull repeated.

From the look in the woman's eyes, Dread had the feeling the skull hadn't been speaking to him.

'If you do not claim fear,' she said, smirking, *'then fear shall claim you.'*

A high-pitched scream tore through the dark. Dread blinked, pain blooming behind his eyes. The woman leapt from the glass, launching herself straight at him.

Claws, rusted and jagged, slashed through the air as he

raised his sword. Steel met talon with a screech, missing his face by inches.

'What are you?' he breathed, his voice rough.

The reflection straightened. Gone were the sleek black locks of Myrenna's hair, replaced by something grey and matted. Her once-smooth skin sagged and peeled, slick with a damp film that caught the dim light in patches. What stood before him was no woman, but a twisted, gnarled banshee, wearing a grin too wide for any human mouth.

The thing laughed, the sound shrill and wet. 'I'm fear.'

Then she lunged.

She moved like a shooting star, fast, bright, and impossible to hold. Dread spun to meet her, his blade flashing. Her claws raked the air, teeth snapping as she vanished and reappeared to his left, a blur of motion and madness.

She flashed around him, meeting steel with skin as she jumped through pockets of the darkness. Vanishing and attacking, then vanishing again.

It took everything in Dread to keep up. His instincts kicked in, the crow inside him peering for potential threats. He shifted as the beast came towards him, her wild eyes and frantic scream rippling along his skin. He was a crow. Then man. Then crow again as they shifted together. The water sloshed as the woman charged. Dread swung his sword only for it to catch in her nails.

He lunged, pushing his sword towards the soft skin between her fingers. Black blood pooled, and her screech disappeared into another void.

He backed up a step, her wail pulsating through his head. With a snarl, she appeared from his left, slashing down his arm with her claws.

Dread yelled. His blade fell, splashing into the pool.

Dread heaved a breath, spots blinking behind his eyes. His skin was torn, the blood dripping down his arm like spilled wine. Sweat peppered his brow.

As she charged forward again, he rolled, narrowly avoiding her. The skull watched it all with haunting eyes. Dread dived for his sword. His hands grasped the hilt, and as he went to raise it, the blade shrunk, turning into a butter knife.

The monster laughed again as it lunged, shoving Dread back. He fell with a splash into the cool water. It soaked his clothes, the weight of his body dragging him down.

Her nails sunk into his chest and he roared.

The water rose, cold liquid burning through his nostrils as the sounds of screaming lulled.

Pushing him down

down

down.

He'd never learnt to swim. Never learnt to hold his breath under water.

Sharp rocks dug into his cheek. With a snarl, Dread pushed with all his might and kicked out, knocking the monster backwards.

He heaved in a breath above water, his clothes soaked. He blinked, the headache pushing behind his eyes as if they were about to explode. The creature squatted before him, tilting her head in a bird-like fashion. Her form changed shape, turning back into that magnificent woman.

Myrenna.

She blew him a kiss. The nightgown was torn, her skin scratched from his blade.

'*It is you, Dread,*' she whispered. '*You are what I desire. Not Hansel. Never Hansel.*'

Dread wiped his face, pushing the hair out of his eyes. She was beautiful. And deadly.

She stalked towards him, her manicured nails soft on his skin as she stroked his arm. *It has always been you.*

His heart froze, and she slapped him.

Dread winced as the monster pinned him down, her body heavier than she looked. She was small, but she had the strength of a beast. A monster.

It's not Myrenna, his mind roared.

He growled as those amethyst eyes met his. *'I take it back,'* she said, her voice dark. *'It was* never *you.'*

Something inside him howled and he thrashed. She pushed down harder, her smirk growing with every struggle, her nails clawing into his skin.

'You are pathetic,' she said. *'Worthless beyond comprehension. It will never be you.'*

She pushed him down further.

And further.

'I will never love you.'

And as the water covered him whole, seeping into his lungs, he saw Hansel. The huntsman glittered above the surface of the water. Golden and righteous. His strong hands cupped Myrenna's face.

Dread roared, bubbles choking from his throat.

'I could never love you.'

The cold cruel water enveloped him, but it was his fear that drowned him.

And as Hansel's lips touched Myrenna's, pain clawed into Dread's heart. Piercing it so thoroughly, that Dread let it take hold.

Myrenna watched as Dread stepped through the black haze, the lantern fairy's screams piercing the stillness. She'd wanted to be the one to do it. To claim what was rightfully hers. But something had shifted.

When a reaper had slithered to her just before dawn, rasping its talons along the stone floor, she hadn't hesitated. Its language was harsh and strange, but she'd understood enough.

The Sanctuary had been breached. The traitors had been found.

Rats, she thought. And she was ready to poison the nest.

Snow, of course, wasn't among them. The little wretch had fled to Felldryn. But the others – those who had dared to steal from her – would not be so lucky.

Dread had made the mistake of leaving the fire burning. A spark was all hope needed.

She'd feasted on maidens before she'd come here, the power still fresh in her bones as the reaper relayed the attack. From what she'd gathered, most had fled north, attempting to escape through the forest or over the lake. Right between two powerful kingdoms bent on destroying them. All she had to do now was snuff them out before they could hide again.

Myrenna had been fortunate with Dread's arrival, the Crow her perfect pet to fetch her prized possession and bait whatever evil lingered inside. His desperation was pathetic, but useful.

She paced along the dirt as they waited, the reaper beside her churning the soil. Unfortunately, she didn't have the option to wait. She would have to act now if she were to find the refugees and traitors.

Turning towards the guards, she pointed to the bone door. 'Nobody follows him,' she ordered. 'Nobody touches what he brings out. And nobody here leaves this chamber. Do you understand?'

The guards nodded.

Anxiety churned within her, but she only had one shot at this. She would just have to trust that Dread would succeed.

The thought made her ill.

She twisted as her body shifted, black ash floating through the caverns towards the sky. She didn't have time to travel, but the tower would do. The creatures howled and the shaiths screamed in glee as the Queen's black mist peaked over the top of a parapet, landing smoothly just outside the window to Dread's tower.

From here, she saw everything. The dips of the valleys, the rise of distant hills. Rock and dead grass stretched to the edge of the world. Below, the pit lay open, its bridges and tunnels forming a maze exposed to the sky. The scent of furnaces clung to the air. Her beasts sang in the deep. The wind moved through her hair like a breath from the gods.

She raised her arms and whispered the spell.

The words from the scroll, decaying and ancient, once buried beneath Bellatorre, burned in her memory as she spoke.

And as a deep, guttural cry split the forest, answering her call, Myrenna grinned.

Her dragon was awake. And hungry.

Flynn held the map in front of him, Piccadilly's messy scrawl outlining the directions to the Peaks of Carfell. Porchid peered over his shoulder, providing a muted light in the dark. She had been brave in the evacuation, leading people out and guiding them with the other fairies, illuminating a path into the forest.

Porchid had seemed wary of him at first, usually opting to stay with the dwarves, but now that he was in charge, she wanted to be the first to know what was happening. She continued to pout, nipping at his ear sometimes when he either annoyed her or did nothing at all. He strangely liked her trust, though he would never admit it out loud.

The trees swallowed the moonlight, cloaking the forest in a darkness that felt heavier than it should. Flynn could make out the peaks just beyond the treetops, jagged silhouettes looming above. They were close. But the group had needed rest.

Hundreds of recruits lay scattered between the trunks, some curled together for warmth. Crickets chirped low in the grass, a lullaby for the weary, and exhaustion pulled at him like a weight. Spring was nearly over, yet the night air still bit at his skin. He regretted leaving his jacket behind.

When they'd stopped, he'd ordered a fire ban. No flames. No warmth. Just the wind and each other. The grumbling had been expected, but Flynn had stood firm. Fire was a call to death. A signal in the dark that screamed, *come find us.*

He knew how the Queen's army operated. How the murders flew in tight formation, swooping down on pockets of resistance like hawks. The dark hounds were worse. Silent.

Unrelenting. Once they caught a scent, they never stopped. That thought alone kept Flynn's heart drumming against his ribs.

To keep the fear at bay, he shifted now and then, wings slicing the sky as he flew overhead, scanning the forest for threats, counting heads. It was the least he could do after letting them fall into enemy hands at the castle.

Piccadilly had stayed behind with Hansel, buying time while Flynn led the others out. He hadn't seen her since.

It had always been part of the plan. A backup. A just in case. But he hadn't expected the weight of it. The twitch in his muscles. The way he kept looking back.

They'd told themselves it was a possibility. A maybe. But when the *boom* had come, loud and shattering, tearing through the Sanctuary like thunder made flesh, Flynn had realised just how unprepared he truly was.

His body still ached from the battle with his brother, the cuts and scars healing slower than other wounds. It worked that way with magical injuries, the pain lingering even after it healed. Surprisingly, shifting had been fine. He'd expected to hear his brother's voice, to receive the threats he was accustomed to, but each time he'd scouted, the connection had remained silent. As if his brothers were also in hiding.

He tried not to think about it too much. He always knew it would end this way. Yet somehow, it didn't stop the pain in his heart, from losing his only family. He'd hoped Trik would at least understand. Love did strange things to people.

He and his brothers loved strong women. Dread with Myrenna. Trik with Artemis. And him, with Piccadilly. She did not love him as he loved her. But he'd chosen to stay anyway. To help those who needed him. It was a sacrifice he'd never expected to make. Considering he was prone to being selfish.

The Riverbell fairy huffed as daylight broke over the trees. Many of the rebels hadn't slept, choosing to keep a watchful eye out for the Queen's men. They were close now, at least, not far from the mines of Carfell, which Piccadilly had chosen as their new place of refuge. They were all tired, broken, and a little battered, but the worst was yet to come.

The dwarves lingered along the edges, their weapons sharp and ready as Bonyx and Bjorn broke through the trees.

'They're all hungry,' Bonyx said, leaning on his cane. 'We ran out of food yesterday and their energy is waning.'

'There is food stashed in the mines,' Flynn replied. 'Though, you'd have a better idea at the length of the journey than me.'

'It's still about half a day away,' Bjorn gruffed, taking a sip from his flask.

'Will they make it?' Flynn asked.

'Most will,' Bonyx said, 'but it's the slower, weaker ones I worry about. Especially Rabbit and Rumple.'

'Rumple can walk, right?'

'He can,' Bonyx nodded, 'but he hides under that cloak of his, afraid of shadows.'

'And Rabbit?'

'Not awake yet,' Bjorn gruffed. 'He's heavier than he looks. Doc almost pulled his back out.'

'Tell him to let someone else carry the injured,' Flynn said. 'He's of no use to us as a patient.'

'You know he won't,' Bonyx replied with a sad smile. 'We'll handle it. You should get some rest.'

'I'm not the one with the cane.'

Bonyx waved away his concerns. 'The cane is an illusion. So is age.'

Flynn snorted, but the dwarf was right, he did need sleep.

Porchid's head drooped until Flynn gave her a gentle shake. 'Come on,' he murmured. 'We'll close our eyes for a minute.'

She flashed an annoyed red, but didn't argue, drifting down as he stretched out on a patch of grass.

Sleep, however, kept its distance. His thoughts turned sour, twisting around the truth he didn't want to face. He wasn't cut out to lead. Not like this. Not when it counted. The weight of it pressed on his chest, and all he could think of was how much easier it would be if Piccadilly were here. She always knew what to do.

Crickets croaked low in the grass, birds beginning to thread morning into the trees. His limbs sagged into the earth. The grass was soft, the world quiet. Just for a moment, Flynn let himself sink into the hush, let the forest fool him into safety.

Then came the scream.

Porchid squealed, her wings trembling as Flynn jolted upright, every nerve flaring. He scanned the camp. No movement. Not yet. They were frozen, all of them, staring at the fog.

It crept between the trunks, thick and black, dragging rot in its wake. Flynn's nose wrinkled. The scent was wrong. Vile, old. Where it touched the forest, the grass shrivelled to ash.

The fog curled around a woman too slow to move. She raised her hand, eyes wide. But the smoke took her, wrapped itself around her limbs and squeezed.

Her scream split the air.

When she crumpled, what hit the ground was no longer human.

Flynn spun, voice cutting through the silence. 'Everyone, move!'

The fog twisted, shaping into a giant shadowy maw as it broke through the trees. Its sharp teeth glistened, the snout sniffing its feast. The fog dragon had arrived.

Bjorn and Bonyx ran, the crowd rushing for the mountains. Some were slower than others, but Flynn waited, pushing them forward. His voice was drowned out as the beast roared, and he whirled on it, releasing a sword.

It grinned. Its black eyes sparkled with hunger.

Flynn had no chance with a sword, but he had limited options. Porchid squealed at the fairies as they scattered, her vibrant warning echoing along the trees.

The fog crept wider, coiling into every hollow. The beast bared its teeth as Flynn swung. The blade met bone with a sharp crack, snapping against the dragon's fangs. Purple smoke curled from its throat.

Flynn ran. He bolted from the camp, crashing through branches, praying the dragon would follow. The air turned sour around him, thick with mould and rot. Each breath clawed at his lungs, his boots crushing leaves into dust as he ran faster. The scent hit him then, raw and undeniable. Death.

He tore over rocks, slipping and recovering, weaving between trees. Behind him, the fog surged forward, hunting. A glance over his shoulder showed a great shadow, moving like it knew him, like it wanted him.

He couldn't outrun it.

His legs burned, thighs trembling with each step. Pain rose in his chest but he didn't slow. When the roar of the river reached his ears, he shifted mid-leap. Bones cracked, wings unfurled, and he shot into the air, breaking through the canopy in a burst of wind and feathers.

Sky. Cold. Empty.

He beat his wings hard, drawing every scrap of strength into flight. The clouds loomed above, pale and still. The birds had vanished.

Behind him, the shadow lunched. Wings. Claws. A maw of

fire. The dragon followed, vast and ancient, its wings stretching like a storm across the sky. Flynn was barely the size of its tooth. Still, he flew. Upward. Eastward. Through the thinning air, every breath tight, every beat of his wings a scream of effort.

The ground had vanished, buried beneath the dragon's shadow.

He cawed once, a shrill cry of defiance. Then he turned, diving east, following the ribbon of silver that was the river. The beast came after him, jaws snapping, breath hissing. Flynn zigzagged through the air, dodging teeth, slipping past smoke, his body burning with fear. But he didn't let it take him. Not yet.

He dived, barely missing the dragon's wing, and saw the group running, the slow bodies and families struggling along the forest. If he didn't survive, neither would they. They would never make it to the mines. Never have the chance to fight. To stand for hope. Or win.

With a caw, he told them to flee, the beast only pixies away.

Spinning fast, Flynn dragged every scrap of energy he held onto and beat his wings harder, flying higher. And higher.

The air thinned and the rumble of the dragon's belly vibrated through the wind.

To save them all, to save Piccadilly, he would have to take a chance. And as he stopped his wings, the world stilling around him, he turned. And dove headfirst towards the dragon's open maw.

XXXII
The Changes of Fate

Trik woke by the fireplace, groggy-eyed and sore. He wasn't sure if he could move. Myrenna had broken him, again and again. Snapping. Twisting. Breaking. Healing. Through it all, Dread had just stood there.

Tears still streaked his cheeks, his shivering body weak and drained. The fire had gone out, the room cool and silent. He'd expected Dread to have left already, for Myrenna to have checked on the key. He should join them. Should support his Queen.

But 'should' was a funny word.

He *should* have left with Artemis when she'd toyed with the idea. When she'd growled at the Queen's poor choices. He'd said 'no,' of course. He couldn't leave his brothers.

The creepy gilded frame that hung behind her throne. He knew the power it wielded. The influence it gave Myrenna as it whispered dark thoughts into her mind. And she was about to obtain another one.

He pulled himself up with a groan, the carpet no longer soft. His arms shook and he dropped, his head cracking on the floor. The pain in his muscles burned as he rolled onto his back. This was what serving Myrenna was like. What serving selfish power entailed.

Dread loved her, Trik understood that. More than anyone, he understood it. It didn't mean he had to like it.

He'd had Snow, he'd had Artemis, and he'd had a plan on how to attack the dead. How to wear down the Princess to then push forward. The Elysian fields were his. They had been his for years. He'd almost had it all. Now, he had nothing.

In the space of a few hours, everything had changed. Snow had escaped. Artemis was killed. The army had attacked without warning, men slaughtered before they could even lift a sword, and Trik had just ... flown away. As if none of them had mattered.

Even Flynn had the conviction to adhere to his beliefs, but Trik had just followed along. Waiting for his rewards like a trained animal.

Flashes of the night before floated along his vision, drowning him in pain. And horror. He wasn't even sure if he could shift, terrified that he'd be frozen again, as if Myrenna waited behind closed doors.

She saw everything. Knew everything. Except for what happened inside his heart.

Artemis.

The huntress had been cruel. Vicious. Spiteful. But at least she'd been his.

What would she think of him now? She would have been furious.

Trik could not follow blindly anymore. Artemis would want revenge. Trik found he wanted it too. Snow would pay. She would drown slowly in her own blood, and he would be thorough in his killing.

A new path lit up before him. One that urged him onwards, towards a different future. One where he followed his own beliefs. It was then, on the floor of his brother's room, Trik decided. He would not bring Myrenna the heart. He would not be a pet.

Not anymore.

His arms shook as he tried to lift himself again, his teeth grinding at the creak in his bones. He took deep breaths and squeezed his eyes shut. His only option was to fly to Felldryn, to find vengeance.

With staggered breaths he reached deep within himself and found the small magic that allowed him to shift. It cowered from him like a frightened child and he coaxed it, pulling it from the shadows and embracing it whole.

Stars dotted his vision as he felt the change. Dizziness cascaded over him as his chest rose and fell. The pain was great, but it was numbed, blending in with the ache already grinding through his bones. There was a snap, his wings forming as he howled towards the ceiling. As his feathers bloomed, the beak taking shape along his face, he almost cried with relief. He was a crow again. Dark feathered and matted, but still a crow.

He tested his feet, the claws still working. Only, when he lifted his wing, a pain shot through his shoulder. He eyed the wing and saw it was bent. Slightly crooked and broken at the back.

He ground his teeth, a groan escaping him as he pushed. He flapped once, then twice. Pain shot through his torso, yet he did not hesitate, and neither did the wing.

With a few flaps, Trik raised himself. It would be enough. It had to be.

He could only hope that Dread would forgive him. That Flynn would understand. Because after the death of Artemis, Trik only played for one side in this war.

And it was for himself.

Cyrene entered her mother's chambers after dark, the only light coming from the translucent fish who swam along the walls.

She hated that about her mother. That she refused to build skylights or brighten up the space. It was why her home was so decorated. To try and animate the suffocating shades of black her mother loved.

Having a merprince complete a trial was a big deal. One hadn't occurred in a long while and especially not by a royal. Cyrene's mother would make a display of it. It would be a masterpiece.

The trial would consist of a banquet, rows of tables lined with delicacies from all over. The castle would be decorated in wreaths, and crowds would fight for the best seats. If Prince

Mizu died, they would party into the night and songs would be written about it. But if he survived ... Cyrene would be wedded. Only to become a widow.

Cyrene was fully aware she was a pawn. Her mother loved the underlying punishment involved as payback for her insolence. She'd still have to marry Edmar and remain stuck here. It was her mother's greatest wish and Cyrene's greatest fear.

At least he was one of the more likeable males she'd grown up with. He wouldn't hurt her, though he'd betrayed her before. The thought left a sour taste in her mouth.

The Queen lounged in her parlour as Cyrene entered, one of her maids brushing her hair with a bone comb.

'Daughter,' she greeted.

'Mother,' Cyrene replied, seating herself by the small games table.

The Queen looked pleased despite Cyrene's underlying tone. She grinned at herself in the mirror, triumph already written over her scaled skin. 'Preparations are underway,' she began. 'The Merking should arrive in two days.'

'Why go through all of this?' Cyrene asked, picking up one of the figurines from the half-finished game of Coral Chess on the table. 'You'll kill the Merprince anyway.'

The Queen pouted. 'My dear child. I would never go back on my bargain.'

Cyrene rolled her eyes, and her mother waved away the maid.

Alone, she said, 'Why should the Prince not prove himself for my daughter's hand?'

'Edmar didn't have to.'

'Edmar and his family already proved their worth. At least he's one of us,' she replied. 'He's also very useful.'

Cyrene crossed her legs. Originally, she'd wanted to come

back to tell her mother about Myrenna. To warn her about the spindle and the mirrors. But now that she was home, and after what Eve had told her, she wondered whether the Queen would even listen. Whether she would heed her words.

Despite the Queen's fear, she was good at hiding her concerns. Waving off the land-dwellers' issues as if they lived on a different continent, and not just above the surface on shared soil.

'I suppose you think I'm cruel, as you always do,' the Queen said. 'I've done nothing but help my kind and love my kingdom. I make bargains to make them happy and to make me happy.'

At what cost?

'I know what you think of me,' she said. 'Like a spiteful teenager, you punish me for it.' The Queen drifted toward the bed, her gaze falling on the gown laid out with care. It shimmered in the low light, the train spilling over the edge like a wave, threaded with beads of sea glass that caught every glint. The bodice was a delicate lattice of netting and bone, each strand stitched with pearls so fine they looked like drops of morning dew. It was breathtaking.

Her mother's fingers trailed over the material. 'All I ever wanted for you was to fight for this kingdom. To rule as I have ruled, and to protect our people.'

'That's all I have ever done,' Cyrene said quietly. 'I always think of Nysa first.'

The Queen's eye twitched. 'You said Nysa was your heart in the throne room.'

'It is.'

'Then why have you done everything to prove otherwise? You bring a human into our realm, not as a pet, but as a guest. Don't even get me started on your previous indiscretions.'

'My previous discretions mean nothing—'

'Oh, but they do, daughter,' her mother said. 'Once upon a time, you chose that *mermaid.* Then later, you chose those *land dwellers,*' she seethed. 'How am I to trust you will put us first when you freely mingle with those *things?* When you choose everything *but* Nysa.'

Cyrene released a breath. Her trail of destruction ran true, her loyalty divided. She hadn't been a good daughter. Or a good princess. She'd left at the first opportunity she could. Left at the first sign of freedom away from the invisible chains her mother wrapped around her.

'I don't know what to say, Mother. I fell in love.'

Something dark flashed behind her mother's eyes. A sorrow and a hatred so foul that Cyrene shrunk under the gaze.

'You could have loved whoever you wanted,' the Queen said. 'Chosen any nymph as your companion. Yet, you chose her. A mermaid. A *princess* of Teal Cove, to be exact.' The Queen shook her head. 'I had such high hopes for you. For a bright and strong future. As did your father.'

Cyrene froze, her bobbing leg going still. The Queen never mentioned her father much, not anymore. He was like a ghost, a faded memory left to the depths of the deepest caverns. Hidden amongst the royal treasure. Hearing her mention the old king unnerved Cyrene. Her mother never did anything without reason.

'He would have been disappointed,' she said. 'He would have started a war over that mess you call love. You are lucky it was only me.'

As if that were any better.

'When you left to search for Pearl, you left a mess that I had to clean-up. Do you know what that does to a reputation? What that kind of betrayal looks like?'

Cyrene could only guess, but from the rising anger in her mother's voice, she assumed it was bad. She hadn't cared at the time. She'd only wanted to find Pearl. To ensure her safety. And when she'd died, Cyrene had gone into a dark place. Waiting for the moment when she could kill the Seeker and pay for the injustice Pearl had endured.

Eve had told her what had happened. Of what had been done to her. Pearl had been innocent, her eyes full of hope and love. She was too beautiful for this realm, and the Ever After had claimed her for it.

'Years, it took me, to rectify that mess,' her mother continued, 'and a lot of bargains to satiate the hunger of a potential rebellion. Edmar's family almost called off the betrothal. The black mark on the family would have been irreversible.'

'I know.'

'Do you?' the Queen hissed. 'Do you understand the work I have put in to protect you and this kingdom? Because it doesn't look like it when you bring a human pet with you.'

'She's not my pet,' Cyrene grumbled.

'Don't be a sullen idiot,' the Queen snapped. 'You and I both know something is happening on land that we cannot control. Something that will ripple through the realm and affect all of us. Yet you waltz back home with an insult to me and your kind.'

'I didn't realise it would be a big deal.'

'For Cauldron's sake, Cyrene! It's as if I've been speaking to a dead shell for years!' the Queen said, raking her nails down her face. 'Have you learnt absolutely nothing from me? You made a statement when you came home. I had no choice *but* to bring the Prince and make him a spectacle.'

Cyrene blinked, taken back by the change in topic.

'If I hadn't made that bargain, you would have been the

gossip. *The insolent princess,*' the Queen continued. 'Think about it, how can I rule a kingdom if I can't even rule my own child? You left me with no alternatives, backing me into a corner as always. So, that is why you have been promised if he wins. That is why you were put on display. And that is why you owe me.'

Cyrene shook her head. 'I thought you were punishing me.'

'I wanted to,' the Queen said, lifting the dress. 'Some small part of me still does. But I also find myself tired of punishing you. I'm exhausted from having the same conversations and holding the same anger. After you left the last time, I realised something.'

'What was that?'

'I realised that you'll do what you please with or without me. In this at least, I tried to protect you.'

Cyrene didn't know what to say. Didn't know how to react as her mother walked over with the dress. She held it before her, the green and silver shimmering against the pale lights. 'I had this made for you, for the trials.'

Cyrene's fingers shook as she took the dress, feeling the soft skirt. Unlike her bony mother, it would hug her hips, bringing out the soft curves of her body. The colour alone would brighten the red in her hair, giving her skin a deeper shade of blue.

'Now that we're finally being honest,' the Queen said, smirking at Cyrene's surprise, 'tell me what it is the Seeker wants.'

Cyrene almost dropped the dress.

She couldn't ask for the mirror. Not with everything else. Whatever even ground her mother and she had found would be lost. Washed away like the tide.

When Cyrene didn't answer, her mother cupped her cheek. 'You never do anything without reason,' she said. 'You are like me in that regard. So, why have you come home, and what is it you want?'

Eve was going to steal from the trove. Was going to take the mirror. And she would be doing it in less than two days. If Cyrene told her mother now, Eve wouldn't survive. She would be taken underground. To a prison so dark she would either grow insane or drown. The other alternative was feeding her to a sea monster. At least that would be quicker.

Neither option looked inviting.

'She killed Pearl,' Cyrene said darkly.

She hated doing it. Hated twisting into the cruel part of herself she hid away. She had no other choice, though; it was the only thing her mother would approve of. The only thing that would keep Eve alive long enough to do what she had to do.

Cyrene knew it was a stretch, but the dress sat heavily on her knees, her mother's watchful gaze looking for any hint of a lie.

The Queen lowered her hand, her frown the only indication of her uncertainty. 'If she killed the one you loved, then why is she here with you?'

'Because ...' Cyrene swallowed. 'Because Nysa is my heart. Not Pearl. It took me a while to realise, but I know that now. Nysa is my choice and Eve is my penance.'

The Queen eyed her suspiciously, silent a moment before saying, 'I knew she was a pet.'

Cyrene didn't correct her. 'Though, I suppose I dislike her less now.'

'Mother ...' Cyrene started, but the Queen waved her away.

'I grieve for your loss. For what love does to you. But I do not grieve for her. I'm just glad you're finally home and coming to your senses.'

Cyrene wanted to be angry but found she couldn't. Soft spoken words between her and her mother were a rare thing, and the child within Cyrene longed for it to never end. If they were swapping truths, then perhaps this was Cyrene's opportunity. A chance to amend.

'I came home to warn you,' Cyrene said, raking her fingers over the netted corset. 'To tell you about the spindle and the shift in the world. A Grimm has died, the very same witch who gave us the Morei. I'm afraid the prophecy has begun, that the one who comes to claim it is close.'

The Queen sat in the chair opposite Cyrene, the Coral Chess pieces lying before them. Cyrene let her fingers trail over the dress's stitching, keeping her centred as she told her mother of what had happened. Of the prison break and the spindle. Of Myrenna's power and the prophecy.

'War is coming, mother. I don't think there is any way to stop it. Creatures that have been sleeping are waking to Myrenna's call. An army of the dead is controlled by a princess barely under twenty. And if Myrenna succeeds in killing the Grimms and taking Snow's heart, then there is no stopping her. She will be all powerful. Immortal. She will outlive and control us all.'

'What makes you think she will come to the sea?'

'We have magic objects forgotten even by our own people. There is power there.'

'Even we do not remember half of what treasures lay below. You have no proof.'

'She wants the Morei,' Cyrene pleaded. 'She needs it to destroy the Grimms. She will come, that is certain.'

'An object long forgotten has now been mentioned twice today,' the Queen said, her nails tapping on the table. She pouted before standing, her chin tilted towards Cyrene. It was the same look Cyrene had seen when her mother was calculating a plan. When she had begun to think three steps ahead in the very game sitting on the table before her.

She had to hope her mother would listen. That her mother would aid where she could. But if she was being honest, she never knew what her mother would do. She could promise you the world but only deliver a jar of sand and it would still fit between the rules of her agreement.

'I have decided, you will stay with me until the trials,' she said. 'It seems we have much to discuss.'

Cyrene frowned. 'But Eveline is at my home, with Edmar.'

'Still worried about the human even after all that?' her mother drawled. 'She will be better off at your home. Hidden away from prying eyes.'

'She is a human in Nysa. I cannot leave her, Mother. I said I wouldn't.'

'Such concern for someone you hate,' the Queen mused. Cyrene bit her bottom lip, holding back the words that would doom her. 'Did you not say she was with Edmar?'

Worry gnawed at Cyrene's insides, chewing away whatever calm she thought she had. 'She will need more scales. The spell will begin to wear off around the trials.'

'Why should I care about all that? You called her a penance. An apology. Is she now not mine?'

'She is still mine,' Cyrene said. 'She is Nysa's.'

The Queen twisted around, her eyes narrowing. 'Why is she here, Daughter?'

'I told you,' Cyrene said, holding back a stammer. 'She had the dream tapestry. She killed Pearl. She was my compensation to you, not an insult.'

'If she is my compensation then why can I not do with her as I please?'

The water grew colder around Cyrene, but she remained steady, the dress her anchor.

'I do not appreciate tales being spun. The lies of the land-dwellers roll off your tongue like seafoam off a wave,' the Queen said. 'If she is the famous Seeker, then she will find another way. That is what she does, after all. Finds lost things.'

'I brought her here in good faith,' Cyrene said. 'I promised her—'

'Did you? Was it sealed with magic?'

Cyrene had only given her word. She shook her head, confirming the promise was not official, terror seizing her as the Queen moved closer.

'You are not as clever as you think you are,' the Queen whispered. 'She is here for a reason, and I doubt it is to pay tribute. If she undermines me, or embarrasses this family, I will have her eaten or drowned or killed. Perhaps she may be a guest at our grand event.'

'You wouldn't,' Cyrene said. 'She'd never survive such a thing.'

The Queen narrowed her eyes, her patience wearing thin. Whatever moment they'd had, it quickly vanished. 'Perhaps you should have thought about that before bringing her into this kingdom,' the Queen seethed. 'I promised to not kill her in the throne room. I even let you feed her as if she were welcome. Whilst your insolence was cute as a child, it does not bode well for you now. I agreed to nothing about letting her live long enough to stain this kingdom. I made no promises about her being comfortable here. She is to stay with Edmar, then she will attend the trials like the rest of the kingdom, or she is to die. Choose.'

Cyrene had no choice at all. Even if Eve managed to escape this place, she'd still not have the mirror, failing their quest before they'd even started. But if she attended the trials, there was no way she could leave and steal it, either. And if she died, well, all hope was lost.

She was stuck. They all were.

'Now you're hesitant,' her mother chastised. 'You are possibly the most infuriating sea nymph I have ever come across.'

The Queen rubbed her temples and Cyrene stared at the glittering dress. She hated saying the words, but they came out smoothly as she said, 'She will come to the trials. I'll tell Edmar to prepare her.'

'Fine,' the Queen said. 'She'll need to sit near us, but not in the royal podium. Edmar's family won't be pleased, but they'll deal with it. I'll have my advisors watch her.'

Cyrene tried not to cringe at the thought. The two slimy eels surrounding Eve like a pet on display.

'Now,' the Queen said, pointing to the dress. 'Try it on. The Merking will arrive soon, and you and I are going to put on a show.'

XXXIII
The Twisting of Ties

The warning from Adanna still clouded Florian's mind as he stepped into the library. He didn't notice the warmth at first, nor the familiar scent of parchment and ink, not until the soft turn of a page drew him back to the present.

Odion was sprawled across a chair before the fire, one leg slung over the armrest with the sort of elegance only a prince could manage without looking foolish. His fingers hovered over a book, eyes darting across the lines as if trying to outrun time. A faint furrow sat between his brows, the only crack in his stony composure.

Florian shifted the weight in his arms. The books pressed against his chest, heavy enough to make his shoulders ache, but the fire cast a golden hush across the room, and for a moment, it felt almost peaceful.

'Hello,' he said, voice low against the crackling wood.

Odion jolted, just slightly, but didn't lift his head.

Florian leaned forward, trying to glimpse the title, but Odion shifted, dragging the book away from view with a sigh.

'What are you reading?' Florian asked.

As expected, there was no smile, no warmth. Just a grunt, low and dismissive, as Odion kept his eyes fixed on the open book resting in his lap.

Florian held back a wince. He didn't know why he still tried. Every interaction was met with silence or the sharp edge of a threat. A fortress would be easier to talk to. Yet something in him refused to stop. Since that dinner, he'd been caught in a loop, drawn back to Odion without reason or sense. Maybe it had been the rare laugh, quick and unguarded. Maybe the eyes, those impossibly sharp and beautiful eyes. Or perhaps it had been the voice, low and precise, rich with an accent that curled around every word like velvet.

Whatever it was, he couldn't shake it.

Endearing.

Useless.

He waited now, seeing if maybe, just maybe, the Prince would look up.

He didn't.

A little deflated, Florian dropped the stack of books on the table and rubbed his arms to warm up. Despite the roaring hearth, the library had a way of always remaining cold.

Much like the dark prince's demeanour.

He'd believed the library would be empty except for the librarian, who seemed to vanish then reappear right before you did something wrong. She was unsettling, to say the least, and Florian was quietly thankful he wasn't alone. Not when the whispers still crawled from the shelves. He was a coward, but at least he was honest about it. And he was trying. That counted for something, right?

Florian crossed the cold floor toward the desk when Odion finally spoke. His voice was flat as he turned the page in his book. 'Petrella isn't here.'

Florian froze mid-step, his throat suddenly dry. Odion had a way of knowing things without being told.

Rubbing his nose out of habit, Florian asked, 'Do you know where she is?'

'Nobody ever knows where she is.'

Helpful.

'What do you need her for?' Odion asked, finally looking up. His mismatched eyes caught the dim light, glowing as if lit from within. They shimmered like something made of pure magic, bright and warm. Florian's breath hitched.

The twins looked almost identical, from the shape of their noses to the sharp cheekbones. But while Adanna shared Odion's eyes, there were vast differences. Hers were cool, clouded, like a storm brewing just beneath the surface. Where Odion's were richer in colour, alive with a warmth that clashed with the coldness in his posture.

Florian's voice was low as he said, 'I wanted to ask about the chained books or the little lord's gifts.'

Odion slammed his book shut and eased from the chair with feline grace. Within a few moments he stood a breath away, the smell of citrus lingering on his skin. Florian gulped, remembering their close proximity only a few stacks from here.

'Those books are off limits. They have nothing we need,' Odion said. 'I tried. You were there.'

The Prince's eyes seared into Florian's as he remembered almost being caught.

Florian flushed. 'We both heard those whispers.'

'Nothing good can come from whispers in the dark,' Odion said quietly. 'As for the little lord's gifts, I've looked for them for years, what makes you think you can waltz in here and find them?'

At least he didn't call me useless again.

'I don't think I can,' Florian replied, a little breathless. 'But I do think Petrella might—'

'Petrella doesn't help anyone,' Odion replied. 'She's been here for a long, *long,* time. If she won't help me then she certainly won't help *you.*'

'What are you doing here, then?'

'What else do you do in a library? I'm reading.'

Florian stepped forward. 'What are you reading?'

Odion turned away. 'It's nothing.'

Florian halted. The flat voice had gone, replaced by something anxious. Florian frowned, trying to peer towards the chair.

Odion pushed him away. 'I said, it was nothing.'

'Then why are you making a fuss?'

'I'm not.'

'Just let me see.' Florian darted forward, ducking under Odion's arm as he lunged for the chair. He nearly made it. His fingers brushed the edge of a page.

But Odion was faster.

A hand clamped around Florian's elbow, yanking him

back. The world spun. Suddenly, they were face to face. Too close.

Their noses touched. Breath mingled. Florian froze, lips parted, heart thudding.

Odion's eyes widened. A flicker of something, surprise, maybe, crossed his face.

Then he shoved Florian away.

Florian's foot caught on the edge of the rug and he stumbled. Instinctively, he grabbed Odion's shirt for balance, but only managed to drag him down too. They crashed onto the worn rug in a tangle of limbs, the fire crackling beside them. The book slipped from the chair as they fell, landing with a dull thump beside them.

Florian might have laughed, if not for the look on Odion's face. Stern. Unamused.

'Don't touch it,' Odion growled, as he untangled himself from Florian. But it was too late, Florian had already picked it up.

It was a *romance.*

The stoic prince of Felldryn sat alone reading romance novels.

Florian laughed. 'I loved this book.'

Odion's cheeks turned crimson as he snatched the book back. 'How dare—'

A *crash* came from a shadowed alcove and both of them were on their feet in an instant. Odion shoved Florian back, a thin dagger already in his palm. His arm lingered in front of Florian, his shoulders taut, and all Florian could wonder was where the blade had come from.

A glass lay broken on the ground, a book scattered nearby.

'Who's there?' Odion growled.

Florian stared at the alcoves, the crackling fire an anthem to his nightmares as he imagined a beast or, worse, a giant. Odion remained firm, his body as still as stone. He was the same height as Florian, but that's where their likeness ended. Where Florian was all pale skin and fair hair, Odion was the night sky. His dark skin shone, the smoothness alluring in a way that made Florian want to reach out and touch him.

Something moved from the shadows.

'Do you think it's a wraith?' Florian whispered.

Odion snarled, and Florian backed up a step. A chuckle came from the shadows as a figure stepped into the light, her arms raised.

Princess Snow.

'Would you believe I used to be good at hiding?' she said.

Her short black hair was pinned back at the sides, and she wore a pair of pants with a fitted top that accentuated her curves. She was taller than Eve – not that it was difficult – but it was this feature that stood out when Florian noted her womanhood. The way she had grown into her jawline, her eyes lined with thick lashes to shape the stark blue colour. If Florian was a pale moon and Odion was the night sky, then Snow was the depths of the ocean.

'Why are you hiding?' Odion asked, not lowering his weapon.

'If you must know,' she sighed, 'I was avoiding people. The library at home was always my favourite place to hide.'

Florian touched Odion's arm, urging him to lower his weapon. Strangely enough, the Prince let him do it.

'Is this because of the bet with Malak?' Florian asked.

Snow huffed, tucking a strand of loose dark hair behind her ear. 'Maybe.'

'This is ridiculous,' Odion scoffed. With two strides, he picked up his book and tucked it under his arm. 'First my privacy is invaded by an annoying prince, and now my last place of enjoyment is ruined by the princess who stole my horse. What is it with you people?'

'You think I'm annoying?' Florian asked, but he shut his mouth at the look Odion gave him.

Odion pointed to Snow. 'You have a room to cry in, do it on your own time,' he said before turning back to Florian. 'And *you* need to back off. The objects are a myth, a children's story.'

'That can't be—'

The Prince wasn't finished. 'Those books are dangerous. Locked away for a *reason*. And even if they weren't deadly or dangerous, do you not think I wouldn't have done it already? The fact is, if Petrella could access those books I would know about it.'

'How?' Snow asked, crossing her arms. 'Have you ever asked her?'

Odion's jaw twitched at the insult. 'Do you eavesdrop as easily as you steal?'

She poked her tongue out, and Odion rubbed his eyes. 'No, I haven't asked her,' he said. 'What do you know about it, anyway?'

'Just what I heard,' she said. 'Something about chained books and secrets.'

Snow has a point. 'How do you know Petrella can't do it?' Florian asked.

Odion raised his arms. 'Because I've never seen her do it!'

'So, you've been watching her every minute of every day, then?' Snow interjected.

'Of course not—'

'Then how do you know?'

'I ...' Odion stammered. 'She's not capable of such a thing.'

'Why is that?' Florian asked.

Odion pressed his fingers against his eyes. 'Why do I feel like I'm being tortured? Both of you are insufferable. Those chains are bound in magic. They are untouchable. They are dangerous.'

'Have you tried?' Florian asked.

Odion's lips thinned. 'I did try. Once. It wasn't a good idea.'

Florian didn't know what had gotten into him, or where this courage had come from. He felt emboldened by Snow somehow. She was backing him up for once. He knew they were short on time. Knew they were short of options. Plus, the shock on Odion's face at this encounter warmed something inside him.

'I know you both think that you're going to be some kind of grand heroes, coming in and saving us all, but you've been here for five minutes,' Odion said. 'In that time, Fabian has managed to fill my sister's head with nonsense, pissed off the librarian, and invaded any private areas I once enjoyed.'

'My name is Florian.'

'I don't *care*,' Odion groaned. 'So far, all I see is a spoilt princess who doesn't worry about anyone but herself and likes to take things that aren't hers. The only two of you worth any medallions are Pip and Malak. And they aren't royal, or human, or *arseholes*.'

He moved closer to Florian, his nostrils flaring. 'What did you not understand about our last conversation? We don't need your help, and we sure as the cauldron don't want to help *you*.'

Florian went to say something, but Snow interrupted, her eyes lighting up in a way that only did when she had a plan.

'What if I told you I could help?' she said.

'I'd call you a liar,' Odion snapped.

She shrugged it off. 'Back in Bellatorre, before Myrenna married my father, we used to have a restricted library.'

'You both just keep talking,' Odion said exasperated.

'It was underneath the castle,' she continued, her voice darkening. 'Filled with scrolls and old tomes. I used to beg my father to let me read them, but he said they were dangerous. Too much for a small child to handle.'

'By the Godmother,' Odion sighed, waving her away as she followed after him. 'You are both relentless. I don't care about your sob story.'

'You would if you stopped being an *idiot* for five seconds. There is power in those scrolls. Lots of it. Why do you think they're locked away like that? I'd swear it on the cauldron.'

He paused, eyeing her up and down with contempt. 'First of all, your word means nothing. You stole from me. You are not here to help anyone else but yourself.'

Snow tapped her foot. 'I'm here to save my kingdom and that means looking at all avenues. Your sister is *dying*.'

Odion stiffened at the comment, his eyes narrowing.

'You say you're looking for a way to stop this war, to aid us if you win, and yet you don't use the resources at your disposal. Myrenna used the scrolls in my kingdom to take over, to build her magic. If you can't use the sword, then find another weapon. I'm offering to help you unlock those scrolls and their power. I'm offering to help you end this war so you can aid mine.'

Odion shook his head. 'You offer me nothing, Princess. Those scrolls only hold death.'

'So does that wooden sword.'

Odion began to turn away, his shoulders taut. 'You both come here with empty solutions. The scrolls. The little lord's artifacts. But neither will help. You know nothing of either of them. Do you think I haven't tried? I have followed every trail, every detail on both of those paths and they have only led me to despair. Let it go.'

As he walked away, Snow followed him, her determined steps on his heels. 'You're going to give up so easily? Walk away when you're finally not alone.'

He ignored her.

Red bloomed along her cheeks. She squealed and smacked him.

He turned in an instant and towered over her, his eyes darkening.

Florian's mouth gaped open.

'Perhaps,' Snow said with venom. 'if you'd stopped flirting so much you'd have been able to seek a new lead.'

Odion growled. 'Flirting? With who? You? You're crazy.'

'Not me,' Snow snapped pointing at Florian. 'Him.'

Florian blanched, but Odion stood firm, his hands clenching by his side. The book bent, and Florian hoped he was never on the bad side of that anger.

'If you *think*—' Odion began.

'I don't *think* anything,' Snow interrupted. 'I know because I watch. You walk around this castle all sullen and "woe is me" but you take delight in putting Florian down. I see the way you watch him when he isn't looking. Like some creep from the window when he's with your sister. I see how you purposely ignore him and then get frustrated when he's around. If that little escapade before didn't prove it, then I don't know what does.'

She poked her finger into his chest. 'You act like you can fix everything, like you have control, but here's something honest. You. Have. None.'

He stepped back and rubbed his chest, his eyes like ice. 'You know nothing about me, or control.'

'And you know nothing about me. Not until you *listen*.'

Florian stood dumbfounded a few pixies away. He sniffed awkwardly, the tense silence lingering a little too long, until something shifted between them. The corner of Snow's mouth lifted, and Odion sighed, leaving Florian confused and feeling a little silly.

What just happened?

'I wasn't flirting,' Odion mumbled.

'Whatever,' Snow said, 'just listen. After my father married Myrenna, when she pretended to be kind, she would go down to the dungeons all the time. She'd tell me about it sometimes, how the scrolls were magic. About how she'd found a way to control the fog dragon.'

'I'm listening,' Odion said.

'She would come to my rooms and tell me little secrets. Snippets of shadow beasts and the simplest of spells. Invisibility. Love potions. Shields,' Snow said. 'She had power before, sure, but after she raided us, she became something else. Something *more*. A goddess, in the eyes of the realm.'

Snow couldn't hide the smugness at Odion's hateful glare. 'With that power, Adanna wouldn't be alone in her burden. You could protect her. Save her.'

Odion looked stricken, some part of him soaking in the Princess's words and the other part willing himself to let go. Florian couldn't comprehend what that kind of pressure felt like. To watch as your twin slowly withered away, unable to help. Unable to stop it.

'If I agree to this,' Odion said through gritted teeth, 'what is it you want in return? Because I doubt it's just our army.'

She hesitated for a moment too long. 'I want more than just your aid.'

'I don't understand,' Florian said quietly from the side. 'That's what we came here for, isn't it? Allies and aid?'

'Did you hear nothing?' she shook her head. 'Those scrolls have power. Enough to defeat Myrenna. If we unlock those ... I want some of it, too.'

Florian blinked, trying to process. She looked hateful, angry and petulant, resembling a small child bargaining with their parents for more chocolate when they'd been told no. Something stirred along his skin, cold and slimy. This conversation didn't bode well with him, though he couldn't put his finger on why.

'Power isn't always magic,' Florian said. 'You already have power. You're a princess. You can fight. You have a rebellion waiting to stand behind you in battle. You have love and a country willing to offer aid if we succeed. You have a kingdom that you'll claim once this is all over.'

Her hateful eyes slid towards him and he felt like shrinking into the fire. Burning to death would be more comfortable than that gaze.

'None of that means anything if I don't kill Myrenna.'

She took careful steps towards him, her eyes piercing as she leaned in close. Florian could see the wrath behind them. The cold fire that had been cultivated since she'd woken from that coffin. He'd seen them change colour in the days after the forest, striking an icy blue instead of the warm summer sky she'd once owned.

He couldn't hold back the shiver of the memory that crawled to the surface in those eyes, the one of her cutting down soldiers on a dirty battlefield, screaming as Artemis found a sword slicing into her back.

'Right now, I'm a figurehead,' she said pointedly. 'I'm in hiding, *if you forgot*. I'm powerless against the threat of Myrenna.' She paused. 'You know the major difference the kingdom of Perridorm has that I don't?'

'Magic,' Odion answered flatly.

Snow gave him a dark grin. 'Correct. Magic. Myrenna has honed it for years. Sure, it started with the Mirror, but it wasn't until she came to my kingdom and killed my father that she found real power. She found it in the scrolls beneath my old home. Taught herself blood magic and spells. She built it from the ground up by locking herself away and playing with it.'

There was a shine behind her eyes that made Florian's stomach twist. Her grin seemed to stretch too wide, teeth catching the light like something waiting to bite. But it was her voice that unsettled him most. Beneath the words, there was a hunger, sharp and thin, like a blade pressed just shy of skin.Myrenna had to be stopped, that was guaranteed, but the how had never been discussed. He'd assumed imprisonment. A fair trial, the banishing of her magic. But this, this dark promise that Snow seethed from her pores, was not what he had envisioned. What stopped them from becoming the monsters when they took that path? Who brought them back when blood was all they could see?

'It won't work,' Florian said, trying to find the piece of courage he'd found earlier. 'Power can help, but it won't save your kingdom. Only your mind can. You can. Your promise can. Your kindness can. Power cannot.'

He waited for Odion to agree, to tell Snow she was crazy, that magic could not be conjured that way. That meeting the Queen with the same poison was as sure as dooming them all.

As the silence fell, Snow's blue eyes homed in on the dark prince like an arrow to a bullseye.

Odion finally said, 'It might.'

Florian spun towards him. 'Have you lost your mind? It won't. Myrenna could use the scrolls because she already had magic. She had the mirror to fuel her. Snow doesn't have that. Snow is ...'

Florian's collar went taut around his neck, Snow snarling as she pulled it tight. 'I'm *what*?'

'I only meant,' Florian stammered, 'you're not a witch. You don't have any natural magic. You don't have a mirror like Myrenna, and I've ... I've never seen you use any magic.'

Odion warily watched the Princess's hands. 'He has a point. How do you know you'll even be able to use them?'

Her grip faltered but her nostrils still flared. 'Everything in this realm has magic,' she gritted, releasing Florian. 'Surely that's enough to try.'

'If we do this,' Odion said, his eyes focused, 'and it works ... What will you do with that power?'

'I'll kill Myrenna. I'll take back what is mine.'

'And what *exactly* is yours?' Odion asked quietly.

She waved him away. 'I'm not interested in Felldryn, so you can stop worrying about an invasion.'

Odion released a breath, and Florian gulped down air. His neck flared a bright red, his eyes feeling a little swollen. For someone so petite, she was strong.

'If you gain this power,' Odion asked, carefully, 'and you succeed, you agree to help save my sister and my home?'

'I'll save your home, but your sister's too far gone.'

Odion's knife was out before they could breathe and Snow took a step back, the point a pinprick from her skin.

'Whoa,' she said, arms raised. 'It was a joke. The answer is yes. Yes, I'll help.'

'My sister is never to be used in jokes. Got it?'

'*Fine,*' she drawled.

Florian unbuttoned the top of his shirt and wiped the nervous sweat from his brow. 'Can I get something straight,' he asked, still catching his breath. 'You fight me about the little lord's gifts and opening the chained secret books, but when Snow – who we all know you hate – asks for power, you somehow agree to it?'

'I haven't agreed to it,' Odion said.

'But you—'

'I've agreed to an alliance where killing Myrenna is a possibility. If she dies, then the sword is no longer used. If the sword is no longer used—'

'Then you save Adanna,' Florian finished.

The Prince nodded before quickly looking away.

Florian wasn't sure, but he swore he saw a hint of uncertainty in his eyes. Shaking it off, he turned to them both. 'So, what happens now?'

'We only have one lead,' Odion said, 'and it's not a pleasant one.'

'You'll finally help me find Petrella?' Florian asked.

'Lucky for you, I already know where she is.'

Florian didn't feel lucky. He felt wrong. Something similar to despair was building inside of him. It was as if the balance of the world had tilted and it was about to swallow them whole.

Adanna tossed and turned in her sleep, her mind spinning and weaving through visions. Normally they came in sharp bursts. Small snippets that only gave her a flash. A taste.

However, tonight was different.

I stand on the cliff, the Lady of the Stars smiling down at me. Purple thunder rolls overhead, stretching across the sky as wind tears at my cheeks. Lightning flashes in bursts, lashing the ground with fury.

Behind me, the dead groan. I feel them rise, clawing through the soil as blood spills from me. And keeps spilling.

A crow caws above, its cry sharp against the storm. It twists mid-air, feathers folding into limbs, wings into arms. A man lands on the parapet and slips into the castle, the twin towers shimmering beneath the rain. Shadows cling to their edges like vines.

I turn back to the Lady of the Stars but she is gone.

The ground shudders beneath me. Stone cracks. I tilt, breath catching as the cliff gives way.

And I fall.

Flailing towards violent waves below.

Adanna woke with a start, the fussing voice of Laurie hovering over her. Her touch was wet, a cool cloth in her hands.

'Your highness,' she whispered. 'I heard you screaming.'

Adanna placed her hand on the handmaiden's arm, soothing her. The princess's breath came out ragged, her skin covered in a sheen of sweat. Despite her condition, she was used to it. It was Laurie she worried about. The handmaiden tended to fret, and Adanna wanted to reassure her.

'I'm okay, Laurie,' she panted. 'It was just a dream.'

'They're more frequent now,' Laurie said quietly.

'Why are you still here?' Adanna asked softly. 'You were due to see your family hours ago.'

Laurie's patted her arm. 'I'm needed here. I've been staying in my old rooms.'

Adanna peeled the sheets off her sticky body. She needed air, something to break the stuffiness of the room. As usual, Laurie knew what she needed and opened the double doors to the outside. The cool night air washed over them, and Adanna loosed a breath as it soothed her skin.

'I worry you spend too much time here,' Adanna said, watching the stars. 'You have children.'

There was no storm. No blood.

'My daughter is close to your age, she's fine. She tells me to stay as well.'

'Ivy is a sweet girl,' Adanna replied.

Laurie nodded, getting another cool cloth as the Princess lay back down.

'The dreams are more frequent,' Laurie remarked, 'The screams worse.'

Adanna's head throbbed and she swallowed. 'I'm grateful you're here.'

Laurie gave her a comforting smile and squeezed her hand. The handmaiden had always been here to help. She'd been her mother's handmaiden for years, now taking up the mantle with Adanna. She was grateful to the stars for that. For letting Laurie be away when the castle had been attacked. It meant she and her family had survived. Others had not been so lucky.

'Were you reliving the deaths again?' Laurie asked.

Adanna shook her head. 'The dreams are different this time. It was a vision, not a memory. Usually, I get a flash of something specific. The storm. The Bellatorrian Queen's eyes. Snow in the cage at the army camp. This time, though ... It was like there were multiple things happening in one scene. Fluent yet confusing. I can't pin it down.'

Laurie fussed with her pillows, plumping them. 'Tonight is

not the night to think on it,' she said. 'However, the only thing that has changed is our visitors.'

'You think their visit is causing them?'

Laurie pursed her lips. 'I think there's a lot going on that we don't know about or understand.'

Adanna rubbed her eyes, exhaustion coating her. 'Tomorrow we'll think on it.'

Laurie placed a kiss on her brow. She swept the princess's loose stands off her face and smiled. 'Tomorrow,' she agreed. Leaving Adanna to fall into a dreamless sleep.

XXXIV
The Fool's Bargain

Bryn clutched the hem of his threadbare shirt, trying to still the tremble in his hands.

The key had worked.

The gate had opened.

And whatever waited below was his fault.

He stood frozen, feet rooted to the stone, unable to look away from the bone door. It loomed ahead, slick with age and carved in symbols he didn't recognise.

Then the sound came.

A lullaby, low and curling, seeped from the cracks in the door. It wasn't soft. It wasn't kind. It slithered through the air like smoke, each note stretched too long, too thin. The melody clawed at the edges of his thoughts, familiar in shape but wrong in tone, like something meant to soothe, twisted into menace.

Dread stepped forward into the dark.

All Bryn could focus on was Erick's wild eyes as he had pleaded with him to stop. To cease crafting the bone. But Bryn had been too consumed. Too proud to admit when it had gone too far. Without his friend, he had nobody left here. Nobody else to lean on.

There would be nobody to bury his friend. To set him into flame and say the sacred words. His body would be left in the tower until the stones caved in on him or he dried into a husk.

Bryn swallowed. He'd fought so hard against Erick's views when he'd built the key, opting to take it from him rather than free their people. Bryn saw now he'd been blind. Taken by a creation and power he'd never experienced before.

He could craft magic. *Actual* magic. Something the dwarves hadn't seen in an age.

He knew Bjorn had come from a royal bloodline. Heard Bonyx and Brufell discuss the War of Thorns. Despite the Seven's histories, Bryn never expected that he too would become a story. Not a story of triumph, or victory. But of grief, and despair.

A story about the first dwarven magic maker in over a century. A dwarf who could carve any material and bring forth life. And it would be wasted serving the Evil Queen.

The Queen's Maker.

He thought of Rabbit, of the others fighting to save Snow. He thought about the Crystal coffin glittering over the pool in the grotto. The toys he'd carved for the younger dwarves. The weapons and tunnels. The carvings and chairs. He still had so much to lose. So much to do outside of these walls.

He was a creator. Not a destroyer.

Myrenna cursed above him, her black skirts trailing the dirt. She'd been agitated since they got there, pulling him free from the prison where he'd lain next to his dead friend all night. With a huff, Myrenna turned to the guards. Tucked into her braids was a small but extravagant crown, its shining silver surface woven with diamonds and rubies. She didn't need it to prove who she was, everybody knew the Queen. She stood out, would always stand out. Bryn hated to admit it, but it looked good on her. A masterfully made piece in its own right.

The Queen pointed to the bone door, her eyes cruel as she ordered, 'Nobody follows him. Nobody touches what he brings out. And nobody here leaves this chamber. Do you understand?'

The guards nodded, standing tall before she swept up her skirts and headed to the exit. In an instant she transformed into ash then floated into the sky.

As the black cloud of the Queen sailed away, the door thrummed, leaving the foul taste of magic on Bryn's tongue.

Bryn eyed the guards and the dwarves in the corner, everybody focused on the flickering black curtain lingering at the door's entryway. Without Erick's distraction, Bryn was left with little room to move. He had to stick to the path, to find Rabbit and the others. The guards whispered amongst themselves, placing bets on whether the crow would survive. Bryn tried to breathe. His chest felt tight, each inhale shallow. He took a step, then another, forcing himself towards the wall. An older dwarf watched from nearby, silent and still.

White petals bloomed along the bone gate, reaching

skyward in slow, deliberate stretches. They clung to the stone like ivy, winding through cracks and carvings, their stems thin but stubborn. A sweet, honeyed scent hung in the air, thick enough to taste. They were beautiful, in a way, shaded along the edges like the colours of a sunset. For something so hard to obtain, they seemed so slight, and as Bryn reached out his thick fingers, a voice made him halt.

'Whatever you're planning, it's stupid.'

Bryn peered over his shoulder to look at the gruff older dwarf standing beside him. His voice was deep, his words well pronounced. His eyes narrowed at Bryn's now-retreating hand. The others in the cavern whispered, ignoring whatever confrontation this was.

'I'm admiring the flowers,' Bryn whispered back, hoping to not gain attention. But the guards were still distracted, anticipation soaking the air as medallions were swapped between hands. The lullaby echoed from below, soft and tempting. It reminded Bryn of a siren song, calling sailors to their death.

'You're looking at them like a prize,' the dwarf replied, nodding towards the flowers. 'They're magic flowers. Nothing good comes from them.'

Bryn frowned. 'What would you know about magic flowers?'

'I know a great deal,' the older dwarf whispered. 'I studied in the halls of Parador.'

'And yet Erick was the one to decipher the text,' Bryn mumbled.

The older dwarf scowled. 'If you had seen the size of Parador, you would understand why I had not yet reached that part of my learning.'

Bryn bit the inside of his cheek, trying not to snap. His fist clenched beside him, the churning in his stomach rearing into something like seasickness.

'I lived in Parador,' Bryn ground out, trying to keep his voice low. 'I know how big the library is.'

The older dwarf stepped back, his eyes roving over Bryn. 'You're too young. Only the Seven ...'

Bryn let him piece it together, remaining silent as he turned back towards the flowers.

'How are you *here*?' the dwarf asked, his voice low. 'You are ...'

'Oi!' one of the guards shouted. 'Back away from the door and stop talking.'

The two of them shrunk away. The older dwarf was only silent a moment before he added, 'You shouldn't be here.'

In three long strides, the guard stood over him and struck, staining his cheek a dark red. Before Bryn could blink, they were shoved to the side, falling into one another as the older dwarf wheezed. The vines pricked Bryn's back, digging in like claws as he shoved the other dwarf off him. The other guards snickered.

'Rotten luck, ending up in here,' the dwarf muttered to Bryn.

'It was on purpose,' Bryn replied, trying to remove the prick in his back.

'Are you mad?'

'I'm mad you won't stop talking.'

The dwarf shook his head. 'Not angry. Are you mad up here?' He tapped his skull. 'Nobody comes in here by choice.'

Bryn had known what he meant but hadn't cared to answer honestly. With a grimace, he said, 'Sometimes I think we're all mad.'

Bryn had wondered more than once if he was crazy since entering this cesspit of a place.

He shifted, wincing as something jabbed his shoulder. A small hole in the wall caught his eye. Behind him, the guards were still laughing, their jeers echoing off the stone. Bryn tuned them out, fingers slipping into the hollow.

Glass met his touch.

He drew it out slowly. A bottle, cool and smooth in his palm. As the light caught it, his breath caught too.

Stardust.

His heart thudded. He glanced around the cavern, eyes now adjusting to the dark. Shadows peeled back, revealing more hollows, small pockets carved along the stone. Each one barely visible. But they were there.

Another glint by the entrance confirmed it. This place was rigged. And if the cavern was set to blow, then so were the mines. All of them.

Bryn's hands shook. He clenched his fists, trying to steady the tremor of fear crawling beneath his skin.

'What happens when Dread finds whatever he's looking for?' Bryn whispered.

'That depends on the Queen,' the older dwarf answered. 'The mines haven't been rich by any means, but she has made some profit. The deeper we go, the more bones we find. It hasn't been productive in a while. We just assume she likes to keep it as a prison of sorts. Why?'

'The place is littered with stardust.'

'I know. We use it to blow up new tunnels.'

'No,' Bryn hissed. 'I mean hidden in the walls. It's all around us.'

It took the dwarf a moment to catch on, but Bryn knew he'd seen it when he noticed the same alcove he had.

'What happens when this much stardust explodes?' Bryn asked.

The dwarf shook his head. 'It would be a calamity. One small bottle creates an explosion. Enough to bring down a wall. Together, with as many as you say, would cause complete destruction. It would kill everyone in here.'

'How far would we need to go to be out of its proximity?' Bryn asked.

'Hard to say,' he replied. 'None of us can even pass the gates.'

'You told me to stop whatever I was planning. That it was stupid.'

The older dwarf's eyes narrowed. 'Yes, because you looked suspicious. And suspicious recruits have a habit of being taken to the pits for a whipping.'

'I was trying to take a flower,' Bryn replied. 'To save my cousin. I'd planned on escaping, on sneaking out alone.'

'That *is* stupid.'

'It is,' Bryn said, gripping the bottle in his pocket. 'But it's also less stupid than what I'm about to suggest next.'

The dwarf stayed silent. At least he hadn't called him stupid again.

'If the Queen gets what she wants,' Bryn said. 'This mine is done for. It's ready to explode. I know you've fought before and failed. I know you've seen death. But this changes everything.' He held out the bottle to the dwarf, letting his old fingers close over it. 'Erick was going to warn the others. To tell them to riot. He died before he could. If the Queen gets that weapon, whatever is hidden behind that door, none of us have a chance at surviving.'

'We have nowhere else to go.'

'I have contacts in the rebellion,' Bryn whispered. 'For those who are strong enough to survive, I can provide refuge.'

'Why should I trust you?' the dwarf asked.

'Because we're kin. Because I'm part of the Seven. I'm the first magic-maker in a century of dwarves. And, because I will do this, with or without you.'

The dwarf hesitated, eyes lingering on the bottle before shifting to the far corner. The other dwarves huddled together, thin limbs pulled close to their bodies. Their eyes were wide and empty, shadows sunken deep into their faces. The fabric of their uniforms hung loose, torn in places and caked with dust. Grime clung to every seam, but here and there, Bryn caught something darker, stains that had once been red, now dried to brown.

'And what of the Mines of Parador, of the beasts that crawl there?' the dwarf asked Bryn.

Bryn was surprised by the question. 'What of them?'

'Will you promise me that Parador will keep its doors open? That we'll relinquish the ghosts of their claim and take it back?'

Bryn remembered the cold calls of the wraiths, the shadows moving amongst the dark. 'You want to reclaim Parador?'

'I want to claim home,' he replied. 'There is nothing else left for me but that.'

Bryn didn't know if it was possible. But he also didn't know if what he was asking now was possible. All he had was chance. Bryn gave him a small nod. 'When the time comes, I will try.'

'Then I'll help you. Tell me what I need to do.'

In hushed tones Bryn outlined his and Erick's original plan. Of how, through a whisper or a signal, the recruits were meant to flee. Erick had mentioned the abandoned tunnels near the north before he'd died. Most of them had been closed off due to the lack of magic and resources. However, some had been cleared from the last escape attempt, but he didn't know how many or which ones.

It was a slim shot. He knew it. Knew that some would follow and others would not. He could only pray to the Godmother that most would listen and take the chance once they knew about the stardust.

When the dwarf handed the bottle back, he gripped Bryn's hands. 'Before you do this, give them time to flee. As much time as you can muster.'

Before Bryn could answer, the dwarf collapsed backwards. His bones groaned with the impact as he slammed into the edge of the bone door, cracking a portion of it. The guards barked curses, rushing over to haul him off.

He was yanked upright, his collar choking him as he rasped, 'Help a poor old dwarf.'

The guard sneered, but the old dwarf went on, dragging out his words with theatrical effort. 'I am weak. I must return to my bed. I need my strength ... for the Queen.'

'The Queen doesn't need you,' the guard snapped, dropping him into the dirt.

His boot lifted, ready to strike, but a shout rang out. 'Wait!'

The boot paused mid-air as the first guard turned. 'He's her translator,' the second said. 'The one who found the door.'

A growl, then a begrudging curse. 'Fine.' He grabbed the old dwarf by the arm. 'You'd better be ready when she gets back. Or I'll be grabbing the whips.'

The dwarf flinched as his shift slipped, revealing a lattice of old scars etched across his back. Bryn said nothing, jaw tight, eyes fixed on the silent exchange as the dwarf was dragged away.

His gnarled fingers twitched in small, deliberate signals. One of the others whimpered but gave a tight nod.

Bryn returned the gesture with a small, steadying nod of his own.

Now or never.

Swallowing hard, he crept towards the wall. Sweat coated his palms, but when he felt the vine nudge his back, he held still, almost sighing with relief. Quickly, he plucked a few of the flowers, tucking them carefully into his pocket.

Behind him, the haunting voice cut off mid-song.

Myrenna hated waiting.

As the fog dragon stirred, somewhere far off and deep, she felt her magic drain like water through cupped hands. At least the rebellion had been handled. One less barb. One less nuisance demanding her attention.

She cracked her neck, braids tugging at her scalp where they sat tight with the crown. The descent into the mines was miserable. Cracked stone, smoke curling through every crevice, the stench of sulphur thick in the air. She rarely came down here. It didn't suit her.

She preferred silk. Diamonds. Clean air and crystal chandeliers. After a lifetime of scrubbing flour from her hair and dodging her drunk father's fists, she'd embraced the luxury like it was her birthright. It had come easily. The manipulation, the flattery, the occasional threat. It was better than poverty. Better than dough under her fingernails.

She flicked her wrist and her heels vanished, replaced with

flats. The stairs were steep, and with her magic waning, she had no interest in falling. She let the residual magic cradle her steps, drifting slowly downward, yawning as she reached the hall outside Dread's quarters.

The fog dragon always took too much. Always left her hollow.

Once she had the second mirror, that would change.

She didn't have much time. Dread would be stepping through the bone door any moment now.

Inside, his chamber was empty. She crossed the room, and knelt at the edge of the bed. Peering underneath, Myrenna dragged out a trunk made of heavy wood, the motion leaving marks on the floor. She unlocked it with a flick of her wrist. The old latch clicked, then snapped open. She shoved aside cloth and scraps until she found what she was looking for. A swath of satin, soaked in dried blood. Peeling it back, she held back her scowl. The mines were warm enough to ruin flesh quickly. Meaning, the heart she'd retrieved had browned and shrivelled at the edges.

'Ugh,' she muttered, and bit into it.

It was tough. Chewy. Dry as ash.

She gagged.

Only by the third bite did she feel the flicker of magic return, like needles dancing along her skin. The bitter taste clung to her tongue, and she paced the room, trying to swallow down the bile.

That's when she noticed it.

The bed was disturbed. The couch crooked. Black feathers scattered. The window wide open, its curtains fluttering like torn sails.

A piece of folded parchment flapped in the breeze, pinned beneath an old tome.

Still chewing, Myrenna lifted the note and read.

Snow falls in Felldryn.

Forgive me, brother.

A snarl tore from the Queen's throat as the heart dropped to the floor with a thud.

Black fire erupted from her fingertips. The note vanished in a hiss, curling into ash before it even touched the stone. But its message still scraped against her ribs like a blade.

She stared at the scorched spot, breathing shallow.

Trik.

His face returned in fragments. The raw look in his eyes. The sound of his brother's scream echoing through the chambers behind them.

Dread couldn't find out his brother had fled. Not yet. Not while the mirror remained out of reach.

Her jaw locked. She turned from the mess, pacing in stiff, clipped strides. The taste of spoiled magic still clung to her tongue. The heart had done enough to wake her, but not enough to steady her. She needed to move. Act. Twist the narrative before it twisted her.

She slid her hands over her skirts. The silk dissolved, replaced by fitted black trousers and high boots that hugged her calves. A sleek tunic shaped to her figure, snug at the waist and sharp at the collar. She coiled her braid tighter, the motion precise. Her nails lengthened, dark and curved to a point.

The tunnels ahead pulsed with noise. Screeches echoed through the stone like knives on bone. She didn't flinch.

One of the shaith's dropped onto the windowsill with a flutter of sinew wings, landing in a crouch. Her eyes shimmered with oil-slick gleam. The voice that rasped from her throat was thick with devotion. 'Mistress.'

Myrenna smiled, showing her teeth.

She stepped closer, close enough to see herself reflected in the black of her eyes. 'I need something,' she said.

The shaith quivered, eyes gleaming brighter. 'Anything.'

Her smile sharpened. 'I need you to go hunting.'

The creature grinned, slow and wicked.

XXXV
The Malice of Mists

A roar echoed over the trees as Piccadilly lugged the boats to shore. They were close to Ivywood and the entrance to the mountain pass towards Carfell.

The sound vibrated along the sandy beach causing Piccadilly's pointed ears to twitch.

Hansel wheezed behind her, his cheeks flushed and soaked in sweat. They'd managed to hold his wound together, stitching it again when it had reopened, with fishing line found in the boat. The group crowded close to each other as the wind picked up, loosening the leaves along the ground.

'Quickly,' Piccadilly urged, pulling them towards the trees.

She at least recognised this part of the forest, where the river cut through the land all the way to the sea. It was what fed the Silver Lake, the water clear and pure from the melted snow on the mountains. A bridge was close by. Not the major one used on the Queen's Road, but a smaller one made of rope and stone. It was a dangerous route, but when she'd planned the escape, she hadn't wanted to take any chances. Though she hoped the rumours of three goats guarding it was untrue.

As the others pushed through the trees, another roar echoed.

'Her power grows,' an old woman said from nearby.

Piccadilly recognised the woman. She had attended the training sessions in the Sanctuary. Her hair was braided, tightly woven with different shades of grey. She was short but stocky and her teeth were the colour of granite. 'That is the roar of the Fog Dragon.'

'How do you know?'

'It attacked my village in the mountains before I came down to the city. Sucking the lifeblood from all it covered. My daughter died protecting us, weaving a minor shielding spell to hold it off. She only lasted seconds before it took her. Shrivelling her body into a decayed shell.'

'I'm sorry,' Piccadilly replied.

The woman shook her head. 'I had a slip of paper just for her name.'

'The Ever After will care for her.'

'Will it?' the old woman mused. 'Or is that a fool's tale, too?'

Another gust of wind blew, pulling the branches at an odd

angle. Piccadilly eyed the sky, goosebumps growing on her skin at the sound.

'I've never heard a beast with a roar like that,' Piccadilly said, the woman coming to stand beside her.

A quiet fell over the trees, the river's torrent seeming to slow. She heard a bird's call. Sharp and piercing. It echoed through the sky as a tiny black shadow flew alone.

Piccadilly pushed the woman lower to the ground as the bird swerved, dodging a great black shadow crawling from the trees. Some of the fog thickened, forming the distinct shape of wings and a maw opening wide.

No.

The bird veered left, and the shadow twisted on itself, under the cover of the clouds. Then lunged.

'Run!' Piccadilly screamed at the woman.

To her credit, the woman didn't hesitate. She grabbed the others and pulled them towards the mountains. Piccadilly ran, too, but she kept her eyes on the skies. The trees gave them coverage as they moved but it didn't protect them.

Piccadilly squinted as the bird veered upwards, barely missing the sharp teeth and bursts of black fire. It cawed, the sound both a warning and a plea.

Fear coated her bones. She knew that bird. Had saved him enough times to recognise his call.

With soundless feet, she shot along the river, jumping over rocks and sand as if the wind carried her. She pulled out her bow as the sky darkened, the clouds spreading thin over the horizon. She only had three arrows, but they were carved from ancient wood, something her mother had discovered in the early days of her childhood. She didn't know the wood's origin or the magic it held, but the arrows had done enough to protect her back then.

Her feet froze as the crow cawed again. The dragon and crow darted through the air, twisting and dodging like twin dancers.

Piccadilly didn't have much time. Grabbing a sturdy branch, she hauled herself up towards the top of an old oak. Thin branches tugged at her hair, but she ignored them.

Another roar shattered the silence.

She balanced the arrow, heart pounding.

A shrill caw sliced through the sky. A black crow flew just above the leaves, the dragon close behind. Its wings were tiny in comparison to the great beast, like a bug caught in a spider's web before the final strike. She held her breath and tracked their movement.

The crow spun sharply, and the dragon snarled, wings slicing through the mist in massive, thunderous beats.

She slipped into that cool, quiet place inside her, the world fading as she focused. The dragon's long neck stretched forward, the thin skin between its webbed wings glowing faintly in the fog.

Flynn was fast, but even he couldn't survive this. As he dove, spiralling toward the forest, Piccadilly exhaled slowly and released her arrow. It spun, flying straight for the space between the two creatures.

The dragon roared as the arrow grazed its ear. Dark purple blood spilled over its eye.

She cursed under her breath. With the wind and speed, she'd need to recalibrate her aim.

For a moment, the dragon forgot about Flynn as its sharp eyes locked on her.

Shit.

The dragon lunged.

Piccadilly leapt, branches slicing her skin.

A loud crack echoed as the dragon crashed where she'd just been, snapping the oak in two.

Dust and splinters rained down, blurring her vision.

The trees offered some cover, but it was no use. Fog slithered across the ground, thick and seething. She dropped, a sharp stab of pain rocking her knees.

A caw echoed overhead as the beast surged forward, grass and roots turning to ash in its wake.

Piccadilly ran. She dodged rocks and tangled roots, flying low over the soil, every ounce of energy driving her forward. But the fog was faster. It flowed like liquid, creeping through the trunks and wilting every living thing it touched, its sticky breath hot on her heels.

Gritting her teeth, she nocked her second arrow.

The ground tilted beneath her. She slipped, skidding down the side of a gully. She smashed along a rock and her leg screamed in protest.

The dragon did not slow. It glided down the hill, hungry, wild.

She raised her bow, twisting her body just as the beast's head sliced through the trees. Its teeth gleamed like jagged knives in the shadows. The mouth opened wide—

Her arrow knocked against the bow, her speed down the gully too fast for her catch a direct shot. She fired anyway.

Missing it by a breath.

Teeth came to claim her. Ripe and greedy and hot.

Just as she thought she was as good as dead, a black bird shot through the trees. His claws slashed across the beast's face, almost meeting teeth before he swivelled with a screech. One shadow against another.

The dragon roared again, rearing back as it tried to bite the bird. But the space was too small. Flynn cawed again and

Piccadilly smashed against a tree. She grunted, pain ricocheting down her back. But she didn't have time to focus on it as the dragon roared again.

With shaking hands Piccadilly raised her bow, her elbow shaking lightly as the fog hissed before her. She would only have this one shot. This last chance.

And as Flynn lured the beast towards Piccadilly, the great mouth opening wide, her arrow flew. Hitting the inside of the beast's throat.

The sound the dragon released was terrifying. The ground shook as it fell, purple light blooming in its mouth. Flynn whooshed past her. His wings spready as he dove through the trees then back into the sky. The dragon loosed a howling roar.

Purple smoke seeped through the crevices, casting the forest in a cold, bleak fire. Piccadilly dove for the other side of the tree. The heat scorched Piccadilly's skin and singed the ends of her hair as she herself pressed against the bark, narrowly escaping the flames. Her feet dug into the soil, refusing to move just yet. When the fire died away, leaving the earth dry and blackened, the dragon dug its clawed feet into the ground and lifted itself into the sky.

Straight towards Flynn.

'No,' Piccadilly panted, running towards them.

She tore through the forest, the thick canopy flickering as the two dark shadows slipped beneath the leaves. Her gaze darted to the horizon, chasing the sharp caw that cut through the air. When she burst into the clearing, there they were.

Flynn plummeted again, his wings sluggish and heavy. He wouldn't outrun it. He would be caught. He would die.

A figure stepped forward nearby, short and off-kilter as he crossed into the open. Piccadilly reached for another arrow but found her quiver empty. Panic gripped her, freezing her in place. The figure lowered his hood, and she met those black pupils. Unblinking, cold, and fixed on her.

'Rumple?' she whispered in surprise.

He stood in the field, alone and untethered, raising the spindle before him with careful reverence. Piccadilly's heart hammered, her blood igniting. Pain shot up the side of her leg, her back, but all she could do was watch.

Green smoke curled from the spindle, twisting through the clearing like a living thing. Above, Flynn cawed sharply, his wings folding close. The dragon, wild and ravenous, pursued, enraged.

Suddenly, Flynn dove. The beast followed like a falling arrow, plummeting toward the earth.

Piccadilly held her breath.

Just before impact, Flynn twisted sharply.

The beast roared, exhaling a torrent of burning purple fire that hissed and writhed through the smoke below.

The earth trembled, a metallic tang thick on Piccadilly's tongue. She dropped to her knees as the soil quaked.

The dragon thrashed, blood spilling from its shattered skull, then stilled. The ground calmed, the smoke thinned and vanished, and Rumple collapsed, trembling on the grass.

With ragged breaths, Piccadilly searched the sky. But she couldn't find Flynn's shadow.

'Flynn?' she called, her voice cracked. 'FLYNN!'

A weak caw came from nearby and she ran, finding the crow lying between two lone trees near the river. His bones snapped as he changed, his black hair unruly and his body tattered.

His skin was burned, stained and twisted from the flames of the dragon.

Piccadilly pulled him into a hug. Relief flooded through her as she beheld him. He was burnt but he was alive.

Alive.

He looked up towards her, blinking back pain filled tears and she smiled. Then he grabbed her cheeks and placed his lips on hers.

'I'm worried about Snow,' Malak commented from across the table.

He held a teacup, his large fingers barely holding on as he managed to take another sip. Pip had let his tea go cold, but Adanna was helping herself to seconds. Today she wore a cool blue dress, almost the colour of stone. Malak thought it washed her out a little, but the longer sleeves and ruffled skirts were pretty on her tiny frame.

'The only thing you should be worried about when it comes to Snow is keeping her on a leash,' Pip murmured.

'I'm being serious, Pip,' Malak said.

The elf shrugged. 'So am I.'

Adanna took a sip from her cup. 'What worries you, Malak?'

'She's behaving differently,' he said. 'I don't know what it is exactly. It's almost like she's a shifter, changing shape in front of my eyes. Recognisable one moment and completely different the next. If that makes sense?'

'The only thing she'd shift into is a snake,' Pip muttered.

'Enough!' Malak snapped. 'Why can't you be serious for once?'

Pip narrowed his eyes. 'I am serious. In fact, I'm so serious about it that I followed you ninnies here after obtaining my freedom. I'm so serious about it that I've put up with the pain you call a princess.'

'If you hate her so much then why are you here?' Malak challenged.

'Because she's a better alternative than the Evil Queen.'

When Malak went to bite Pip's head off, Adanna's crisp voice broke between them. 'Trauma affects us all differently.'

Malak nodded, remembering how she'd said the same thing after meeting Snow the first time. Still, it didn't stop the knot in his gut from tightening. They hardly ever fought. He'd never even raised his voice at her before, but after the clash during training, something had shifted. As if the troll beneath his skin had simmered too long and was now desperate to break free.

He dragged a palm down his face, his grip unsteady on the teacup. She was his princess. The fire in his heart, his home. All he'd ever wanted was for her to be happy. Safe. But since the crystal coffin and the camp, she'd changed. Become sullen. Angry. Not like Eve. This was heavier. Something darker, more dangerous.

He'd noticed it after the wood nymphs. The way her eyes flickered with colour during conversation. Even her fighting had changed. Fewer blocks, more strikes. She wasn't protecting any more. She was *attacking*.

But of all the signs, it was the picnic that stayed with him. The moment he found her with Odion's horse. She'd spoken to him then, told him pieces of what happened. Just slivers. Enough to sense the horror she'd survived. Enough to know she was planning something. A distraction, she'd said. A plan that wouldn't hurt anyone, but would help them all.

He believed her. Of course he did. He was loyal.

But her voice had changed that day. There had been a strange quiet in it, like a whisper you were never meant to hear. It wasn't what she said, but how she said the words, that haunted him.

Still, he'd done what she asked. And somehow, he felt like he was hanging from a rope with no idea why it had been tied.

Now, his companions sat in a foreign kingdom, petitioning for aid, inching further from everything they once knew. The castle keep. The gardens. The stargazing. All gone. Strange, really. He'd spent more time with her these past weeks than he ever had before. And yet, she was slipping further away. Like a loose thread slowly unravelling with every hour. And there was absolutely nothing he could do about it.

'I know both of you dislike her,' he said, a little defeated, 'but I'm concerned. Without Hansel, she—'

'I don't dislike her,' Adanna interrupted. 'I know she dislikes me.'

There was no malice behind the Princess's tone, only hard honesty as she placed her teacup down. 'I don't know her very well but I can see the love between you two. There is a bond, and if something in that bond is threatened or challenges you, then it's unsettling.'

Pip remained silent but Malak stood, leaving his tea forgotten. 'I think I'll go find her.'

Adanna gave him a nod. 'I think that's a good idea.'

As Malak left the room, he couldn't help but think about Adanna's smile. Something about it was knowing, a crack in the universe that had been revealed but he didn't know what it meant. She was a strange princess, full of pretty words and odd smiles.

As he wandered through the halls, Malak turned the recent events over in his mind. The losses. The grotto. A part of him still wanted to trust Snow. To believe in her plan. But another part – the old, buried troll – longed to reach for his club and protect what he knew was safe.

Myrenna lived in many places. Shadows, birds, magic. She had a knack for slipping through the cracks of the world and digging in with sharpened nails.

Everyone but Snow seemed settled here. Pip was aloof, of course, never fully present, but that was the way of elves. Curious, yet always on the outside. Odion moved like a ghost, only appearing when needed. And Snow ... Snow came to the dinners, but since their lessons had stopped, she'd all but vanished.

The corridors shifted from clean to forgotten. Cobwebs clung to corners like old wounds, the spiders filling in for the people who once lived here. He'd told Adanna he liked the quiet, but now that he walked through it, the silence felt colder than he remembered.

He couldn't let Snow slip away. Couldn't let the space between them stretch any further. He had to find her. Say sorry for what he'd said, for how he'd been. Maybe he could make her a picnic. Read to her like he used to. Remind her of the parts of them that were still whole.

A housekeeper passed. He called out, and she paused. Her eyes darted to him, wide and wary. She looked like someone who hadn't seen many trolls before, let alone spoken one.

'Have you seen Princess Snow around?' he asked.

The tray in her hand shook. 'Not in a while, Sir.'

'Any inkling on where she might be?'

She shook her head and Malak sighed. With a nod, he let her go, her quick steps turning into a light run as she escaped.

'Please don't be in the stables again,' he muttered to himself, hoping she hadn't stolen yet another horse.

It wasn't until he turned a corner and saw the flicker of shadow in his mind's eye that Malak stopped. The window beside him was hazed in shades of brown, the glass smudged by time and weather. Outside, the sky had dimmed, stretching over the land like a hand smothering the sun. Night came quickly here. Thick. Veiled. Like a curtain falling, drawing stars out of hiding.

But it wasn't the stars that held him.

A bird fought the wind, one wing crumpled, its shape staggering against the dark. Malak watched as it dipped, tumbling through the air before crashing into the rose trellis.

Malak was moving before he realised, boots heavy on the stairwell. The door slammed open, the grass crunched beneath him as he stormed across it, club in hand. By the time he reached the fountain, a man lay slumped against the rim. His head was unevenly shaved, blood streaking his scalp. His clothes were ragged, the fabric stiff with brown stains that told their own story.

Malak grabbed the man's collar and hauled him upright. The growl that left him rumbled low in the night.

The man's head lolled, but his gaze met Malak's without fear. Weary, yes. Defiant, too. And it was the scar, long and jagged, running like a fault line across his scalp, that made Malak hesitate.

He knew that scar.

But before he could speak, the man gave a tired grin.

'I was looking for a beauty,' he said. 'Not a beast.'

XXXVI
The Reflection of Fate

Dread remembered nothing but darkness and pain.

He saw his brothers die. He saw Myrenna. Hansel. His parents. The yard lined with stakes, fire licking the sky, their names already turned to ash.

Monster. Shifter. *Beast.*

The creature from the mirror drove its claws into his chest, tearing through the threads of his heart. Would Myrenna care? Or forget him, like the others?

Water closed over him, soaking him through. His lungs screamed as the cold pressed in. The beast shredded him, piece by piece.

Hansel.

Myrenna.

Trik.

Flynn.

Dread lost himself. To the pain. To the fear. To the silence inside his scream.

And just as everything slipped—

The beast let go.

Hands gripped him, sharp nails biting skin. He surfaced with a choke, the cold roaring in his ears.

Amethyst eyes glared down at him.

Myrenna.

He blinked twice, then vomited.

'Get up,' Myrenna growled.

His queen wore britches, her hair braided back like a warrior. And unlike the mirror, this one looked real.

Felt real.

He was ashamed he'd almost believed the reflection.

The creature growled from the dark as Myrenna strode forward. He knew she'd seen the mirror. Seen the damage spread along the ground. The water was stained with his blood, pooling along the rock edges.

Her shoulders twisted back as her nails grew, sharpening into her own personal knives. She was power. And fury. And might.

Dread wanted to bow. To cave. To serve.

She'd come for him. Had *saved* him. When nobody else had.

The Queen was merciless as she stood, grinning as if she had already won. With the long stroke of her finger, she beckoned the creature forward.

Dread didn't breathe as the creature growled back.

The Queen unleashed herself.

'Is there a special knock?' Snow asked as the three of them stood before a large door.

Florian watched as Odion bit the inside of his cheek, waiting for him to do something. After their agreement in the library, Odion had led them to a hallway at the back of the stacks where an unassuming, curved stairway guarded a hollow room below. There, they'd arrived at a door, looking very untouched and very dusty.

'No,' Odion replied, before he lifted his hand and knocked.

'I don't understand what the fuss is all about,' Snow said.

'Petrella is ...' Florian started.

'—I'm what?'

They jumped, turning to see Petrella. She stood on the top step glaring at the three of them as if they were horse dung she'd just scraped off her shoe.

Florian gulped. This had been a bad idea. They were intruding. Waltzing to her personal quarters as if she would welcome them with tea. Petrella isn't a tea person, Florian thought. She seemed like a spirits drinker.

Odion was the one to speak first. 'We came to ask about a few things ... Madam.'

Madam?

Florian cocked his eyebrow, but the Prince stepped in front of him. Petrella eyed them, almost floating on the step like an impossible ghost.

Florian's back pressed against the door, the lock creaking at his touch. He noticed rust etched along the edges of the doorhandle, a cobweb coating the lock.

Odd, he thought. *Considering these are her chambers.*

She stared down her nose at them, her eyes dark and piercing. 'Did I not tell you as a boy that you should not peek into things that were best left forgotten? Dark and dangerous times lurk behind them.'

Odion nodded. 'You did.'

'Is it the chains you wish to ask about, or the little lord's gifts?' she asked.

Odion and Florian's eyes met in question at the mention of the little lord, but they didn't say anything. Instead Odion looked up at her, choosing his next words carefully. 'Can I ask about both?'

She considered him. 'You may. But you have never asked before. Why change now?'

Snow stepped forward. 'Because we're desperate.'

'The princess who speaks so freely on other's behalf,' the librarian mused. The look on her face was pure ice. She sneered at Snow, the disdain a dark force reaching towards Snow's fair skin. Florian swore he saw the princess flinch before she, too, raised her nose in defiance.

He wished he could be more like that. Brave in the face of fear.

His fingers trembled as the cobwebs stuck to his nails. The handle was stained, the gold still smooth despite its age, and he had the strange urge to open it.

'I would not suggest looking into things long untouched,' Petrella said.

Florian turned and noticed she was not replying to Snow but responding to Odion.

'Secrets remain secrets because they do not wish to be found.'

'Don't secrets always have a way of setting themselves free?' Florian replied, swallowing.

Petrella watched him for a moment, eyes curious, before she floated – *actually floated* – down the stairs.

Even Odion froze, the only movement his outstretched arm. His hand stopped just in front of Florian, as if forming a barrier. The prince blinked, confused, unsure why—

Petrella was suddenly in front of him, nose inches from his. She smelt of dust and old parchment, her clothes barely more than a whisper against her skin.

'We haven't come to fight,' Odion said.

'Oh?' she asked, eyeing his arm in front of Florian. 'Then why protect the blonde prince from an ally?'

Odion dropped his hand. 'My family have always had the utmost respect for you. You have lived here for a while and—'

She cackled, the sound deafening in the confines of the stairwell. 'For a while? I have seen three generations grow old and die. I have seen your feasts and famines. I have recorded the histories and the battles and the noise. I witnessed the massacre of your parents and yet I remain. Protecting the past, the present, and our future. I see you brood and wander my halls. I see your sister bleed and raise the dead. Her screams are a hollow anthem along these halls. A while, you say? I say eternity.'

'What *are* you?' Florian whispered.

Her hollow eyes turned to him and she grinned. Dust

plumed off her dress, and his nose twitched. It wasn't the smell that did him in. Or the cluttered quarters. Instead, fate had other plans. Apparently, that meant always being the idiot who ruined a perfectly good moment.

With a staggered inhale a sneeze worked its way along his throat, lifting like a bird in flight through his nose and scratching behind his eyes. He tried to hold it, to halt the inevitable, but even with his tea, the dust that came from her was too much.

With the thrash of his head, he sneezed, a great billowing thing, as his nose turned crimson. He stumbled, his back hitting wood, turning the handle, and falling into Petrella's quarters.

Snow's face contorted in contempt. Petrella only smiled. And Odion ... well, he just stood there. Florian curled inwards, the embarrassment more painful than the fall. He shivered on the cold floor, looking up to Petrella's cold face with a meek and apologetic look.

Surprisingly, she didn't chastise him. 'Fate always plays its cards right.'

Snow moved first, ignoring the librarian with the swish of her hips as she entered. Florian reached out his hand, Snow scoffed and stepped over him.

He figured she wouldn't help, but it still hurt anyway.

It was Odion who stopped, his eyes hard and shoulders stiff. His warm, calloused hand reached out, giving Florian a steady lift as they stood, shoulder to shoulder.

Something ignited within Florian at the touch. He breathed in the scent of metal and citrus and let it soothe him. Odion shifted, his arm grazing Florian's ever so slightly.

A hum reverberated along his skin, the heat from his cheeks burning.

Did he do it on purpose?

Snow shoved aside a stack of yellowed papers, sending them fluttering to the floor. She moved without caution, brushing past hanging tools and brittle scrolls, her fingers trailing across delicate surfaces like she owned the place.

Florian didn't pay her any mind as he took in the space. The room was larger than expected, but unlike the other places in the palace, it was cluttered. Books, scrolls, paper, machines, and vials lay endlessly scattered, reaching into the far corners. Florian imagined the spiders having a discussion on where to build their webs, their eight legs cramped amongst the forgotten things.

Snow coughed, bringing his ridiculous thoughts to a close. She lifted a blanket, revealing a large wooden desk with an array of drawers. Scratches embedded the surface, matching the floor which displayed dents and bruises, as if things had been dragged across its surface carelessly.

'I thought I was messy,' the princess commented.

Florian chose to ignore the comment as Odion left his side. It wasn't until Petrella stepped forward that he noticed her more. She *looked* human, even solid, it was just that she gave no body heat. Not even a flicker.

Florian's voice shook, finally asking what he'd been wondering at the doorway. 'Are you a ghost?'

She laughed, the sound hollow. 'Of course not, you dolt. I'm an air nymph.'

He took a step back, and she frowned. He hadn't meant to, it was a reflex, like his running from the wood nymphs when they attacked them so fervently in the forest. 'I—'

'Humans are all the same.' There was a flatness to her voice, something empty and dull as she peered at the others. 'The chained books are off limits, but you should find what you need here. It only needed a push.'

'A push? All I did was sneeze.'

'Yes,' she replied, 'but you entered.'

He looked at her quizzically and she sighed. 'Look around you. When was the last time I had a visitor? I don't think anybody has been here since the King and Queen decided to visit before their last dinner.'

Florian blanched. 'They visited you the night they died?'

'They seemed odd at the time, whispering of dreams and prophecies. I shooed them away, but they wouldn't have it, barging in here with piles of scrolls and the like.'

Odion tilted his head. 'Did they say anything?'

She frowned, dredging up the memory like a boot on a fishing line. 'They said something about them needing to be hidden, to be found when one finally opens the door.' She looked at him then, expectant.

'What?' he asked.

She raised her eyebrow before opening her arm out the room. 'You opened the door.'

'Anyone could have opened the door.'

'But they didn't.'

'They could have.'

She groaned, her shimmering form blinking in and out. 'I'm getting tired of you now. I'm leaving.'

'Wait,' Florian panted, quickly eyeing Odion and Snow before he turned. 'Why help us now when before you seemed so—'

'Bitter?' she laughed. 'I am a protector. I cannot open the door for you, I can only guide you once you pass the threshold. You've passed it.'

'What does that mean exactly?' Odion asked.

She eyed him coolly. 'It means you have a new path.'

'Where are they?' Florian asked. 'The scrolls they left?'

She rolled her eyes but did as he bid, pointing towards the discarded piano.

'Thank you.' he replied.

But she had already vanished.

XXXVII
The Prince of Teal Cove

Cyrene may have not been allowed to leave the keep, but the Queen mentioned nothing about having visitors.

She waited by the back gate near the garden, the garden's green seaweed spreading over rock like the hair from a maiden. It floated with the current, swirling against the ongoing storm above.

The moon offered no light from behind the black clouds and the flashing thunder above was the only reprieve from its violent darkness. It was the kind of weather that made Cyrene appreciate the cold stillness of her kingdom.

Here in the royal gardens, it was another world. One full of luminescent light from the blooming flowers. They swayed too, but more like ballerinas floating along with their partners. It always amused Cyrene, the amount of colour the flowers shed. It was just about the only colour the queen allowed and it swallowed her whole backyard.

Cyrene used to love it here as a child, frolicking amongst the gardens as if she lived in a palace made of rainbows. She'd envisioned it to be the merkingdom. Though she'd never seen Teal Cove, she'd dreamt about it enough times to create her own vision of the place. The coral and shells made of glittering gold. The sea glass towers and endless music.

The garden was the closest she had ever come to it, except for when she'd had Pearl. The mermaid who had stolen her breath and heart. Who had told her stories about the plays and concerts. The games and balls.

It had all sounded like a dream.

Cyrene used to envision going there, playing pretend with Pearl until she had been beckoned home, where her mother shared another lesson and yelled at her. During that time, it wasn't until Cyrene came home that she'd felt alone. Lost amongst the black rock and quiet halls.

Getting her own place had been her first step to happiness, and even that had taken a lot of convincing. She'd had to deal with the politics, attend her mother's events, and play the good daughter.

The royal life hadn't suited her, but she played the game all the same. For the small freedom it promised.

Shadows crawled along the wall as the flowers danced, interrupted by a sharp hiss to Cyrene's right. She turned as Eve knocked into Edmar, the sea nymph scowling at the touch as they snuck towards the gate.

'Could you two be any louder?' Cyrene chastised.

'She swims like a guppy,' Edmar grumbled.

Eve hissed. 'Just because you're useless with directions and I don't have magic eyes that adjust in the dark, doesn't mean you can pin blame on the human.'

'I can blame you all I want.'

Cyrene frowned. 'The scales I gave you should have helped with your vision.'

'They did,' Eve said, 'but the more I swim, the worse my vision gets. As if everything is getting foggier.'

The scales were wearing off quicker than Cyrene intended, giving them short windows of time. Eve might hate the transition, but with their new timeline, the Seeker had little choice. 'I'll have to give you more before you leave. The transformation might be wearing off.'

She ignored Eve's groans as she locked the gates behind them. Cyrene ushered them towards a hidden entrance bathed in coral and seagrass, and checked the perimeter for guards.

The glowing fish swam slowly down the halls of the castle as Cyrene pulled Eve and Edmar along through the shadows. Luckily for them, the Queen liked her beauty sleep. It had been a blessing for Cyrene when she was younger, prone to sneaking out instead of sneaking people in.

How times have changed.

'Do you know where we're going?' Eve asked, hugging herself tightly in the cold current.

Cyrene's brows furrowed at the human changes in her. If they weren't careful, Eve wouldn't just be cold and blind. She would be suffocated and squashed, falling to the pressure of the depths. Drowning was a slow, cold death and it was not something Cyrene wanted to happen to her friend.

As they veered a corner, another craggy tunnel appeared, black moss covering most of the surface. The moss looked like little hairs, as if the three of them swam beside a great bear.

Eve reached out to touch but Cyrene swatted her hand away. 'That's poisonous fungi, and yes, I do know where we are going.'

'Do you want to share?' Edmar asked, eyeing the fungi with contempt.

'Not with you.'

Cyrene shoved a blooming flower into his palm. It glowed a soft pink, the light creeping over his scowl like a wraith luring wanderers into the dark.

'Let me guess,' he drawled. 'I'm to stay here and keep watch like a trained seahorse.'

Cyrene gave him a smug smile and patted him on the shoulder. 'What a good little horsey you are. You already know what to do.'

'This is ridiculous,' he said. 'I came to help, not to be left behind like some accessory you forgot.'

'At least you know your place,' Eve replied.

'Why can the human stay?' Edmar argued, ignoring her. 'She can hardly swim.'

'Should I even pretend to answer that?' Cyrene asked. 'Or are you going to use some common sense?'

'Ugh,' he sighed. 'Why? Because she's the Seeker she's so important? It's a load of sea mucus.'

'If it's a load of mucus then why are you here?'

'I told you.'

'You've told me a lot of things and most of them have been lies. You'll stay here, or you'll wait outside.'

He gave Eve a look of contempt before placing the flower behind his ear. 'Fine, but I'll not sit amongst the fungi.'

'The hall it is.'

'Whatever,' he replied, before swimming away.

As Cyrene pulled Eve forward, careful of the black moss, Eve whispered, 'I'm assuming he doesn't need to stand guard?'

'No, he doesn't. This area of the castle is almost empty, but there's always a chance. Plus, I don't want him with us when we speak to Mizu. He might find his odds are better elsewhere.'

'He betrayed you that badly?'

'He really did.'

Eve moved closer and her fingers dug into her arm as Cyrene pulled her along. Her breaths were harsher the deeper they swam and her strange, coloured skin produced bumps along her arms.

Eve wasn't the first human to see the dungeons of Nysa, but she was the first to openly swim in them whilst free. Others had seen a darker fate, one where the Queen toyed with them and left them to drown. Shrivelling in the cold with bloated bodies and a sheen of ghastly blue.

'Why do we need to speak with Mizu anyway?' Eve whispered.

'His timing is too coincidental. Plus, you'll be stuck with us during the trials, so if he really is here for an alliance, I want to suss him out first, see if he can help.'

'You'd trust a mermaid?'

'I trusted his sister,' she said, quietly.

Pearl.

'Can you promise me something?' Cyrene asked as the tunnels narrowed, the water getting cooler. 'Can you make sure you don't pull that heroic fairy shit. Drowning is the easiest death down here, and I'm worried about your bones getting crushed. Just tell me when you need more scales, okay?'

Eve bit her lip before she nodded. She looked uncomfortable but at least she was alive. Even Cyrene felt the pressure down here, the heavy weight of the water pulling her down. It was why the prisons were here. Buried deep beneath the cold rock, away from the light. A mermaid would have struggled breathing down here, their energy sapped from merely staying alive.

Another tactic of the Queen. A weak prince was less likely to win.

A cough echoed from ahead and Cyrene slowed down. She pulled out a pouch and pale pink light pierced the darkness.

'Use these as a light,' she said, handing Eve a couple of the flowers. Eve clutched them like a lifeline as Cyrene lifted out the rest from her pouch. When she veered near an alcove, she recognised Mizu's shining tail, the large fins barely fitting behind the bars.

The prince sat against the wall, his eyes bright despite his heavy breathing. His shoulders sagged, his tail squashed as it pressed against him. His chest was broad, the milky skin still beautiful despite this miserable place.

'Prince Mizu?' Eve asked.

Cyrene pulled her back, her eyes watchful as the Prince's hands twitched. Even locked away he was a threat. Years of training honed into every instinct. He ignored Eve, his eyes boring into Cyrene with an intensity that made her want to squirm.

'I thought it was only your mother with a fear for Merpeople.' he said lazily, the accent coming off his tongue in strange lilts. 'I expected more from the princess who loved my *Lokei*.'

'I do not fear you,' Cyrene said.

'Then why do you tremble?' he asked.

Her jaw clenched but she answered honestly. 'I tremble because you look like her.'

He gave her a sad smile, his grief somehow heavier down here amongst the shadowed walls.

'Who have you brought to see me?' he asked.

Eve gave Cyrene a glance and waved her forward. 'This is Eve. The Seeker. She's a land dweller.'

'A human alive in the Kingdom of Nysa is rare. Does the Queen not usually collect their corpses?' His eyes glittered at the question, curious and lovely.

Cyrene tried to deny it, but something about him was alluring. Mysterious.

Betrothed, her mind echoed.

Her nostrils flared at the thought, despair creeping along her skin with the current. He was so like his sister. The smooth jawline, the sheen of his skin. His eyes were different, though. Depthless, like a night without stars.

'She does collect corpses,' Cyrene answered. 'But I swayed her.'

'Just as I did?' he asked.

'Not quite.'

A ripple shuddered through the walls and they froze.

Eve grabbed Cyrene's wrist. 'Is it just me or was that ripple stronger than before.'

'The Evil Queen grows closer to the Morei,' Mizu murmured.

Cyrene whirled on him, but it was Eve who asked, 'Are you truly here for an alliance, or is this some ploy to get the mirror back from the nymphs? That's what this war between your people is about, right?'

Mizu watched her for a moment before replying. 'The

mermaids were always the true keepers. The ones to share the burden.'

'That is a lie,' Cyrene hissed. 'We were also given the mirror to protect.'

Mizu nodded. 'Yes, but only until the next black moon. You have kept it for many more moons than agreed.'

That was true. The last changeover was to happen when Cyrene had been a child, but her mother had refused. Stating the mirror was better here. Safer amongst the treasures she hoarded. Being so young, Cyrene had believed her.

'Why come for the mirror now, then?' Cyrene asked. 'Why not years ago, when it was owed? Myrenna has been growing in power for years.'

'Because the ripple has come,' he said, matter of factly. 'Because my father feels it and he knows it is time.'

'Time for what?' Eve asked.

'Time for the Morei to go to the one who will claim it before the Evil Queen can. The land is not safe and neither are we.'

'You will die tomorrow,' Cyrene said. 'You understand that, right? My mother has no intention of giving you that mirror.'

He gave her a sad smile. 'It was always a risk.'

Eve backed away. 'And you accept that?'

'I accept what the prophecy foretells and what the Seer told my father. Even if we managed an alliance, the Sea Queen is powerful. I'm here for more than a marriage proposal. I'm here to ensure the prophecy is fulfilled.'

'What did the Seer tell your father?' Cyrene asked.

He gripped the bars and leaned in. 'She told my father that he would have no heir.'

'But ... he had two of you,' Cyrene stammered. 'You and Pearl.'

'Yet, one of us is already dead and the other is close to it.'

'Will you not fight it?' Eve asked. 'Will you not at least try?'

'Of course, I will try, *nagin*, I am a warrior. I will fight.' Mizu shuffled, making himself comfortable again. 'I hope for a better future. One where all kingdoms may live side by side. Whether that is by life or death. I accept.'

'You accept death?'

'I accept fate.'

'Fate is a load of *fairy shit!*' Eve spat.

'For a *nagin*,' he said, 'you have a lot of spirit.'

'Why?' Eve asked. 'Why blindly follow?'

'Because I believe in the pre-told story. I believe in the author who wrote our fate and designed us. I believe in the destiny that defines us and the history it'll create.'

'You're a fool,' Cyrene seethed.

'I'm many things,' he replied, 'but I'm no fool. I won't give up. I'll face your trial and I'll prevail.'

'Only to marry me,' Cyrene said. 'What a bleak ending.'

'Yet, it was a gift Pearl would have gladly accepted.'

Cyrene swallowed at his words, trying to squash down the ache in her chest. She licked her lips before voicing their true reason for coming here.

Edmar rounded the corner and frowned at the sight of them. 'The light guards are coming.'

His eyes narrowed on the prince, but the mermaid only smiled back. *'Sesik null moreil tukail.'*

Cyrene pulled Eve. 'It's time to go.'

'But we didn't get what we came for. We have no idea where the trial will be and we need to know if he'll give us the mi—'

Cyrene didn't let her finish as she pulled Eve along, following Edmar out of the tunnels and back to the gardens. The guards floated in formation as the three of them passed like shadows, only stopping at the castle's border.

When they broke off, Cyrene closing the gate between them, Eve paused, pressing her hands against the bars. She looked so frail, so weak amongst the depths of the water that Cyrene wondered if she'd made a mistake bringing her here.

But the Seeker's eyes were determined as she leaned in, her face coated in fury as she asked, 'Why didn't you ask for his help?'

'Because he can't help us,' Cyrene said. 'He'll die tomorrow.'

Eve gave her a look of scepticism but thankfully changed topic. 'What did he say back there?'

Cyrene shook her head, the wonder of Pearl's likeness still floating through her mind. She gave Edmar a wary glance as she said, 'He called Edmar the "Man of two faces."'

XXXVIII
The Fear and the Feat

Malak tapped his foot against the stone floor, watching the crow from behind the enchanted bars.

'Where did he come from?' Pip asked.

'He's from the Silver City,' Malak said. 'I saw him crash from the sky as a crow, and there's few who have that particular talent.'

Laurie, Malak, Adanna, and Pip stood in the dungeons, observing the intruder inside the cell. His hands were bound behind his back, his body sprawled on the ground. So far, he remained unconscious.

Adanna frowned in the low lamplight, her hair loose around her shoulders. She wore a crimson dress, the shorter sleeves doing little to cover her arms. Malak noted the scars peppering her skin, some raw and others long faded to silver. He tried to avert his gaze as she said, 'He's Myrenna's general.'

'Why is he not on the border leading her army?' Pip asked.

'And here of all places,' Laurie said to nobody in particular. She stood behind Adanna like a second shadow.

'Do you think he defected?' Malak asked, his words sharper than usual.

When the crow had descended, Malak hadn't time to think, not until the stranger had uttered, *I was looking for a beauty. Not a beast.*

Laurie had been the one to find Malak dragging the unconscious man through the gardens, before she'd rushed to tell the others. The only ones she'd been able to find had been Pip and Adanna. Nobody had seen the two princes, or Snow.

'The bars are enchanted,' Adanna said.

'Good,' Pip said. 'Best to leave him to rot.'

Malak only stared at the man. The scar that ran down his skull was jagged, a battle wound no doubt. His skin was covered in bruises, certain areas already swelling from whatever had happened to him.

This was Snow's captor. The man who had threatened her. Tortured her.

A growl escaped his throat.

'The troll awakens,' Pip muttered.

Malak paced, hoping to ease the building tension in his chest.

It had been a shock, finding a crow lost amongst the sky.

He'd seen them at the castle, floating in groups in succinct and even lines. An aerial army. Eyes that roamed the realm. But they'd always been distant, a hazy dream of some sort. The closest they'd been was from glimpses in the sky when they'd travelled to Perridorm, the birds hiding in whatever brush they could.

This man was the General. The man who attacked these very borders. But he hadn't come with his army, he had come alone, his wing broken, his body beaten.

Malak stopped pacing. 'We should kill him.'

He meant it.

He would.

He should.

But the more he thought about it, the more he hated himself for it. The words felt foul in his mouth.

'If I were in your position, I would have killed me on sight,' a deep voice said.

Malak whirled, finding the shifter's eyes wide open. He watched them all with a hateful smirk, his eyes glinting.

'Why are you here?' Adanna asked, her chair by the back door. She'd insisted on standing for this encounter, to look down at the intruder who invaded her land even though Laurie scowled at the decision.

Malak commended her for it.

The man looked up at her. 'The Undead Princess,' he mused. 'It's a pleasure to finally meet you.'

She raised her eyebrow.

'Are you a spy?' Malak asked. 'Why are you here?'

The prisoner ignored him, staring at the Princess, who did not back down.

Adanna lifted her chin. 'Explain what you're doing in my kingdom.'

'Shouldn't you know?' he asked, grinning wide. 'You saw me coming, after all.'

Adanna did not waver. 'I see many things.'

'Let me guess, I was mostly shadow?'

Laurie stepped forward and squeezed the Princess's shoulder in quiet reassurance. Her voice was a whisper as she asked, 'What do we do with him?'

'If you're not going to kill him, then we'll see what he has to say,' Pip said, taking a puff of his pipe. 'For the Queen's general to come sailing into enemy territory alone, it must be dire ... or suicidal. Much of a muchness these days.'

The elf was right: they had to do something.

'It's death or interrogation,' Malak said to the crow. His club hung by his side, the spikes a whisper away from the bars to his cage.

Trik's gaze skimmed over the group, landing on Adanna the longest before he finally looked up at Malak. 'I'm here to bargain.'

Malak opened his mouth, but Adanna spoke first. 'You have nothing to bargain with. We are about to win.'

He smiled. 'Are you sure about that?'

'She is,' Pip said. 'You wouldn't be here otherwise.'

The General flicked his eyes to Pip, before he turned back to Adanna and assessed her. Somehow his stare seared beneath the robe she wore as if he could see all her secrets, her scars, and count them.

Malak noticed Adanna's flinch, though it was small.

But so did the man. 'Wouldn't I?'

'Enough,' Malak said, smacking his club into the bars, the metal echoing.

'I have information,' the General said. '*Loads* of it. You think your little army can save you? It can't. I know what is happening east of the border. I know what the Queen has planned, and only I know how to save your *pitiful* kingdom.'

'You risk a lot coming here,' Adanna said.

'That's something we can agree on.'

Malak shifted on his feet. The crow's arrival itched at him like a storm waiting to break. This wasn't chance.

'Who are you?' he asked, the words low and rough.

'I'm a—'

'None of that crow fairy shit. Your name.'

He frowned. 'Trik. My name is Trik.'

'How fitting,' Pip commented.

'Why are you here?' Malak prodded.

'I'm a deserter,' Trik replied, 'like you said. I'll either die by Myrenna's hand or Perridorm's sword. I'm here because I have no other option, *troll*.' He said troll with disdain, as if it tasted foul in his mouth.

Malak had heard the tone before, whispered amongst villagers and creatures alike. But tonight, he held little patience and a growl ripped through his throat. A touch held him back, the petite hand strong despite its size. Adanna gave him a comforting smile.

He swallowed.

You are not a beast. Control yourself.

He stepped back. He was not a killer, he was far from it, but when it came to Snow, something always unleashed within him.

The smell of tobacco lingered in the air, the smoke rising with Pip's exhale. 'What is it you seek in return for this information?' the elf asked. 'Only an idiot would come to their enemy's doors. Especially when you've threatened the lives of their royalty.'

'Which one?' Trik asked. 'I have threatened two royals and

lived. Though, one hasn't claimed her title yet,' he mused. 'She has debts to pay first.'

Malak froze. 'What do you mean?' he growled lowly.

The corner of Trik's mouth raised, his watchful, hateful eyes falling on Adanna. 'You are already a queen. You just won't do the formalities.' He shrugged, lounging against the wall. 'Myrenna seeks to hurt me and Snow. Though Snow would be a larger target. The ripe apple, ready for a juicy bite.'

Malak smashed his club into the metal bars. Trik only laughed.

'I will tell you what I know,' Trik said. 'For a price.'

'And what, exactly,' Malak hissed, 'is that price?'

Malak knew the answer before it came. Smothering and vengeful and cold. It cut through him like the steel of a blade, piercing right into the depths of his heart.

Before Malak could blink, Trik grinned again.

'The price is Snow.'

Myrenna and the creature jumped through pockets of darkness. Each one reappearing to attack the other with claws and fangs and teeth.

The mirror had been the first thing Myrenna had seen when she'd entered. Her eyes latching onto it with the hunger of a starved child.

It was hers.

It had always been hers.

She'd held her fears at bay for years. There was nothing the mirror could do that its sibling hadn't already wrought.

Black blood leaked from the banshee's wrinkly skin. An unearthly scream rang through the space, as if it had come from the cauldron itself.

Myrenna screamed in triumph as she portal-jumped again, appearing on the other side of the mirror. The eyes of the skull watched her with absent curiosity.

If the bone mirror wanted fear, she'd show them fear. She'd drown them in terror until they choked on her. Her whole life, she'd never asked for anything – she *took* it.

With a cackle, she reappeared before the mirror. Her reflection twisted and *wicked*. She saw the beast behind her, its wild white hair shaped like a lion's mane.

Myrenna flashed the monster a wicked smile and beckoned it forward.

The beast pounced straight for her.

Myrenna stepped back into a pocket of night as the beast rushed forward. Straight into the mirror's glass surface.

Myrenna was back in a blink, her hand outstretched as she chanted a spell. The mirror shimmered and the creature roared, clawing against the glass on the other side. Its limbs were warped, its teeth sharp and rotten. Gone was the pathetic copy it had made of Myrenna, back to its former self, resembling a ghoul or half-dead woman.

Myrenna's power churned, bending and fading with the spell. The old heart she'd eaten wasn't enough to hold her, and with each of the beast's attacks, her power waned.

She eyed the skull, silent yet watchful.

'Dread!' she shrieked.

The shifter made it to her side, his body hunched and worn.

'Lift me,' she ordered.

His arms shook as he grabbed her hips, lifting her towards the top of the mirror, the beast screaming behind the glass.

Dread lifted her until she was face-to-face with the skull.

'You cannot contain fear,' the skull's clattering teeth said. 'It will always claw its way out.'

Words. It was always words with these things. Promises and smoke and whispers.

She'd had enough.

Raising her hands, she stared into its depthless eyes. 'Not if I claw into it first.'

She latched her hands around the skull and yanked, hard. She focused on every inch of power she had left into that pull. Her nails bit into bone and the skull wailed at the touch. Bone cracked, teeth fell.

Myrenna released a howl and the skull shattered.

The mirror's reflection flickered and the beast inside thrashed, pushing against her magic like a tsunami. Her magic wavered, shimmering into nothing for a fraction of a second before it roared again.

The beast screamed. Stars floated across her vision, but all she had to do was hold on for one. More. Second.

A *crack* rang throughout the darkness, followed by a scream. Then the bone frame fractured, the glow dimming to almost nothing.

Myrenna's heel scraped stone as Dread eased her down and she staggered.

'I own you,' she whispered, fingers splaying across the mirror's surface. 'Come to me.'

The beast whimpered. A tremble ran through its limbs as it inched closer. Myrenna lowered to one knee. 'I'm taking you,' she said. 'You're mine.'

Its eyes were made of shadow and fury. Yet it pressed its head to the glass, mirroring her.

And the mirror gave in. It sighed, darkly, and belonged to her.

Myrenna's lips curled into a smirk—

Then the world shattered.

The explosion hit like thunder breaking through bone. She slammed into Dread, his arms folding around her as rock and air roared above them.

The beast screamed.

Stone rained in sheets, sealing the entrance.

Locking them both in.

XXXIX

The Trial and the Treasure Trove

'It looks like Yulemas, not an execution,' Eve muttered under her breath.

She followed Edmar towards the castle, taking in the mayhem and excitement of Nysa.

Creatures whispered from one end of the kingdom to the other. Flowers bloomed from every window, and nymphs excitedly made their bets. Children had ribbons in their hair, and adults carried large swaths of food in preparation for the festivities.

The Queen's announcement didn't need a grand speech; word had spread fast enough, even reaching the farthest dunes lining the border of the three kingdoms.

As they approached the main town, guards lined the walkway, their breastplates shining against the bright sun flickering through the water. The storm from the night before was all but forgotten.

'Before you ask,' Edmar started. 'It's for the Merking. He's due to arrive today.'

Eve wanted to slap that arrogant face of his as he puffed out his chest.

She wondered how the king felt, having his son put on display like this. Or how Mizu's beautiful tail had been cramped beneath the dungeons.

Man of two faces.

Edmar greeted courtiers, smiling as he moved slowly through the ever-growing crowd.

Today would end in one of two ways: Mizu's marriage, or his death. And if the Queen had her way, it would be the latter.

Eve twisted her fingers around the outfit she'd been given. The dress hadn't been her choice, or Edmar's. It was a sickly green, layered with netting that snagged on anything drifting past. Barnacles clung to the sides, stubborn and sharp. Around her hips, the fabric pinched, each kick catching in the too-long skirts. The top stretched to her neck, itching like sandpaper against her skin.

'I don't suppose you have any better dresses available?' she'd asked that morning, trying to ignore the pain from the new scales she'd just applied. Edmar hadn't been happy about providing them, but with Cyrene's insistence he'd obliged, leaving both of them in a foul mood.

He'd been insufferable, if not a little rude. Without Cyrene to stop the bickering, they'd been at each other's throats. She supposed when all this was done, maybe she could stab him.

Prick the prick.

'This was given to you by the Queen,' he'd said. 'You're lucky it doesn't involve chains.'

She supposed that had been a benefit, but it didn't relieve the spark of annoyance at the sea nymph's contempt for humans. Either way, she'd been left with little choice.

Again.

They entered the outer gates of the castle, the crowd teeming with sea nymphs. It grew thicker with each passing minute, the chatter alive and vibrant. She tried not to shrink under the nymphs' glares, at the way some stared in pity and others in hunger.

'How am I supposed to sneak away when I'm on display like *this*?' Eve asked.

He waved away her concerns. 'Once the trials start, you'll be quickly forgotten.' He smiled as a female nymph covered in shells passed them by. 'A trial like this hasn't happened in a long time. The nymphs are itching for it. Just look around you.'

Groups whispered with nervous energy, their drinks never empty.

Eve scratched under her armpit. Not only was this dress hideous, the netting and slimy material itched her skin. The fabric didn't give much room to move, and the skirt was ridiculously long. Probably to hide her very human feet.

Edmar didn't comment as they merged into the crowd bustling into the halls. She recognised some courtiers from the throne room. Like Edmar, they all wore their finery. Except their finery was made of metal, outlining their bodies with a thin layer of armour. Edmar had specifically matched his to the beads in his hair, lining his eyes with a shade of kohl.

He did look striking, but Eve found herself too distracted to care.

They were to attend a lunch to welcome the Merking before heading towards the arena. Wherever that was. Edmar had advised that there were a few arenas dotted along the seafloor pending what type of trial it was. Some were designed to end conflicts when two families were in a disagreement. Some arenas were purely for skill sets or demonstrating certain talents, such as dance, or weaponry.

Edmar had also mentioned some were built within darker chasms, usually near a sea monster of some kind. He'd said those were rare, the risk to the people too great for the Queen to consider.

'But for a prince,' he'd said, 'the Queen may risk it.'

Eve shuddered at the thought, Edmar having gone on a ramble. 'There are far more sea monsters than you think. Most of them dwell near The Channel and Black Cove further west. But there's a few here. Mainly the Drakon, the Crimson, and the Jormungandr. We have smaller ones, of course, but those three are the terrifying ones.'

'The others aren't terrifying?'

He'd laughed. 'Of course they are. They are smaller, though, younger. The Jormungandr was always my favourite as a child. It's a giant serpent with teeth sharper than ours. It swallows kingdoms whole and digs its way under the seafloor. When I got in trouble as a child, my father would tell me the serpent would come and eat me. I used to dream about having to live inside this giant creature's stomach.'

'That's absurd.'

'Is it?' he asked. 'Many strange things are created in a land of magic. The Crimson, for example, was created by the same makers as you and I. The Grimms. There's a story that it sleeps *within the depths of the chasms, made of claws and several mouths.'*

Eve moved closer to Edmar, itching to escape the touches of those around her. 'Edmar?' she asked. 'Tell me about the Drakon.'

'The Drakon is a sea dragon that has existed since the beginning of our kind. He's always lived in the trove. It's a good story actually. The royal family made a deal with him when arriving here. Supposedly, the creature had no home. So, they gave him the trove in exchange for protecting the treasures and being left alone. The only people allowed in the trove without harm are the royal family, each gifted with a special ring. The Queen wears hers in her hair.'

Bodies bumped against them as they made their way through the crowd.

'Does Cyrene have one?' Eve asked.

Edmar shook his head. 'Only one is left, and the Queen took it when the King passed away. Cyrene will inherit it one day, if the Queen ever concedes the throne.'

'So, the ring keeps the beast away. Not blood?'

Edmar frowned. 'I'd never thought that much into it, but it would make sense.'

Horns blared and the crowd silenced. Edmar grabbed Eve's hand and dragged her closer to the throne.

Cyrene stood on the podium, her bright red hair braided with pearls. She wore a dress of emerald, cinching in her waist to bring out her curves.

She looked incredible.

Eve looked like a shipwreck.

The crowd parted as the Merking entered, holding a trident the size of two men. It was made of gold, diamonds etched into its surface with precision. Guards followed him in succinct lines, each with smaller tridents. But where Nysa was renowned for dark tones, this group was covered in beams of pale sunlight, as if the gems carried them in a moving rainbow.

The Queen welcomed them, her smirk one of dark promise as Mizu was brought forward. Eve didn't know why she expected chains, or a defeated prince, but she was pleasantly surprised when Mizu exited from behind the throne and embraced his father. The grip from the King was strong. His trident glowed as the royals whispered their welcomes.

As if some unspoken command had been announced, the crowd began to chatter again, soaking up their drinks and eating the banquet. The King sat in a chair situated by the Queen, who spoke to him in hushed tones.

Edmar left her by the platter of raw fish, vanishing into another cluster of courtiers. Eve picked at the offerings, choosing prawns over the slimier things she knew would turn her stomach.

She was half-tuned out, letting the noise blur around her, when a shift in the water behind made her fingers twitch toward her knife.

A merman drifted into view, his fin brushing the hem of her dress as he plucked a prawn straight from her plate.

'I haven't seen your kind in the depths for a very long time,' he said, voice smooth as sea glass.

'So people keep saying,' Eve muttered, resisting the urge to slap his hand away.

His eyes shimmered gold. Iridescent scales caught the lanternlight across his shoulders and collarbone. The chest piece he wore clung like kelp silk, armour light and ceremonial. She recognised him now. He had been one of the King's guards when Mizu had been brought before the Queen, flanked by shadowed fins and silent glances.

Still, he smiled at her. And unlike the others, it wasn't with arrogance or awe. It was quiet. Curious. Almost kind.

'I expected sea nymphs and blood,' he said, throwing the last prawn in his mouth. 'I'm intrigued by a human in these parts.'

'Yet, you're not surprised,' Eve said, giving him a glare as he reached for another prawn.

'Could you not?' she seethed, pulling her plate away. 'This is all I can eat, and you're stuffing them in your face.'

'Apologies, Seeker.'

Eve looked up at him and let the poison seep into her tone as she said, 'Silly bunch of gossips.'

He chuckled. 'Nysa is not known for its subtlety.'

'Is Teal Cove?'

He was silent a moment. 'No. The water likes to transport noise, and the sea creatures use it to their advantage.'

She laughed at that, catching Cyrene's warning gaze from her post. Eve scowled back.

The guard leaned in. 'I'm Akio,' he said by way of greeting.

'Eveline.'

As the music halted, the Queen raised her glass and seized the attention in the room. 'We welcome Teal Cove to Nysa. May they be swept by the currents and honour our treasures.'

'May they honour our treasures,' the crowd repeated.

Akio bowed low before swimming away, taking his place by the Prince. Mizu gave him a warm smile as he approached, clapping him on the back in welcome.

Most of the next hour was coated in pretty speeches about the honour of the trials, outlining the victors of the past, and speaking of previous deaths in gruesome detail.

Eve's muscles hurt, her body fighting against the water without fins. Whilst others floated in one place, she was swept several pixies to the side with every current. Edmar gripped her elbow as she began to float away again, his hand solid on her arm. His smile was plastered on, his eyes alight as the Queen continued her speech. Everyone clapped on cue, cheering in unison as the Queen smiled.

Only the Merking remained unfazed, his grimace permanently etched on his face. Eve supposed she matched him, her boredom evident in the roll of her eyes at every longwinded comment about Nysa's history.

'The trial will start in three hours,' the Queen mused, and the crowd applauded again. 'Today we may see our kingdoms united. A feat not done by any ancestor before us.'

'Or he'll die,' Eve muttered.

'Today we mark history. We mark a moment in time that will be ingrained in our futures. A prince against a beast.'

At that, Eve's head perked up.

'The trial will be at sunset when the water glows gold. When the beast is at its hungriest. For the heart of a princess is not easily won.'

Eve sighed. 'She likes to talk.'

'*Shut it,*' Edmar growled.

'For the trial, I give you Prince Mizu'—she paused—'and the Drakon.'

The crowd gasped.

Edmar gripped Eve's arm to the point of pain.

The Drakon.

Cyrene stared at her mother, her mouth ajar as the Queen sipped her wine. The Merking remained stoic, silent and stern. And Mizu, he stood taller, raising himself like a true warrior.

As the crowd bickered, Eve turned to Edmar. 'Does this mean ...?'

'Yes.'

'But we can't. The Drakon guards the royal treasure. That's where the mirror is. Where the beast lives.'

'I'm well aware, Seeker,' Edmar ground out.

Eve shook her head, biting her bottom lip as she leaned in. 'Our plan's doomed,' she whispered. 'There's no way we'll find the mirror with the whole kingdom watching.'

He breathed out through his nostrils, eyes flicking to Cyrene before settling back on her. 'It's fine,' he said, though the words sounded more like he was trying to convince himself than her.

He tugged her toward the back wall, away from the crowd, just as a guard's gaze landed on them with suspicion. Eve's stomach churned, nausea curling like a wave.

'We'll have to move once the trial's over,' Edmar murmured. 'If he dies, they'll feast through the night. If he lives, that's one less beast you'll have to face when the celebrations start. Either way, there's still a chance.'

He lowered his voice further. 'Let me pull some strings. I'll get you out after the trial. I have connections. Cyrene can keep the Queen distracted.'

Something inside Eve twisted. 'We have no other choice, do we?'

'I'll make the rounds now. We'll only have a short amount of time.'

Eve hugged herself as Edmar swam away, trying to bite back the tide of cold fear covering her bones.

'It's fine,' she said to herself. 'Everything is fine.'

She wouldn't only need to sneak away. She'd have to find the mirror amongst the hordes of treasure, and face one of the meanest sea creatures ever to grace this land.

I can adapt. It's fine.

But no matter how many times she told herself it was fine,

it wasn't. Fear coiled within her, tight and painful. Her heart clenched, the claws of the cavern whispering along her memory. She longed for the cottage. For the warm hearth and the imps that fed her. She longed for the grotto. For her father's touch. For Dante's calm voice to whisper some of his wisdom. For Hansel's brave words.

She stood on the precipice of a cliff, her body dangling over its edge, and she hugged herself tighter.

It's fine.

Because even if it wasn't, she would have to go through with the plan anyway. Because she had no other choice. Because she'd never had one to begin with.

XL

The Map of Memories

Princess Snowfall Anabella Aurelia Whitmore ignored the bossy librarian as she ventured around Petrella's rooms. It was full of knick-knacks. Peculiar things like snake hides, warped animals, instruments, and oddities. The objects lingered along every surface, and on top of that there were books and books and more books.

Snow stepped over another stack and pushed aside a bear's head, revealing a makeshift cot. It looked like nobody had lived in this room in over a century. Everything brought up dust and even she wanted to sneeze. Though she wouldn't dare admit it to Florian.

She eyed the two princes by the door. One dark and one light. They stood closely, Odion watching the door as his hand twitched by his side. In her ignorance she might have assumed it twitched for his knife, but she saw it shuddered towards Florian's hand, an inch separating them.

Ugh.

The voices in her mind echoed their agreement. *They don't deserve it.*

Perhaps it was jealousy, two people finding a magnetism she'd only felt for Hansel.

She was a woman now, her beauty unsurpassable, even with the shorter hair. She was a lotus flower, delicate and alive, full of promise and sweet smells. It was why Myrenna wanted her heart. She was pure. *Perfect.*

Yet, even with those traits, love had a funny way of staining things. It was a strange thing after all.

Malak's love had woken her from the Queen's curse. Had been her lifeline when she could have been only half alive and left forgotten. She felt bad sometimes about not reciprocating it in the same way, but for her, it had always been Hansel.

It always would be.

When the creepy librarian left, the two princes looked closely at a piano in the corner.

'What is it?' she asked. Odion looked shaken, his usually steady nature slightly unhinged. She pushed her way over and dusted herself off before she placed her hands on her hips. 'Come on. Share the details.'

It was Florian who responded. 'Petrella said there are scrolls in the piano. Things left from the King and Queen.'

'As in, your parents?' she asked Odion.

He nodded, his face a little pale.

'Did you want to wait and find Adanna?' Florian asked softly. 'She might want to—'

'No,' the Prince ground out.

Florian looked stricken, but Snow didn't care. She was more concerned about *what* the old rulers had left. She eyed the piano. She wanted those scrolls.

She could already taste the magic. Could feel the blade sinking into Myrenna's skin. Her stepmother had always underestimated her, and Snow looked forward to wiping the smug smile off her face.

Myrenna's life was Snow's to take. *Only* Snow's.

After that, she would marry Hansel and make him her king consort. Her own personal hero to warm her bed and kill her enemies. Then, and only then, would she find her happily ever after. A thrill raced through her at the thought.

The piano's lid creaked stiffly as she heaved it open. With the princes' help, it came free, the hinges snapping apart after long neglect. Inside, the hidden scrolls lay sealed like a treasure chest, and she almost giggled with delight. It had been ages since she'd felt this close to success. Her promise. Her future. Her throne.

Odion grunted beside her, shifting away from Florian's shadow, but the prince paid him no mind.

Or he's just dim.

Petty little romances didn't matter now. Only the scrolls did. Somewhere in here lay the secret to unlocking those chains. Her hands dived in and cracked open a box, snatching a journal. She unravelled the string holding it closed, the edges faded and aged. The cover cracked open stiffly, revealing cursive writing.

Odion was more careful, dusting them off with a soft reverence. Snow rolled her eyes and stepped away.

For hours, they trailed through scrolls and journals, each one holding nothing more than the history of Perridorm's line. Some rubbish about a little lord and his gifts and how the wooden sword worked with his bloodline only. Odion looked focused, Florian eyeing them both at intervals as they sat on the floor. Her frustration grew with each passing page, impatience prickling under her skin to a near rage. She threw the journal.

'This is useless,' she snapped.

Florian cut through her frustration with a bright grin. 'I've found something!'

Snow sprang to her feet, Odion quick behind, as the prince spread out a large parchment. The castle's layout sprawled before them, lines traced in quill with smooth, precise strokes. What caught her eye were the tiny crosses scattered across it, spaced like marks on an old treasure map.

Unimpressed, Snow pursed her lips. 'It's a map.'

'Exactly,' Florian said. 'I thought it was more myth and gibberish, but the more I read, the more I understood.'

'About the chains?' she asked.

He shook his head. 'Not about the chains. About the little lord's gifts.'

'What do you mean?'

'I know we aimed to unlock the chains, but most of the scrolls here relate to Odion's family history,' he said, looking towards the Prince. 'Towards the sword and the Lady of the Stars. I kept reading, thinking that maybe they were all linked, but those books haven't been mentioned. Only the Lord's gifts have. In one of your father's journals, he mentioned he'd hidden them and had to keep doing so due to you and Adanna looking for them. Your sister told me about the treasure hunts you both had as children, scoping the castle for clues.'

An odd smile crossed Odion's lips at the memory. 'We were so adamant we'd find them, but we never did.'

'That's the thing,' Florian said. 'You almost did, several times.' He pointed to the map. 'The journal mentions you and Adanna being scolded in the west wing and his guilt for getting angry with you. He'd only hidden the object because you'd been so close and one of the staff reported you.'

'I remember,' Odion said. 'Adanna cried for hours afterwards, scared that Father was disappointed in us. We stopped playing after that. His wrath wasn't worth it, and by that point we'd become too old for games. He'd said the quill and the horse were a myth. That it was time for us to grow up.'

'Well, he did it because one of the objects was in the room next door to yours.'

Florian's finger trailed to another cross. 'Here it says you almost found the quill on the night of the Queen's birthday.' His finger moved to another cross. 'And here it mentions you'd almost found the horse on the night of the Lady of the Stars celebration.'

'What does this have to do with the restricted section?' Snow asked impatiently.

Florian blinked at her, a little confused. 'It doesn't have anything to do with the restricted section.'

She held back a growl. 'Then why do we care?'

'Because the journal leads to the other gifts. To the objects that match the sword.'

Odion pointed to an 'X' in one of the glass towers. 'I recognise most of these places from my and Adanna's treasure hunts, but there's three or four I don't. This one in the tower is new.

It's not somewhere my sister and I went. The glass was fragile, and Adanna never liked heights.'

'Do you see what this means?' Florian asked, stepping towards Odion.

'You think this leads to the horse and the quill?'

'We could reunite them all,' Florian said quietly. 'You could use them to help your sister. To help your kingdom. Without resorting to chained books and unknown magic.'

Odion didn't look convinced, and Snow definitely wasn't.

Florian took Odion's hand, his eyes pleading. 'I know you said it was a myth, but we have a map. We have written confirmation from your father. They are real. Why take a chance on a "maybe" with the chained scrolls when you have something tangible in front of you?'

Florian held his breath and Snow saw the uncertainty bloom from Odion. His hand remained in Florian's, unmoving and still. She didn't know how, but she felt the shift. The quietness of the both of them pondering the possibilities.

Florian's excitement bubbled under the surface. Yet, it wasn't excitement in Snow's veins. It was rage. Emotionless and cruel.

Her voice was cold as she asked, 'What about the scrolls?'

They ignored her.

'We could help Adanna,' Florian said. 'We could save the kingdom.'

Odion was quiet a moment before he whispered. 'What if I can't use them?'

'Everything in the journals leads me to believe you can.'

Snow wanted to pull out her knife. To stab them both and make them listen to her. They were fools. Total and utter *fools*.

Do it, the voices echoed. *Take the brooding one first.*

Odion would be the hardest to kill, his honed skills and

warrior instincts potentially better than hers. She swallowed down the thought.

'Hello?' she yelled as her fingers snapped in front of their faces. 'What about the scrolls?'

They both looked at her, their eyes half in dream land.

Complete idiots, she thought.

Kill them.

No.

Unfortunately, the urge remained, but she held back the leash on her rage. They may have been idiots, but they were idiots who could give her what she wanted.

'We don't need them anymore,' Florian said, finally answering her question. 'With the little lord's gifts, Odion can protect Adanna, he can share the burden and win the war. The objects hold magical properties.'

The spiteful, hateful side of her clawed its way out at his words. Odion noticed and stood in front of Florian, his blade already out. Hers was out too, but she had no recollection of doing it.

Kill them.

'We had a deal,' she seethed.

Odion was cool as he replied. 'We still do. This is just another way to the same outcome.'

'Those scrolls are the only way to get what we want.'

He shook his head. 'I agreed to your bargain on the premise there were no other leads to the gifts. If we have an alternative, one less dangerous than those scrolls, we should take it.'

'*Coward,*' she hissed, but he didn't back down.

Odion eyed her strangely, his head tilting as he assessed her. Florian watched over the prince's shoulder, wide-eyed and pathetic.

'So, this is it, then?' she asked. 'You rescind our deal and follow the path of dead maps and maybes?'

'It was always a maybe with both options, Snow,' Florian said quietly. 'This one just has more promise. It has more hope.'

Hope. A word she was beginning to hate. The only hope she'd felt simmered away at the mention of the map and the stupid markings.

'You can come with us?' Florian asked. 'You can still keep the deal intact.'

Kill them.

She was a storm. A flood. Clamping down on all that rage, she stamped her foot. 'I will not deal with two fickle pieces of—'

She halted. A new plan rapidly forming in her mind.

They'd barely even covered half the paperwork in here. Just because she hadn't read anything about the scrolls didn't mean they didn't exist. And with Florian and Odion too busy treasure hunting in their sick little love bubble, she would be free to break the chains herself. And keep the power those books revealed.

She wouldn't have to share. Or justify the spells she took. She would only have to choose.

The voices hissed inside her, angry at being ignored.

She lowered her knife. 'You know what?' she said. 'Do whatever you want.'

Leaving them stunned, she stormed out.

Snow had barely reached the library door, still seething at the princes' betrayal, when she heard them. The whispers.

The voices inside her echoed, calling in familiar greeting.

At this stage, the last thing she wanted to do was sit, and

lying on her bed seemed like a pathetic thing to do. She needed to sweat, or run, or eat. Anything that would distract her from the brewing storm in her chest. With careful steps she followed the sounds, letting them guide her until she rounded the book stacks, arriving in the restricted section. The chains glowed silver, moving as if there were a slight wind. Her hand lingered, itching to touch but knowing she couldn't without being zapped.

Some copies were stitched into bound books, others tied with a thread, and along the top, the scrolls curved into themselves, ready to be unravelled. She walked in front of them, eyeing the ink and getting frustrated when the faded font on the spines didn't show her anything. It was like there was a shield, invisible and tangible that coated the shelf in a hazy sheen.

'Again, she finds herself alone.'

Snow jumped, whirling around to find Petrella.

Snow schooled her face into the sneer she'd perfected. 'Hello, old crone. Come to keep this lonely princess company amongst the forgotten stacks?'

The woman eyed her up and down, her mouth puckering into something unimpressed. 'The only *crones* in this realm are the Sisters Grimm, and they lie north of here in Grimms' Grove.'

Snow raised her eyebrow. She didn't care about the Grimms and she sure as the cauldron didn't like Petrella's attitude. 'What game are you playing?' she asked. 'Leading us to those journals only to find nothing about what we're searching for.'

'Speak for yourself,' Petrella said, the side of her lip quirking. '*You* did not find what you were looking for. Who's to say the two princes did not?'

Snow rolled her eyes. 'Tell me about the chains, old lady. How do I unlock them?'

Petrella's eyes darkened as she stepped forward. For a small woman, she took up a lot of space. The air thickened and something cold crawled up Snow's spine.

Snow raised her chin. 'Tell me.'

Petrella shook her head. 'You are all demand and no give. To receive something, you must provide first. What will you give to unlock the secrets inside?'

'If I wanted idiotic comments I would have gone to Pip. If you're not going to help, you can leave.' She paused. 'Why are you even here, anyway?'

'I came to tell you all there is a visitor.'

'Okay?' Snow said. 'And?'

'And he's someone you'll be very interested in, though I don't really feel like telling you about him anymore.'

'Him?' she asked. 'Who is it?'

Snow wanted to punch her, but something in her tone lured the princess in. Who would visit? Snow didn't know anybody who would risk it except for ... could it be?

'Hansel?' she breathed.

Petrella laughed. A hateful, mocking sound, causing Snow to raise her blade.

The princess lowered her voice, sounding out each syllable in a dark threat. 'Who. Is. It?'

Petrella smirked.

Snow's rage hit its peak, her knife twitching in her small hands. She would do it. She could feel the itch rising within her.

Do it.

I will.

Just as Snow was about to charge, the woman spoke, humour lacing her words. 'It's your favourite crow.'

My what?

The moment froze, her mind ticking over as her rage dissipated into a wisp of ice and wind. Realisation dawned on her. She only knew one crow who would dare fly this far. Who belonged on the edges of Perridorm's borders. Belonged at her stepmother's side, raising an army to control the other kingdoms.

A hard shiver ran through her. 'Trik?'

Petrella vanished, her lingering laughter the only reply.

XLI

The Cry of the Drakon

The stadium was carved into the rib bones of a once-great beast, its seating uneven yet worn smooth by time. The floor beneath was black rock, veined with cracks and lined with adjoining chambers where the crowd trickled through in slow, murmuring waves.

Eve's gift flared as they poured in, slipping past curtains made of seaweed that swayed like breath. Her dress itched at the seams, stiff and too fine, chosen by someone who thought the human should suffer. Behind her, the higher-level families pottered about, voices light and careless as they placed bets and traded barbed compliments.

She had never seen anything like this. Not even whispers of what a trial like this would entail. Cyrene had kept quiet about the deeper customs of her people, and now Eve understood why.

Music drifted from an orchestra nestled near the royal podium, low and haunting. The currents carried it gently, and the orange sun filtered through the watery roof in fractured beams. It should have been beautiful. But the ground rumbled beneath her feet, subtle and slow, as if something stirred far below.

'I used to make jokes about the Drakon's snoring,' Cyrene said, appearing at Eve's side. 'It made me feel calmer about it.'

'I don't think being calm is something I'm capable of doing right now,' Eve whispered.

Cyrene reached for her hand, giving it a soft squeeze. Her touch was warm, grounding. 'Edmar will get you in safely. He's good at charming people to do what he wants.'

It didn't help. Not really. Either way, Eve would be going deeper. Further into the sea. Into the heavy, suffocating dark, for a mirror she had never seen, and a fate she couldn't yet name.

Cyrene leaned in. 'If anyone can find the mirror, it's you.'

'I'm not worried about not finding it,' Eve said, her palms clammy. 'I'm worried about drowning, or getting eaten, or being unable to carry it. I'm worried about what happens after, even if we do succeed. I can't swim the whole way in this dress. I can barely even float in it.'

'You won't have to,' Cyrene said. 'You'll take the mirror to my place, from there you can get changed. Edmar has organised for some old friends to help you. Ones that actually like land dwellers.'

Eve snorted. 'Nobody likes land dwellers down here.'

'The dolphins do.'

'You're joking, right? Dolphins?' Eve waited for the joke but Cyrene didn't waiver.

'I'm not going to be carried away by a pod of dolphins to shore like some weird fantastical dream,' Eve hissed. 'It's absurd.'

Cyrene grimaced. 'I'm getting really tired of your negativity.'

'It's not negativity. It's realism.'

'Whatever it is, it's exhausting.'

A new song carried up towards them as the Queen laughed, her courtiers copying her every movement. The Merking stared straight ahead, his trident high.

'I don't want to die,' Eve admitted.

Cyrene's face softened. 'If this so-called prophecy is real, then death was never on the cards.'

They stepped back as trumpets blared and the curtains drew open. The crowd erupted into wild cheers while Eve was shoved aside, the sharp tug of a hook catching her dress. She winced as the fabric ripped, the Queen's cold sneer locking onto her like a dagger.

'Keep your pet under control,' the Queen hissed at Cyrene.

Cyrene pulled Eve back. 'Keep three pixies behind me. Don't speak. Don't make eye contact.'

'Where do I go?'

'Just follow me,' Edmar said, appearing behind them. He pulled down his cuffs then smoothed down his hair. 'There will be a spot marked for us on the podium below, just beside the royal box.'

The crowd roared, setting off a ringing in Eve's ears. Cyrene straightened her back. Eve took hold of Edmar's arm as they floated out into the arena. Her dress now trailed behind her, the torn material leaving a long ribbon of netting that snagged on the ground. Eve yanked on it, barely holding herself together as she followed them out.

The crowd grew louder as she entered the open ocean, the rib cage towering over them. The ground shook, the chasm trembling with the applause. When Edmar broke off, she followed him, trailing down the carved stairs until she arrived at her seat.

As the Queen lifted her arms, a sly grin spread across her face. Eve caught the flash of a ring nestled in her hair, sea glass entwined with diamond, glinting like a shard of the ocean itself.

The ocean floor groaned beneath them and suddenly ink burst upward in thick black plumes, like fireworks made of shadow, ash drifting down in dizzying swirls.

The crowd gasped. Eve's breath caught as the ground split open, a searing wound tearing the earth apart. Inside, arches of black stone framed shelves, ramps and staircases carved from darkness itself.

But her eyes were drawn to the treasure, where heaps of gold, silver, gems, paintings, weapons, and silks were piled without end or beginning. At first, it looked like chaos. Yet as she stared deeper, Eve saw a pattern emerge. The treasure traced a winding path, guiding toward a throne forged of gold and vines. Sharp thorns curled from its backrest, twisting into a giant rose.

From afar, Prince Mizu appeared, a small figure amidst the turmoil. The Merking's jaw clenched tight as his son was led forward to the throne.

'He doesn't look too scared,' Eve said to Edmar.

'The fear is always there, even if we cannot see it,' Edmar said. 'But he won't look so brave when the Drakon arrives. The Queen is keeping it at bay for now. She will be the only one who can if it decides the Prince hasn't been enough to satisfy it.'

Eve shivered.

'May you be swept by the currents and honour our treasures, Prince Mizu,' the Queen said. 'Find the Morei you so desperately seek, before the Drakon finds you.'

Mizu stared up at her, his face grim, and bowed. Eve couldn't figure out how he did it. How he remained stoic in a time like this, when her skin was ablaze with anxiety as the nymphs crammed around her. She could barely breathe. Barely think. It was too much.

The Prince held her gaze as he replied. 'Let your trial begin.'

With a sneer, the Queen twisted the ring in her hair. Allowing a roar to shatter the air.

XLII
The Stardust and the Dwarf

In the eastern tunnels of the Queen's Mines, the silence pierced Bryn's ears. Even the guards had stopped their laughter, the money halted between hands. The bone door stilled, the skeletons hardening somehow as the song died.

Bryn touched the flower in his pocket, the soft petals creasing under his touch. Would something so fragile survive what he was about to do?

He'd seen the recruits communicate. Seen them speak to each other with hand signals and whispers. He just didn't know how long it would take to spread the message. To evacuate.

It was a risk, a big one. And with the Queen gone, Bryn wasn't sure how far he could go.

The younger dwarves hovered along the wall, their pickaxes forgotten. There were five dwarves, including him, and twelve guards. If they could all fight, they stood a chance, but not whilst the beasts roamed the caverns as well. Most had come to escort the Queen, to seek the bone door. Erick had been right about that.

Bryn froze as the beasts fell silent, every face turning toward the quiet door. The cavern's magic trembled, the air holding its breath before the storm.

He edged closer to the doorway, eyes fixed on the shimmering black wall that pulsed like a living thing. He'd seen the Queen return through it, her presence setting his nerves ablaze, his heart pounding like a wild choir.

A sharp shout from a guard snapped him back. 'Get back!' the voice bellowed, but then a scream tore through the air, raw and desperate.

The sound rattled the caves like a falling star. Bryn spun just as a shadow plummeted from above.

A body hit the ground with a sickening crack, no more than three pixie lengths away. Dark blood seeped into the sand, dripping from the shattered skull of one of the Queen's hounds. Its thick limbs twisted unnaturally, the mouth agape, teeth scattered across the floor.

Chaos erupted in an instant.

Bryn was moving before the guards could release their swords. He'd only just gripped the rough handle of a pickaxe when a guard lunged for him, teeth bared. Bryn didn't think, didn't falter as he raised the weapon and swung, hitting flesh with a sick crunch.

The handle protruded from the guard's stomach as blood spurted from his mouth, falling over Bryn's front.

Time stood still, his hands barely registering the new pain. He blinked and time swung back into motion. The chasm echoed with the growls and shots and screams and pain. What had it been? A minute? A second?

Bryn didn't bother trying to make sense of the chaos. It was time. With new determination, he pulled the pickaxe free with a grunt and turned towards the tunnel's entrance. Prisoners smothered the floor and swung their weapons with a fervour he'd not seen in an age. Others yelled from above as bodies fell to the floor, cracking and crying out with flailing arms.

Weapons were freed, blood was sprayed, and screams rang out. The old dwarf had done what he promised. He'd told them of what was to come. Bryn panted, twisting towards the dwarves as they shivered in the corner.

'Fight!' he yelled, but they only stared at him wide-eyed as a growl came from his back.

Bryn turned just as one of the black-skinned reapers shot out from the fray, his double set of teeth shining mid-lunge.

Bryn dived, barely avoiding its claws as he rolled across the dirt. He swung out his axe, his weight like an anchor as the beast charged again. The point hit its mark, searing into the flesh of the reaper's throat.

More blood. More shrieks.

He tasted dirt and stumbled back, his gaze landing on one of the guard's swords. The hilt was slick in his palms as he picked it up.

A scream loosed from the dwarves as two guards brought

down their swords. Quick and succinct. Gone in the blink of an eye.

Gone, gone, gone.

Bryn stared at the detached heads, a roar in his ears. He should have protected them. He should have never entered the mines. Never started this wretched mission.

Each step, each choice blinked before him as he stood, his eyes wild.

What have I done?

A growl came from his left and Bryn swung again, cutting the legs off a wounded bloodhound. It wheezed as it fell, blood sinking into the sand. He was thankful to Bjorn and Brufell for the fighting lessons as he met each blow that came for him.

A reaper came from his left, a guard from his right. And all through it, the ringing in his ears grew louder and louder. He slid across the dirt as another guard shot towards him, his sword arching as he swung again. Metal hit metal, clanging amongst the screams. Bryn ignored the gurgled sighs, the falling bodies, the agony sawing through the cavern walls.

Instead, he kept cutting. And cutting. And cutting.

Murder.

He ran across the dirt, aiming for the exit, and wiped blood from his eyes. There were hundreds, maybe even thousands of recruits locked in these mines. Together, they were a force to be reckoned with.

A shaith shot from the sky and picked up a changeling before she clawed into his skin and shrieked. More shaiths did the same. Bodies plunged from everywhere. Some from the ceiling, others from the narrow shelves lining the chasm, and some from the small battles echoing along the floor.

The only thing that remained untouched was the bone door.

It was hard to tell who was winning. Who was killing more than the other. All Bryn knew was the need to run.

His fingers clenched the pickaxe as he sprinted across the cavern. Just as he pulled the stardust bottle from his pocket, a snarl sliced through the air. A reaper charged, and Bryn dropped low, the weapon slicing flesh.

He fought down the whirl of thoughts. How many had escaped, how many hadn't, who he might have doomed with this reckless plan. One hand gripped the jar, the other the pickaxe. He hacked through everything in his way. Purple and red uniforms, black jaws and taut skin. Sharp teeth and dead eyes all blended into one nightmare as he neared the pits.

Bodies writhed, staining the earth with blood. Prisoners locked with the Queen's army. Changelings, witches, dwarves, fairies. Men, trolls, shaiths, beasts. They charged with vengeance in their eyes and fury burning in their veins. Flesh tore from bone.

Bryn licked his cracked lips. He'd only been little when the War of Thorns had raged. Had been hidden during the battle that infected his home, losing his family in the process. But no matter how many stories Bonyx had told, it never truly showed you what battle was like.

Life blinked out around him as blood sprayed. He dodged bodies, urging himself forward and bringing his axe down whenever he could. He battled his way through, the holes in the walls filled with stardust laughing at him in morbid warning.

It will all blow. You will all die.

Another shaith screamed, diving with a cry of delight as a troll fell. Bryn glanced briefly, trying to gauge the chaos.

That was his mistake.

Pain flared down his arm as he was thrown sideways. Teeth

sank into his skin as a bloodhound clamped on, froth bubbling from its jaws. Darkness edged his vision before the beast was flung against the wall by a changeling. The axe smashed into its skull.

The female changeling spun to Bryn, growling.

His arm went limp.

'You're Erick's friend,' she said.

Bryn clenched his teeth through the pain and took her hand, swaying to his feet. 'You must get out of here,' he said.

'This is it, isn't it? What Erick warned us about?'

'I can't explain now. But you have to go. Take whoever you can.' He opened his palm to reveal the stardust bottle. 'It's about to blow.'

She didn't flinch. 'We'll hold them off. I'll warn whoever I can. But get out. For Erick.'

'For Erick,' Bryn replied as she leapt back into the fight.

He wavered, guilt and survival twisting inside him. Luck or fate, he didn't know which was laughing now.

Stumbling through another tunnel, recruits fled past him. But some stayed to fight. Bodies tangled, fighting their way out. Bryn pushed forward until light blinded him.

Another bloodhound charged, blood soaking his side. Pain lashed his arm.

Murder.

But he didn't stop. Not as he cut down the monster with a swipe. Not as he ran up the stairs. And not as he reached the barren fields above.

Outside, creatures poured from the cavern, screaming as the shaiths dove from the skies. He ran, helping those he could, clenching the bottle in his fist, the wall of the mines growing larger with each step. All he could hear were screams. All he could see was the dead sprawled before him. War and blood and death.

Still, he ran.

As the wall loomed above him, the crowd grew by the gate, fighting against the iron doors trapping them inside. A shriek broke out as a group of recruits raided the tower, climbing the steps with shouts of freedom.

Bryn wavered.

He would need to buy them time, buy them safety.

He swung out as another reaper charged towards a witch. The gates groaned.

More time. I need more time.

With blood coating his face, Bryn turned towards the gaping wound in the earth, the forges still burning despite the battle. Bryn's fingers brushed the flower in his pocket, Rabbit's breath warm at his ear. His lips parted. He took a steadying breath and ran. Back towards the mines.

Some stared as if he'd lost his mind or chosen death. But he did not slow. His boots thudded against the soil, his body pushing past those trying to pull him back.

At the edge of the chasm, where the opening of the mines lay, the recruits scattered like leaves in the wind. Bryn lifted his eyes and sent a silent prayer skyward, begging the cauldron to save them all. He didn't dare breathe as he closed his eyes, whispering the words that clung to hope.

Then he let go of the stardust bottle.

He did not watch it fall. Nor did he hesitate as he dropped his pickaxe and ran.

And ran.

And ran.

The mines walls loomed overhead, mocking him as his short legs pounded the earth. Time twisted. Hours, minutes, seconds melting together. Faces of everyone he loved flickered through his mind, calling him forward.

Run. Run. Run.

Just as he neared the gates ...

BOOM.

The earth trembled, spinning beneath his feet. Screams tore through the air, human and beast alike. He risked a glance behind him as the mine collapsed, swallowing all who remained inside in a roar of stone and dust.

XLIII

The Drakon and its Prince

Eve let out a gasp.

Scales of moonlight, rimmed in red, broke through the cavern. The Drakon's tail was as large as a whale, the body smooth and feline as it cut through water. The roar shook the arena, vibrating along the bone beside her and rattling the piles of treasure below. The monsters teeth were jagged, missing in places and full of bones.

'This isn't a trial,' Eve whispered to Edmar. 'This is an execution.'

The Drakon was beautiful. And terrifying.

Prince Mizu twisted to follow the Drakon's long tail as it slipped between the caverns, vanishing as swiftly as it had appeared. He lowered himself from the podium, partially obscuring himself by a pile of gold coins where he floated, with slow, cautious movements. The thorned throne stood like a shield nearby, hiding him from the terrible beast that had been unleashed.

'What is he doing?' Edmar asked.

The crowd was electric, the hum of bodies creating its own anthem as they waited with bated breaths. Eve wanted to close her eyes, to wish it all away, but found she couldn't as her panicked eyes locked onto the prince.

The Drakon watched from the shadows, waiting, a low purr vibrating in its throat.

Mizu glanced at the crowd, then at his father. The Merking leaned forward, terror carved into his face. Eve felt the familiar churn of dread, a sick knot tightening whenever the cursed object was near. It pulled at her, but she forced it down.

The Drakon circled, its great head shimmering before it slipped behind another cavern wall.

Mizu's tail flicked sharply as he moved around a pile of treasure, using it as cover. He ducked, keeping his tail close, as the sea monster crept into the open.

Its nostrils flared, cautious and curious. Scales glinting, the Drakon slid toward the throne, coiling around it like a living shadow.

The crowd held its breath.

The Drakon sniffed the salty currents and let out a low growl.

Mizu weighed some coins in his hands, still as stone. There was the faintest flicker of tension in his unblinking eyes. He pushed aside some gold and moved the paintings nearby, steeling himself.

'He won't find the mirror amongst all that,' she whispered.

Edmar's only response was a frown.

Mizu pushed aside a trophy, its delicate hilt fracturing at the touch. He lunged, trying to catch the broken piece, but it was too late. The rim of the trophy clattered to the ground. As if an earthquake had split, the pile of treasure groaned, toppling to the side like the slice of a knife, exposing him.

It was like a dinner bell, loud and shrill and urgent. The beast roared, its body unfurling and rushed towards the prince. Mizu pushed off the ground, swerving around as the Drakon collided with the trinkets. Mizu's tail barely missed teeth as he twisted, dodging the Drakon's claws by a pixie.

This is madness.

Eve turned to the Queen, who clapped slowly, a cruel smile lighting her face.

This battle was unfair from the start. Eve knew it, but hearing it and seeing it were worlds apart. A wave of sickness churned in her gut, twisting between disgust and the sharp pull of her gift.

Treasure burst into the air in clouds as Mizu darted through the tunnels, weaving behind jagged rock. The Drakon lunged after him and snapped its teeth mere pixies away. Just as the Prince seemed cornered, he pivoted, diving into a narrow alcove too small for the monster to follow.

Eve's eyes flicked between the Prince, thrashing through the water, and the Drakon, slicing through currents as if bending the water to its will.

A thunderous crash shook the cavern as Mizu plunged into the treasure. The Drakon slammed after him with a deafening boom. Trinkets scattered like shattered stardust.

The Prince surfaced, clutching a small trident. He twisted it in his hands, steady and unyielding. Eve went taut as the Drakon reared up behind him. Gold coins dripped from its scales like metal rain.

The crowd roared as the beast attacked. The Queen smirked from her seat as the Prince hesitated. Eve hesitating with him.

Mizu's torn fin left a bloody trail in the water behind him and it triggered the beast. The creature flared its nostrils, its chest rumbling at the scent. But when Eve expected it to shoot forward, it slowed down its movements, circling the Prince with the ease of a predator who knew its prey was cornered. The Prince shook, his trident out before him as he followed the movements, attempting to hide his shaking hands.

'The Drakon's dragging it out,' Eve said. 'Why?'

'Perhaps he likes the chase,' Edmar commented.

Collectively the crowd gasped as the Drakon disappeared. And just as the silence was at its heaviest, the Merking screamed. 'Mizu!'

The Prince spun toward his father just as the Drakon's tail whipped out.

It struck Mizu hard, knocking the trident from his grasp. He slammed against the cavern wall with a crack. The Drakon roared and lunged, claws scraping across his torso and shrouding them both in a veil of blood.

'This is wrong,' Eve whispered, her eyes cutting through the arena below.

The blood darkened, swirling like a thick cloud. Fragments of the creature shimmered beneath the surface as the Drakon twisted, roaring its victory.

The crowd leaned in, breath held tight. The Merking sat frozen, lost. Somehow, Eve had fought through the crowd. Her hands gripped the railing near the edge of the stadium, white-knuckled and trembling.

Through a narrow gap, Eve caught sight of the wheezing prince. His tail curled around him like a wounded pup. The trident rested just beyond reach, and the Drakon prowled close. Mizu struggled to rise but faltered. Eve leaned forward. And as the Drakon arched its back, like a cat with a mouse, something inside Eve broke.

I hope for a better future. One where all kingdoms may live side by side. Whether that is by life or death. I accept.

But Eve did not accept it.

She'd had enough death. Enough blood.

She was sick of it.

So, as the Drakon outstretched its claws, Eve lost all control.

She released a scream and threw herself over the railing. The crowd roared, but it was white noise as she dived towards the chasm. Freeing her blade, Eve sliced her palm and let the blood trail behind her.

It was all she needed.

Just one moment.

One distraction.

The Drakon's head shot towards her, its teeth bared. A ripple tumbled down its spine as it twisted towards her and lunged. And in the span of a second, as the dark water pulled her down, she whispered a prayer. Then let her knife fly free.

'Is she always that erratic?' Odion asked.

'Snow is always upset,' Florian said quietly, straightening a cloth on one of the tables in Petrella's forgotten rooms.

He regretted the words as soon as they left his mouth, the sound of his voice not quite right. 'I only meant, since this whole mess started, she's not been herself.'

Odion nodded, his shoulders stiff. He gripped a journal, his mother's handwriting faint and broken.

'War does that to people, you know,' Odion said. 'Adanna and I used to be different, too. Happier.'

Florian only blinked, unable to respond. He breathed softly, fearful that any sudden movement would stop Odion's words. He braved a look upwards, noticing Odion's gilded eye shimmering like a pool of gold.

Beautiful.

For the first time since being here, there was nothing hard in his accent. Nothing flat about his words. It was all colour and regret.

'I was the only one to believe Adanna when she said she'd seen the Evil Queen,' Odion said as he shook his head. 'Not even my mother – who doted on her – believed her. Her dreams were stories, something she would grow out of. But the gifts of my family are strange and always have been.'

Florian shuffled as Odion moved closer. The dark prince grazed his fingers along the map, his voice soft as he said, 'I'm sorry for the things I said to you.'

Florian swallowed. 'It's fine.'

'It's not. I was brought up better than that. I believed you to be a threat, someone unknown in our castle of secrets.' His head tilted up, meeting Florian's gaze with startling clarity. Odion's eyes seared into him, burning and bright.

Florian felt tethered in that moment, as if a golden string loomed between them. Florian raised his hand. Under usual circumstances, Odion would have flinched, hissed at him or berated him. Instead, he stood deadly still, letting Florian's palm cup his cheek.

'I don't want to share your secrets,' Florian said quietly. 'I want to keep them.'

Florian rubbed his thumb along Odion's stubble, entranced by the smooth skin underneath. Odion leaned in, stunning Florian into a freeze where he couldn't quite breathe.

'Forgive me,' Odion asked.

Florian's answer was a resounding yes. With careful fingers, Odion gripped Florian's upheld hand and stroked the back of it. Florian could feel the rough calluses, the skin worn from a sword's hilt, and it felt like home.

Time halted in a way that tilted the axis of Florian's world. His lips parted, his chest heavy, and just as he pulled forth some bravery, an inch of him moving forward, Odion let go.

'Where do we start?' he asked, pointing to the map.

Florian gulped and Odion's eyes focused, trailing the paths of the map, the little lord's gifts now at the forefront of everything they stood to gain.

Florian turned to help and bit his lip. The moment was gone. But the urge to touch Odion again was not.

XLIV
The Cost of Survival

Malak paced. 'Surely, you're not agreeing to this?'

They were in the dining hall, Adanna seated at the head of the table. Pip smoked his pipe from the other side, not touching the food laid out in front of him for the first time since being here. Laurie just watched from the wall.

Trik had been left in the dungeons, but his laughing eyes still lingered in Malak's mind even though it had been over an hour. Snow and the others hadn't been seen. Adanna creased her brows, focusing on the tablecloth as if it would speak and provide some answers.

'He is valuable,' Pip replied. 'His information could change the entire course of this war.'

'What if he's lying?' Malak said. 'What if he's just puffing up his feathers so we take the bait? We can't consider this. Adanna *can't* consider this.'

The Princess was quiet for a moment. 'We must consider all options.'

'Are you kidding?' Malak hissed. 'It's *Snow*. We have an *alliance*. Or does that mean nothing to you?'

She lifted her head, piercing him with those strange eyes of hers. 'It means a great deal. I'm just trying to process what this means and what we do moving forward. Pip is right, we cannot kill him. The information he holds is too valuable. We must decide now. You and I do not think Snow is worth the cost, despite how she loathes me. But there will be a cost. What is it you're willing to pay if it's not the Princess?'

'Anything,' he said. 'I will give anything but her.'

Pip scoffed, waving Laurie over for a glass of wine. 'Love baffles me.'

'You say you would give anything,' Adanna continued, 'but it still leaves us with little choice. What can we offer that he doesn't already have?'

'He wants Snow for vengeance,' Pip said. 'He thinks she killed his lover. Unless we can give him something else that's similar, or of equal value, he won't talk.'

'Snow didn't kill her' Adanna said.

'Odion did,' Malak replied.

Pip only cocked his brow. 'Does the crow know that?'

'He seemed to know a lot,' Laurie murmured. The group

turned towards her. 'He mentioned you'd seen him in your visions.'

Adanna frowned. 'The dreams only show me shadows. Some I understand and others I do not. I only saw a bird for his arrival. The rest is hazy. Pooled blood, knives, a dragon, I think. It doesn't show me anything about whether it's linked to him or if it's a year from now. I'm sorry.'

Malak shook his head. He wanted to kill the crow. To drag a blade across his throat and be done with it. A quick death would be mercy, far more than Trik deserved after what he had done to Snow in the army camp. But Malak was not a killer.

He clenched and unclenched his fists, jaw tight. The taste of blood filled his mouth. Hunger flared through him. Not for food, but to protect. To shield. To tear. Still, he forced himself to breathe. He was logical. Smart.

Trik was valuable. The information he held could help them reclaim Perridorm. Could free it. Could turn the tide and bring the rebellion, give them the ally they so desperately needed. That was the point of all this. To unite the kingdoms. To stop the rot at the root.

Malak exhaled through his nose, the animal in him still snarling beneath his skin. He scraped out a chair and sank into it. Then he raised a hand, gesturing to Laurie for a glass of wine. Maybe it would help drown the beast inside him.

'Let's start with what we know,' Malak said first, taking a swig. 'We know Trik's the General. We know he works for Myrenna, or at least, he did work for Myrenna.'

'We know he's a shifter,' Pip said. 'One that turns into a crow.'

'He's one of her murders,' Malak said. 'He loved the Huntress and now he seeks to kill Snow for her death.'

'If he is here to kill Snow,' Pip said, 'then that at least tells us he's definitely left Myrenna's employ. If Snow's dead, then her heart is useless.'

Adanna nodded. 'What else do we know?'

'I don't know,' Malak replied. 'Surely, he has family or something? Do we know how many of the Queen's crows are shifters? I was never privy to that kind of information.'

'There are only three,' Adanna said.

'How do you—?'

'My dreams. There have always been three crows. Always together. Brothers of sorts. Don't ask me how I know, just trust me that I do.'

Pip tapped his fingers on the table. 'Three brothers. Three crows. How many do you think work for the Queen?'

The double set doors swung open as Snow entered.

Malak stood as she glared at the group.

'Was anyone going to tell me about my torturer arriving, or were you waiting for dessert to be served?'

'Snow,' Malak said.

She looked dishevelled, her lips puckered like she'd eaten something sour. He leaned to the side, trying to see if Florian and Odion followed behind her. They didn't.

'Out of everyone here,' Snow said, eyeing Malak with distaste, 'I expected you to have my back. When did lying become part of our friendship?'

'I couldn't find you.'

She snatched the glass of wine in front of Pip and swigged it back. Pip held back his retort as Laurie poured him another, glaring at Snow from behind. The princess pulled out a chair and slumped in it. 'What did he offer you, and when did he ask about killing me?'

Adanna's lip quirked at Snow's entrance, her keen eyes

watchful. 'We were just discussing what else we could offer in your place.'

'Surely he has *other* priorities besides you,' Laurie chimed in.

Snow glared at her.

'We were also covering what we know about him,' Malak said, stealing her attention. 'I don't remember him at the palace.'

'I do,' she said, lifting her boots onto the table.

Adanna raised her brow, but halted Laurie as the maid's mouth formed into a thin line.

Snow was in a mood. She was actively finding trigger points, buttons to press, and that usually meant something had happened to set her off. Malak only saw these moods after Snow had seen Myrenna or when she'd been caught creeping in the castle and was whisked back to her rooms. Normally they were small, brittle complaints that shattered when she saw reason. But the further they travelled, the more she burned. Not with golden light like a warm day, but like the molten lava boiling down a black mountain.

Malak eyed the empty doorway again but there was still no sign of the princes.

'He has two brothers,' Snow said. 'I don't know much, but they both worked for the Queen. I'd seen Trik with Artemis before, in the gardens when I was young. They were ... *intimate.* The other one I've seen shift in the eyrie. He used to visit her tower a lot. Carried scrolls and all that. His name is Dread. Trik tried to threaten me with his name in the camp. The last one I've never met, but I've heard them speak of him. He's the one that remains a mystery.'

'What's their relationship like?' Adanna asked.

Snow swirled her glass. 'They seemed off and on, like a

troubled bond. They either partied together or fought like bloodhounds. The other one seemed younger, like he's got it easier. I'd put medallions on him being the weakest link though I've never seen him.'

'We'll try the brother as leverage, then,' Malak said. 'I'll talk to the crow tomorrow morning. Leave him to stew in a dark cage for a night.'

'I'll come,' Adanna said.

'No, Princess,' Laurie urged. 'Let Odion accompany him. You haven't slept well. You need to rest.'

She gave Laurie a nod. 'Fine. You will tell him?'

'I will.'

'So will I,' said Malak.

'The more I stick around, the less hopeful I become,' Pip said sourly, swallowing the rest of his drink.

'Shut it,' Snow snapped.

Pip waved her away, unconcerned as he jumped off his seat. 'I'm going to bed. It's too late of an hour to deal with this much hostility.'

'I'm tired, too,' Adanna said. 'I'll see you both tomorrow.'

Laurie wheeled her out, leaving Snow and Malak alone.

Snow dropped her boots, gliding off the seat to the exit, when Malak stopped her.

'Hey,' he said, moving around the table. 'I was hoping to talk to you.'

'You could've done that when Trik arrived,' she said, trying to push past him.

His frown deepened. 'I couldn't find you. I've searched everywhere since our fight. We parted on bad terms and I just ... I just wanted to fix it. Apologise. Go back to how it was.'

Her eyes softened, just for a breath, before she blinked it

away and stepped back. 'I'm not sure anything will ever go back to how it was.'

Something clawed at his chest, sharp and unseen, ripping past skin and into the meat of him. Myrenna didn't need to use her nails to tear out his heart. Snow was already doing it, bit by bit, with every cold glance, every fading word.

He didn't know where to start. How to reach her. How to make her laugh again. Had he already lost her, and only now noticed the empty space she'd left behind?

'Snow,' he said quietly. Almost pleading. 'I'm trying. Where were you today? It was like you vanished.'

'I don't have to tell you where I go.'

'No,' he said, voice stumbling. 'You don't. It's just ... you usually do. So, I know where to find you.'

'You found me when I stole the horse,' she said, her tone flat. 'If you know me so well, shouldn't you have been able to do the same this time?'

'The horse was a fluke.'

'A fluke,' she echoed, and her shoulders sagged. 'It doesn't matter. I'm tired. I've had a bad day and I'm exhausted. Can we talk about this later?'

He didn't want later. He didn't want to carry this hollow feeling through another sleepless night. He wanted her grin, her sharp wit, the warmth she used to hold for him like it was second nature.

But instead, he said, 'Okay.'

She squeezed his elbow, a gesture that usually comforted him but felt empty. 'Good night, Malak,' she said.

His throat bobbed. 'Good night, Princess.'

And even though she hadn't closed the door behind her, he still felt like one had been slammed in his face.

Snow wanted to feel guilty about Malak. She really did. But she couldn't.

His constant need to smooth things over made her skin crawl. She'd told him how she felt, time and time again, and he'd batted her concerns away like flies. Always with the better plan. The better answer. The better tone. He loved the sound of his own voice, and she was done listening to it.

Whenever he came near, she felt small. Like she had back at the grotto. A fledgling under scrutiny, surrounded and picked apart, as if she didn't know her own mind.

He needed too much. She didn't have anything left to give him.

After the forest, after the disaster with her deal between Florian and Odion, Snow had found peace in being alone again. Nothing got broken that way. No one tried to reshape her, or correct her, or make her into someone easier to love. She was free. Even if her only companion now was the quiet hum of her own dark thoughts.

She'd waited until everyone else had gone to bed before she'd snuck out of her rooms. The library was haunting at this time, the grey clouds halting the cool starlight that should have glowed through the ceiling windows. Her steps were light as whispered voices snaked through the night.

Friends, the voices inside her echoed.

The two sounds caressed each other, familiar and broken and cold. She didn't have time to ponder it as she snuck across the floors and hid within the shadows. Soon she would have

Hansel. She would have her throne. She only needed power first.

Snow wondered if Myrenna knew, if somehow the Queen could feel her from here. Did she hear the echo of Snow's heart in her dreams, the quiet breath of the Princess as she hid from the prying eyes of Myrenna's monsters?

Sometimes, in Snow's dreams she felt Myrenna. As if she were the ghost of a shadow, skimming along the edges. She felt Trik, too. And the cage that locked her away.

Hurt. Alone. Afraid.

Weak.

If everything went her way, she would never be weak again. Never feel powerless. Or afraid. Or small.

The door to Petrella's rooms creeped open. The dust and stale air crinkled her nose. The piano lay forgotten, and their footprints and white sheets trailed a clear path from where they'd entered earlier.

She scoped through the papers, scattering them one by one as night crept in. Her candle burned low, the crackle a warm song as she read over the journals. She skimmed mostly, hunting for key words. Chain. Book. Scroll. Magic. None revealed what she wanted.

When a clock chimed within the library and reverberated along the hallway, she sighed. It was almost three in the morning. Her lids were heavy, her body sore from hunching over.

'I'll have to try again tomorrow,' she mumbled.

She rubbed her chest as a yawn escaped her lips.

Whispers lingered down the steps. Enticing her. Urging her.

Her candle sputtered, the dying light almost out.

Friendsss.

But even she wasn't sure if the whispers in the library were friends. Whether she even had those anymore. She supposed she didn't need them. She would wear her crown. She would win. And her people would become her friends.

It didn't sound so lonely when she envisioned it.

The candle sputtered out as she reached the halls. The only light visible coming from the pale shimmer of stars through the windows. Snow followed, idly wandering as the sounds of night crawled in. Her voices were unsettled, whispering to her as her eyes drooped.

They sang for the scrolls in the library, writhing beneath her, yearning for it.

Soon, she soothed. *We will have them soon.*

Yesss, they whispered back.

The voices still hummed under her skin as she finally approached her room. Nearby, Malak's snore echoed under his door.

He was so loud.

Feral. Ugly.

They were the words that came to her now when she thought of him, like some disgusting snot that crawled from his nose. You knew it was a part of you, but it was hideous and needed to be forgotten.

Malak's desperate plea to make things right replayed through her thoughts. The way he had practically *begged.* There was a part of her that pitied him for the display. It wasn't that she couldn't make things right exactly, it's just that she didn't want to. Especially after the forest. After the camp.

Forget him, the voices urged. *Forget them all.*

'Hush now.'

She reached the other hallway, her door in view. How could she open the chains? What if it led to something else entirely? How could she get what she needed? The only other person she'd known who'd done something similar was Myrenna. With the magic hidden under Bellatorre. She didn't know how her stepmother had done it, how she had opened something that heavily protected. But she had. And Snow was afraid that the secret would stay with her.

Surely, Myrenna hadn't been the first. She'd also not be the last.

The key slid into the lock, her door opening with a slight creak as she entered.

She is not the only one, the voices whispered.

Snow frowned at the voices, throwing her gear onto the table in the small sitting room. Her room, for the most part, was pleasant. Not as lavish as the suites in Bellatorre, but it held the essentials. A modest living area, a fireplace that crackled softly, a bed tucked against the back wall, and an arched entryway leading to a bathroom with a deep tub and a shelf crowded with glass bottles and creams.

While most people would find comfort in the space, her room looked untouched, the sheets still tucked in. The curtains were teal, the air lifting them in soft waves as Snow moved to close the window.

She tried to remember Myrenna's arrival. The slow sickness taking over her father's body as she cooed to him. Feeding him poisoned tea.

Snow rubbed her eyes as she lay on the bed. Sleep beckoned her, but her body was wired as something nagged in the back of her mind.

She is not the only keeper of secrets.

Myrenna had been alone when she'd arrived in Bellatorre. She had spent most of her days with Snow or running the palace whilst the King slept.

As Snow drifted off, she recalled the days after her father

died. The funeral. The black banners and gifts. She remembered looking for Myrenna, only to find the cold hard shell of a woman. A woman who tried to erase the old rulers. Who changed the castle, and laws, and expectations. A gilded mirror hung from the throne room, the silky voice lingering along the tiles. Then the birds. So many birds. They cawed in the sky. A loud cacophony erupting from their vicious beaks.

Memories swam over her, overlapping and twisting. A shifter, wandering the eyrie. Malak behind the stables. Hansel with his hollow eyes after a visit with the Queen. And then the scrolls. Scattered along the floors of her tower.

She had not been alone. She'd had the mirror. Her murders.

The crow, the voices said, burning through her.

Her eyes flew open at the sound of the curtains flapping despite the closed windows.

'Trik.'

Memories of his hateful smile still haunted her. His cruel voice as he cut and cut and cut. She shuddered as crimson combed along her vision. She wanted to kill him. To have him bleed for what he did. For helping Myrenna. For unleashing his lover. For the pain he'd inflicted on her.

She reached for the knife under her pillow, finding it a frail shield against the fear creeping within her.

It is okay, the voices said. *He can help.*

'He can die,' she bit back.

After. He can die after.

Would she be skilled enough to kill him? She remembered the feel of her blade in flesh, the dead crawling from the soil. She'd been empowered that day, emboldened, as if some dark part of her had awoken.

After, they cooed.

And she listened.

She could kill him still. After she got what she needed. After he told her of the scrolls and how Myrenna did it. After he had no more uses other than to bleed at the mercy of her knife.

She was still in her clothes, the sky still flecked with stars. If she was lucky, she had time before the others woke. With new fervour, she snatched her jacket and made her way to the dungeons.

When she arrived, Trik stood free of his binds and she tried not to show her surprise. She halted near the cell, but he didn't look up, though she knew he saw her. It was clear in the slight upward curve of his lip as he picked at his nails.

'I wondered when you would visit.'

Snow pulled out her knife and held it in front of her. She tried to still her shaking hands, but the memory of what he had done to her was too clear. Too focused.

After, the voices said.

She straightened her shoulders and lifted her chin. Fear held back her words, lodging them in her throat. He casually leaned against the bars and Snow noted they didn't zap him.

Usually, wards meant a crackle or pain, much like the chains in the library, but he seemed content in his prison. Comfortable, even.

He nodded towards her small blade. 'Have you come to kill me?' His eyes lingered on her in a way that made her feel trivial and useless.

She held the blade high. 'Maybe.' Her mouth was dry and her body trembled. She wanted to say yes. Wanted to lunge for him. Yet another part of her couldn't bring herself to move.

'I do want to kill you,' she said, licking her lips. 'Instead, I have a proposal.'

'Oh?' he asked, stepping away from the bars. He stood on the other side, close enough to reach through and touch her. He didn't. 'And what would warrant a change like that?'

'You have something I need,' Snow said.

'And what might that be?'

'Information.'

He eyed her up and down in a way that made her want to crawl under a table and hide. Instead of answering her question, his lips curled into a sinister smile. 'You have a beautiful scream.'

She snarled.

He chuckled. 'I will give you only the death you deserve and nothing else.'

'You dismiss my offer before you even hear me out? Who knew you and the crippled princess had so much in common?' She let the venom seep into her voice, the disdain for her new allies dripping like spilled wine.

Trik arched his eyebrow. 'Interesting.'

'What is?'

'That you isolate yourself from the ones who help you. Did the twins not save you from my camp?'

'The Prince did. The Princess is ... less than you would expect.'

'She seems pretty powerful on the battlefield when her army is raised,' he said darkly. 'My men would disagree with you.'

'A lot of people disagree with me,' she said, stepping closer.

He didn't flinch, didn't move. Her heart raced under her chest, her knife a pinprick from his throat, but he watched her. Waiting.

'Let's cut right down to it,' she said. 'I just need one little piece of help, to unlock these forgotten books. I know you can help. You helped Myrenna.'

'Did I?'

'Don't play dumb,' she hissed, pressing the knife into his throat.

'One more inch and I'll come out to play,' he said, jaw twitching. She pressed it harder, enjoying the lick of blood that fell.

A snap echoed and Trik grinned. The Princess froze as his bones began to break, twisting and folding with sickening precision. Flesh warped. Limbs shrank. Feathers burst from skin. In seconds, a bird stood where he had been.

She staggered back, heart hammering, as the creature darted through the bars. Mid-air, he shifted again, bones stretching, feathers retreating, landing in a crouch with a grimace, as if the transformation had torn something loose inside him.

She spun, ready to run, when he appeared behind her. His eyes were wild, lips curled in a hungry snarl. She swung instinctively. Steel met flesh. His arm jerked up to block, but not fast enough. Her blade sliced deep.

A low growl loosed from him, one made of revenge and promise.

Snow held the knife out, eyes wide. Fear threatened to gobble her whole. Flashes of the camp, the cross. The cage. It blinded her as she stumbled and hit the wall behind her.

He moved fast, *too* fast. And before Snow knew it, he was cupping his hand around her throat, her knife clattering to the floor.

'I warned you,' he said.

She choked, a grunting sound escaping her lips as terror

slid over her skin. She couldn't hide it as she said, 'Those bars were enchanted.'

'That explains the itch,' he snarled. He tightened his grip on her throat.

'I came to bargain.'

He eyed her knife on the ground. 'I believed you until you drew blood.' He pushed harder, his body warm against the chill of her bones. 'I came here to kill you,' he said. 'Did you know that? I asked for you from the others.' His free hand trailed along her collarbone before stopping near her heart. 'Half the kingdoms' problems are because of you. Without your heart, Myrenna remains mortal. Not to mention the fact that you killed Artemis. It's only fair that I kill you, too.'

Her hands fumbled, shaky and erratic. She wouldn't escape this. Couldn't. The voices within her hissed, battering against his hold as she squeezed her eyes shut. She couldn't find his logic about Myrenna, but she could deny killing his lover.

'I didn't kill her,' Snow wheezed. Her head was light now from Trik's grip. She fumbled, her hands cradling his, pulling without success. 'You want to kill me, but I didn't do it. There are bigger things at play.'

He growled. 'Liar.'

'*Please,*' she begged.

His eyes narrowed.

Blood pulsed under her skin, her face heated. 'I want to kill you, too,' she coughed. 'For what you did, for what you will do. But I won't because you have something I need.'

'You have *nothing* I need,' he spat.

She smiled, trying to rein back control. At least his grip had eased. 'That's where you're wrong.'

'And what, pray tell, do you have to bargain with?'

After.

'I can tell you who did it. Who killed your huntress.'

She saw no point in playing around. She was here for one thing, and she needed it sooner rather than later. She'd leave the games to Myrenna. For now, she just needed his skills.

He laughed, eyeing her up and down as he stood over her, leering in that murderous way of his. 'I already know who killed Artemis.'

'I didn't do it,' she said.

'Why would I believe you?'

'Because I'd *claim* it if I had.'

His jaw tightened, his mouth set. 'You would just hand over their name?'

'If I get what I need, then yes.'

At that, he dropped her, leaving her heaving on the floor as he waited, arms crossed. 'And your heart?' he asked.

She rubbed her throat, anger boiling under the surface. 'Myrenna won't need it if I kill her first.'

He raised his brow. 'Is this what my help is for? To find a way to kill the Evil Queen.'

'Of sorts,' she replied. 'How did you get out, anyway? There's supposed to be magic on those bars.'

'This isn't my first imprisonment, *Princess*. I can work basic spells. I'm a Murder. Get to the point before I kill you.'

She looked up at him, her face scrunched. 'Did you ever go under the castle in Bellatorre? To the caverns built deep within?' He watched her, his eye twitching, and she smiled. 'I know you have. You were with her.'

'Your point?'

'The magic scrolls down there are not the only ones to exist. They're here, too.'

His eyes narrowed but he let her continue.

'They are protected, wrapped in chains which stop anyone

getting close. I can't unlock them, but you can. You saw how Myrenna did it. You know.'

'Let's say I do know,' he replied as he flicked dirt out from under his fingernails. 'What's stopping me from killing you when we unlock them?'

'What's to stop me from doing the same?'

'So eager for blood, *Princess*.'

She glared at him, hating the way he said her title.

He held her stare. 'Tell me who killed Artemis and I'll agree.'

'No,' she said, 'not until after you help.'

He tilted his head as she stood up and dusted herself off. Not knowing what to do with her hands, she rested them on her hips, stifling the shaking that wracked her body.

'Do we have a deal?' she asked.

'I haven't been offered anything better.'

She hated herself for this. Hated him for having what she needed. She sucked in her breath and held out her hand. 'Deal.'

After, the voices echoed.

And as his hand clasped over hers, he leaned in and whispered, 'If you're lying to me, I'll do worse things than just cut your skin.'

She gulped. Hating how hard he squeezed her hand.

After.

Then she would watch him bleed out.

XLV
The Seekers Watery Grave

Eve had done a lot of things in her life. She had been a merchant's daughter. A circus performer. A Seeker. A wolf slayer. A friend. A foe. What she had never been was self-sacrificial. That trait was left for those in stories. For those who wanted glory. All she had ever wanted was something she could claim for her father's sacrifice.

She didn't recognise this part of herself. The part of her who'd screamed Mizu's name. The part of her that had allowed her body to lean forward, that allowed her instincts to take over.

The rational part of her, the part that pushed her to survive, had been lost under the roar of the crowd. Sunk into the depths as something else broke free. A need to right a wrong.

Mizu lay bleeding, Cyrene's voice hidden behind the bursts of noise as Eve sank.

And sank.

And sank.

The Drakon swam towards her, slick and smooth against the current. The crowd was a blur as the gilded handle of her knife glittered amongst the treasure and shot like a brazen arrow towards the monster.

Her awful dress pulled her down, flailing behind like a lost piece of seaweed. A siren drowning a sailor.

She let it.

The beast locked its red-rimmed eyes on her.

This was it. The moment fate bared its teeth.

Her knife flew, spinning through the water, and struck true. Straight into the beast's eye.

The Drakon reared back, a guttural cry ripping from its throat. Its tail whipped through the air.

Eve didn't move in time. The blow struck like a wave, lifting her off her feet. She slammed into the treasure pile, gold and steel clattering beneath her. Pain bloomed sharp and sudden as something jagged tore through her thigh.

She gasped.

Her dress twisted around her limbs, tightening like a snare. Every breath caught. Her chest heaved, but the fabric held fast.

All around her, the roar filled the water. The crowd. The beast. Its pain bled into the ocean like smoke, thick and alive.

She fought against the current and tumbled through the water, leaving a trail of blood behind her. She scrambled over the treasure, and pushed towards Mizu.

The Drakon thrashed. His claws raked towards his eyes, forcing waves through the water.

Her dress snagged on the edge of a birdcage, the fabric tugging tight. She yanked hard, and the material tore with a sharp rip that freed her legs. Eve scrambled upright, slipping over scattered treasure, coins clinking, gems skittering beneath her palms. She crawled toward the shadows, searching for cover.

The currents surged around her, relentless. Each kick dragged her sideways, each stroke a fight against the pull. Water pressed in from all sides, cold and heavy, as if the sea itself wanted to claim her.

The Drakon roared, raw and thunderous. The sound shook the walls and rattled the treasure beneath them. Its claw gripped Eve's knife and tore it free from its eye, blood steaming. The rage behind that roar raised bumps along Eve's skin, a primal warning that pulsed through her bones.

This has to be most idiotic thing you've ever done.

Down here, Eve was prey. A fish amongst sharks. And she had served herself on a platter.

Blood coated her tongue, sharp and metallic, as if she'd bitten iron. Pain lanced through her leg, the gash so deep it scraped bone. She kicked, floundering, the water thick around her limbs. Mizu's voice cut through the chaos, but she couldn't make out the words. Roars echoed off the cavern walls, mingling with the beast's screech and the shriek of shifting stone.

A sudden current surged beneath her, dragging her sideways, straight toward the thorny throne. She twisted mid-pull, just as the Drakon slashed past, claws raking her arm, heat blooming along her skin. The force flung her upside down. Her breath caught, a gasp torn from her throat as the world spun.

Blood blurred her vision. The cavern tilted. And somewhere in the dark, the Drakon circled again.

Before she could right herself, the beast smacked into her side, and she crashed into an old table. Spots coated her vision, blinking in and out like the starlit sky.

Strong arms wrapped around her, hot against her skin, fire to the ocean's ice, and she blinked. Mizu's long hair tickled her nose but his grip was firm.

'*Frik Nagin,*' he hissed.

She didn't need to ask what he meant. The venom in his voice told her enough. She was a stupid girl. A rash one. A weak one. She wasn't a warrior. She wasn't even brave.

The Prince yanked her behind a towering shield, its silver surface dulled by age and battle. Splintered wood scraped her spine as he pressed her into cover, the jagged edges biting through fabric. His grip was unyielding, steady, but she had no strength left to resist. Her limbs hung heavy, breath shallow, the fight draining from her faster than the blood in the water. She hissed as the Merprince pressed against the wound on her side. His hands were shaking. Bruises covered his chest, and one eye was swollen nearly shut. His breath came shallow, rough.

He didn't argue when she pushed him away. Just leaned against the shield and peered into the gloom, tracking the Drakon as it slithered out of sight.

Above them, the crowd was a blurred hum, their shapes like shadows in a hive. The pressure in her limbs pulsed like a drumbeat. Eve wished for a Halopod, something to suck the pain from her bones.

'You have ruined everything,' Mizu rasped, dropping to one knee. Blood trickled between his fingers as he clutched his side.

'I'm sorry for trying to save your life,' Eve shot back. 'Next time I'll let the monster eat you.'

'You do not understand their culture. Their reasons.'

'You were going to die!'

'And now you will, too.' His voice cracked. 'I had every intention of winning. Of uniting the undersea realms.'

'Forgive me for not interpreting your riddles and half-truths! You looked like you were ready to die.'

His jaw clenched as he leaned in further. 'To be ready to die, and to want death are two different things, *Nagin*. I will embrace death when the time comes, but that does not mean I will not fight for life.'

Eve clenched her teeth as she sat up, pain rippling through her body.

She choked back a sob as she saw her wound, the gash on her leg jagged and unruly.

Mizu was already moving, shoving aside coins and shattered relics, hands diving into the glittering mess until he pulled free a tangle of sea grass and weeds. He didn't speak. His fingers worked fast, grinding the strands into a thick, green paste against the stone.

Then he struck.

The paste slapped onto her wound, cold and biting. Eve hissed, breath sharp through clenched teeth.

He wrapped it in seaweed, knotting it tight with practiced hands. The dressing was crude, but it held.

'Can you still win?' she asked, her legs trembling.

'Even if I defeat it, I won't be granted victory,' he said. 'Your interference broke the terms. The bargain is void.'

'I'm sorry,' Eve said. And meant it.

He looked at her, surprised. 'You sound like you don't say that often.'

'It was hard,' she admitted.

But true.

'I'm rarely ever wrong,' she joked, a sad laugh escaping.

'With a gift like yours, I don't doubt it, Nagin.'

In response to his words, Eve's gift flared and fired through her spine. White blinded her vision, and she gasped.

Mizu's rough hands grasped her. 'What's wrong?'

Her power thrummed, the call beating from everywhere and nowhere. With stilted breaths she focused, following the thread like the north star leading a sailor. It flickered on her left.

'I feel it,' she said. 'The Morei.'

'Is that why you are here?' he asked.

A grumble echoed through the darkness, the Drakon crawling closer.

'*Mirrors of Glass in a watery cage,*' he echoed. 'You are the one.'

Eve didn't reply, pushing back the onslaught raging inside her. The stone thrummed in her pocket.

Mizu peered into the dark, his shoulders set. 'I know you killed my sister.'

She flinched. 'I didn't—'

'I forgive you,' he said, taking her hand. 'I knew what she was like. How she dreamed. How she behaved. She was petulant. And brash. And vibrant. But she was also kind.'

'She asked me to do it. She couldn't ...'

'I know,' Mizu replied. 'I spent many years after her death following the trail. Paid my price to walk amongst the land dwellers for truths.'

Eve swallowed, barely breathing.

'And all roads led to the same conclusion. That her dream was not as bright as she had hoped. And at the end, her death was a blessing. Do not hold that guilt. Or that pain. I forgive you.'

I forgive you.

If only she'd done the same with Hansel earlier.

Eve's gift throbbed, pulling her to the side as it sucked the air from her lungs. Bile rose to her throat, the magic taking hold as she fought against it.

'Find the Morei,' Mizu said. 'Save us, *Nagin*.' He let go of her just as the Drakon slithered past.

Mizu dove for the trident, his shout tearing through the water. A *crash* followed, then a *boom*, and treasures exploded like falling stars. The chasm walls groaned.

Eve's gift tugged at her like puppet strings. She crawled to the shield and peered around its edge. Through the watery haze, she spotted Mizu darting between fallen gold and shattered glass.

The Drakon loomed behind him, a mass of shadow and fury, its rumble vibrating through the cavern walls.

Mizu dove behind a toppled statue of a human prince, face cracked and half-buried in coins. The Prince looked at Eve, eyes sharp, and gave a single nod.

He wasn't running.

He was buying her time.

Save us, Nagin.

She shut her eyes and drew a shaky breath. It was now or never.

The beast turned. Mizu roared, lunging with his trident raised.

Eve pushed off the cavern floor, arms slicing through the

water in wild, uneven strokes. The current clawed at her, slowing her down.

She wasn't made for this.

The deep had always been something she watched from the shore, toes barely brushing its edge. Now it swallowed her whole, and every kick reminded her of the choice she never made.

Regret bloomed in her chest, bitter and rising.

Through the haze, something caught her eye.

It sat alone, half-buried beneath a spill of gold coins and shattered gems. Its surface was smooth, dark as ink, untouched by dust or time. A black mirror.

The mirror was small, delicate, the kind once cradled in a noblewoman's hand, used to check rouge and powder beneath candlelight. The frame was wrought from blackened silver, tarnished in places, but still etched with curling vines and tiny stars. Its handle tapered like a stem, smooth and cold, ending in a flourish of filigree.

Despite the centuries buried beneath treasure, the glass remained untouched. No rust, no cracks. Just a perfect, obsidian reflection.

It hummed with quiet power, as if it had been waiting for her.

Mizu screamed, but she didn't turn. The mirror glinted in the dark. She reached for it, hunger flaring deep in her gut, unfamiliar and sharp. The current slammed her against a jagged rock and she hissed in pain. She braced herself and launched off it, arm outstretched.

Her fingers closed around the mirror's handle.

And then the pain hit.

It was like lightning down her spine. She writhed, flailing through the water as the mirror pulsed in her grip.

The Drakon aimed for her.

Eve kicked through the water, dodging just in time, the beast's claw tearing through the space where she'd been. She darted between stone walls, treasure piled high on either side, the weight of it pressing in.

'Mizu?' she gasped.

No answer. Only the echo of her breath.

Eve clutched the mirror in one hand, the other dragging along jagged stone as she struggled to stay upright. Her vision blurred, dark spots blooming as she slammed into the wall again. The gash in her leg spilled warmth into the water, a crimson trail curling behind her.

The Drakon rose, massive and furious. Its pale and crimson scales were torn, patches of hide missing, raw muscle exposed beneath. Steam hissed from its flared nostrils, and its teeth gleamed.

She was cornered. No escape. No help.

This is how I die.

The mirror dug into her skin, the blackened frame shifting, curling around her palm like it had a will of its own. The stone was hot, burning into her side as the beast readied itself to pounce. Eve chanced a look towards the stadium, to the podium where she knew her friend stood, and said a prayer.

Forgive me.

And as the beast charged, Eve screamed and thrust the mirror before her. She waited for the impact. For death.

But it didn't come.

She blinked, back pressed hard to the wall, her dress torn in places beyond mending. Instead of pain, she found herself staring into the eye of the Drakon.

The mirror, barely the size of one of his scales, hung in her grip, modest and unthreatening. Yet the Drakon was caught in it. His eye locked on the glass, a strange gurgle bubbling from his throat.

The Morei glowed. Its frame melted into tendrils of inky black that stretched towards the beast.

Voices whispered from within the glass. *Let us take it.*

Like oil spilled through water, the ink spread across the Drakon's scales, clinging to the monster like fire to dry leaves. White scales turned obsidian. Hardened. Changed. Eve didn't breathe. Her hand trembled against the pulse of magic. The stone in her pocket blazed, searing her skin. Still, she didn't cry out.

Not when the black consumed the Drakon's eyes. Not when her gilded knife floated down before her, gleaming. Not when the Drakon twisted. Seethed. *Changed.* Until it floated before her, no longer flesh but a statue of shadow and death.

Somewhere beyond the hum of power, she heard Mizu scream her name.

But she couldn't move.

The current roared around her. She was upside down, inside out, her skin turned raw and her bones painted in shadow.

Master, the mirror whispered. *Feed us.*

Eve could smell her skin cooking, scorched to the core. Her leg shrieked as pain flared where the stone's magic touched it.

Still, she could not move.

Golden light tore through the gloom as Mizu leapt, the trident blazing in his grip. He landed beside the Drakon, frozen mid-snarl, its pale and crimson scales locked in place, claws raised in eternal fury.

With a cry, Mizu swung.

The trident struck the beast's head, and the impact rang out like a bell. Cracks spidered across its surface, light pouring through the fractures. Then, with a sound like shattering ice, the Drakon's head exploded into shards of black glass, scattering across the cavern floor.

The mirror dropped from Eve's hand. Mizu caught it.

She vomited into the water.

Eve's hand trembled as she pulled the stone from her pocket, its silver veins pulsing like lightning. She crawled to Mizu, each movement a battle against pain and the crushing depths. He was motionless, his body beaten, and his eyes locked on the mirror with a hollow, unblinking stare.

The frame slithered toward him, slow and deliberate, its edges dripping in thick black sludge that coiled around his tail. His mouth opened. Closed. Caught in silence.

Eve stumbled forward, her vision lurching like a ship caught in a storm. The mirror pulsed, dark and hungry. She reached it, raised the stone high, and brought it down onto the glass with everything she had left.

A crack split the air.

The cavern shuddered. And as Eve felt the blood drain from her body, the last thing she saw was the lapis stone drinking the mirror whole, vanishing it into shadow.

XLVI

The Triks of The Trade

Malak drove the club into the dummy's gut with a grunt, sweat flicking from his brow. The sky was still pale, the sun slow to rise, but he'd been here for a while now, hammering his body through motion, through breath, through anything that might silence his thoughts. But they clung to him like the mist that skirted over his skin.

Snow's voice still echoed through him, that flat edge she used when speaking to him. When she had given up. He should have found better words last night, should have pushed through the fog of frustration and hurt, but instead he'd only made it worse. Again.

He ducked, swung wide, then twisted the club and landed a strike against the post that splintered some of the wood. The force jolted up his arm, but he welcomed the ache.

Malak turned, began again, drilling footwork Hansel had taught him long ago, grounding himself in each motion. He was heavier now, stronger, but some stances still pulled at old bruises and half-healed memories. That was fine. That was part of the ritual.

A shout rang out overhead.

He paused, the hairs on his arms rising.

Another shout, clearer this time, followed by the jangle of bells. The castle stirred.

Malak's hand gripped the club tighter. He scanned the walls, the rising towers, and caught the burst of movement as a window flew open and Pip leaned out, pointing down with his crooked finger.

Malak followed the line of his hand. And saw him. Trik. Walking through the mist like a shadow from some half-remembered nightmare.

His pale scar shone pink in the soft light, slicing across the base of his skull like a brand. He didn't run. Didn't hide. Just walked forward with that same easy arrogance.

Malak's blood chilled.

What in the cauldron was he doing loose?

Malak growled, the sound feral as the crow approached. He seemed unconcerned, casually walking along the grass as a few guards ran out after him. He raised his arms in silent surrender as more shouts rang out.

'*How* in the cauldron did you get out?' Malak growled, raising his weapon.

Trik shrugged. 'I told you, I'm not here to cause trouble. Just to make a bargain.'

'That's not what I asked. Try again.'

'I thought they said you were smart for a troll.' Trik picked some invisible lint off his shirt. His clothes were fresh, probably stolen from one of the many empty rooms. 'I shifted, of course. No rope or bars can keep a crow from slipping through.'

'The magic should have.'

'Oh, that,' he replied, grinning. 'That was more challenging, but not impossible. I've been working with Myrenna a while, I've picked up some tricks. Get it? Trik.' He chuckled.

Malak didn't.

One night. *Less* than one night and their enemy had escaped, looking more like he was on holiday than a prisoner amongst enemies. Incompetent didn't even begin to describe how he felt about this turn of events.

'Calm down,' Trik said, shrugging. 'I won't go anywhere.'

'It helps that you have nowhere else to go,' Pip said, puffing as he reached the training platform.

Trik just rolled his eyes.

Malak clutched his weapon, his body radiating nervous energy despite the workout. If Trik's escape had been as breezy as he implied, then where had the crow been until now?

Malak nodded to the guards. They backed up, but remained at the ready.

'We haven't yet decided on your offer,' Malak said low, his voice laced with warning.

Trik's brows raised, utterly unaffected. 'Really? I assumed it was a flat out *no,* considering your history.'

'If you knew it was a "no,"' Malak asked, watching his every move, 'then why ask for Snow?'

Trik picked up one of the training swords and swung it

smoothly through the air. Testing its weight and feel. 'To unsettle you.'

Malak scrutinized the movements, precise and unyielding. 'Where have you been since you decided to break free of your chains?'

'Here and there,' Trik mused, eyeing Malak's stance.

Malak shivered at the thought of them all asleep whilst this monster roamed their halls. Anything could have happened. *Anything.*

'I know what you're thinking,' Trik said. 'That I could have slit your throats in your sleep.'

'You could have,' Malak said. 'So, why didn't you?'

'As I said last night, it's not in my interest.'

Malak eyed Trik carefully as he stepped onto the training platform, his gait light and confident. He didn't fear Malak, that much was clear.

'What is it you want, then?' Malak asked.

Trik cracked his shoulders. 'The usual. Revenge. Freedom. Family.'

'Simple requests,' Pip replied drily as Trik twirled the sword, bending his knees with a dark grin.

'Simple words. Complicated requests.'

Something primal reared inside Malak. Snow had been asleep. Snow had been in that castle. One minor mistake and she could have been taken. The whole rebellion overthrown with the swipe of a knife.

Trik's eyes gleamed in challenge. 'I find the best way to know your opponent is to face them. Preferably in battle. You can gather a lot of truths about someone without saying a word.'

Malak didn't respond, opting to throw the sword in favour of his club. He matched Trik's steps as they circled each other.

Pip grunted from the sideline as Trik said, 'If you attack too quick, you learn they are brash. If the technique is weak, they have no commitment. If they parry, they like to play.'

Trik's sword shot out and Malak met it with a swipe, knocking it back with ease. There was a rumble in his throat, his killer instincts shifting into overdrive.

'If the opponent is slow, well,' Trik said, 'they're just slow.'

'I assure you, *Crow*, I'm not slow.'

'Neither am I.'

With that, he lurched forward, jolting the sword in a feigned attack before he spun, bringing it towards Malak's side. Malak saw it clearly and turned with a graceful spin before raising his club high. The sword clanged on the spikes attached to Malak's club.

The shifter grinned as he stepped back and swung his sword in a smooth arc. Malak met blow for blow, his club holding against steel. Their feet shuffled like two dancers. Each spike bit into the sword and each edge came crashing back towards him.

After another hit, Trik swerved again, ducking before he pushed his sword forward, barely missing Malak's abdomen as the troll careened back. And on it went, the two of them parrying and dancing and clashing until sweat dripped from them both, their weapons gleaming in the high, burning sun.

'Tell us what you really want,' Malak said as he lunged. His club collided with the sword, catching on the edge as it twisted the crow's wrist. He turned, and Malak went for the hit, punching him in the ribs.

The crow grunted but jumped back, his sword firmly in hand. 'I told you. I want to get away from *her.*'

They'd drawn a crowd now, some of the staff lingering nearby.

'Convenient that we're the ones you come to,' Malak said. 'The very people who slayed your lover.'

Trik's brow twitched. Only slightly, but enough that Malak knew he'd hit a sore spot. The crow gracefully dodged Malak's next attack, pushed the club back, and kicked Malak's thigh.

The troll stumbled back, a growl in his throat. 'You shouldn't be here.'

'You can lock me up and I'll stay this time if it makes you feel safer,' Trik replied.

The crow was playing with him, luring him into a slow creeping anger. Malak saw what he was doing, his parents had done the same with the intention of breaking him. But he wouldn't break.

He had to unnerve Trik, to put him off if he wanted to win.

'What will it take you make you leave?' Malak growled.

'I told you,' Trik said, 'a bargain.'

'Snow isn't on the table.'

Trik swung again and Malk deflected, side stepping the crow and creating space between them. He hated what he was about to do, but with so little choices available, what else could he do?

'Then you have nothing I want.' Trik sneered, prowling forward.

Malak raised his club, ready for a strike. 'What about your brother?'

Trik halted. His face twisted into something Malak couldn't pin. Trik flung the sword from his hands, letting it clatter a few feet away. Then he ran at Malak.

Malak swung again, aiming for the crow's stomach, but missed when Trik pivoted.

'What do you know of my brother?' Trik hissed, fury in his eyes.

'I know something has happened with you and Dread. Something big if you left him like this.' Malak was only guessing, of course, but from the narrowed eyes and clenched jaw, he had hit bullseye. 'But I'm not offering Dread. You know that.'

The crow didn't respond.

Malak circled him, his blood thrumming under the surface. He felt the gaze of the guards, the others coming from the castle to see the spectacle. He was surrounded, and Malak had an opportunity.

Trik was still as he snarled, 'Where's Flynn?'

Flynn.

Malak watched Trik pace, taking in his features in a new light. The brothers looked different, of course, but there were similarities. The gait, the shape of their jaws, the sharp eyes. Malak smirked at the realisation.

'I know where he's been.' Malak said.

He hadn't known before this moment, riding on a hunch of discord and lost family. But as soon as the shifter had revealed his weakness, he gambled that the Flynn they'd seen at the Skinny Piglet and the crow's brother were one and the same.

I can guarantee one of her crows has their eyes on you right now.

'Liar,' Trik hissed.

Malak took another gamble.

'Is he about this height?' Malak said, lifting his green hand. 'With slicked black hair and piercing green eyes? A little cocky, and likes to grin?'

Trik's throat bobbed, and the air tightened. A subtle vibration that prickled along Malak's skin. He'd felt it before he saw it, the quiet thrum of fury building behind Trik's eyes. That kind of silence never lasted long.

Malak braced himself.

Trik was going to blow, and if he did something stupid, Malak would be more than happy to put him down.

Trik's voice was low. 'Where is he?'

'You wanted a bargain?' Malak asked. 'Here it is. You tell us when Myrenna's next strike will happen, and I'll tell you where I saw Flynn last.'

Trik laughed, loud and piercing. 'That's your first question? You're terrible at this.'

Malak blinked, trying to understand, when Trik pointed to Adanna who sat near the edge of the castle in her chair. Laurie stood behind her, both women frowning.

'She already knows when the Queen will arrive. When the skies will darken with churning black smoke and the flying death will descend. She has seen it coming and it is only a matter of days.' He smiled wickedly at Malak. 'Perhaps you should stop lying to each other first before you seek truths from me.'

A matter of days. By the cauldron.

'That's enough from you,' Malak growled, raising his club.

'I disagree, it's my turn,' Trik said. 'Where's my brother?'

Malak turned to Adanna who nodded permission for him to speak. 'We saw him a few weeks ago,' he replied coldly. 'Near Roserock. He'd stopped at a tavern called the Skinny Piglet.'

'Why?'

Now Malak grinned. 'Tell me why you defected first.'

'Her Majesty, my brother, and I had an altercation,' Trik said. 'It was not in my favour. What was Flynn doing at the Skinny Piglet?'

They continued to circle each other.

'He was trading,' Malak replied. 'And before you ask for what, I don't know. He was shady about it.'

Trik nodded, as if that was a common occurrence for his brother.

'Why does the Queen want Perridorm?' Malak asked.

Trik sighed. 'Do you not follow anything?'

'Just answer the question.'

'She wants the scrolls and the sword. The southern parts of Bellatorre and Perridorm align with the merkingdom and the Isle of Nysa. This kingdom holds strange magic, and the sea holds treasures. She wants them. *Needs* them.'

'I thought she only needed Snow's heart.'

'Just as a man only needs water to survive,' Trik sneered. 'Snow's heart will sustain her, but only for what comes next.'

'What comes next?'

'I think you're out of questions.'

Malak held up his club. 'Flynn is with the rebellion. He's on our side.'

Trik paused and ran his hand over his face. 'Shit.'

'You don't seem surprised.'

'Dread insinuated, but I never thought he'd do it. Not truly.'

Malak didn't care about his brother. Didn't care about whatever squabble happened between them. He stepped forward, the spikes close to Trik's head as he growled, 'What. Comes. Next?'

Something like regret crossed Trik's features. 'Death comes next. She comes as soon as she finds the mirror in that mine of hers.'

Trik had gone silently as Malak ordered the guards to lock him up. This time, the enchantments would be stronger with multiple guards on watch at every interval. They'd given him a room this time.

The crowd had dispersed quickly after the match, the weight of Trik's words lying heavily on them.

'Death comes next. She comes as soon as she finds the mirror in that mine of hers.'

Malak tried to not pay it any heed as he followed Snow from the training grounds, keeping up with her quick pace.

'Are you ready to talk now?' he asked.

She stopped. 'After that spectacle, you want to talk?'

'It's better than thinking about Myrenna coming with another mirror in her possession.'

Her blue eyes glittered, losing herself in some dark place within.

He asked, 'Are you holding up okay?'

'What do you want, Malak?'

'I want to talk, to figure out whatever is going on with you. I feel like ...' he struggled for words. 'I feel like there's this chasm between us, and every time I try to cross it, it collapses. I just want to close it and stand on the same ground as you again.'

She was silent a moment, watching the trees and unruly gardens with keen eyes. 'What if I don't want that?'

He frowned. 'I don't understand.'

She shook her head. 'That's the problem. You never do.'

'I—'

'Leave me alone, Malak,' she said, walking away. She didn't look back.

They were simple words with a simple request. But as his chest bled from within, a crack forming in his heart, he knew it was far more complicated than that.

That night, Snow lingered in the shadows, her eyes fixed on Trik's door. The youngest of the guards yawned and rubbed at his eyes, shifting from foot to foot. He was barely past boyhood, and his uniform – green and cream trimmed with charcoal – looked more suited to a court page than a soldier. Compared to Bellatorre's red and purple, his colours looked soft, like something pulled from a storybook rather than a warfront. He would have been better suited to guarding her crystal coffin than the dark corridors of a half-forgotten castle.

The stars had disappeared, swallowed by low clouds crawling across the sky. Earlier, the air had clung warm and wet to her skin, teasing rain and frizzing the tips of her short curls. Summer crept closer, drying the earth and stretching the hours of light thin as glass.

Snow pressed into the stone wall behind her. The soles of her feet throbbed, still a little raw from being barefoot on the battlefield when she had faced Artemis. It had been nearly three hours, and the only soul to approach had been Laurie, carrying a tray of tea into Trik's room. Since then, nothing. No whispers, no footsteps, only the occasional creak of wood or groan of wind through the windows.

Snow lightly trailed her fingers along the letter she'd written, the parchment already crinkled.

Footsteps echoed again. She shrank further into the alcove, watching as a pair of guards rounded the corner, their conversation low.

'Trey's late again,' one muttered. 'He's meant to take second watch. I'm not covering for him twice in a week.'

The younger boy at the door perked up. 'He said he'll be here in a few minutes. Overslept. Did you want to grab a bite before the next round?'

The older man shook his head. 'No, I think I'll sleep. If he's here soon, I might run home before the Prince and Princess wake. I've got first light tomorrow.'

He leaned his ear against the door, listening to the soft breathing of the prisoner within. 'I reckon you'll be alright. I'll walk you to the gate. Your mother'll kill me if you pass out before getting home.'

They moved off together, boots tapping against stone, their voices fading.

Snow didn't hesitate. She darted forward, pressed her ear to the door, then slipped the paper beneath it with a swift flick of her fingers. She knocked softly then ran, not daring to wait for the other guard's arrival. She ducked back into the shadows, peering around the corner, hoping Trik was awake.

A lone black feather slid under the door.

With a grin, she slipped away, scurrying along the hallways. She reached the library in minutes, pushing against the heavy doors with a grunt.

'Snow?' a voice said from behind her.

She swore under her breath as Malak emerged from the shadows. He looked at her like a stranger, as if one wrong word would set her off.

'Are you following me?' she asked, unable to hide the venom in her voice.

'I don't need to,' he said. 'It seems fate keeps bringing us together.'

She rolled her eyes, and he looked at the doors behind her.

'Why are you going to the library this late?'

Get rid of him, the voices said.

I'm trying.

'I'm getting a book, if you must know,' she replied. 'It helps me sleep.'

It wasn't unusual for her to want a book for bed; she'd lived in them for most of her life, wishing she could obtain the freedom they had. The adventure.

'Did you want me to help?' he asked.

'Not particularly.'

He flinched and she bit her bottom lip. Trik would be meeting her any moment. She had to get rid of him.

'I told you to leave me alone,' she said. 'Why won't you?'

'Because ...' he said. 'I love you. I'll always love you.'

The words struck like a knife, soft but sharp, slicing somewhere deep. When she had woken in the grotto to find him half-dead and bleeding, the sound of his voice had guided her back. The glow worms had blinked overhead like stars caught underground and for an impossible moment, they had shared something real. Then Eveline crept into her thoughts, slick as poison, and the memory curdled.

Her voice came out hard. 'I don't love you.'

His face twisted, as if she'd run him through. She felt her hand tighten over her chest, the other gripping the door handle.

'I know you love Hansel,' Malak said, quieter now. 'You may never love me the way I love you, but I'll be here anyway.

Protecting you. Guiding you. Saving you. I made a vow and I plan on keeping it.'

Snow laughed. It was bitter, sharp around the edges. That vow again. 'I don't want it,' she spat.

Malak flinched, the sound of it like a slap. 'You don't mean that.'

'I do.' Her voice trembled, but not with doubt. 'I relieve you of your vow. I don't want it. Not when it costs me my freedom. My voice. I need to do this on my own.'

'I—'

'Get out, Malak.'

He stood frozen.

'I said, get out.'

His head bowed, heartbreak written across every inch of him. Still, all he said was, 'Goodnight, Princess.' Malak shut the door behind him.

Snow rubbed her temple. She'd been reckless and horrible. Callous and cruel. But it needed to be done for what she had to do.

Have I been too harsh?

No, the voices replied. *You have been kind. Trolls have no place in history.*

I always imagined we'd rule together. Hansel and Malak and me.

You are perfect. Better to rule alone with Hansel by your side as consort.

'I don't know if that was cute or disturbing,' a voice said from the fireplace.

She jumped, but steadied her breathing when she saw it was Trik. 'He means well.'

'He's a troll,' Trik said, standing. 'Trolls don't love, or make vows, or ever end up with a human. I retain my previous statement. It was disturbing.'

Snow scowled. 'He's a half-breed. Part human, part troll. He can feel all of the above.'

'How sweet,' he mused. 'Sticking up for the creature who stalks you.'

She wanted to smack that smirk off his face. 'He doesn't stalk me. He protects me.'

And suffocates you.

Trik followed as she left for the stacks, his lurking hulk of a body close behind her. She eyed the shelves, ensuring Petrella wasn't going to appear.

'It's not my business,' Trik said, breathing in her ear. 'But one word of advice, *Princess*. If I were to become Queen, I would use that obsession to its fullest capability.'

'What's that supposed to mean?' she said, turning around.

His eyes glittered. 'It means, if you don't have to be alone, don't be. I learnt that the hard way.'

He shuffled past her, seeming to follow the thrum of power echoing through the stacks.

Don't trust him, the voices said, *he's a liar.*

He was a liar. And a torturer.

After.

'After,' she whispered to herself, pulling her knife free.

XLVII
The Crashing of a Kingdom

The Queen struck first.

A backhand across Cyrene's face, sharp and sudden, sent her reeling through the water. Her cheek burned. Before she could recover, the Merking's hand closed around the Queen's throat.

His grief poured from him like poison in the water. He'd lost both his children to fates twisted beyond imagining. Now, he promised the Queen nothing less.

They surged toward the chasm, limbs tangled, teeth bared.

The seabed trembled beneath them, the quake rippling outward. Chunks of rock splintered from the cliffs and fell, swallowed by the mouth of the deep. The treasure trove, once a symbol of glory, now cracked and crumbled, becoming a tomb.

All thanks to Eveline and that mirror.

Cyrene floated in the current, stunned, her body spinning in the chaos. The magic that once guarded the Drakon's hoard was gone. The sea had turned on itself.

The stadium above fractured into madness. Bodies drifted, some lifeless, others thrashing in panic. The podium hung at an angle, one side collapsed under the weight of the fleeing nobles. Screams echoed through the water. Nymphs clawed toward open sea, scales flashing as they dodged falling debris. Somewhere, a child cried out, the sound sharp enough to cut through stone and current alike.

Cyrene didn't move. She only watched as the sea tore itself apart.

Edmar appeared beside her and pulled her back. 'We have to leave.'

But her eyes were fixed on the King and Queen, still in the royal box. Her mother lunged, ripping a knife from her belt and slashing at the Merking. There was no hesitation. Only fury. The blade sank deep. Blood bloomed across his chest like ink in water, but he didn't waver.

Around them, guards clashed with panicked nymphs. The crowd surged and fractured. But Cyrene could only think of one thing: Eveline.

She thrashed in Edmar's grip, fighting the weight of him as he pulled her back. His stupid soft hair brushed her cheek. Her feet tangled in her gown and rage flared in her chest. She wanted trousers, her spear, anything but this silk prison and empty hands.

'They're dead' he yelled over the chaos.

'NO!' she screamed.

The ground rumbled as another giant bone shifted and fell, the undercurrent pulling at the shadowed nymphs trying to escape. It landed on a podium, crushing her people beneath it.

This was what her kingdom had become. A bloodbath.

'Cyrene!' Edmar yelled. 'Stop fighting me.'

Her elbow crunched into his stomach. He stumbled back, gasping. She turned just in time to see her mother transform, tentacles unfurling from her scales like sea snakes, coiling around the Merking.

He struggled, pushing against her, but the Queen only laughed, a shrill, piercing sound that split the water.

'What have you done!?' Cyrene screamed.

A tentacle lashed out, slamming her to the seafloor. Pain laced her body.

'There will be no more bargains,' the Queen said.

'At what cost?' she asked. 'We had a chance at peace.'

The Queen only cackled. 'Peace will come. The Merking has no heirs left. I will be Queen of Nysa *and* Teal Cove.'

'Stop it,' Cyrene begged. 'Please.'

Tentacles wrapped around the Merking's mouth and pulled tight. His skin flushed red, eyes wide with horror as the Queen grew and grew.

'This won't stop what's coming,' Cyrene begged, pushing herself to stand. 'It won't stop the ripple. It won't stop Myrenna.'

Her mother ignored her, transfixed on the choking king.

Cyrene dodged another tentacle and turned to Edmar. He stood a few pixies away, his eyes wide as another giant bone fell from the sky.

'Edmar,' she yelled. 'Give me your knife.

He flinched, eyes blank with terror.

'Give me the knife,' she urged again.

He backed away as a tentacle reached towards him.

'Edmar!' Cyrene snapped.

But a fleeing body slammed into him, and he shook his head. Her hand was outstretched, ready to offer help. Instead, Edmar fled.

'Coward!' she screamed, just as one of her mother's tentacles latched onto her arm. It yanked her backward, slime clinging to her scales. She barely missed a fleeing child as she was dragged through the water, until she was face to face with the Queen.

'Why have you always fought against me?' her mother raged. 'We are about to *win* and yet you still act like a stubborn child. This is for *us*.'

Breathless and heartbroken, Cyrene stared into her mother's eyes. Eyes that had once cared for her. Loved her. Taught her. She knew she would bleed for it, but her mother was right in one thing. She *was* stubborn.

Her hand gripped the tentacle, her nails digging into flesh. 'You say "us." Not them.'

Her mother frowned, the Merking kneeling before her. 'Everything I do is for us,' she replied.

Cyrene saw the glint of her mother's knife. She took in her mother's face one last time. 'Who will fight for them if it is just us?'

With a jolt, Cyrene seized the knife and slashed. The Queen screamed as a lock of her hair fell, the ring of their bloodline tumbling to the seafloor. Cyrene cut the tentacle next, freeing her arm.

The Queen slithered back, eyes blazing. 'I taught you everything!' she seethed. 'And you learnt nothing.'

'I learnt *everything*,' Cyrene said as she snatched the ring. 'Just not from you.'

The Queen screeched and lunged. Black tentacles flew. Cyrene rolled, dodging their grasp by a hair. The ground cracked beneath the Queen's feet, splitting like a web.

'I loved you,' Cyrene said.

'To love is to die!'

Cyrene drove the knife into the seafloor. The crack widened, splintering under the Queen. The distraction was enough for the Merking to slip free.

The floor gave way, and a chasm opened beneath them. Thunder roared overhead, and the pressure of the currents drove them downward. A massive bone plummeted from above, the last remnant of the stadium's architecture collapsing into ruin.

Cyrene saw it coming.

She screamed, arm stretched out through the water. 'Mother!'

The Queen looked too late. The bone struck with brutal force, crushing her on impact.

Then her mother was gone. Lost to the chasm and debris.

Something deep cracked inside Cyrene. Grief surged, sharp and sudden, but there was no time to drown in it. The sea rumbled again, and her body moved before her mind could catch up.

She grabbed the Merking's arm and hauled it over her shoulders. He was heavy, half-conscious and twice her size. She kicked off the seafloor, fighting the current.

The water roared around her, thick with debris and cries. Bones fell like thunder. Shadows twisted through the wreckage. She didn't look back.

Her muscles burned. Her lungs ached. But she kept swimming.

The current tugged at her, tried to drag her down, but she angled upward, toward the light. Her gown tore against jagged stone. Her shoulder throbbed beneath the weight of the king. Still, she rose.

It wasn't until the water thinned and the pressure eased that she realised they'd broken through. The ruins of Nysa's stadium faded behind her, consumed by distance and dust. The sea turned pale, the light clearer, the silence louder.

She reached a shelf of rock and collapsed onto it, dragging the Merking beside her. He coughed once, then lay still, his chest rising slow and shallow.

Cyrene sat back, her body trembling. Her fingers curled into the stone. She turned toward the wreckage.

The stadium was gone. The treasure. The Seeker. Her people scattered or dead. The Queen – her mother – crushed beneath the weight of her own fury.

Salt stung her eyes, but she didn't blink it away.

She had fought. She had survived. But the cost bled through her bones.

Cyrene bowed her head, the ring of her bloodline clutched in her palm. The sea around her was quiet now, but inside, everything screamed.

She mourned.

For the kingdom that had raised her. For the mother who had ruined it. For the girl she had been.

And the queen she was forced to become.

XLVIII
The Breaking of Innocence

Snow followed Trik towards the restricted section, where chains glowed faintly in the dark. The whispers were silent this time. 'She's not coming,' Trik said, drifting ahead of her between the shelves.

'Who?' she asked.

'The air nymph,' he replied flatly. 'The librarian.'

'Petrella?'

He shrugged. 'I don't care for her name.'

Snow stepped forward, unease prickling beneath her skin.

Something felt off. She couldn't place it, just a sharp, quiet dread at the base of her spine. Was she making a mistake? After all, Florian and Odion had found another way. But the map would only help the twins. Not her.

She breathed in and tried to steady herself. Maybe it was Malak. Maybe his words had unsettled her more than she realised.

Trik pulled a jar from the shelf, snapping her attention back. It was made of thick glass, small enough to sit in his palm, shaped like a coiled spiral. Snow leaned closer, curiosity pushing aside caution.

To her surprise, it moved. A grey wind swirled within, fast and furious, like a storm bottled tight.

'It looks like a mini tornado,' she commented.

Trik shook the bottle a little and a scowling, angry face appeared.

Snow jolted back with a gasp. 'Petrella?'

Trik smiled at her. 'So easily shocked, Princess? I thought you'd have more gumption, considering what you achieved on the battlefield.'

She scowled at him. 'I was just ... surprised.'

'Surprised gets you killed.'

He poked the bottle. 'I'll admit,' he began, taking in the bottle, 'she was harder to catch than the others.'

'Others?'

He sighed. 'Yes, other air nymphs. Their cousins by the sea love violence and treasures. The wood nymphs are a little simpler, preferring the world to be covered in forests with rules and committees. But the air nymphs,' he said with intrigue, 'like to remain solo. They find homes and settle. Much like your troll, they like to protect.'

Snow eyed the bottle then glanced up at the chains. 'This is what she protects?'

He nodded. 'Nymphs may all be slightly different,' he said, moving towards a lock hanging from a low shelf. 'but the one common denominator is treasure. And this, princess, is a treasure.'

'What do we do with her?'

The voices inside her bloomed, dancing to some unknown song as Trik loosened the cap of the jar. The smoke whirled inside.

This is happening, she thought. *It is finally happening.*

Excitement thrummed in her bones, the hum from the lock urging her forward as Petrella screamed inside.

He smirked. 'Her death, will be our key.'

Trik stepped back and crushed the bottle beneath his boot. Air burst out, slamming into Snow's skin like a wave. She staggered as a tiny tornado spun from the floor, shrieking with Petrella's voice. The librarian's nails raked down her cheeks as she screamed.

The whirlwind twisted, faster and faster, until it slammed into the lock.

A sharp crack split the dark. Metal hissed and splintered.

Trik reached for it, fingers closing around the broken latch.

A voice rang out from behind them.

'Stop what you're doing.'

Snow turned slowly, hands raised on instinct, and met Laurie's wide, terrified eyes. The woman stood stiff in the aisle, both hands clutching a sword that looked far too heavy for her. Its point dipped with her shaking arms, but it was still aimed squarely at Trik.

'Let the lock go,' Laurie said. 'Get away from that bookcase.'

Trik didn't move. He only smiled.

Snow stood frozen, heart hammering.

We've been caught.

She was so close. A breath away from answers. From something powerful enough to tip the scales. But now, that hope shrank behind Laurie's trembling stance. A dull roar filled her head, loud enough to drown reason.

Her fingers twitched toward the blade at her side. 'Did you follow me?' she asked, her voice quieter than expected.

Laurie only gulped, the confession in her eyes enough. She was untrained, that much was clear from her unsteady breathing. The shake in her arms. She wasn't comfortable with a sword, not like Snow was.

Trik spoke. 'Are you sure you know what you're doing?'

'I know enough,' Laurie spat. 'I know that you're a prisoner and should be asleep. I put enough potion in that bread to knock you out for a week.'

He only smiled at her in triumph.

'And you,' she said, poking the sword towards Snow, 'are selfish and a brat. I expected betrayal, but not like this. You sacrifice an alliance for this? For *him*?' Her breaths were heavy, her eyes wild. 'He tortured you. He was about to hand you over to the Queen. This is crazy. You're crazy.'

Crazy.

The word ground against Snow's bones. She swallowed fire, the bellowing heat of her anger crawling through her stomach, up through her chest.

She'll take everything. Ruin everything.

Snow's nostrils flared, her heart beating at a hammering pace.

The maid's foot moved forward.

In half a breath, Snow's knife was in hand, in the other

half, her knees hit the ground. Snow twisted and sliced through Laurie's torso.

Laurie's sword clattered to the floor, her hands reaching for her stomach. Her insides fell with a squelch to the ground and blood pooled around Snow's legs.

Snow watched absently as the maid fell, her body thudding on the floor.

Trik squeezed her shoulder. His breath was hot on her ear as he said, 'What's it feel like to be the bad apple?'

Snow stared at Laurie, blade still in hand. She felt Trik leave. Felt the cool kiss of air on her skin. But she didn't move.

Thinking about his question, only one answer came to mind.

It felt powerful.

Adanna rocked in her sheets, sweat coating her brow. Purple smoke and ash hailed through her dreams. Amethyst eyes and setting suns. And blood.

She woke with a start as the breeze rustled the sheer curtains of her rooms. Her sheets lay tangled around her, the silk stark with patches of her sweat, and she pushed it off.

'Laurie?' she called, waiting for the maid to rush in with water.

When there was no response, she wiped her brow with her sleeve.

She must have gone home.

Adanna had begged as much. She had a family, a husband and children. Most nights the maid stayed here, especially after the visitors had arrived, but Laurie was only human. She needed rest.

Adanna did too.

With staggered steps, Adanna lifted her nightgown and shuffled over to her basin. Laurie usually left her a few sleeping concoctions to help with the nightmares, but tonight, it was empty.

Strange.

Laurie never left her without. She was like Adanna's second mother.

Perhaps I missed something.

Perhaps she was a little dazed, as they all were.

Adanna poured some water and sipped, her eyes fixed on the cloth by the door. The sword hummed, beckoning her. She felt the dead too, the ghosts and the soldiers. Even when they slumbered amongst the fields of her lands. It was her curse. Her gift.

Unease coated her shoulders, but she put it down to exhaustion. She had enough to worry about. Enough to carry. Laurie would be okay.

But as she laid down, the soft feathers of her pillow embracing her head, she felt it linger. As if something had gone horribly, horribly awry.

Epilogue

The strength of the mirror seared through Myrenna. Magic blazed, her back arching as black poured from her fingers. Smoke rippled over her skin like a second body. Wild, viscous, alive.

A monster had awoken.

Her eyes pierced the dark. Her laugh echoed like thunder in the silence. Power rolled off her in waves, thrumming its own brutal melody. A thousand suns, burning in rhythm.

Who needed hearts when this – this glorious, boundless well – was hers?

The mines trembled. Distant explosions buzzed in her ears as the walls cracked and groaned.

Stones sliced her bare feet as she rose from the pit. Bones turned to dust beneath her, their symbols vanishing into rock. The exit loomed, sealed shut. Ash drifted from the ceiling.

She raised her arms. Black smoke erupted, carving a tunnel through stone.

Dread followed behind, dragging the mirror like a chained beast.

Cool air kissed her skin as she stepped forward, power streaming in tendrils from her hands. They curled through corpses and ruin, tasting blood and fear. She drank it in. Craved it.

Sunlight slashed through the tunnel mouth as she emerged. Her eyes glowed. Her body thrummed. She was darkness incarnate. A creature born of smoke and hunger.

She was beauty.

She was energy.

She was death.

Dread wheezed behind her as she broke from the tunnel. He blinked in the dusky afternoon sun and gasped as he saw the destruction. The mines were gone, crumbled and caved and broken. They didn't say a word as they trailed towards the high black walls, the sun beckoning her towards the horizon.

She was so close. So near to her dream. Her own happily ever after. Myrenna could almost taste it as Dread stood beside her and kissed her hand. She was no longer afraid.

She had two mirrors and Snow's heart left. The only heart that needed to perish before she finally faced the Sister's Grimm. And it lay in a kingdom surrounded by the dead.

With her newfound wickedness, the Queen looked to the west.

Perridorm had no idea what was coming.

End of Book Four

The Sea Nymph and her Pearl

A SHORT STORY

Faraway, within the murky depths of the wild sea, lived two rivalling kingdoms. One kingdom was etched in sea glass, the other in pearl. Both were a promise. The beating twin-hearts of the great abyss, and though their kingdoms shone in beauty and light, a seed of darkness had been buried. And with it, the burden of blood.

Beneath these waters, with these warring kingdoms, lay two small princesses, each one half of the other. One had that of darkest blue skin and scales which shone under the wilting sun that filtered through the depths of the realm. The other had the tail of a fish, coated in pearlescent scales, its hues of red and silver melting like the dawn of a new day.

Though their families lay in hatred for each other, a war long raged, it did not matter to the two children. For together they were two halves of the same shell. The pearl mermaid was a beacon to the small nymph with blue scales. And like a ship is tied to its captain, so was the sea nymph to the pearl mermaid.

For years they played games, finding each other in the darkest corners of the sea. It was their calling to find lost treasure. And as they reached the age of thirteen, the year they became grown, the girls ventured further towards the land.

The sea nymph was caution, the pearl mermaid a wild storm.

Upon a cool evening, as the starlit sky tickled the surface of the oceans blue, the sea nymph felt a shift in the currents. It brushed against her skin, cooler than usual, threading through the water like a whisper. The pearl mermaid drifted between the coral nearby, unaware, while the sea stirred with something new. It was then a dark shadow crossed over them. A beast above the surface.

The sea nymph shook as the silhouette grew, sucking in the moonlight that spread across the coral. In panic, the two children hid within a shallow cave, the sharp edges of the rock pricking their scales. They watched in awe as the shadow stretched, growing like a gaping abyss. So large it was, that even the coral shivered. The pearl mermaid gasped at the sight. And just when they thought the beast upon them, they saw only barnacles and wood. For above them was not a monster, but a great ship, floating across the seas.

The mermaid pushed herself from the cave as it drifted above them, her eyes shining in new curiosity. The nymph was more hesitant, waiting a breath.

Moonlight danced across the waves, catching on something silver. A glint. A flicker. Then, the surface broke.

A necklace slipped through, delicate and gleaming, its chain twisting as it sank. The light clung to it, casting ripples across the water. It fell slowly, drifting past startled fish and coral spires, sinking deeper into the sea's quiet hush.

In her glee, the pearl mermaid reached forward, her small hands closing over the necklace. And as quickly as the ship came, it was gone.

The mermaid's eyes went wide. Her pale fingers found a latch carved into the necklace's side.

'My pearl,' the sea nymph said. 'It's time for us to go home. We have seen all we can, and are too close to where humans roam.'

But the pearl mermaid ignored the little nymph, her blue eyes only focusing on the small silver treasure she held in her hands. With the flick of the latch, the necklace opened and the pearl mermaid gasped. For inside the necklace was a picture of a man and a human child.

'It's a human!' the mermaid cried. 'Like the skeletons we've seen! This is a true treasure to find indeed!'

But the nymph was not as trusting as the mermaid, doubt having been sown into her bones from her mother, who ruled with an iron fist amongst the kingdom of Nysa.

'Be careful, my pearl,' the sea nymph warned. 'That shadow brings death. We could be harmed. Or take our last breath.'

But the pearl mermaid laughed as she always did, her warm smile calming the rising fear in the nymph's stomach. 'You tread too carefully, as you always do. But if you wish to go home, then I shall come, too.'

The two girls swam home, the sea nymph listening as the mermaid spoke of the secrets they'd unravelled, her heart full of glee. But even in the pearl's happiness, the sea nymph's heart sat heavy. The ship was a shadow, a warning of doom.

The mermaid began to sing a lullaby that echoed through even the darkest caverns of the sea.

Fathoms below, the coffin of men,
Where the water is Death.
And the land is a breath.
Fathoms below, in the sea creatures' den,

Where the beautiful play,
And the sirens stray,
Fathoms below, of tourmaline black,
Where treasures lay deep,
In the sea nymphs' keep.
Fathoms below, humans beware.
For it'll steal your soul,
Enter if you dare.

As each cycle passed, the girls grew into themselves. Under the cover of darkness, the sea nymph would find her pearl amongst the coral they had come to love, and each time the mermaid wore the locket around her neck. But as the nights grew long, and they met each kingdom's demands, the sea nymph found herself more alone amongst that familiar coral, with no pearl mermaid in sight.

On one winter night, as the dark sea chilled, the sea nymph snuck out to find her friend. She swam to that shining city amongst the Merpeople, and she called to her pearl. It was forbidden, but the love in her heart lay no boundaries.

But her pearl no longer answered. She only answered to the locket, her heart consumed by a human man and child.

Three years later, as the nymph sat in her kingdom upon her sixteenth birthday, beside her mother's black throne, she felt a sudden longing in her heart. An ache to see her friend who would also be sixteen this year. It was an age where expectations sat upon the royalty, allowing them to charter their own course.

But it was not new adventures, nor new worlds the sea nymph dreamed of. She only thought of her pearl.

The nymph feared telling her mother such things, as the Queen was known for her powerful potions and powerful temper. To leave Nysa and enter the Merkingdom was treason.

But as her heart went heavy, the stars decided to play their own game that day. For, little did the nymph know, her pearl had finally come.

The doors to the throne room spread wide, allowing her pearl to enter. But she was not the same mermaid who had flittered amongst the coral, nor was she familiar. Her once pearlescent tail was a pale comparison to its former glory, the shimmer dulled and grey. Her cheeks were hollow, but there still remained that spark behind her eyes. The one that called for adventure. Still, against the dark crystallised walls of the throne room and the sea witch, she was a small fading light.

The sea nymph took a step forward and her mother's dark eyes shot her a warning glare. For though the Queen lived for her people, and she ruled fair for her own, she took pleasure in tormenting those who were other. The sea nymph's mouth went dry as her once shining pearl swam forward. Her delicate fingers brushed against a rusted locket, and she bowed before the Queen of Nysa.

'The Princess of Teal Cove has come to my door,' the Queen said. 'Tell me, dear child, why do you taint these floors?'

'I have come to seek help, as I find my soul bleeds. I will give you anything for I'm in dire need. I wish for legs that will never frail, and a human heart, instead of a tail.'

The Queen gave a cruel smile. 'Human legs indeed. What an odd little request. I can give you what you want, but it comes at my behest. If granted to me, it will be your greatest test.'

'Anything you want,' the little mermaid said.

The Queen flashed her teeth and glided down from her throne. 'You have three days to decide on what to trade, little one. But to ensure my secrets, you'll have no tongue.'

The sea nymph stood frozen. The Queen's onyx blade

sliced out her pearl's tongue, dribbling blood onto the floor. When the mermaid collapsed, a small tear slid free. And the sea nymph knew she would never again hear one of the mermaid's songs.

Three days passed, and her pearl did return, though her face held scars and her scales no longer glowed. With small shaking hands, she gave over the necklace, and the sea nymph queen cackled in glee.

The nymph clutched her chest, for she knew what was next, the wicked smile on her mother's lips familiar. As the Queen's sharp teeth flashed, her cauldron opened up from within the floor, its blackened carcass reaching towards the ceiling with arms of bone and seaweed.

'A pity you merfolk only have those tails, your prize and prison in your kingdom of betrayals,' the Queen said. 'I shall grant your wish, but heed my warning: when the potion is drunk, you'll be cut by morning. No more Teal Cove, or family, or scales, and no more singing, or swimming, or tails. Your life will be mortal, so, your years sliced in two, your magic stripped away with years so few. You have one year to seek what you love, and if you fail you, will die above. Your soul will not have refuge, in the Ever After it will not roam. For if you fail, your body becomes sea foam.'

'No!' the nymph cried as she swam to her friend. 'You cannot do this! Its price is your end.'

With a sad little smile, the pearl mermaid kissed her friend and turned to the Queen, ready for her fate.

In a blazing flash of red, magic filled the tourmaline court, filling each crevice as the potion was brewed. With the slice of a coral blade, the Queen cut the pearl's tail. But little to the Queen's knowledge, her daughter's heart was also broken.

In the sea nymph's despair, she begged the Queen to give

her pearl more time, for one cycle was barely a blink in the life-span of a nymph or mermaid. But the Queen did not care. Her eyes burned with the need to bring the Merking sorrow. The Queen did not bargain to help the pearl, but to claim a prize she had long desired. The death of mermaid royalty.

As the mermaid morphed, growing legs from her once pearlescent scales, her sad eyes met the sea nymph princess. And inside that small moment, years of friendship and love and hope echoed back.

The mermaid gasped, her throat choking in the cold waters of Nysa. 'You have dealt your own hand,' the Queen laughed. 'I did not promise to take you to land.'

In horror, the sea nymph dived, grasping her pearl and pulling her from the dark. She would have only moments before the water swallowed her whole. And though she knew her treason, the sea nymph ignored the warning shouts of her mother, and clutched onto her pearl.

They broke through the surface just as her pearl turned blue. The sand felt hard under the sea nymph's feet. She had never trodden on land. Had never dreamed of visiting those who dwelled here. But for now, her fear was gone, for all she had loved lay dying before her. Her pearl as cold as the dark caverns below.

Yet, as the stars shone above them, fate would play another card.

The nymph choked on a sob and the light of a lantern crested the hill. Though she did not wish to leave her, she still wished to save her. She called forth her siren song, letting it drift over the sand. Two men and a girl sighted them, following the song to the shore. They ran down the hill, hissing curses at the nymph who lay by the girl's side.

The land dwellers surrounded her pearl, pumping the

mermaid's chest before the pearl's eyes opened and she coughed out sea water. The sea nymph, dived back into the depths of the ocean and watched as her pearl took the arm of the man, her small steps cautious and clumsy. And upon that night, as she watched the lanterns retreat, the sea nymph's heart cracked, frozen mid beat.

As punishment, her mother, her Queen, hid her away and trained her in the dark. And as she grew, her nature turned to stone. She hid inside herself a small pocket of happiness. For each night, as she dreamt, she dreamt of her pearl. Of the rainbow coral and the secret messages. Of the small hand that grasped hers in comfort when she was frightened. And sometimes, under the depths of a black tourmaline kingdom, when that fear crept in again, the Princess felt the shadow of a soft hand grasp hers.

One year later, when an early dawn filtered through the water like rain, the Princess stepped forward as the royal emissary. She had pled her case and beat her opponents, becoming the youngest the court had ever seen. The Queen, in her displeasure, obliged, and the sea nymph made her way to shore.

As the sand crunched under her steps, she felt the familiar twinge in her heart. The waves crashed to shore, sea foam bubbling at her feet. And though the sea nymph carried out her duties for her court, she always wandered the way other lost hearts do, hoping to find a treasure once lost.

For though she had not found her pearl yet, she would spend all her hundred years doing so.

And she would start by finding the Seeker.

The End

For updates and bonus scenes, you can
join K E Barden's Newsletter by
scanning the QR Code below.

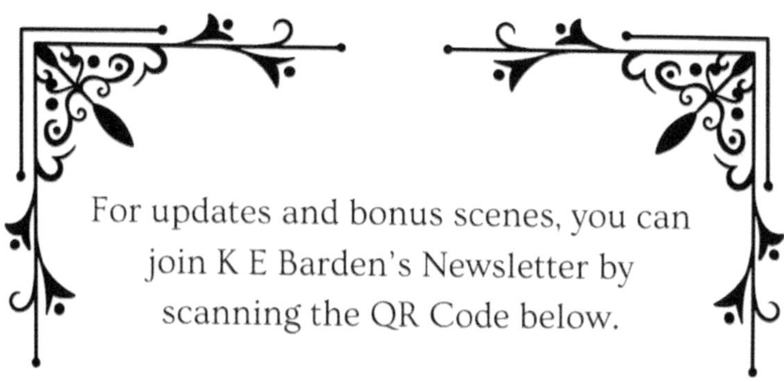

Acknowledgements

Wow. I cannot believe another book is done. Every time I think it should feel different, finishing a book is always a shock to the system. (In the best kind of way).

This book feels extra special because its been drafted for roughly four years. That's right, it has just been sitting there on my laptop, waiting patiently. Not to mention the fact that TGH is the first new book I've published since the rerelease of the first three. This book marks a HUGE milestone for me. Because it's never been put into readers hands.

But more than that, it was also written around the time my brother died. Dante is a tribute to him and a lot of the scenes involving grief within these pages reflected my own journey of grief. Nobody mourns the same way and it's never a linear path forward, but it's extremely personal. So, I hope you were kind while reading through Eve's grief too. RIP Trent.

While writing is a solo endeavour, there's always a tonne of people to thank because getting a book to the publishing stage takes a whole village.

Firstly, thank you to Jared, my fiancé, my best friend, my confidant. You're my favourite person and I would never have gotten this far without you. Thank you for talking through idea's, for letting me disappear for hours, for accepting that my mind will forever be wandering into far off worlds. You are so patient and kind and supportive. It makes all the difference in the world. These books would not exist without you and I'm forever grateful.

To my Lady Dungeons. (hehe) Thank you for being a safe space to talk to about books and writing blocks and just life in general. You make me smile everyday and are the best beta readers a girl could ask for.

To my friends and family. Every single one of you have supported me in this dream. I have not had one person question why I write, or tell me that it's a waste of time. To be surrounded by people who do nothing but support me is a gift, one I treasure every single day. Thank you.

To all the bookstores who have taken a chance on this series, you have changed my life. The owners, the managers, the community. All of it blows me away. You are magical people who thrive on dreams and creativity and I cannot scream about you all enough. Thank you for existing. For being a safe space. For encouraging dreams to exist.

Thank you to my editor, Daniel. I thank you in every single book but to edit the fourth instalment in the series with you has honestly been an honour. When I reached out asking you to commit to five books over the next 3 years, I didn't think you would actually say yes, but you did. You have been in the trenches with these characters, and with me. Thank you for believing in this story. For believing in me. And for sticking around until the end (which is so close now!)

To the authors and bookish businesses I have connected with (You know who you are). Thank you for the group chats and the tips and the cookie on my birthday. Thank you for the advice, for the updates in the literary world and for making this little indie author feel welcome. Trad or Indie. You are all so special to me and I love you all so much.

To the artists, for creating each artwork and bringing my characters to life. For being patient with me when I try and put what's in my head into a brief and for just being so damn talented.

Lastly, to my readers. This wouldn't be happening without your support. Thank you for loving these characters fiercely and loudly. For screaming about these books on social media. For reviewing and coming to events to see me. For creating art and beautiful posts and telling your friends. I see the book clubs, the orders, the recommendations, the shares and I can never thank you enough.

Thank you. Thank you. Thank you.

Kim xx

About the Author

K E Barden is an independent author based in Brisbane.

Her first book, The Gilded Mirror was written entirely on a mobile phone and the dent in her pinkie finger proves it.

When she isn't writing, you can usually find her spoiling her high maintenance cat, building fairy castles, or comparing her real boyfriend with her book boyfriends.

Her books are a combination of fiction, romance and fantasy with the express intent of stealing you away from reality and creating characters that will become your entire personality.

You can find Kim on social media @ KEBardenAuthor

Authors Note

Thank you for making it this far. I hope you enjoyed These Grave Hearts.

Reviews are the lifeblood of indie authors. Without them, there's a very high chance our books fade into obscurity. If you

are enjoying the Finding Ever After series please take the time
to leave a review on GoodReads, Amazon, Social Media, or
anywhere you want to share.

Thank you, Kim xx

www.ingramcontent.com/pod-product-compliance
Lightning Source LLC
Chambersburg PA
CBHW050943210726
48287CB00004B/1120